NOTES
ON
INFINITY

NOTES ON INFINITY

A Novel

AUSTIN TAYLOR

CELADON
BOOKS

NEW YORK

NOTES ON INFINITY. Copyright © 2025 by Austin Taylor. All rights reserved. Printed in the United States of America. For information, address Celadon Books, a division of Macmillan Publishers, 120 Broadway, New York, NY 10271.

www.celadonbooks.com

Designed by Omar Chapa

Library of Congress Cataloging-in-Publication Data

Names: Taylor, Austin, 1999– author.
Title: Notes on infinity : a novel / Austin Taylor.
Description: First edition. | New York, NY : Celadon Books, 2025.
Identifiers: LCCN 2024047950 | ISBN 9781250376107 (hardcover) |
    ISBN 9781250376114 (ebook)
Subjects: LCGFT: Bildungsromans. | Novels.
Classification: LCC PS3620.A928 N68 2025 | DDC 813/.6—dc23/
    eng/20241217
LC record available at https://lccn.loc.gov/2024047950

Our books may be purchased in bulk for promotional, educational, or business use. Please contact your local bookseller or the Macmillan Corporate and Premium Sales Department at 1-800-221-7945, extension 5442, or by email at MacmillanSpecialMarkets@macmillan.com.

First Edition: 2025

10 9 8 7 6 5 4 3 2 1

For JMT and NEA. Thank you.

NOTES
ON
INFINITY

Zoe is in the dressing room staring into the mirror, gripping the edges of the vanity below. Her hair is fine, but she's ruined her makeup—she'll have to have someone fix it. She's never been able to do it herself.

The tears have stopped. It's a beautiful mirror, she thinks. Frame carved with boughs and leaves and fruits. And, reflected in it, a nice dressing room. Very old Harvard, all dark wood and stained glass windows. It reminds her of her parents' house. There are tiny bottles of San Pellegrino in an ice bucket on the low table, the sides of which are weeping enough that she can hear her mother saying "Put something under that before it stains." The flowers in the cut glass vase are lilies, which symbolize life. Somebody thought they were quite clever.

Zoe tries to remember how she did this before. Smiles at her reflection. Tilts her chin up. Then she stops smiling, closes her eyes, sucks in her cheeks, shakes her head. Opens her eyes and tries again. Better. She starts to say her first few lines. "My name is—" Stops, clears her throat. "Hello. My name—" Shakes her head, pinches her nose in two fingers. "Thank you so much for having me. It's great to be back."

Pause, let them applaud.

Except during the pause she laughs, her eyebrows raising, and she can't stop laughing, because this is everything she ever wanted, isn't it, and she clamps a hand over her mouth, and the mania in her eyes could be amusement but could also be fear, no, terror—hysteria, supplies some more rational voice from the back of her mind—and she can't stop look-ing into them, into her own eyes, which are the eyes of an animal. An animal that's cornered. A lab rat you've just picked up by the tail.

It doesn't matter if she remembers how she did it before because she will never be able to do it like that again because that Zoe, the before Zoe, is dead.

She takes three shaky steps backward and thuds against the wall. Someone knocks softly. "Ms. Kyriakidis, are you all right?" They must be on Harvard's staff; her own would know not to follow her.

She swallows hard and clears her throat and says, "Yes, just a sec-ond." The voice that comes out is a woman's, but the eyes of the person in the mirror are a child's. The child who came here as a supplicant, not a god.

She slides down the wall and sits with her knees up to her chest. If my parents weren't outside, she thinks, maybe then. And Alex. And Jack. And Professor Hall, who, Christ, sent me a congratulatory email and said she'd be excited to hear my talk.

"Zoe, five." It's Phoebe's voice outside, with an edge in it.

She stands up, wrenches open the door. "I'm so sorry, I've just been sick, and I need—" but Phoebe has already seen and is tapping at her phone, and in seconds a woman with a little bag comes running. Phoebe gives Zoe a hard look before swirling out of the room. "Here," the woman says, "wipe off what's there and I'll just start over. You have beautiful skin, there's really not much to do."

Zoe laughs. "That's very kind of you." It is. Zoe's skin used to be beautiful, but now it's pale and thin, purple under her eyes. Has been for months. "It's stupid," she says, "that I can't do my own. My mother would be horrified." She takes refuge in the darkness behind her eye-lids while the woman applies concealer, eyeliner, mascara with cool, soft strokes. Once she found a stranger's hands on her face awkward, but now the ritual is soothing.

Then she says "Thank you" and she means more than thank you for fixing my makeup, she means thank you for helping me put my mask back on, thank you for not flinching when you saw what was behind it all the time, and the woman nods. Then the woman says "Are you ready?" and Zoe says "If you could just give me a second" and smiles and waits for the woman to leave before pulling the small bottle from her suit pocket. She tips three, no, four pills into her palm and knocks them all back at once, swallows them dry.

She leaves the dressing room and shuts the door carefully and the woman leads her down the hall and Zoe can hear that they are about halfway through her introduction, which means she still has some time.

Someone comes and mics her. Lifts her hair gently to loop the wire over her ear.

The woman says, "You look great," and pats her on the shoulder.

When she climbs onstage there is a hush. She hears her mother's voice, as she always does: "Long neck, shoulders back." The honey-colored wood of Sanders Theatre glows in the dim light of the chandelier. Every seat is full. Zoe glances up at the arched green ceiling, built to carry words to the audience, and feels the microphone against her cheek, waiting to immortalize them. There is a moment in which she thinks she cannot do it. Not again. In which it feels like something—a snake, a snake, of course—is twisting itself around her neck and slowly, slowly squeezing.

But she clears her throat and the snake loosens, just enough. And she looks out into the audience and she sees the upturned faces, so young. And she smiles, and she knows it is reaching her eyes. And she lifts her hand. And she says, "Hello, thank you all so much for having me. It's good to be back." There is applause. She clasps her hands in front of her and bends at the waist, tipping her head to gesture at a bow. "My name is Zoe Kyriakidis," she says. She raises her chin and looks out. "And I would like to tell you a story."

I

GENESIS

There is nothing in biology yet found that indicates the inevitability of death. This suggests to me that it is not at all inevitable, and that it is only a matter of time before the biologists discover what it is that is causing us the trouble.

—RICHARD P. FEYNMAN, *THE PLEASURE OF FINDING THINGS OUT*

1

There are two types of students in the first semester of organic chemistry. Those who arrive ten minutes early and sit primly in the second row, notebook out in case the professor lets go of any wisdom before the clock strikes the hour, and those who jog in four minutes late, unshowered and unshaven, with no bag and no notebook, and slump into a seat at the end of the aisle.

Zoe was very carefully being neither, and so she was well positioned to notice Jack, who was also neither, but perhaps less intentionally.

He might have been unshaven, or not—she wasn't sure you'd be able to tell either way. He was tall, had unruly dark hair, and walked with a leftward lean. He was too early to be in the second category, but she slotted him there anyway. Except then he sat in the front, next to an older guy in a beat-up leather jacket who she'd assumed was the teaching fellow. She leaned forward in her chair, interest piqued. Perhaps he was a very young-looking TF himself. He had taken out a notebook—from where she wasn't sure, he had no backpack—but he hadn't unfolded the arm table. This was, she realized as he twirled a crappy ballpoint pen between long fingers, because he was left-handed. He hunched over to scribble something in the notebook, which he propped on his knee, and Zoe could see where his leftward lean came from.

The professor, late, introduced himself and his teaching staff. Leather Jacket was the head TF, Ben. Left-Handed, then, was a student.

Through the lecture, Zoe had half her attention on the blackboard and the other half on Left-Handed's notes. He had drawn a line down the middle of the page (starting right after whatever notes were previous, not bothering with a fresh page, which set Zoe on edge), and seemed to be taking class notes in the left column and sketching some sort of experimental setup in the right.

When Professor Norton asked for questions, Left-Handed gestured vaguely upward.

"Jack?"

Zoe prickled. The professor already knew him by name?

"Could you explain a bit more the role of chirality in organocatalysis here?" They were covering Lewis bases.

"Mm," Professor Norton hummed, leaning back on the table and stretching out his khaki-clad legs. "So a chiral catalyst allows you to select for one enantiomer over another in your product."

"Right—I've been reading about the new superactive chiral transition metal catalysts, and I don't think I fully understand them."

Professor Norton laughed—laughed! "That might be a tad beyond the scope of today's class. If you want to talk about them, though, feel free to come to my office hours."

Jack nodded. Zoe felt the beginnings of jealousy.

"Speaking of which, my office hours," Professor Norton said as people packed up, "are going to be Thursdays, today, directly after lecture. If any of you have a significant conflict with that, reschedule it." The class laughed nervously.

Zoe had not planned to attend Professor Norton's office hours.

She had been forced into this very much intro-level, very much requirement—"practically a *gen ed*," she'd said on the phone to her brother—by her adviser, who told her that if she didn't take orgo as a sophomore with everyone else she would not have the required credits to graduate as a chemistry major. Plus Norton was a pure experimentalist, working on drug delivery—might as well be in pharma, really. Zoe was interested in theory, and so felt no need to impress him. Since applying to Harvard she'd been set on working with Daniel Fen, who was doing really interesting work in neuro theory. She still hadn't gotten through his PA, but she'd heard from someone who'd heard from someone else that he had a senior from the College in his lab, so she persisted.

And yet she found herself still in her seat when Professor Norton, Jack, and another girl were the only people remaining in the room.

"Alrighty," said Professor Norton, tapping his folder on the table. "You three?"

They walked out of the lecture hall and into the bowels of Mallinckrodt. Built in 1929 but renovated in the 1970s, the chemistry building sat in that dingy middle ground between old and grand and new and shiny. They descended a dim stairwell to a subbasement level Zoe didn't know existed, then crossed the entire building to a different stairwell, halfway up which Professor Norton said, "I hope everyone's fine with stairs." Crossed back through what Zoe thought was the third floor, past glass-walled labs full of masked and goggled scientists with double-thick blue gloves up to their elbows, under pipes that sprouted like weeds over the ceiling. Swung a hard right, then a hard left, and came to an elevator bank with two dinky elevators.

"And to two," said Professor Norton.

"Why didn't we take the stairs to the second floor?" Zoe ventured.

Professor Norton raised his eyebrows. "Because that stairwell doesn't get you to my office."

"You can't get there from here," Jack said wryly, in a faux-thick Northeast accent Zoe couldn't quite place.

She frowned.

The elevator dinged, rattled open.

In Professor Norton's office, Jack set his notebook down, pulled out the same kind of clear plastic Bic, and started spinning it again, flinging it through his pointer and middle fingers, then middle and ring, then ring and thumb, then back. Zoe wondered how far it would go if he made a mistake. She imagined it flying across the table and striking Professor Norton in the eye, sticking straight out of the socket like an old cartoon.

Zoe looked up at Jack's face, and found it was looking back. She was startled by his eyes. They were pale blue, with long, straight eyelashes, and she was confused that someone who she had not bothered to evaluate for attractiveness had such a beautiful feature. Jack nodded at her to go first.

Zoe cleared her throat, realized she didn't have a question prepared. "I'd be interested to hear the answer to the catalysis question that—I'm sorry, I don't know your name," she said, pretending not to remember.

"Jack."

"That Jack asked."

"Great." Professor Norton stood, picked up the chalk, went to the blackboard behind him. "So as you all know, a Lewis base works"—he pressed hard with the chalk, and excess sifted down the board—"by donating an electron pair to activate the electrophile. And a chiral Lewis base . . ."

The pen was a blur across Jack's fingers.

Professor Norton droned. Something about ligands, tunable reactivity, activation of inert bonds, catalyst stability.

Jack interjected. "Can you use a chiral Brønsted acid as the ligand? Instead of a Lewis base?" Zoe squinted, trying to follow.

Professor Norton tilted his head. "Interesting. I don't . . . well, frankly, I'm not completely certain. I don't work on these. But I would think not, because I don't imagine you could form a stable complex with electron-poor ligands."

Jack nodded, scribbled a note.

"I can't imagine that's relevant to your work with Daniel?"

You're kidding, Zoe thought. Daniel Fen?

"No, no. I was just curious."

Professor Norton nodded, put both hands on the table, leaned onto them. "Either of you ladies?"

Zoe was mute.

"Um . . ." The other girl scooched forward to lean onto the desk. "I'm not sure I completely understand, uh, how you end up with a double bond in the resonance structure we went over today?"

"You—what's your name?"

"Zoe."

"Zoe, can you help her with that? I'm going to check on something, I'll be just a moment."

Well. It was a basic question. "Let me see," Zoe said, and she pulled the paper toward herself. Jack had his notebook on his knee again and was sketching something with long, sharp strokes. She drew out the answer, walked through it aloud.

"Does that make sense?"

"Yeah, thanks so much!" The girl looked nervous. She stuffed her paper into her bag and stood. "I'm gonna go," she said unnecessarily. Zoe watched her leave. Jack wasn't paying attention.

Zoe waited for him to say something, but he just kept sketching. When he filled the page he was working on he turned it, flipped the notebook over, and started another. Zoe searched her own notes for an intelligent question to ask Professor Norton when he returned.

She caved. "I heard the undergraduate who worked for Daniel Fen was a senior."

"Mm?" He looked up.

"Are . . . you a senior?"

"No."

Zoe nodded.

He said nothing, returning to his notebook.

She pretended to check the time. Packed her things. Moved to leave the room.

"Bye," he called at the last minute, just as she was stepping through the doorway.

"Bye."

The scoreboard read: 1–0.

2

Organic chemistry quickly became a game. Zoe found herself pre-paring the most esoteric theoretical questions to ask during lecture and familiarizing herself with the most esoteric experimental applications that she knew Jack would ask about so she could ask a follow-up question as though his initial questions had been common knowledge. She was dumping far too much time into the class. The problem of whether or not Jack also saw it as a game did nag at her at first, because he seemed so detached, but he never failed to engage, to signal with two fingers then meander through some long-winded but brilliant nonquestion, and anyway she was aloof, too, which was part of the game. So it stopped bothering her, because how could he not be playing, everyone saw it for what it was. Indeed, the rest of the class sat through their gymnastics with grim irritation. Even Professor Norton had grown bored of the performance.

But the sparring brought her such unexpected pleasure.

And in the back of her mind, though she'd never admit it, was the thought that if she impressed him enough, he might introduce her to Fen.

The day of the first midterm Zoe was not nervous. She was, because of the game, overprepared. She sat in her usual midterm seat, which was different from her lecture seat: to the right, on the aisle, about halfway back. And she watched the doors, curious about when Jack would arrive and where he would sit.

The answer was that he didn't. The head TF, Ben, walked in with a stack of exams and began handing them out at two past the hour, and Jack was not present. Zoe almost asked Ben where he was but caught herself and took a packet. She wrote her name neatly on the front and signed the honor code attestation.

"Okay, guys. You can get started." Paper shuffled. The air, when it met the back of her throat, was tinged with college kid anxiety.

Zoe hesitated, eyes on the door, before flipping into the test. She liked her games fair.

The first question was difficult, so she skipped it, and then she skipped the second, too. She felt off-kilter and kept glancing up at the clock. Fifteen past. Eighteen.

She was staring at the door again when it opened and Jack walked in. He didn't even have the decency to look rushed. When they made eye contact, she thought the left corner of his mouth turned up just slightly. He took an exam from the table at the front of the room and then walked up the aisle to sit somewhere behind her.

Twenty-two past. She thought, Your time is really going to have been wasted if you bomb this exam because you're distracted by his antics. So she stood up, mouthed, "Bathroom?" to the TF, put her cell phone face down on the table at the front (it was switched off, anyway), and left the lecture hall. This was her favorite trick for refocusing during an exam. She'd read somewhere once that doorways do a peculiar thing to your brain, which is why you might go into another room to retrieve something and find yourself there with no idea what you needed. Walking through a doorway is like a brain reset switch. When she reentered the lecture hall, she'd solved question two and had a rough idea of where to start on question one.

She finished writing just as time was called, confident that she was handing in a perfect paper, and allowed herself to glance back, like scratching an itch. He was already gone.

When she'd thought of the exam as a round of the game, she hadn't thought of ways to break a potential tie. But Jack had. Time.

She begrudgingly adjusted the scoreboard. Plus one, Jack.

The next class, he wasn't there.

He had never been late to a lecture, so when Professor Norton walked in before he did, she was surprised. And by fifteen past the hour, she knew he wasn't going to show at all.

"Questions?" Professor Norton asked after he'd filled the first two blackboards. She thought about asking hers, but it felt stupid and shallow without her target audience, so she played with her pen instead, twisting it apart, pulling out the spring, putting it back in, screwing it together.

"Zoe? No?" Professor Norton looked amused.

She felt herself blush. "Well, I was wondering . . ." She asked her question. It would have been more embarrassing not to.

She sank into the grubby upholstery of the flip-down stadium chair, breaking one of her mother's cardinal rules. ("No slouching. You should be proud to be a tall woman.") She felt a buzzy anxious something in her chest. And the class was unbearably boring again.

They got their exams back after class the next Tuesday. Hers was perfect, but it gave her none of the usual thrill.

As she walked out into the sunshine, too bright off the windows of the labs across the way, she wondered if he had dropped the class. Which was stupid, she chided herself, because regardless she had other goals to attend to, significant ones, which would in fact be much better served by her focus now that she wasn't in a ridiculous organic chemistry arms race with a boy. She pulled her notebook out of her bag and, still walking, began jotting down a list of professors to reach out to about lab work. She should have done this weeks ago. She wrote Daniel Fen at the top, out of habit, but then scratched it out. If he didn't want her, she would go elsewhere.

She barely glanced over her shoulder before stepping out onto Oxford Street. A car had to brake for her. It is a crosswalk, she thought.

"Dumb bitch!" a man standing on the other side of the road yelled.

She didn't look at him. But as she passed through the grand brick gate, "Enter to Grow in Wisdom" across the top, she glanced down at her clothing. Took note of the short skirt she was wearing. Thought, first, that she should stop wearing it, and then that she should keep wearing it, and then that she might productively mull over the problem of appearances.

3

"I just feel like getting it out of the way now would be nice. While my classes are easier," Sophia said. Three of Zoe's four roommates were sitting around the common room of their suite. Gabby was at her unfortunate Friday afternoon lab.

"But you won't have taken second semester orgo," Hanna said, looking up from the homework she was balancing on her lap.

"I'll just self-study it."

"That . . . is insane," Hanna said. "I diagnose you a masochist."

The corners of Zoe's mouth turned up as she sipped from her water bottle.

"How long is it good for again?"

"Three years." Sophia pushed back to tilt her desk chair into its semirecline.

"What if you want to take some time off?"

Sophia looked scandalized. "Time off before what might be nine years of graduate school? I mean, hopefully nine years."

"Or," Zoe offered, "you could skip the whole medical school thing. MCAT, schmemCAT." She was already laughing before Sophia could throw her hands up. "I'm just *say*ing, it's an option."

"Self-study second semester orgo," Hanna was still muttering. "I can't even study first semester orgo."

"I was just finishing up my orgo p-set, actually."

"Great, do this for me then?" Hanna tossed Zoe her crumpled packet, the staple torn out of the top left corner. Zoe drew in the arrow pushing to solve the problem with the pencil she'd been bouncing, eraser first, on the floor. Tossed the packet back.

"You are so irritating."

"You are so welcome."

Zoe paused, and then said, "Speaking of orgo, do you guys know anyone in chem named Jack?"

Hanna slid down to sprawl across the love seat, hung her head over the armrest, pale blond hair nearly touching the floor. "Nope."

Zoe turned to Sophia.

"Hmm." Sophia was looking at her curiously. "Is this a love interest?"

How could she have picked up anything of tone from just eight words? "No," Zoe said too quickly, annoyed with herself for sounding shady when she wasn't lying. Jack wasn't a love interest. "Not at all. He was just in my orgo class and stopped showing up."

"Drop the class?"

"Yeah, have you had a midterm yet?" Hanna asked.

"Just. But there's no way he bombed the midterm. He was . . ." Keeping up with me, she wanted to say, but she didn't want to sound like a jerk. "Probably the smartest kid in the class."

"So it *is* a love interest," Sophia said, triumphant.

"No, really, guys." Zoe fluttered her eyes shut for a moment, cursing her blush, wondering how she could possibly explain the game. "We just had a . . . friendly competition running. Who could be, you know, the biggest section kid. I'm sure it was really annoying to everyone else. So I was just wondering why he stopped coming to class. That's all."

"Alternatively, he could've aced the midterm and decided he didn't need to show up for the rest of the class," Sophia said.

Zoe nodded, and then leaned her head back against the wall. She hadn't thought of that.

Sophia cleared her throat delicately. "I do know who he is."

"Oh?" Zoe tried to sound casual. Because, damn it, she was.

"Jack Leahy. He took LS50 with me last year." So he was a sophomore.

"Did you know he's working with Daniel Fen? Well, I think."

"Interesting," Sophia said, tucking a strand of hair behind her ear. She had medium brown hair of a medium length, which she kept securely tucked behind both ears at all times. "No. I thought the storied undergrad in Fen's lab was a senior."

"Apparently not."

"He is smart, although I didn't think he was that impressive. Seemed like he had his own stuff going on, you know? Didn't care too much." Sophia narrowed her eyes at Zoe. "I wouldn't have pegged him as your type."

Zoe laughed. "What, exactly, is my type?"

Sophia just shook her head, a small smile on her lips. "You know, I don't know. Not him."

Zoe hadn't had a boyfriend since she'd gotten to college. Nor, if she was being honest, before that. Neither was particularly unusual: some very high percentage of Harvard students enter as virgins, and most don't start pairing off into real couples until sometime late sophomore or junior year.

Sophia's comment about type made her think of Danny, though, who she hadn't thought of in a while. Danny Hess—of course she remembered his last name, she'd repeated Zoe Hess over and over and over in her mind like a spell, like saying it enough times would make him see past the fact that she was sixteen and he was in his mid-twenties, make him sweep her off her feet and run away with her. Funny how someone you thought of every waking moment for months, how a type of longing that was so significant it became a building block of your identity, eventually slips wholly from your mind.

He was one of four working with her father that summer. Since they were all young men and since young men tend to take up far more space than necessary, the four plus her father plus her brother, all draped over the furniture, the picture of ease, seemed to fill the living room. Which left no place for Zoe.

In the evening they, plus Zoe and her mother, made eight, which was the number of chairs at the dining room table.

Zoe had spent the better part of her childhood squeezed between two strange men at dinners, because her mother believed in mixing people at the table and her father believed in treating children like adults. Since he'd taken the first job at MIT when Zoe was just a baby, he'd been hosting his students—and those of his colleagues, in the years when he had only enough funding for one—for dinner most nights in the summer months when the campus quieted and graduate students had to worry about only their research. Like the old days, Zoe's father would reminisce, before all this teaching and class-taking nonsense, when the scientists could hear themselves think and take time to talk, and the men would laugh (then they had seemed like men, but perhaps now she would call them boys, Zoe thought, and it amused her).

When she was little, six or seven, they'd carry on conversations literally over her head while she leaned forward to eat her dinner. When her father held court, she would sometimes answer one of his rhetorical questions or proposals in a small, high voice: "Your reasoning sounds flawed," or "Did you check your math there, Daddy?"

Everyone thought this was adorable. The men would offer her high fives or fist bumps, and she would grin, crinkling up until she was all straight Greek nose and straight Greek eyebrows, both too big for her tiny face.

By eleven or twelve, the summers brought with them a vague sense of constant embarrassment, the unease of being unsure what space you're meant to take up. But she always sat in on her father's living room seminars, as she was starting to learn physics in school and was fascinated by the ideas that would murmur around the room like they had a life of their own. By the time she was conscious enough to actually understand what he was researching, he was working on quantum field theory. Then there had been a period of rebellion, a few summers where she thought physics was stupid and her father was overrated and she wanted nothing to do with him or his students and she spent most evenings rotating through other kids' houses where she practiced her Yes ma'ams and No ma'ams and Can I help you with that, sirs, her mother's southern charm slightly disarming from the mouth of an olive-skinned girl with tangled black hair who was caught in a painfully gangly phase of growth. And then she turned sixteen, and there was Danny.

She'd taken her first real math class that year, linear algebra, which made her feel very grown-up, but she'd also failed her driver's test, which made her feel like a stupid trapped child, and so she rambled around their house (the restored four-story Victorian in mid-Cambridge toward Harvard that MIT owned and was loaning them for the duration of her father being impressive and sought-after, which had felt enormous after a string of two-bedroom apartments paid for by postdoc stipends), slamming doors and cupboards and being generally irritating, until her mother said, Honey, let's be polite now, and her father said, If you wanted your license, you should've been a better driver, and her brother, Alex, didn't say anything, knew it was too soon, although later he'd offer her driving lessons because, at root, they were friends, even though he nearly always made her feel like her parents' girly accessory to their golden boy.

She'd been sitting on the couch when Danny arrived. He was early, so her mother was in the kitchen up to her elbows in dinner and her father was upstairs in his office working.

"Can you get that, Zoe?" her mother called, and Zoe blew out through her nose, tossed her cell phone on the couch, and stalked to the door. She swung it open and leaned against the frame, cocking a hip to one side. She was newly tall, had hit five nine that year. Danny, standing on the step below the threshold, was perfectly eye level, which meant (mental math was not a challenge for Zoe) he would be about six two.

"Can I help you?" she said before she had fully taken him in.

"I hope so. I'm here for dinner? With Professor Kyriakidis?" He'd practiced the name. She looked into his face. Blond hair, longish, tousled. Mouth that turned down slightly at the corners, like he was holding in a laugh. She blinked.

"Uh, right. That's my dad." She opened the door to let him in and found her mother over her shoulder.

"Zo-e! What kind of welcome was that? Hi, dear, I'm Mrs. Kyriakidis. It's so nice to meet you. What was your name?"

Danny's smile crept across his face like a surprise, creasing his cheeks and narrowing his eyes, blue, and Zoe was lost. "Danny. It's nice to meet you, Mrs. Kyriakidis. And your sister?"

She laughed, exactly as he'd intended, and Zoe blushed deeper.

"Daughter," Zoe's mother said, "don't you be silly. She gets the hair from her father. And the manners, too."

Zoe wanted to dissolve into the floorboards and never reassemble. "Zoe," she managed, "nice to meet you."

"And yourself, Zoe." Danny nodded, looked inside. "It smells great from all the way out here!"

"Oh! Aren't you delightful." Zoe's mother opened her arm and led him in. "Can I get you a drink?"

Sitting between two men in their twenties at dinner that night—neither of them Danny—made Zoe feel mortified and hot and miserable. Every time one of them brushed her with an elbow as he reached across the table for the salt or one of the family-style plates she'd flinch, apologize.

She watched him when she thought he wouldn't notice, only half listening to the conversation. Studied the way the muscles in his jaw moved as he chewed, the way the muscles in his arm moved as he picked up a plate, a fork. He was wearing a white button-up worn thin, against which his skin was caramelly tan. He was from Stanford, she learned, visiting, and her father had sat him next to Alex, who was off to Stanford himself the next year. They were already chatting animatedly about research on campus, the best bars to drink at, which professors to make friends with. Zoe burned with jealousy.

When she helped her mother clear the table, he smiled up at her— "Thanks, Zoe"—and the miserable dinner was worth it after all, and she had to spend a moment in the kitchen collecting herself, which her mother pretended to ignore.

The next morning she was awake at five, sweating in her sheets, fresh June air moving a few strands of hair across her face, burning from a terribly vivid dream about Danny. How had she even remembered his appearance well enough to render it with such granularity?

She stretched, felt herself vibrate like an overtightened string. And then she pulled her laptop from her desk to her bed, sat up, and searched his name. Eight publications, first author on three. She crossed her legs, perched her laptop between her knees, and started to read.

Over the next few weeks she'd slip into her father's office when she knew he'd be taking what he called breaks and what others would call working at a less frenetic pace and ask him to explain some of the finer points of various research threads. She made some small effort to disguise the fact that she only cared about threads adjacent to Danny's, which was plenty for her father, whose attention to detail with regards to human relationships was marginal.

She'd make sure she was downstairs on the couch when Danny arrived, always early, to chat up her mother and help in the kitchen. Her mother, whose attention to detail with regards to human relationships was extraordinary, thought this was probably a healthy diversion.

Danny would slip off his shoes at the door, Tevas or sneakers, to walk barefoot through the house in his rolled-up khakis. He never wore socks, and Zoe found his ankles (slender, with light blond hair) and long feet (crossed with tan lines, flexing as he walked) unbearably erotic.

He and her brother were fast friends, which meant that when Alex offered Zoe driving lessons, Danny was there, and jumped in immediately to offer lessons of his own—"family should never try to teach family to drive"—which simultaneously made Zoe want to disappear and to glide into the clear lavender sky.

She'd listen to the clink of glasses and the pours of whiskey and the trailing ends of after-dinner conversations from the stairwell just around the corner. She'd tasted whiskey before, of course—most of her friends' parents had well-stocked liquor cabinets, and they'd notice when some was gone but they wouldn't care, better the kids do it in the house—so she was well equipped to imagine how it would taste on Danny's mouth.

It took her weeks to work up the courage to join them. When she finally moved to follow the men into the living room after dessert one evening her mother called her back, "Zoe, could you help me clear the table, please?" and Zoe snapped, quietly, "Alex doesn't have to," and her mother said, "Well Alex helps set." Which was true, but there wasn't anything to miss before the meal. Zoe gathered the plates, smudged with the bright purple remnants of a blueberry cobbler, clattered them into the sink, and then slunk into the living room, where all the obvious seats were taken. She paused and glanced around furtively for a place where she wouldn't feel in the way. When her father finally noticed her, he said, "My Zoe! What do you need?" and she choked on her words, "I just wanted to listen," and Danny said, "Little mouse! Deciding to join us rather than hide around the corner?" and her face flamed bright red, and it took everything she had not to run from the room. Alex took pity on her, moved to sit on the floor with his back against his chair so that she could have it, and continued talking from down there, gesturing, while she perched above him, the princess. Could it be worse? But she could do it. She was here now and there were tracks of sweat down the insides of her arms and it would all be wasted if she didn't speak. So when the conversation rolled around to Danny's work, she cleared her throat and edged her way in with what she'd prepared, a hole she'd noticed in one of his papers and an experiment that she thought could fill it, and Danny looked at her and nodded and smiled and she thought, Yes! I've contributed something, until her father said, "Mm, we pointed that out and Danny offered a pretty solid defense of himself." No one bothered to fill her in on what the defense was, and when she looked back at Danny, he was already talking to somebody else.

* * *

Mortification: pure, hot, horrible. Still strong enough, all these years later, to taste.

She would stand nude in front of her mirror and look at herself. Small breasts, narrow hips, but a newly pinched waist. Collarbones that had just emerged from her baby fat cut clean planes under her face, which, nearly big enough now for her eyes and nose and brows, almost looked dramatic rather than ridiculous.

Some days, she thought she was a woman, and others she was hopelessly a child.

Danny didn't seem to remember the after-dinner episode. Was that better or worse? He was funny, and quick to laugh, and he did give her driving lessons, she dripping sweat and clenching her teeth and slamming on the brakes, he just laughing in the passenger seat, saying, "Zoe, kid, you've gotta relax. You've gotta go with the flow."

When he left Cambridge at the end of the summer, he hugged her and her brother both, said he'd see Alex soon, told Zoe "Don't forget to write" with a smile in his voice. She went up to her room and masturbated, and then cried, and then lay despondent in her bed for the last week before school started, hot August sun beating through the window. Of course she didn't write.

She shook her head, thinking about how ridiculous she'd been. She wondered what Danny would think of her now. If she'd still be a kid to him. If she still *was* a kid, after all.

4

She ran into Jack a few weeks later. She was walking to an evening section, eight thirty in the Science Center, and he was trekking back across the Yard. It was dark and an early first snow had fallen, dusting the brownish grass.

The combination of height and leftward lean was distinctive. As he got closer, Zoe could see he was wearing a worn military-style parka, dark green, lots of pockets, and his usual threadbare jeans and scuffed boots. He was always pale, but today he looked exhausted, crescents under his eyes puffy and dark.

Zoe's interest flared. She jammed her hands in her pockets. He wasn't looking at her. Did she really want to be the one who said something? But if she didn't, she might never speak to him again. Which—

"Jack?" She said his name before she could talk herself out of it.

He stopped, and they faced each other. Zoe shifted her weight to one leg. "Zoe."

"What are you . . . did you drop orgo?"

"Oh, no," he said, "I've just been busy."

"Oh." So he hadn't been enjoying the game as much as she had.

In fact, maybe she'd made the whole thing up. She was grateful it was dark, because she could feel herself blushing.

"How has it been?"

"Fine, fine." Boring, without you, she thought, but of course she couldn't say that now.

He shook a curl out of his face.

"What are you busy with?"

"Oh, just the lab. Some involved experiments. Back and forth at odd hours." He nodded backward.

All she could think was that his nod was in the wrong direction. Wyss was the other way. "Isn't Daniel Fen at the Wyss Institute?"

"Uh, yeah. He is."

Zoe looked at him.

"Well, uh. I should get something to eat," he said.

"Okay," she said. She wished she had something interesting to say, something funny or smart that would pique his interest, give her the upper hand. But she didn't.

He half-smiled and then loped off, cutting straight across the lawn instead of using the diagonal pathways, leaving a line of dark prints on the frosted grass.

She wished she'd been keeping score physically, on a piece of paper, so that she could scribble the whole thing out. Crumple it up. Throw it away.

She promised herself that was the end of the Jack affair, whatever it had been. From now on, she'd just be as bitter toward him as she would've been toward any undergrad who had snuck their way into Fen's lab.

Except that the following day, when she walked into orgo, he was sitting in the seat next to hers. He smiled, with just his lips, and lifted his left fingers off his notebook in a wave.

She thought, He's playing with me.

She sat, and waited for him to speak. He smelled sort of smoky.

He didn't. Speak, that is. Professor Norton sauntered in a few minutes past the hour and picked up his chalk. Jack and Zoe were both quiet, leaning in opposite directions to take notes.

It was a Thursday, which meant there would be office hours after the lecture. Zoe wondered if Jack was going. If she made the first move, would he follow? If he did, would she?

No, she resolved, this was ridiculous. She would go get herself some lunch. She packed her things, headed outside.

Jack, tucking his notebook under his left arm, followed her.

"Are you going to get something to eat?" he asked.

"I was, yeah."

"So." He gestured with his head down the street toward the Yard and, beyond it, the river houses and their dining halls.

He walked with his hands in his pockets. She wondered what he was thinking, and she wished she didn't care quite so much about the answer. Her eyes flicked from face to face in the flow of oncoming students. Single frames: a laugh, a pair of zoned-out eyes, a smile down at a cell phone, a look of disgust and a hand holding a phone to a face, the blur of a turning head.

"So." The combination of her curiosity and her mother's vehement lessons on small talk rendered her unable to keep the silence. She looked over at him. "What are you working on that leaves you so confused you can't remember where your lab is?"

He snorted, smiled. "Gene therapy."

"What kind of gene therapy?"

"TERT."

"The antiaging stuff?"

He nodded. "Yeah, exactly."

A sophomore was working on something that almost certainly would go to startup within two years? "That's very cool."

He nodded. "I think so, yeah."

She paused a moment, cleared her throat. "I assume it's applied?"

"Yeah. Daniel . . . well, you know how prolific he is with startups."

"So there's going to be a startup."

Jack cocked his head, shrugged. "It's applied, is what I meant."

"Are you going to work on it?"

He raised his eyebrows, shrugged again.

"Are you going to drop out to work on it?"

Finally, Jack laughed. "Persistent."

"Nothing if not," Zoe said, smiling.

"So what are *you* working on?"

"Oh." Zoe's mouth twisted. She didn't want to admit she didn't have lab experience, especially to him. But she restored her pleasant, neutral expression and said brightly: "Nothing, right now. Kind of playing around with some options." That is, until three weeks ago I'd been so set on working with your PI that I refused to consider other options, but he is completely uninterested in me, and so now I'm scrambling.

"Really?" He sounded genuinely surprised. They'd passed by the Science Center, through the plaza with the food trucks and chairs, full of bundled tourists eating pizza and fancy grilled cheese sandwiches, slipped through one of the gates, and were in the Yard. It was a gray day, dreary, the sky matte, turning the red brick brown.

"Why?" she asked, fishing.

"Oh, I just . . ." He raised his eyebrows, one shoulder, one corner of his lips in an asymmetrical sort of you-got-me gesture. "What are you interested in?"

"Well," she said, "when I was in high school, I was more on the physics side of things. Did a lot of quantum." Quantum computing, because that was what Danny was doing, as related to her father's work in quantum field theory. "Now I'm more interested in the bio application. Neuro specifically. Understanding neuronal activity."

"So you're interested in some of Daniel's other projects."

It was Zoe's turn to be embarrassed. And he was on a first-name basis with Daniel Fen. "Who isn't interested in at least one of Daniel's projects?"

Jack just nodded. They were nearly across the Yard, passing Wigglesworth and through the gate behind, reaching Mass. Ave. "So, Zoe," he said. She looked at him. His hands were in his pockets. He didn't look back, but the corner of his mouth was pulling down slightly, like he was holding back a smile. "What *is* consciousness, then?"

She laughed, surprised. "I have no idea. That's why I want to work in neuro. It's the next . . . it's the ocean of human biology."

"Ninety-five percent unexplored."

She flipped the question back on him. "What do *you* think is the nature of consciousness?"

He shrugged. "I work in aging. I have no idea."

"They're not unrelated."

He tilted his head, looking down Holyoke Street. Zoe wondered if she'd offended him. A drip fell from a fire escape above, hitting Zoe's ear, clammy. She flinched and brushed it away on reflex.

They reached the side door of Lowell House. "This is me," Zoe said. She figured he must be in Winthrop or Eliot, two of the other residential houses that were beyond Lowell. She wondered what to say, what might keep the conversation going. "I'll see you Tuesday?"

He nodded, offered an awkward wave, and turned to walk in the other direction, back the way they'd come. Zoe watched him, hand on the wrought iron gate that she'd just unlocked, which was growing insistently heavy as it tried to close. He must be in Adams, she thought.

He reached into his pocket and pulled out a square object, fiddled with it, put something in his mouth. Gum, perhaps. He cut a rather dramatic figure on the empty street: longish coat flapping about his legs, leaning forward into that ambling gait, hair curling up a good three inches above the top of his head.

And also, she thought, Did he just walk me home?

5

"I'm so glad you reached out," Professor Hall said as they were wrapping up their meeting. Professor Hall was extraordinarily impressive. She was the first female tenured professor in chemistry at Harvard, and she was in quantum, a man's field in a man's field. She was arguably as cool as Fen, but she'd responded immediately and personally to Zoe's outreach a few weeks before with an offer to meet and discuss potential lab work. "I should tell you, before I let you go, that I did talk to Lawrence"—that would be Lawrence Trill, one of Zoe's professors from the year prior—"and he couldn't speak highly enough of you."

It felt good. That she might be sought after. And then Professor Hall said, crossing her right leg over her left and putting both hands on her right knee, "I think you'd fit in very well in my lab—I really prioritize mentoring promising young women." Which also could have felt good, but didn't. It felt like cheating.

Science, to Zoe, was a boy's sport. Like football. All of the scientists her father brought home were men, and so the work was inextricably tied up in maleness. In boastful talking; in the particularities of male friendship, those linked ideas of brotherhood and hierarchy;

in eating twice your body weight at dinner because you were so lost in the work you'd not eaten all day; in being slightly shabby in that unshaven, exhausted way and slightly awkward in that *I don't care about social niceties* way; all of which show you're working very hard and thinking deep thoughts and do not have time for the soft, polished things of femaledom. Of course, it felt unfair when her brother had been allowed—encouraged—to fit into these half-feral groups. Her mother did make him wash his hair, but his voice could be rough and loud, his clothes wrinkled and baggy, his conduct peculiar. These things would not do for Zoe.

Not that she was ever told she couldn't do science. In fact, when her father was starting to teach her brother long division and multiplication on the kitchen table and saw Zoe, two years younger, watching curiously, he lifted her up onto his lap and put a pencil in her hand and was delighted when she got it quicker than Alex did. Both children were brilliant—or at least cultivated to be so—and it was never necessarily about which child was smarter than the other. It was just that Zoe, in addition to being smart, also had to be inoffensive. Which did, she mused, leave Alex more time for being brilliant.

"I've asked one of my postdocs to give you a tour after this." Professor Hall was still speaking. She was one of the best-dressed chemistry professors Zoe had ever seen, in a blue-gray pantsuit with the blazer draped over the back of her rolling chair. "I think you might be particularly interested in the tunneling project I mentioned."

"That would be fantastic, thank you so much," Zoe said.

Professor Hall's secretary showed Zoe where to wait for the postdoc, and Zoe waited, trying to push down the mean voice in the back of her head that was saying, Maybe you do need a leg up. Maybe the problem isn't that science is a boy's sport, it's that you aren't a good enough player.

The postdoc emerged, and Zoe stood and reached out a hand to shake. As she was doing so, her phone buzzed in her pocket.

Such a small buzz, to knock her off one course and onto another.

She didn't read the notification until 5:15, after the walkthrough, standing in the coatroom with her bag slung over one shoulder.

Daniel Fen. Subject: meet. Body: might you be available for a quick chat at 6pm?

The tall glass building didn't even say Wyss, just the address, 3 Blackfan Circle. She retucked in her shirt, smoothed her hair, hoped she didn't look like she'd run all the way across campus to catch a shuttle to Longwood, took a deep breath, and walked into the lobby.

The receptionist was politely unimpressed, even when Zoe flashed the email from Professor Fen, and asked her to have a seat while she called down to his PA.

"He'll see you in a few minutes," she said as she hung up. "Someone will come get you."

Zoe nodded. She realized her hands were shaking and chastised herself for feeling nervous, tried to focus on her surroundings. The ceilings were double or even triple height, the back wall lined with huge digital screens that flashed articles and press releases about Wyss work. Zoe was too far away to read them, but she could see the staged photos of smiling scientists, perfectly coiffed, behind artfully blurred flasks and petri dishes. She'd never seen a scientist at work look that joyful, or have makeup that well done. She wondered who those pictures were for.

At 5:58 a sharp-looking blond woman pushed through the doors into the lobby. "Zoe?" she said, and Zoe stood up like she'd been shocked, smiled broadly, and extended her hand.

"Nice to meet you. I'm Professor Fen's PA," the woman said,

barely touching Zoe's hand before turning on her heel and leading
Zoe back.

Professor Fen had a corner office, of course, which was entirely
glass. So Zoe saw, before she went in, that there was already someone
on the near side of the conference table, facing away from her. Tall,
curly hair, leaning onto his left elbow, spinning a pen in his left hand.
Over his middle finger, around his index, under middle, around ring.
She flushed with some uncomfortable, unidentifiable emotion.

Fen's PA opened the door and ushered Zoe in. "Here's Zoe," she
said, and Professor Fen stood up from the other side of the table,
leaning forward. Zoe shook his hand, taking in his jet-black hair
and unlined face, his casual T-shirt and jeans, the spareness of his
movements, the brightness of his eyes. He could pass for early thirties, which made him incredibly young-looking for fifty-two—but of
course he would be.

She sat as Professor Fen sat, and looked over at Jack, who hadn't
moved. He nodded at her, tapping his pen on his open notebook.

"Zoe, it's nice to meet you." Professor Fen spoke like a radio host.

"It's nice to meet you," she replied, and her mother's words echoed
in her ears. Long neck, shoulders back. Smile. She straightened in her
chair.

"Jack speaks highly of you." Professor Fen pressed the tips of his
fingers together in a steeple, elbows on the glass table.

Zoe blushed. She didn't know what she was supposed to say to
that, especially with him sitting beside her. So she laughed, awkwardly, and said, "Well, thank you."

"Could you summarize the work being done in my lab? It is
perfectly fine that you do not have the technical details—nor, of
course, the proprietary details—but please give me a sense of the
landscape. As though I were a, say, PhD student in an adjacent
science, perhaps engineering, perhaps at MIT."

Zoe's stomach clenched. She should have put him off and prepared. And even worse to be unprepared in front of Jack. But then she remembered herself, took a deep breath, placed her folded hands on the desk in front of her, and launched.

"In no particular order. Professor Fen is working on several strands of antiaging research, including TERT and longevity-associated genes. The TERT work is based on our knowledge of how destructive telomere shortening is, indicating a higher risk of, for example, heart disease, and seems to be the most clinically promising." She hesitated, and then leaned into it. "His lab is known for being particularly secretive around blockbuster new tech in order to maximize startup impact."

If she revealed she'd read all of his papers on TERT, it would be clear to Jack that she'd been doing the scientific equivalent of Facebook stalking him. But wouldn't the appearance of some expertise be worth the embarrassment?

"His last paper showed, incredibly, that CMV—a particular viral vector—is an effective delivery device for TERT and FST, and that the two can extend mouse life span by, if I'm remembering correctly"—she knew she was remembering correctly—"about forty percent.

"The area of his work"—she wondered how much to couch it—"that I'm perhaps most interested in is applied artificial intelligence. He's using AI neural networks to understand biological neural networks and the processes of thinking." She cleared her throat. "He's also—"

"That's fine," Fen interrupted. "What are you working on currently?"

"I'm not working in a lab yet. I've spent some time shadowing, I've just come from the Hall—"

"I mean, what are *you* working on?"

I'm not working on anything, Zoe thought, I'm a sophomore, I know absolutely nothing, let alone enough to be creative. But that was not the answer he wanted. "I'm interested in the idea that we can better understand neural networks using AI proxies. I think that eventually we'll see that mechanics are the answer to our consciousness problem."

Fen nodded. "Good. What classes have you taken?"

Zoe listed her courses, thanking herself for taking five a semester and graduate-level electives. When she finished, Fen said, "Not that it matters—nothing can prepare you for creative work," and Zoe just smiled and nodded, trying to look eager but not overeager, trying to seem calm and self-assured but appropriately deferent.

"Jack brought you up as a potential addition to the team he's working with. He said you're clever on the theory side of things, and that you would balance out his skill set well."

Zoe nodded, feeling a vibrating sort of excitement. Had she passed whatever test this was?

"It's not what you are working on. His project is TERT-based—antiaging. Is that okay with you?"

She pretended to consider it before giving her answer, which was in fact immediate. "Yes."

"Great." Fen stood suddenly, resting his fingertips on the table, so Zoe stood, too. Jack remained seated, left foot propped on his right knee, leaning back in his chair. "Someone will be in touch with you about details. And you should think about it. Take the week. If you're not passionate about the work, you won't do well here." He paused. "If you do decide to join us, I'm sure I'll see you." He nodded crisply, once, and then left the conference room.

Zoe hesitated, and then sat back down, spinning her chair to face Jack.

"Good to see you," he said.

"And yourself," she said.

They were both silent.

"You didn't need to do that," she said.

"It wasn't a favor," he said. And then he tilted his chin back and looked at her down the bridge of his nose—had she noticed before that it was slightly crooked?—before flipping his notebook shut, sliding his pen into the metal spiral, which was loose and coming undone at the top, and standing. Zoe stood, too.

"I'll see you in orgo," he said, and he left.

Zoe looked out the window, which faced another glass building that faced another, all the mirrored surfaces making it so bright one might want sunglasses even inside.

"Zoe?" A woman's voice. "I can show you out." It was the PA. She took Zoe back via a route different from the way they'd come, this one through the middle of the floor and therefore the labs. Through the glass walls, Zoe could see what seemed like an infinite number of bright young people working on completely varied projects—bits of machinery, vials of liquid, biological samples, mice. They passed a coffee nook, with three twentysomethings leaning over a table strewn with papers and speaking with an intensity that made Zoe want to stop and listen, one of them raising his voice nearly to a yell as he tapped his finger on one of the papers and detailed what sounded like a complex objection to a particular data interpretation, another sitting back in his chair and crossing his arms, smirking slightly, waiting for the first to finish, and then simply saying "You're wrong," which made all three of them break into raucous laughter. Zoe felt pulled toward them, wanted desperately to be one of them, she and Jack, to argue vehemently and then burst into companionable joy, to feel the heat of working on something that, if you got it right, would most certainly change the world.

The PA accompanied Zoe all the way to the ground floor. Zoe thanked her as she stepped out of the elevator. The PA nodded, the doors closed, and she was whisked back up into the future, leaving Zoe with her feet firmly in the present.

6

At several points, Zoe would think Professor Hall was the right choice of PI. Much later, after everything; a point in the middle, when things were overwhelming and the traditional path seemed so cozily mundane; and now, trying to decide, ego screaming that she should not be clinging to the coattails of another student.

She wanted to discuss it with her roommates, but every time she started to bring it up she flinched away. It was embarrassing. Both because she didn't want to admit she wasn't good enough for Fen by herself, and because talking about Hall's offer felt like bragging. The first half her father, the second her mother.

Her father's perspective would be helpful, too, but she'd not asked him for anything thus far and refused to break now. She wanted to know that her achievements were her own, as much as they could be. Thus Harvard, not MIT or Stanford; thus chemistry, not physics. Thus sitting in silence when he offered advice, folding her hands on the dinner table, eyes focused on the dark whorls in the wood, feeling the anxiety radiate off her mother, a reaction to her disengagement, and the certainty radiate off her father, who either didn't notice his daughter was ignoring him or didn't care. (Her brother had no such qualms, not that he needed help. In fact, he'd come home this Christmas with news to share that warranted opening one of her father's fancy old bottles of wine, which was that he'd be staying at Stanford for his PhD.)

The most notable thing about her first day of work in Fen's lab was that Jack—who sauntered in at about eleven in the morning, after she'd been there for two and a half hours, raised a hand to her in greeting, and then disappeared into the depths of the space—had a spectacular black eye. Dark purple rolling into green into yellow, streaky down the side of his nose like the blood had started to drain before solidifying. It was clearly not new; both his eyes opened all the way, and the puffiness was pretty localized. Against his white skin the whole thing looked ridiculous, like movie makeup. She had to physically shake the image out of her head to pay attention to the postdoc, Jerry, again, who was explaining how to feed the mice.

"You should see the other guy," Jerry joked.

"That looks so bad!" Zoe was grateful for the acknowledgment.

"Yeah, and it's at least two weeks old. You should've seen it right after he got it."

She wanted to ask Jerry if he knew what it was from, and then thought that would be weird. So instead, she shook her head sympathetically, thinking, If Jerry saw it right after Jack got it, and it was at least two weeks old, Jack must've come back to the lab January 2, right after Christmas and New Year's, which was a little strange. Did he not want to spend time with his family? Probably, she thought, he just wanted to get ahead in the lab before the semester—in fact, she thought, I should've come back that early. Then, Why wasn't I invited to come back that early?

The thought made her burn briefly with jealousy, a sense of missing out, before she shoved it away to focus.

At about three, when Zoe's head was full to bursting with new information and her eyes were blurry from the fluorescent lights (several of the lab rats she'd seen wore the orange- or pink-tinted anti-headache glasses, and now she understood why), Jerry said, "Why don't you take a break, get some fresh air, and then I'm going to hand you off to Jack for his portion of the training today."

The first half of that sentence was so welcome that Zoe wilted, but the second made her stiffen again. Was she going to be trained by Jack? Another undergraduate who should still be a trainee? But she just smiled, said, "Thank you so much! I could definitely use some fresh air," and walked down the hall.

"Faster to go left," Jerry called after her. Face burning, she looked over her shoulder and smiled sheepishly before turning and hurrying toward the elevator banks.

The frigid air was welcome, cooling her blush and the heat of her general upset. She tilted her face up, closing her eyes, and felt her snot freeze as she drew a deep breath.

This is exactly where you want to be, she reminded herself.

The door opened behind her, and after a short delay warm air reached her ankles. She looked over her shoulder to smile at whoever was leaving, and realized that whoever was leaving was in fact making their way over to where she stood with her back against the building, and also that whoever was leaving had an enormous shiner, nearly fluorescent in the winter-white light.

He stood beside her and nodded once, pulling a pack of gum from his pocket and holding it out to her. The packaging looked weird, clinical, and she flipped it over to read "Nicorette," then blinked up at him.

"Nicotine gum?"

He looked amused. "My stimulant of choice. No pressure, of course."

She shook her head. "No, thanks. Caffeine is fine for me."

"Smoking is much more satisfying, but you can't work in antiaging and also smoke. The irony would be too delicious."

Zoe laughed, shook her head. She couldn't tell if he was kidding.

"How's your first day?"

"Good," she said, watching cars pass. A black BMW, a silver Toyota. "A lot of info, of course."

"Well, yeah. But you find the work interesting?" He sounded strangely earnest, almost worried. Like a little kid.

"I . . . of course. It's incredible. Cutting edge."

He chewed, fluttered his eyes shut like a smoker taking a drag. She cut a glance up at him, looking at the shadows his eyelashes cast on his cheekbones. The black eye was on the other side of his face, but she could see the edge of the bruise where it touched the tall bridge of his nose. It, his nose, had a slight bump just below his eyebrows, nearly aquiline but for the lack of hook at the end. A second bump toward the middle made Zoe wonder if it had been broken.

"It is. Cutting edge."

She nodded slowly, feeling awkward. "So, um. How'd you get that?"

"Bar fight."

She raised her eyebrows. "Ah."

Jack seemed comfortable in the silence that made Zoe itchy, so she didn't speak.

He moved over to a trash can, took his gum delicately from his mouth, threw it away, returned with his hands jammed in his pockets. He wasn't wearing a jacket, just a gray flannel that hung on his bony shoulders, unbuttoned, over his short-sleeved T-shirt, and he looked cold. Zoe shrugged her own shoulders up inside her wool in sympathy.

"Well," he said, looking across the street. Zoe glanced over, but there was nothing special to see, only a rack of bikes. "Should we get started?"

"Sure," Zoe said, and she followed him inside.

7

The third Monday of the semester, Jack wasn't in the lab. Which was strange only because Jack was always in the lab. She figured he was just taking a day off, and probably for the better. Zoe, at least, was tired: thirty hours a week in the lab plus classes was a lot. Last Monday, she'd been so asleep she'd reflexively gotten on the 7:00 a.m. shuttle and made it across the Charles before remembering that school had started and she needed to go to class before she went to Wyss. It was no wonder Jack had stopped attending orgo in the fall.

But then Jack didn't show up Tuesday, either, and they were supposed to check the group C mice together. Zoe did it herself, and then asked Jerry if he knew where Jack was, and Jerry just shrugged and said he'd last seen him on Saturday. Which made it triply odd.

"He's probably catching up on sleep," Jerry said, "I wish I could do the same thing." Jerry did look exhausted. Zoe wouldn't have understood the urgency with which he worked on this project—PhD students, sure, are trying to finish a dissertation, but postdocs can relax a little—except that she was in it, too, caught in the flow of it, every day a new bend in the river, a mouse living a little longer, running a little farther on a tiny treadmill. She'd picture her grandparents and, worse, her father and mother, the lines that she felt like she was just starting to notice on their faces, more so now that she'd go weeks or even months at a time without seeing them (how ridiculous, how artificial, to stay away from home the whole semester when home was a twenty-minute walk away, and yet it felt crucial), the way her father's back hurt, the way her mother was beginning to sag in places that must have mortified her. And she'd look at the gray-haired, stooped mice, and give them their drugs that activated the gene written into their DNA by the pens of scientists and watch them grow stronger, more energetic, their hair get silkier, their eyes clear. It wasn't her thing, except that it was everybody's thing. Death, that is. Mortality. And so she understood perfectly well.

By Wednesday, Zoe had asked everybody on the team where Jack was, and no one knew nor really seemed to care. She didn't understand how blasé they were being. There had been a campus suicide the year prior, no one Zoe knew, an upperclassman who'd taken a year off and then tried to come back for the fall semester. She had to keep pushing the thought of it out of her head. After her shift, she stopped by to see Stephanie, Fen's PA. Her office sat so that everybody going in and out walked by.

"Have you seen Jack?"

"No," Stephanie answered. "I wasn't here this weekend, but the last time I saw him was Friday."

"Have you heard from him?"

"No. I take it you haven't either." Stephanie was curt; had to be. She wore her pale hair parted in the middle, sleek down both sides of her head, and had a sharp, upturned nose.

"Do you have a way to get in touch with him?"

"Let's see." There was a laptop in front of her, an iPhone at her right hand, and a desktop computer to her left. She typed on the laptop. "I have his college email, which I can give to you, and his dorm

number. No cell. Email is . . ." Stephanie looked up, perfectly plucked
eyebrows arched, and Zoe scrambled in her bag for a piece of paper
and a pen.

"Okay."

"J Leahy, that's *l-e-a-h-y*, at college."

"Got it."

"Dorm is Randolph 243."

"Oh . . . kay." Zoe hadn't expected Stephanie to tell her that.

"He doesn't respond to emails. So that might be easier."

Stephanie turned back to her screen. Zoe thanked her, and left.

On the bus ride home, she wondered whether she should bother with
the email, or just go knock on his door, and then backtracked into
thinking she shouldn't do anything at all.

Outside, the sun was setting, a tight light-yellow ball. It was
that stretch of February when Zoe deeply regretted living in a
northern climate and thought perhaps she'd pack up and start
walking south, stop when the air contained moisture and smelled
of anything more than cold. She felt she looked worse in the winter,
too; olive skin washed out to a greenish pallor, hair tragically dry
and straight, round brown eyes suddenly too big in a sort of con-
sumptive look. The opposite of Nordic Hanna, who got rosy in the
winter, like she'd just been out for some vigorous and healthful ice-
skating. Zoe liked to attribute the pull of the warmth (or perhaps
it was the repulsive force of the cold) to her Greek genes, but it just
as likely came from her mother's family, no member of which had
ventured north of the Mason-Dixon line until Margaret (known by
some as Meg) herself.

Zoe stepped out of the bus and onto the curb, the brick wall
around Harvard Yard curving away from her in both directions, and
picked at the dry skin on her lip with her teeth. She put her hands

in her pockets and walked east along Mass. Ave., took a right down Plympton Street, and ducked into a courtyard.

She was pretty sure this was the right place. Randolph was part of Adams House, and she'd gotten lunch in the Adams dining hall before, which was across the street, but that was the Adams thing, right, that the dining hall wasn't in the same building as the dorms and so they had that warren of tunnels underground (wallpapered with bizarre and brilliant student artwork, or so she'd heard) to get from building to building without going outside.

"I'm looking for Randolph 243?" she said to a student coming at her, a boy, who had a tattered backpack slung over his shoulder and must've just gotten out of bed without brushing his hair, which was flat on the right side and peaked on the left.

"Uh, right. Quickest would be through that door." He pointed, and Zoe realized that there were doors at every corner of the courtyard, "and then up two flights, take a"—he paused, seemed to be trying to figure out the directions in his head—"right, I think, and then you'll find it." He gestured vaguely and kept walking.

The staircase was narrow and low-ceilinged. The dark stain on the intricate wooden banister was worn to blond on the top. The hallway was narrow, too.

Room 243 had no name tag, just a sticky square where one might've been pasted earlier in the year by a well-meaning tutor. Zoe paused for a moment, wondering if she was being stupid, and then knocked and waited, hoping Stephanie had the number right.

An overweight boy with glasses and a remarkably round face opened the door. "I'm looking for Jack?" Zoe said, smiling big.

"Sure," the boy said, "I think he's in his room."

Zoe wanted to ask Are you sure? but didn't. He stepped to the side, as though to let her in. She could see a hall to the right with two narrow doors, both closed, and a common room to the left with too much furniture, one wall papered with screens. Another boy was lying with his feet up on the arm of the sagging couch, ankles crossed.

"Uh, hi," she said, "sorry." The boy on the couch was Black, with high cheekbones and a straight nose. He was wearing worn-looking khakis that draped on his legs. He pushed his hair—twists that fell nearly to his shoulders—back with one hand, and Zoe blushed. He was very attractive. "Um, would you mind just getting him for me?" Zoe asked. "I don't mean to . . . intrude."

The boy with the glasses made his way to one of the doors. "Jack?" he called, "girl here to see you. What did you say your name was?"

"Zoe."

"Says her name is Zoe." As though it might be something else.

There was no noise from inside the room. The boy with the glasses looked at her.

"Would you maybe knock?"

He knocked.

They waited.

"When was the last time you saw him?"

The boy shrugged. "I dunno. Couple days ago? Figured he was keeping weird hours."

The boy on the couch spoke. "Weirder than you?"

"My hours are the correct hours, anything different is weird." The boy with the glasses nodded definitively. The boy on the couch snorted, shook his head.

Zoe tried to reel the conversation back in. "He hasn't shown up to the lab in four days, and he's usually there every day. And no one has heard from him." She could feel herself getting strangely panicky. The room smelled like too many boys in too small a space, and it was seeping out into the hallway, and the boy on the couch hadn't stopped looking at her, and his gaze was making her nervous.

"Did you call him?"

"Oh, uh. I don't have his cell."

The boy with the glasses pulled his out, punched a number and then the speakerphone button as if to prove a point. The phone rang once, and then went straight to voicemail. Jack hadn't recorded a personalized greeting, so it was the stock "You have reached . . ."

The boy on the couch swung up and walked toward Jack's door. He moved easily, like a dancer. He knocked, said, "Jack, if you don't make some sign of life, I'm coming in, so get your hand out of your pants," and then waited a beat before opening the door.

Jack was in bed, asleep. Zoe took a step over the doorframe, heard herself saying, "Oh," at the same time she thought, Is he dead?, which was probably an overreaction.

The boy from the couch walked over to the bed and shook his shoulder. "Dude. You okay? Your girlfriend says you've been MIA." He glanced back at Zoe, but Zoe was looking at Jack, who didn't move. Her fear blossomed in her stomach. The boy with the glasses leaned against the wall, peeling a hangnail.

Then Jack groaned, and Zoe relaxed.

"My fucking head is killing me. Does anyone have some juice?"

There was a long pause.

"Uh," Zoe said, "I can go get some?"

"I think there's some in my fridge." Jack was sitting up, wincing, holding his head. He looked unshowered, and his room smelled weird, sweet. Zoe looked where he was looking to see a knee-high minifridge tucked under the right side of his desk, which was piled with papers that seemed like they'd been blown around, though the window was closed. She crouched and retrieved a small bottle of apple juice, the only thing inside, and handed it to Jack. His sheets were gray flannel. There was hardly anything in the room, she noticed, as he cracked the plastic seal and started gulping. Just spiral-bound notebooks and piles of printed-out scientific papers. Zoe had thought her posters, stack of piano music (there were hundreds of pianos at Harvard, no need to bring a keyboard), tennis racket, bicycle, and yoga mat sparse. Hanna had wallpapered her room with photos and drawings; Gabby'd lugged in three musical instruments, including a pared-down drum set, which was technically forbidden, and two shelves of books in three different languages.

"When did you go to bed?" Zoe asked slowly.

"Uh. Last night?"

"Which was?"

He took a while to answer. "Sunday? Well, it was morning, really." He coughed. "Monday morning."

"It's Wednesday," said the boy from the couch.

Jack frowned. Propped himself up on his elbow, leaned his arm across the headboard. "Fuck. I was supposed to check group C yesterday."

"I did it," Zoe said.

He nodded, shut his eyes. "So that's why you're in my room."

"Yes."

"You good, dude? I have shit to do." The boy with the glasses jabbed his head backward.

"Yeah. Thanks, Mitchell."

The boy from the couch stayed. "Do you need to go to HUHS?"

"No, no," Jack said quickly, "I'm good. Just need some sugar."

The boy from the couch looked at Zoe, then back at Jack. Then back at Zoe.

"I'm Carter," he said, "by the way."

"Zoe," she said, still looking at Jack.

"You gonna stay with him? Someone should probably make sure he actually gets up." Jack did look like he might doze back off.

Zoe spoke before thinking. "Yeah. I can stay."

Carter hesitated, and then left, swinging the door shut behind him.

"You're still in my room." Jack was leaning his head back, eyes still shut. His eyelashes were so dark. Zoe noticed herself noticing them, and that she'd noticed them before.

She thought about how Carter had closed the door.

"We need to get you something to eat." She checked her watch. "The dining hall is closing in fifteen. Do you want to change?"

"I want to go back to sleep."

"You can't. Do you want to change, or do you want to go like that?" He was wearing a T-shirt that was so old the collar was tearing away from the body. She thought going anywhere like that would be criminal but tried not to show it.

He swung his legs over the side of the bed, set his bare feet flat on the floor. On his lower half were very wrinkled jeans. Had he really slept in jeans? "I'll change," he said. He rubbed his face with his hands. "Is it really Wednesday?"

"Yes."

"Fuck. Is Fen pissed?"

"I don't think anyone noticed you were gone." Except me. The unspoken words bounced around the room.

"I'll change. Could you—"

"Yeah, of course." She let herself out and leaned against the wall outside, trying not to make eye contact with Carter, who was back on the couch. She crossed her arms over her chest. He was sitting, looking up at one of the screens with his elbows on his knees, a video game controller in his right hand, a vape pen in his left. Every so often he raised it to his mouth and sipped fashionably. Not like those people who handle vapes like asthma inhalers.

He gestured up without looking at her. "Want a hit?"

"No, I'm good." She felt suddenly young, vulnerable. The dream she'd had the night before crashed into her, re-remembered. She'd gone to CVS, desperate for Band-Aids or tampons or something else both mundane and critical, but when she'd gone in, she'd realized she was nude from the waist up.

Jack emerged, dressed in a hoodie and jeans that looked relatively clean, and went straight out the door.

"Um, thanks, Carter," she said before following Jack. Carter gave them a backward nod.

Jack led her down a different staircase, looping around one corner and then another. They passed an open space with a rack of thirty or more beat-up bikes. Through a door and out onto the street, the cold air waking Zoe as if from a dream. The gate to the dining hall was in front of them. The gilt on it was, supposedly, real gold.

He checked her in as a guest and she followed him to the buffet. He got a tray and piled one plate with spaghetti and meatballs, another with a stewed chicken dish attempting to be Middle Eastern. Zoe made herself a salad and waited for him to finish perusing the desserts, and then they ventured back into the dining hall and tucked themselves at one end of a long table whose other end was occupied by a pack of fratty-looking athletes.

"No one will sit there," Jack said, nodding at the chairs between them and the athletes.

"You're right."

She picked at her salad while he ate methodically, shoveling in the spaghetti and then the chicken. As he went, some color returned to his face, a pink blotch high on each cheekbone. He really needed to wash his hair, which was oily at the temples and frizzed at the ends.

"Lucky half the people here look like hell, else someone might try to send me to HUHS."

A weak attempt at a joke. Zoe wondered where her boundaries were. "What happened?"

"I was up all night Sunday working on something. I went to sleep at, I don't know, nine a.m. Monday. I remember waking up, kind of, a couple times, and thinking it was the middle of the day and I should try to get some more sleep before I went to lab."

"Do you not have Monday classes?"

"Yeah, I do, but it's not a big deal." He shrugged, rested his elbows on the table, and cracked his knuckles in front of his face.

"So you slept for more than two days."

"Well. I was awake for a bit of it. But yeah, I guess."

Zoe slid her tongue over her fixed retainer, something she did when she was thinking. "Why?"

Jack raised his eyebrows and shrugged.

"I think we need to take you to HUHS. There's no way you sleep for over forty-eight hours unless there's something wrong."

"It was probably a blood sugar thing."

"I mean, yes, if you don't eat for forty-eight hours your blood sugar will drop."

"No, I mean, when I went to bed I was probably really hypo. It makes me—" He gestured with one hand. Zoe had no idea what the gesture meant.

"Wait." Zoe cringed at her own insensitivity. "Are you diabetic?"

"Yeah, a bit."

A bit? She wanted to ask, So were you, literally, in a diabetic coma? But she just nodded. The athletes were getting up, scraping their wooden chairs across the floor and shaking the table, rattling Jack's tray. She looked at the empty pasta plate, smeared with tomato sauce.

"What else should we get you?" she asked, and she meant, Don't you need insulin after probably two thousand calories of straight carbs?

"Nothing. I'll feel like shit for a while."

She breathed through her nose. Considered, again, her boundaries. But the boy in front of her felt very much like that, a boy, and the bags under his eyes were puffy and creased, and his hands, folded now in front of him, were too white and tendony, and the high color that hadn't receded from his cheekbones was now unsettling to her, too pink, like face paint. "Don't you need insulin?"

"Oh." He sat back in his chair, and she felt his height again, and he shrugged one shoulder up, and she felt his control again, and he said, "It's not that severe."

Then he smiled, for the first time since he'd woken up, eyes bright, and leaned forward onto his elbows. "Don't you want to know what I was working on that kept me up all night?"

8

Though they wouldn't say it this way, not yet, what he was working on was how to make cells live forever.

They finished their frantic brainstorming session around eleven, sheets of scribbles scattered over his bed. They were both fading out of scientific usefulness, coming down from the high of creativity and into a placid, satisfied zen. Zoe was sitting in Jack's desk chair, legs stretched in front of her and feet crossed at the ankles, and Jack had moved to lie flat on his back on the floor.

"Do you want to watch a movie?" he asked. "I have something I've been meaning to see."

She wasn't one to stay up until 2:00 a.m. the night before class (or any night, really). But she didn't even think twice. "Do you have any snacks?"

"Under the bed."

While she was digging through the shoe box of chips and packaged bagels pilfered from the dining hall, he went out into the common room, where she could hear him messing with a DVD player. She helped herself to pretzels and took a bag of SunChips for him with the vague idea that they were healthier and would better stabilize his blood sugar.

When she padded out, in her socks, she found him sitting on the couch. The title screen was up; the film was called *Dogma*. Matt Damon was in it (of course). She sat beside Jack. It was interesting, how she felt no flare of uncertain thrill about his intentions. They had slipped into grooves already somehow worn deep and familiar, grooves that ran in close parallel but never crossed.

When the movie went to credits, they sat in silence for a while. Zoe had her head slightly tilted, eyes thoughtful, still on the now-dark screen. Jack cracked his knuckles slowly, one by one.

Zoe wasn't into film, preferred to read, but even books didn't often move her. (Jack, for his part, loved film, and he'd force her later to watch his personal list of classics. She agreed with his assessment of *Crouching Tiger, Hidden Dragon*; *Tombstone*; *Spirited Away*; and *Inception*; but not *When Harry Met Sally*.) When Zoe was moved, though, she was moved great distances.

She almost didn't want to try to put into words the idea she was trying to untangle. She knew that spoken, it would lose its magic. And yet.

"I cannot imagine a better God than Alanis Morrisette." She tilted her head back and looked up at the ceiling. It was too dim to see the network of thin cracks in the old plaster.

He nodded. "Me neither."

"How else . . . how else could we have this mess"—she gestured around herself—"if God wasn't a . . . playful . . . if she didn't have such a sense of humor." She shook her head. She'd known she wouldn't be able to explain. "Fucking Skee-Ball."

"I know." She looked at him, and he was grinning, and when their eyes met she could see that he did know, that they had watched the same thing and it had made them feel precisely the same way.

She swallowed, shook her head, nodded, smiled at him. And she knew then that she'd go with him wherever he asked her to, though she'd often pretend she wouldn't.

"Do you know"—he sat back, languid—"about the chimney in Jefferson Lab?"

"No." She should've been tired—it must've been close to two—but she wasn't, just buzzy. Happy. Like she had arrived somewhere.

"There's a chimney in Jefferson lab that runs from the basement of the building out through the roof. But there's no fireplace or boiler or anything in the basement."

"Weird."

"There's no cell service in Jefferson either. Have you noticed?"

Zoe hadn't ever taken a class in Jefferson—she'd taken her physics classes in other departments (like quantum in the chemistry department). She shook her head.

"The chimney is lined with lead. It interferes with cell signal."

"They used it for experiments, then?"

He was nodding. "Wanted to know what stuff souls are made of."

"Mm," Zoe hummed. "I don't think souls are made of stuff."

"So they dropped cats down the chimney. The impact would kill them. Since they were in a lead-lined chimney, the souls would be forced straight up—or so went the hypothesis. Of course, it's completely possible that a soul can pass through lead."

She flinched. "Ugh," she said, and then, "but of course. About the lead."

"They set up various devices at the top of the chimney, trying to detect changes as the soul passed by. Pressure, temperature, air composition."

"The poor cats." She pictured them crumpled at the bottom of the chute. Pictured the assistant who must've had to clean the mess, opening a little lead-lined door and scooping out the remains, dumping them in a bag already full of other small bodies.

"I know. They tried other animals, too. They weren't sure rats had souls, though, so they only went up from cats." She assumed he meant monkeys. She hoped he didn't mean people. He paused for a long time, squinting up at the ceiling. "They could never find anything."

"That would have made Her really sad," Zoe said. "Don't you think?"

When she was little, Zoe had been the too-serious kid that other kids found odd. And when she got to middle school, the girl that other girls' parents compared them to (Well you don't see Zoe Kyriakidis making out with her boyfriend on the corner/getting a C on her math exam/skipping tennis practice/getting drunk, do you? That's because she's going to go to MIT), which doesn't exactly engender good feeling. It only made it worse when Alex (Alex to whom it came easy, who was just charming, and who had never really not been handsome, one of those prepubescent boys who middle-aged women say is going to be a lady killer) included her in his social circles, because she knew it was out of pity.

So by the time she started high school, she'd developed this aloof persona. Which meant that while she had friends, became pretty popular, actually, she never had close friends. It was the same in college, with her roommates, though she and Sophia had had some flashes, had a lot in common. Probably, if she had given it more time, they could have become close.

But with Jack, she didn't need to give it time.

Which was probably why, when she and Jack crashed into each other, when all at once there was no distance between herself and another person, and she felt known, and she felt like she knew, there was never any letting go. Not even after everything.

9

About a week passed.

It was almost March and finally felt like it, the weather teasing warmth. The smell was somewhere between new growth and rot, flowers and decay. It was midmorning, and Zoe was out for a walk. She breathed deeply, unbuttoned her jacket, shoved her hands in her pockets.

Their work in Fen's lab was dragging. The group C mice hadn't turned out as expected—in fact, they'd developed an odd disorder that seemed to be affecting their motor cortexes, and everybody was frustrated.

Her phone buzzed against her hand, and then kept buzzing. A call. She pulled it out of her pocket and looked at the screen, tough to see in the bright sunlight. Jack. He hadn't called her since they'd exchanged cell phone numbers. Why would he? They saw each other every day, usually more than once a day. And they'd started commuting together, the bouncing of the shuttle bumping their shoulders and knees into each other's as they pored over papers or a notebook. They discovered that he could sit on the left and she on the right and they could both write on the same page at the same time without jostling elbows.

They worked on Fen stuff, even though what had looped around them and was tightening, lacing them together, was their own idea, the one that had come into being in Jack's dorm room. Sometimes, when it was really early or really late and the bus was empty, they'd mention it in half-coded whispers, like if they said anything specific aloud or did any concrete work the spell would be broken and the magic would be gone.

"Do you have a few minutes?"

"Sure," she said. "What's up? Did you have an idea about what happened with group C?"

"No," he said, "the opposite. Where are you?"

She looked up. "Somewhere behind the Science Center? Toward Northwest. There's a big gray Harvard building, looks old."

"The Divinity School. I'm really close to you—just stay where you are, I'll find you."

"Wait, why—" she started, but he had already hung up.

She followed directions, sitting on a convenient bench. Cambridge is full of benches, all with those little nameplates—donated by so-and-so, class of such-and-such. Within five minutes she saw him, walking at her with big strides, hunched forward like he was in a hurry.

"Are you okay?" she asked when he was within earshot.

"Of course I'm okay," he said, stopping in front of her. Then he cleared his throat, ran a hand through his hair. "I have a proposal for you."

Which is how, ten minutes later, she found herself standing in front of a secretary's desk in the Biological Labs on Divinity Avenue. He'd walked her there so quickly she hadn't caught the nameplate on the door. The secretary was older than Zoe was used to, in her late fifties or early sixties, with a short haircut, a dress that came past her knees, and small heels, like an archetype from a time gone by. A far cry from sleek, modern Stephanie.

"He's here?" Jack asked.

"Yes, he's in his office. I'll get him. Nice to meet you, hon," she said to Zoe, smiling and nodding, and Zoe smiled back.

"He'll be just a moment," the secretary said when she returned. Zoe perched obediently in a chair. Jack stayed standing, leaning to one side. He looked somehow even rangier than usual.

A very old man with bushy white eyebrows emerged a few minutes later from the door behind the secretary's desk. Zoe had read recently about the effect of aging on eyebrow growth in men—it has to do with the way hair follicles interact with testosterone over time—and she thought idly about this now. Long-term exposure to testosterone makes hair follicles get stuck in the growth phase, or lengthens the growth phase, or something like that.

"Jack!" he said, holding out a hand. "How are you?"

"Good. I have someone I want you to meet."

"Oh?" He seemed to notice Zoe for the first time. "Who might this young lady be?"

If she had known who he was, she might have bristled at "young lady." But because he was, to her, just another old white man with an outdated worldview, she simply smiled and held out her hand. "Zoe," she said, "nice to meet you."

His skin was thin, moved easily under her fingers. But his grip was tight.

"This is my partner," Jack said. Zoe warmed. She hadn't ever thought of them like that, but it felt right.

"Oh!" The old man's eyebrows shot up, and he looked at Zoe again. "She's lovely."

"Not my girlfriend. My partner. In the epigenetics work."

"Well, then. I didn't realize you had a partner."

"Zoe, this is Professor Brenna. He—"

"Oh! Of course," she said. Even for someone who'd been around a lot of famous professors, Brenna was a lot. Why hadn't Jack warned her? "Semiconservative replication," she added, to fill the silence. He and Meselson and Stahl had figured out how DNA duplicates itself in one of the most elegant experiments ever designed. Much later, Zoe would explain it in a Q and A in which she was asked about her and Jack's time in Brenna's lab.

But she wasn't thinking then about giving presentations to thousands of people, having her makeup done professionally, wearing one of those little microphones that curves down your cheek. She was thinking about the fact that a legend was standing in front of her, and that he had assumed she was not a scientist but a girlfriend.

They moved into his office. On his desk was a thick book of Sumerian poetry, a fountain pen, a desktop computer, and an empty mug. They sat at the coffee table in the middle of the room.

"I myself am most concerned with what it is that makes us human," Brenna said. His voice quivered slightly all the time. "Now that we have gene editing capability, we must figure out exactly what we value about being human, so that we don't snip it out." He laced his fingers together over one knee. His legs were crossed. "What boundaries we need to draw for ourselves. It's perhaps the only question that really matters. Because there won't be any going back."

Zoe nodded. "I'm interested in the neurology problem."

"Then we are thinking in the same direction." He gestured at his book of poetry. "These of course are the fundamental questions of philosophy, of creation, art: What is it that makes our experience what it is? Jack, however, continues to preoccupy himself with the question of immortality."

"It takes all kinds," Jack said, and Brenna's face split into a smile. His teeth were small and widely spaced. He still had most of them. In a strange way, Zoe thought, his face was childish. Round, skin so fragile in spots that it had become smooth again.

"I am too old to care about immortality."

He coughed, as if to prove his point, and it rattled around his chest.

"However, I think Jack asks some elegant questions. You've read Byrne's most recent paper, I imagine."

Jack had thrust it at her the night she'd gone to his dorm room. Then he'd changed his mind, pulled it back and read it aloud.

"Yes, I have."

"And?"

"And I think that the question of how one might safely use the Yamanaka factors to reverse the symptoms of aging in a controlled manner is very promising and very difficult."

That was part of what they'd discussed that night. The factors had been used before to change aged cells all the way back to stem cells (already astounding, because before this we'd thought that cellular differentiation was a one-way street), but the process had never been stopped in the middle. The Byrne paper showed that the Yamanaka factors could turn an old skin cell into a young skin cell, an old muscle cell into a young muscle cell—huge news for potential applications in living organisms.

However, delivery was a problem—it's one thing to target a single cell, and quite another to target every cell of the body and reverse-age an entire organism—and effective dosages almost always caused cancer. So Jack and Zoe talked delivery devices and dosage tweaks, like using some factors but not others.

"Sure, sure. And?"

She tilted her chin up. She wasn't certain she wanted to explain the other thing they'd discussed. The part that made her feel physically as if the top of her head had been taken off. (The description floated up from some half-forgotten reading. She'd find it later—

Emily Dickinson on poetry, from that time she'd been floored by *I heard a fly buzz* in her ninth-grade English class and subsequently decided to read every piece of Dickinson published.)

Eventually, Jack spoke. "The bigger questions are in where and how the cells store the information they need to age backward. But we're explaining this all wrong. I asked the stupid, narrow questions. Drug delivery, dosage, side effect mitigation. Zoe asked the right ones."

Zoe thought she might blush, but she didn't. It was true. She'd been standing there behind Jack in his dorm room, leaning on his chair, watching his hands as he scribbled something to explain what he was working on, and her mind had gone elsewhere, and her heart had started racing, and she'd said "Jack," and there was something in the sound of her voice that made him pause his writing and look up at her. "Why haven't—have you read Mark Fraser?"

"Yes," he'd said, "epigenetics. Of course."

Then her words had come out in a rush, and he'd watched her, rapt, and she'd drunk the wonder in his eyes and kept going.

The idea expelled, she'd sunk to the side, knocking his pen to the floor when she reached out to steady herself on his desk.

"You're a genius," Jack had said simply, and she'd shaken her head, still lost in the idea.

"Do you think that . . ."

"Yes, you're right, and if we could find and unlock that information, you could reset the cell . . . you could age every cell in your body backward to youth"—he'd gestured down Zoe's body—"not to mention we would completely . . ." He'd swallowed and shook his head, and then started writing. She'd moved over to his bed, the glow from the courtyard spilling through the window and over his crumpled sheets, and sat, cross-legged, staring hazily across the room.

He'd spun around in his chair and looked at her. "Zoe. We could change the world. We would change the world."

But now Brenna was speaking. "Ah. Zoe?"

"I asked—if you take Fraser's work on epigenetics to be true, it follows that the mechanism by which the Yamanaka factors age a cell backward is by restoring the organization of the DNA within the cell. The epigenome. Which means that the cell must store, somehow, a copy of what its epigenome should look like. Postdifferentiation. So where is that information, how is it stored, and how can we read it." She forgot to raise her voice at the end, so she added, "Are my questions." The last question was implied: How can we tell an old cell to reread it, to reset itself back to youth?

Brenna nodded slowly. "Very good," he said, but he wasn't looking at her, he was looking at Jack. She couldn't tell if he had already asked these questions himself or, and this seemed more likely, Jack had already told him all of this. She wished she could hit pause on the rest of the world, pull Jack aside, ask him to explain what the hell was going on.

It was then that Jack pulled out his notebook and took a few printed pages from inside the front cover.

"I, uh. Think I found something."

He spread the sheets out, and she noticed his hands were trembling slightly.

"I was playing with applying the factors to yeast."

Where'd he get yeast? she thought. But she was soon too absorbed by his story to care.

"It was an accident, actually. I intended to put a little DSB in, induce aging, and then use the Yamanaka factors. But they didn't work, for some reason. I sequenced the genome, so that if nothing else, I'd know if my edit had worked. I compared it to the original strain's genome. I realized I'd chopped off an additional little sequence of DNA, accidentally.

"I repeated the experiment, this time on purpose, and it held. So this little chunk here—if you knock it out, the factors stop working."

Zoe's heart was thudding. "So that's it. Or part of it. Or codes for it."

"Well, I don't know, but . . ."

"But that could be it. Do you know—"

"I don't know anything else. I just did this."

Zoe bit the inside of her lip, hard. Brenna was already speaking.

"I'm not taking students," he said. "I have a part-time postdoc who's just about finished with his work."

Zoe was still trying to wrap her head around the data.

"However, my lab is open to you, should you wish to pursue these questions." He stood up by pushing off the arms of his chair.

Zoe looked at Jack. He wasn't looking at her. She couldn't think. Everything was moving too fast, blurry. Brenna nodded, and the secretary bustled in and saw them out.

Standing outside the building, Zoe came back to reality, snapping into herself, the February afternoon cold, clouds hurried across the sun by the wind. "What was that?"

"What?"

She wrapped her coat tighter around herself. Her overwhelm had twisted and morphed into anger. That he'd shared the precious, unspoken idea with someone else without telling her. That he'd run an experiment without her. That Brenna, one of the best scientists alive, had assumed she was a girlfriend. That he and Jack had made this whole plan to pursue a project based on her ideas without her input or consent—because they must have, because Brenna wouldn't have offered his lab so quickly unless Jack had already talked to him. That Jack had sprung the data on her in front of Brenna, and that she didn't yet understand the implications of the data, and that she was obsessed with figuring them out.

"You went behind my back to talk to another PI about my ideas?"

Jack blinked at her. "You're not—"

"What the fuck, Jack?"

"Why are you angry?" His eyebrows knit together, and his voice raised slightly. "You're a fucking genius, your idea is brilliant, and we have to pursue it. It would be a waste of—this could make our careers. This could change the way the world thinks about mortality. I found us a way to do that, no questions asked, functionally unlimited resources. It's Dick fucking Brenna, Zoe. He does whatever he wants! And he wants to give us the cash and the space to do this!"

Professor Brenna, she thought, and then, bitterly, that he probably was Dick to Jack. "Why didn't you show me the data first?"

"What do you *mean*? It's new, I literally made those figures today. I finished the second run last night."

His ignorance pissed her off more. "I can't believe you just—while you were fucking around, I was working at our real job. We're a little bit in the middle of something with Daniel Fen, who, I hate to remind you, is actually of this century." She wanted to say something, anything, to tear down Brenna, who both was Jack's conspirator and hadn't taken her seriously. And she really wanted to ask the question that had been burning at her since Jack had walked into orgo what felt like a lifetime ago, which was, Who the fuck are you? Who are you and why are you being given so much? But knowing what that would sound like coming from her, she didn't.

"Daniel . . . there's no way Daniel gives us the freedom to do this. No way."

"Yeah, probably because we shouldn't *have* the freedom to do this! We don't know what we're doing!" They stood, both panting, staring at each other. "Did you show him?"

"No—he'd take it, and he'd give it to some other team. And it'd go to startup, and he'd get the patent. Without us, because we're just fucking interns, Zoe. That's how he oper—that's how this whole fucked-up system operates!"

Now, passersby were staring. They looked, probably, like they were in the throes of a lovers' quarrel, Zoe leaning forward and punctuating with her hands, Jack running his hands through his already wild hair.

"We do know what we're doing. And outside of the bureaucratic bullshit of today's science, we can move *so much faster.*"

"Science isn't fast, Jack! Don't be delusional!"

"It can be way faster than it is, and you know it. You were just complaining the other night that everything is too niche and no one is asking the big questions anymore."

True. She remembered the sun, setting over the Charles, had stained Jack's face red as she said it. "There's a difference between asking big questions and going off the rails. Clearly Brenna isn't in his right mind. We aren't even old enough to *drink*. I don't even know how we would start this thing." But her mind was already racing toward how to break down her questions, how to ask the right subquestions to edge around the core, to move in a tightening spiral until they reached the center.

Jack smirked. "You're thinking about it."

"Agh!" She threw up her hands. Wished she had something devastating to say. Settled for turning on her heel, coat swirling dramatically, and stalking away across the grass.

She had no idea where she was going, and so she was surprised when she emerged onto Oxford Street, right across from Gordon McKay labs. She waited until she was in front of Mallinckrodt, the chem building where they'd had orgo together, until she looked back over her shoulder. Just for the poetry of it. Jack was nowhere to be seen.

Zoe read the Brenna, Meselson, and Stahl paper, 1958, for the first time the night after the meeting. Of course she'd studied semiconservative replication and their experiment. But she'd never really thought about how elegant it all had been. How a paper could, in seven pages of 12-point, 1.5-spaced text, prove beyond reasonable doubt the mechanism by which life remembers itself. How three young men, three students, could discover that mechanism in less than a year. It was the glory days of science, the cowboy days, before the endless slog to reach your own pointless niche, before the twenty-page, two-column, 10-point, single-spaced papers so thick with jargon and citations that a person even one subtopic removed could never hope to understand.

She saw her future: an undergrad gunning for a top PhD program, slogging her way through hours on hours in Fen's lab, where, since starting, she had not once spoken to Fen, then a PhD student gunning for a top postdoc appointment, then a postdoc gunning for another top postdoc appointment and then, finally, that assistant professorship, tenure track, all the while doing the grunt work for someone else's ideas. Feeding mice. Pipetting liquids. Never really getting to think. And maybe one day she'd finally walk into her own lab, in her mid-thirties at the earliest, early forties more likely. And she'd have ensconced herself by then in a bizarre little niche, some single function of some single protein, so deep she wouldn't have any hope of seeing the big picture. She'd be middle-aged, and bored, and unable to remember why she started.

At the end of their conclusion, Brenna, Meselson, and Stahl asked: What are the molecular subunits of DNA? How are they structured, and how do they interact? By what mechanism do they combine and dissociate in vivo? As she read under the yellow light that was built into her stock dorm desk, her overhead light off, her roommates asleep, something moved in Zoe's stomach. What beautiful, fundamental questions, she thought. They stood at a precipice, and looked off into the fog, and asked how life worked, and then built a bridge forward until they reached the answers. She stood up and looked out the window into the Lowell courtyard. It was after midnight. There were lights on in maybe a third of the windows. She opened hers, leaning out, and drank in the cold air. It felt good on her face, raised goose bumps on her legs.

Fuck, she thought, I need to see that data again.

She picked up her phone and called Jack. He answered on the first ring.

"Yes," she said.

II

DOGMA

10

At first, and for a while, and then in sharp pulses when things were going well, the drive was metallic behind her teeth. There was no greater joy than to be consumed by such an obsession, to be successful in inquiry, to stretch the mind to its fullest extent in service of understanding a problem no person had ever understood before. It was like being a kid and running as fast as you can, stretching your legs and pumping your arms and feeling like you're flying over the grass, hundreds of muscles all working perfectly in conjunction, the legs and the core and the heart and the lungs, so many components all in sync, incomprehensible, like magic, to produce this wonderful movement, the sensation of the ground under you and the sky above you and the air rushing past your ears.

They subsisted on Diet Coke from the Biolabs vending machine no one else seemed to use and FlyBy lunches from the basement of the freshman dining hall, far closer to the Biolabs than their own dining halls, which Zoe begged the lunch ladies to let them take despite being sophomores. Jack, broody and awkward, was no help in this negotiation. They spent every waking moment together, save when Zoe went to class.

As Cambridge thawed and the sun began to penetrate the air enough to warm the skin, they'd take midafternoon breaks in the courtyard. It was a quirky courtyard, with two enormous rhino statues flanking the double Biolab doors, a perpetually empty volleyball pit, and a frieze of various animals in the red brick around the tops of the buildings: a wolf looking back over its shoulder, a mountain goat midclimb, a sinewy group of lounging tigers.

In the lab they spoke only about the work, and even then they often preferred symbols and numbers and diagrams to words; would go into the break room and pull Brenna's single dinged-up whiteboard over the bumpy gray carpet that was always shedding long fibers up to the couch and sit, Zoe on the right and Jack on the left, to sketch things out. But outside they talked endlessly about everything: whether computers could ever be conscious (Jack said no, Zoe yes), what it would mean to be immortal, whether you'd rather have infinite money or infinite intelligence (Jack said money, Zoe said intelligence), the ethics of gene editing a fetus, whether or not we have free will and if it matters (Jack said yes, Zoe said no, they agreed it probably doesn't matter), what it means to be a person.

If she thought about it, Zoe would realize she still had no idea what town he was from, what his parents' names were, if he had pets, if he had a favorite color. They'd skipped all of that to get to the deep stuff, the important stuff, like, How does your mind work and What do you believe in, and it'd be ridiculous to go back now.

In retrospect, Brenna was the only one who understood quite how far their idea was from fruition. It was good, but the value of an idea is in its execution, not its conception.

Both Zoe and Jack had experienced the drudgery of the lab, but they hadn't owned it. It was never their project, always someone else's, and anyway undergraduates almost never see a whole project from idea to publication, usually come in halfway through and leave just in time to slide their name onto the paper.

A yeast setup appeared in Brenna's lab overnight. They were able to replicate Jack's initial experiments, and then they got stuck. The yeast genome is more similar to the human genome than you would think, and so Jack and Zoe figured that if the Yamanaka factors work in yeast and in humans, the mechanism must be analogous, and therefore the crucial chunk of DNA that probably—hopefully—encoded epigenetic instructions would be somewhere in the human genome, too.

But weeks passed, and finding it was proving difficult. And she and Jack had significant skill deficits: neither of them had worked much with yeast, and neither of them had the computer science background they needed to do complex genome analysis.

Zoe started to lose weight. She found a slight edge of hunger kept her sharp, awake. And she liked the way her clothes hung off her frame. She thought that, plus the dark circles under her eyes, made it clear to everyone how hard she was working.

Jack started tearing through at least a pack of nicotine gum a day.

Zoe had always been worried about leaving Fen's lab. But at first, when the idea was fresh and she was high on the small rebellion, the leap of faith, she could easily cover up her doubts with the image of the paper by Kyriakidis, Z., Leahy, J., and Brenna, R.; her ticket out of the drudgery of doing other people's science, forever, punched before she'd even graduated college.

As the summer loomed, her image of that paper got hazier, flickered in and out of existence, and she began to spend more time wondering how she could have left the shiny glass of Wyss to come to this dull, old-fashioned building with the musty stairwell and the eighty-year-old janitor who'd been cleaning since before even Brenna had been hired and the chalky ceiling tiles with occasional concerning dark spots. To Brenna's lab, with its twisty, outdated glassware and rows of empty benches, which was, 100 percent of the time, absent Brenna.

"How the hell are we supposed to do this?" Zoe asked one morning, frustrated, hands under the silver hood with the glass sash set about three-quarters of the way down. You wouldn't know it, but the light pink plate in Zoe's gloved hands was covered in fragile human fibroblasts. "I don't even really know how to keep these alive."

"Well, if we can figure out how to keep them alive . . ." Jack began from across the room.

"Don't even." Zoe closed her eyes. Then she set down the plate, snapped off her gloves, and went outside to get some air. Before she was out the door, Jack was already moving into her position at the hood, adjusting his safety glasses, picking up a pipette.

One night in April, when they'd been holed up working in Jack's bedroom for several hours, Zoe gave up and slipped out into the common room, leaving Jack at his computer. They always went to Jack's when they wanted to work outside of the lab, and so by now she didn't feel weird about hanging out with his roommates alone. James was in the chair, talking to Mitchell, who was cross-legged on the floor looking up at a screen where a blue avatar was shooting a green avatar. Zoe couldn't tell if Mitchell was shooting or being shot. Carter was there, too, on the couch. Which was unusual—it seemed like whenever she saw him, he was on his way out.

The only open seat was next to Carter. She sat. Her neck hurt, and she reached up, wincing, to rub at it.

"The genius emerges!" he said. Zoe rolled her eyes. "Here." He reached for her shoulder.

She raised her eyebrows but dropped her hand into her lap, and he sank a thumb directly into the largest knot. She'd seen that Carter was touchy, she reminded herself, seen him kiss his friends—most of whom were women—on the cheek in greeting, drape an arm around them as they waltzed down the hall en route to a show at the American Repertory Theater or an opening at the Harvard Art Museums or a concert in Boston. Still, she couldn't help the adrenaline rush. She'd been harboring a bit of a harmless crush on Carter.

The rest of the roommates were, for lack of a less pejorative term, nerds: Mitchell was a computer science freak who didn't go to class, spent sixteen hours a day writing code and the rest playing video games; Rafael was a premed obsessed with his cancer research; James was an applied math–econ kid who talked too much. And Jack, of course, was Jack. Carter, on the other hand, seemed to have friends in every sphere, or every interesting sphere. He'd gone to Groton, was mixed, Black and white, studied philosophy, wore loose V-neck sweaters, and was the type of Harvard student who does nothing but everything, who self-deprecatingly calls himself a jack-of-all-trades-master-of-none but is better than you at all of them. Zoe hadn't asked what his parents did, and yet someone, at some point, had told her: his father was head of neurosurgery at Weill Cornell, his mother a cardiac surgeon. To be honest, Zoe thought as he moved his hand toward her spine and goose bumps rose up the back of her neck, I don't really get why he's here.

"James," Carter said, "that reminds me of Caty's mural in the tunnels." He laughed. "I mean, it's really just a vagina. Very Georgia O'Keeffe." Zoe had met Caty once, actually, when she'd come to the room to meet Carter. She had winged eyeliner and long black hair with the bangs dyed bright pink. There was a guy dangling off her arm who was a bit of a campus celebrity, a guitarist with square glasses whose cheekbones were just sharp enough to create his status.

"I've never been down there," Zoe said.

"Been down where?" Jack asked. Zoe hadn't realized he'd come out of his room, and she blushed, conscious of the way she was leaning back onto Carter's hand, which felt suddenly very middle school. But Jack didn't seem to notice, or perhaps just didn't care.

"The tunnels."

"Oh." Jack paused, studying her face. "Do you want to have been down there?"

She shrugged, too embarrassed to say yes.

"Let's go, then," he said, heading toward the door.

Carter lifted his hand as she stood, leaving a cold spot where it had been. She trailed Jack out and down the staircase and then into the hall, all the way to a different corner of the building. "You can get down this way," he said, nodding at a narrow door.

"After you."

It was dark. She kept her eyes fixed on the fuzzy halo of Jack's hair, feeling a strange, nervous giggle in her chest. He flicked on a light at the bottom of the stairwell, and there was a sudden expansive skittering, and the reddish floor was moving, and then she realized it had been covered with cockroaches and now they were fleeing the light. She held in her nausea and backed up a few steps.

"Classic," Jack said.

The tunnels were exactly what they sound like. The basement of a dorm, divided into a warren of hallways lined with pipes and wires, bricks painted white and then covered with student art. Some seemed old, caricatures of professors and jangly limericks.

There once was a student called Max
Studied 'stotle and Marx in the stacks
But the problem you see
Had to make some money
Now it's Nietzsche and Goldman and Sachs

Zoe walked at Jack's shoulder, peeking over it like an adventurer. Through one doorway, a black blob with downcast cartoon eyes was captioned "sometimes all the gazing / makes the Abyss nervous." Jack looked back. "I don't think the abyss gets nervous. Do you?"

"Maybe not. But I like the thought. Makes me feel less intimidated."

"Healthy to be intimidated by the abyss."

They walked past a window with no glass that looked down onto a room on an even lower level—a subbasement—with a pool table, abandoned midgame, and several ratty couches. Staring at the scene from up here made it seem like a set piece from a play, absent the actors. Or a diorama in a museum of obsolescence. Leisure Time, College, approx. 2010 CE. Zoe leaned her forearms on the windowsill and stared down. "So weird."

Jack leaned beside her, arm pressing into hers companionably. "So weird." They didn't move. Zoe wondered how long ago the game had been abandoned.

"I've been thinking about how nature doesn't want us to live forever."

"Me, too," Zoe said lightly. "But what do you mean?" Jack didn't answer. "Nature doesn't *want* us to live at all. Nature is trying to kill us every day."

"I mean that every organism is built to decay. It's built to allow itself to break down. Geriatrics is by nature, excuse the pun, a losing battle."

"Yes."

"What I'm trying to say is . . . it's not a mechanical failure. Like, we build—or we used to build—a car wanting it to last as long as possible, but you can't help the fact that things wear out. Our genetic code isn't trying to build something that lives past the time we reproduce and raise successful offspring. Because our genetic code only cares about getting carried to the next generation."

Zoe nodded.

They were both quiet for a few beats.

"One thing that does . . . confuse me, I guess," Zoe said, "is, how could our genes create a thing, consciousness, that doesn't share precisely their interests?" She stopped and looked up, thinking she'd felt someone walking toward them. But the hall was empty.

"It's not going to be selected *against*, probably. Longer life. Although maybe, if longer-lived organisms take up resources that don't allow younger ones to reproduce."

"But why do I *want* to live forever, if it's quite literally not in my DNA? Or . . . maybe not forever. But longer than I live now." Not forever but longer than now was a loose thread in her reasoning. If she pulled, things would unravel, so she didn't.

"Do you think," she continued instead, "does that mean there has to be a soul? That comes from . . . somewhere else."

"There doesn't have to be anything," Jack said, but his tone was playful. He was either saying Yes, duh, of course there has to be a soul; or No, quit being stupid, of course there's no soul. Zoe couldn't tell which and didn't quite know how to ask.

She thought about the cats dropped down the chimney.

"I don't want to live forever," Jack said, closing his eyes. "I just don't want to die."

When she got back to her dorm, it was three. Sophia was still at her desk. Zoe was drunk, metaphorically, from walking and laughing with Jack, and high, literally, from a few drags she'd taken, coughing, of the joint he'd pulled from the pocket of his jeans. It might help her sleep, he'd said, but no pressure. She couldn't tell if it would, but she felt looser, less attached to herself.

Sophia turned around. "Are you all right?"

"Yeah, of course," Zoe said, smiling a little stupidly. "I'm fine. Why?"

"You smell like weed."

"My friends were smoking a joint. I had some."

Sophia kept looking at her. "Since when do you smoke?"

"Since I can't figure out—" She paused. She hadn't explicitly told her roommates about leaving Fen's lab to work with—not with, more in the general vicinity of—Brenna. "Tough problem in the lab."

If she wasn't high, she would've turned the questioning back on Sophia. What are you doing up still? she would have said. Are *you* okay? But her edges were dulled.

"I feel like I haven't seen you in ages," Sophia said.

"Mm. It's been crazy busy."

"Nothing makes you busy. You're the queen of doing a hundred things and still seeming relaxed."

"Sprezzatura," Zoe supplied. And then she floated back to the time Sophia had heard her sobbing through her bedroom door in the middle of the night freshman fall, when she was having an I'm-not-special-anymore breakdown like everybody else, thinking about how kids were probably saying she didn't even need the affirmative action of being a woman in STEM because she'd gotten in on her father's name anyway, thinking they were right, how Sophia had knocked and said, softly, Are you okay? and Zoe had choked out a yes, remained where she was on the floor, and how in the morning Sophia had left a chocolate muffin from the dining hall on her desk. Yes. Sprezzatura.

Sophia rolled her eyes. "Whatever. Are you and Jack official?"

"No," Zoe said, slouching onto the love seat. "We're working together."

"Are those two things mutually exclusive?"

Zoe's thoughts were slow, still half in freshman year, so she just said, "Yes."

Sophia was exasperated. "Look. We're worried about you."

"We?" Something inside her crouched into a defensive posture. Who gave them the right to gang up on her behind her back?

"Yes, we . . . those of us who live here, with you."

"There's nothing to worry about." She thought of Jack's roommates, probably still sitting around his common room. Jack would've gone back to work, or maybe tried to sleep, but Carter and James and Raf and Mitchell would still be there, laughing about something, maybe playing a video game. They wouldn't get all judgy and accusatory like this.

"You're hardly sleeping, you're showing up to class late, you're working all the time. You're never in the dining hall here, because you have all your meals with Jack. You've probably not spoken to anyone but him for the past month, and you're not dating?"

She's just jealous, Zoe thought, rolling her eyes internally, and then she realized that she'd rolled her eyes externally and cringed, moved to say something to make it better, apologize, maybe, but Sophia was already turning back to her laptop and closing it. She picked it up and carried it into her room, shut the door behind her. Zoe stood up and then paused for a moment in the middle of the common space, studying a precarious pile of books (Gabby's), a basket of fruit (Hanna's), the papers Sophia had left on the desk. Then she went into her room and fell into her bed and was asleep before she could consider turning off the lights.

She was disgusted by it while she was still in it, which was, in Zoe's experience, fairly unusual for a sex dream. Perhaps *disgusted* wasn't right. *Conflicted? Upset?* There wasn't a good word for the feeling, she decided, once she had woken up and was lying on her stomach, one foot dangling off the side of her bed.

It had started innocuously. They were out for a walk. It was summer and raining, and the rain was falling on Zoe's face but she wasn't getting wet. Neither was Jack.

They were talking about something serious. An experiment. But Zoe couldn't quite keep track of the conversation: she was watching herself speak more than speaking. They came to Mass Ave Diner. Cambridge was utterly deserted and impressively gray, even for the rain. The street was slick and reflective.

They went inside like this had been their destination, which it would never be, because Jack wouldn't buy food when he could eat for free in the dining hall. They seated themselves, neither of them stopping the stream of discussion. There was no waitress in sight.

Then Jack leaned forward over the table and kissed her, and goose bumps prickled over her arms and blossomed across her back, and suddenly they were in her parents' house, upstairs, standing in the hall outside her room. She could see into her room over his shoulder, and it wasn't her room, it was his dorm room. He was telling her good news and then he pulled her into a hug and she hugged him back, still aroused from being kissed at the diner (when was that, last night? So vivid, like it happened just a moment ago), and he said in her ear, voice low and light, like he was pleasantly surprised, "You want to have sex with me." She didn't know how her body could have given her away so she wondered if he was in her head somehow and this disturbed her. She pulled away from him and said, "I don't think that's a good idea," which it wasn't. And then they were back in the diner and somehow she'd ended up on his side of the booth and he was slipping a hand under her shirt, she could feel rough calluses on the fingertips he was brushing lightly over her skin before pressing his hand against her back and pulling her toward him and her whole body was hot, and they were back in her house and he was saying, "I completely agree," and her stomach was a twirl of confusion and the whole thing made her think of kissing her brother, kissing Alex, and she became nauseated, and then they were back in the diner and they were still making out and he had her left breast in his hand and she was saying into his mouth "We can't do this here," and so they got up and left, still no waitress in sight, no one in sight at all, started walking, and slid back into the conversation they'd been having and the rain cooled her skin and she was out of her body again, watching the two of them pace back toward the lab.

When she woke up she spent a few short moments in craving—perhaps him, perhaps someone else—before it stopped and she realized she had no desire to be with him sexually, and she asked herself, Really? and her self answered, Pretty sure, actually, and she looked at the clock—five—and got out of bed for a few minutes because she didn't like lying in her own warm spot, in the middle of all that feeling.

When she woke up the second time, midmorning light coming through the gap under the shade, it was from a dream about being rejected by every PhD program to which she'd applied. She rubbed her eyes and groaned. Come on, she thought, give me a break.

She got up, dressed, brushed her teeth (dry, she'd run out of toothpaste a few days ago), checked her watch. Jack would either still be in bed or would have not gone to bed. She decided to stop by his room on her way to the Biolabs. She didn't want to face the bench alone.

Carter answered the door. "Hey, Zoe," he said. He was more unkempt than she'd ever seen him, his hair, at least the top half of which was usually tied back from his face, falling into his eyes and puffy at the ends, his eyes narrow, like he wasn't quite awake yet, wearing a pair of sweatpants with Groton down the leg and no shirt. She tried not to look down at his chest and stomach, which were—oh, well, she was looking now—chiseled. "I just got up," he said, "sorry."

She shook her head, looking down. "Is Jack still here? Or did he go in already."

"He's not here," Carter said. "Is, uh. Everything okay?"

"God, do I look that bad?" Zoe asked, laughing nervously.

"No, no, you look great," Carter said, pushing back his hair with one hand. He was wearing rings: one on his pointer finger and one on his pinkie. Must sleep in them, Zoe thought, which made her think of him in bed. She felt herself growing hot. "Jack just seemed on edge when he left and so do you."

"Oh, yeah. Well. You know."

"I don't."

Zoe offered a lopsided smile, shrugged. "I'm gonna head over, then." But she didn't move.

"Come on," he said, "take a break. Coffee? Espresso? Tea? Whiskey, neat?"

"I'm okay," she said. But she followed him in.

She was going to tell someone. She had to. It had been too big of a risk, and it was going too poorly, and those dreams had knocked her off-balance. It should have been Sophia, probably, and would have been, if she'd gone straight home rather than smoking half that joint, if she hadn't picked a fight. But now, in the clean morning light, it would be Carter, who was handing her a cup of tea and smiling, who had procured a shirt, which was good, because now she didn't have to worry about where her eyes were, and who was sitting down across from her and speaking softly.

"So what's the rush? Why are you two putting so much pressure on? You're only sophomores. There's no way Fen expects you to do some crazy project all by yourselves."

"We left Fen's lab to work on this independent thing, and I just—I think it was stupid." It came out abruptly, unceremoniously.

"What?" Carter raised his eyebrows. "What are you working on? And with who?"

"With Richard Brenna. You know—"

"*Brenna?* As in Brenna, Meselson, and Stahl? Really—wow."

She put her elbows on her knees and her face in her hands. "We took this . . . project to him so that we could, like, have creative control and space and time and money. But we have no idea what the fuck we're doing, and he's never around. And if I'm not published next year, I mean, goodbye to a decent PhD program. And if I'm not published at all before I graduate, goodbye to a PhD. Jesus. I mean . . ." She realized she was rambling, boring him, and she cringed. "Ah, you don't care about all of that. I'm sorry."

"No, no, keep going."

"I mean, it's not like I didn't know the risk." She didn't say that part of her—her pride—had wanted the risk, because normal success would be expected of someone with her academic pedigree, but developing a new, groundbreaking theory of aging, alone? That would get people's attention. Would be *hers*. "Like, I knew how much runway we'd need, how much time it would take. I guess I just got swept up in the idea."

Carter put his elbows on his knees, too. She could feel him looking at her.

"So." She faked a laugh, looked up at him, swallowed. "What should I do?"

"Get a second opinion from someone you trust in the space," Carter said, "so you know whether you should cut your losses now or stick with it."

Zoe hadn't expected any advice, let alone good advice, and it snapped her out of whatever strange place she'd been in, where the light was catching in Carter's eyes and the tea smelled soothing and the sun coming in the window was warm on her arm.

"That's a good idea," she said.

And then, "Fuck. Don't tell Jack I told you, he'd be pissed."

Carter mimed zipping his lips, throwing away the key.

"All right, but hear me out," Carter said.

They were sitting by the river, a few days later. So were other groups of students, all scattered across the lawn. Some groups fused (Zoe thought of water droplets coalescing), girls introducing themselves to boys and beers getting passed around. Theirs did not merge with any others.

It was one of the first really warm nights. Zoe had worn a fleece but didn't need it so had spread it over the grass to sit on. Jack was there, of course, and Mitchell and James and Rafael. Carter. And a girl Mitchell was seeing, who was very pretty and had a soft southern accent. She was sharing the edge of Zoe's fleece in companionable silence, and Zoe felt a warm camaraderie growing between them, which was probably just the weed but was nice anyway.

"So if Daniel Fen . . ." Carter took another drag, blew it out in a long stream, eyes shut. "Figured out how to make human life, say, forty years longer."

"Conservative," Jack said with a sharp smile. Zoe knew Jack was referring to them, not to Fen. And, for that matter, so was Carter, who looked at her steadily as he said, "Fine. Sixty. How old was Methuselah?"

Like anyone but him would know the answer. The girl Mitchell had brought, her name was Anna Lee, shook her head and raised her eyebrows gamely.

"Nine hundred sixty-nine."

"Ow, ow," said James, with his usual cringing smile. "Sorry. Are you religious, Anna Lee? I didn't mean to be, you know."

"You're good," she drawled sweetly.

"It doesn't matter the number. That's my *point*, in fact. The actual length of the human life doesn't matter at all. It's like, do you think ants think their lives are extraordinarily short? Or do they think their lives are exactly the right length? The *experienced* length, the *felt* or *perceived* length—no matter the absolute length, it's going to be exactly the same."

The group chewed on that for a while. Finally, Carter passed the joint, and it circled lazily, a bobbing point of light. A firefly. Carter to Mitchell, then Rafael, then Jack, Zoe, Anna Lee, James. Zoe faced the college, her back to the river.

The cluster closest to them let out a raucous string of laughter.

"Okay," Rafael said, "except . . . you could do nine times as many things."

"But could you? I mean, do you think we do three times as many things now as we did when life expectancy was thirty?" Carter asked.

"I mean, yeah. Probably."

"But do we—what are the major events in a human life?"

"Birth, puberty, marriage, childbirth, death," Zoe supplied.

"Did we add any, when we changed the life span?"

"Sure. A career, a second career sometimes, grandkids, retirement . . ." Rafael said.

"I wouldn't put those in the same category, though. They're not as . . . fundamental," Zoe said.

Carter nodded his approval. The joint had made its way back to him.

"Ants don't think anything about the length of their life, because ants don't think." Jack's eyes were half closed, and he leaned back on his hands, legs stretched in front of him and crossed at the ankles.

"You just want to feel good about our stupid research," Zoe said. He tilted his chin down and looked at her.

"Well, if it's stupid, consider it your research. It was your idea."

Zoe snorted, shook her head. He was treading close to giving something away, but it was nice to joke about it. Carter, across the circle, raised his eyebrows.

"But," Jack went on, turning to Carter, "you're taking the most selfish possible frame. Think of it from the perspective of a second person. If the first person lives thirty years longer—well, don't tell me thirty more years with, say, your parents, wouldn't matter to you."

"But if I had thirty more, too, our sum time together would feel the same." Carter caught Zoe's eye and smiled, just slightly, like they were in on a joke together. Which they were. She felt guilty, then. Less for telling him and more that she hadn't told Jack she'd told him.

Jack shook his head. It wasn't like him to back down. There was genuine upset in his face.

The joint was making its way around again. She passed. Her throat was starting to feel sore. Anna Lee took a long drag, handed it on to James.

"Length of life only matters in its difference from the expected value," Carter concluded.

"But what if life were infinite?" Anna Lee said. She sat easily cross-legged, back straight, with her hands in her lap.

"Mm." Carter's smile spread slowly across his face. Zoe was struck with the realization that he wanted Anna Lee, followed by a pang of jealousy to which she had no right. She wondered if Mitchell knew. She wouldn't have thought Anna Lee was Carter's type. Then again, what was Carter's type? "You know, I don't know. That would fundamentally change things, wouldn't it?"

"Mortality could be the defining variable of humanity," Anna Lee said. "Without the end, what would we be?"

Zoe's head was fuzzy. She tilted her head back and could just barely see the stars, pinpricks in the hazy sky. Over her shoulder, the river moved, slow and dark and irresistible.

"We won't know until it happens," Jack said. In his silence, Zoe had forgotten his sadness. Now she looked for it in his face, and it was gone.

"Always in a rush, you scientists," said Anna Lee.

"Well as we just discussed, we have finite time," Jack almost snapped.

"Oh, but is it? I think we might have infinite time, actually. The moment is as long as you feel it." Her eyes were closed.

"Didn't you just say—"

"I said mortality *could* be the defining variable."

The group was quiet. Zoe didn't like the tension. She was relieved when James awkwardly changed the subject, and then when time blurred and she found herself lying on her back next to Jack, staring up at the sky.

The next day, remembering Carter's advice, Zoe called her brother.

"Zo!" he exclaimed. "What the hell! You haven't responded to my texts for"—she could hear him scrolling—"six weeks? What kind of project are you working on?"

She was lying on her bed, fresh out of the first shower she'd taken in, god, she didn't know how long. Her hair was wet on her shoulders, soaking her pillow. She draped her arm over her eyes, which flinched away from the midmorning light.

"It's complicated."

"It must be fantastic, for you to be so distracted." She could hear Alex's keys jangling, backpack zipping. "Sorry, just heading to class. We can keep talking."

"I don't mean to keep you," Zoe said, but she stayed on the phone.

"You're not. So? Spill."

She sighed. "You can't tell Dad. Or Mom."

"Oh?" She heard him open and then lock his door. "How the tables have turned."

"It's worse than getting drunk behind Joe Francini's house and throwing up on your new dress shoes."

"Worse than *that*? Mom was so attached to those shoes." He laughed.

"And better, too. In a way. Maybe."

"Zoe, c'mon. You're killing me."

"I left Fen's lab." She lowered her voice. She was decently sure all three of her roommates had left, but she wasn't familiar with their schedules anymore. Usually at this point in the day she'd either be asleep or heading across the Yard to the Biolabs.

"Yeah? To go where?"

"That's the . . . my partner and I left to start an independent project. In Richard Brenna's lab space. Which sounds cool, except that he's retired."

"Oh?" She could see his eyebrows, thick and straight like hers, rising. "What's this project? And who's this partner?"

"His name is Jack."

"Jack who?"

"Jack Leahy, but he's not—he's an undergrad, too."

"You and another twenty-year-old went rogue and are working solo? Zoe, how daring of you. Have you had more than half a beer, now, too? I mean, in one sitting." He was teasing, but she could tell from his tone that he was surprised. And, maybe, a little impressed. "So, what's the project?"

"Well, it started because I had an idea . . . about epigenetics and antiaging . . . kind of a crazy idea, but we're running with it."

"What's the idea?"

She hesitated. But she'd committed now. "It's a bit . . . well, have you read Byrne's most recent paper?"

"Who's Byrne?"

"Right. So—well, I can send you the papers. But basically Byrne found that it's possible to reverse-age cells in steps. So, without turning them all the way back into stem cells. Then Fraser has this idea that there's one single central cause of aging, epigenome degradation. Your epigenome is—so you know that every cell has the same DNA, but a muscle cell is different from a skin cell? That's because different types of cells have different epigenomes, the way that DNA is packaged, to tell them what genes to express. So the idea is when you age, your cells are losing their identity. Turning into sort of generic, functionless mush. Following?"

"Sure."

"The method Byrne has used isn't really workable, because it has these horrible side effects, among other reasons. But if you combine these points, you get that Byrne has found a way to repair the epigenome of an old cell. Which means that a copy of that epigenetic information has to be stored somewhere. Else we couldn't age cells backward without going all the way back to stem cells. Or, I think that's what it means. We're making a few leaps. We have some preliminary data that might show where that backup is." Zoe's words were running into each other. "We want to confirm that data. And see if we can . . . access the backup safely."

Her brother was quiet. "Wait, this is your idea? No one else is working on this?"

"I mean, they could be. No one else is writing on it, anyway. The epigenome stuff is a bit niche, and people—Fen, too—are really focused on stuff you can apply right now. This is kind of—"

"Basic sciencey. Yeah, no, I get it. Are you making progress? Do you have replicable work?" His voice had changed from big brother to accomplished young scientist. Zoe shrunk a bit in the face of it.

"We're still really, really preliminary. We're trying to . . . we found the locus in yeast, and we're trying to find it in human cells."

He was quiet again. Her heart was racing. She hadn't realized quite how desperately she needed his approval. She picked at her sheets, white with tiny blue flowers. Drew her knees up to her chest and wrapped her arms around them.

"Have you told anyone else about this?"

"No," Zoe said, "not really. Brenna. My roommates don't even know I've left Fen's lab."

"Good. Don't tell anyone else. Zoe"—she cringed, waiting for him to tell her she'd made the biggest mistake of her life—"this is brilliant. I really think this could . . . can we talk about this again, when I'm not on the street?"

She blinked, stunned. "You . . . really?"

"Yes. I don't want to give anyone around here any ideas. But I want to talk more. I mean, I don't know the space. But I think you have something. Can I meet this Jack, too?"

"I . . ." Zoe had been preparing for an indictment, a scolding, a problem-solving session. How to extract herself from the situation, recover her grades, start afresh, nurse her pride. "Yeah. Yeah, of course."

"Good. I have to go to class." Indeed, she could hear the low hum of conversation around him. "But keep me posted. Talk soon."

"Love you," she said.

He paused, and then said, "Love you, too." Almost like he'd forgotten he was talking to his little sister.

11

Outside Darwin's, Alex sized Jack up. Jack was taller, but Alex was heavier. While Alex was just moderately, and at this point deliberately, unkempt (khakis a little baggy, Oxford shirt untucked and unbuttoned at the top), Jack was actually unkempt (jeans faded and then stained pale brown at the tops of the legs, boots ragged). She realized, as she watched them shake hands, that she had never shaken either's, but she knew what her mother had drilled into her brother and couldn't imagine anything but a firm grip from Jack.

Then they went inside, into the awkward stretch of a café meeting when you're waiting to order and feel you can't properly start your discussion but there's nothing else to talk about. When a couple left a tiny table in the corner beneath a shelf with a trailing ivy and some haphazard stacks of books, Jack peeled off to snag it.

It was May, reading period. Alex had finished his finals already—his last of college; the whole family would be flying out to Stanford to watch him graduate in just a few weeks—and was home for the weekend to see his Boston friends and ship out some stuff for his new apartment. And, though he wouldn't say it out loud, to spare her pride, to help Zoe tell their parents about the project. It was one thing to be vague about her pursuits during the semester. It was another to let them believe she was still in Fen's lab for the whole summer.

Zoe pretended not to notice the clerk flirting with Alex as he ordered English Breakfast, black. Then she ordered for herself and Jack, an iced coffee with milk and a black coffee, respectively, and Alex pretended not to notice she knew Jack's order without asking.

Zoe pulled out her wallet, but Alex shouldered by her to pay, rolling his eyes at the clerk, who giggled, flicking her long brown ponytail over her shoulder.

When Zoe and Alex edged themselves through the crowded room and set the drinks down, their table wobbled precariously. Jack narrowed his eyes, steadying it with long fingers splayed flat across the top, before tearing the cardboard sleeve from Zoe's iced coffee, already damp with condensation, folding it up, and ducking under the table to wedge it beneath the culprit short leg. When he reemerged, hair fluffed up higher than before, he put his hands flat on top again and pressed to check his work.

Alex watched, amused. When Jack was finished, Zoe sat beside him, on the bench side, and Alex folded himself into the wooden chair across and leaned forward, lacing his fingers together over his steaming mug. "So, protégés. Tell me everything."

After, Zoe stood up to walk Alex out, grabbing his teacup on reflex and bringing it with her own cup to the tray by the door.

She set them down, and he hugged her. "I'm proud of you," he said, and then, "and I like Jack. I've got Mom on this one. I think you'll need to convince him"—meaning their father—"but you will."

"Are you sure?" She wasn't sure what she was asking about. The project, Jack, their parents.

"There's no such thing as sure." They left the café, bell on the door jingling. It was cool outside, and Alex pulled on his jacket. Zoe had left hers with Jack. She crossed her arms. "When you have a bit more, I'll connect you to my VC friend at Stanford."

She snorted, shook her head.

"Do you guys have a name yet?"

"A name?"

"For the project. For your startup."

Zoe laughed. "Come on."

"You should start thinking of one," he said. "Names are everything."

"What's in a name?" Zoe said automatically. "That which we call a rose . . ."

"By any other word would smell as sweet. Except what if we called a rose Vomit Flower? Or Foot Fungus?"

"*Alex.*"

He grinned mischievously, and she rolled her eyes, and they were twelve and fourteen again. He punched her lightly on the shoulder and strode off into the bright afternoon.

Freshman summer was the summer to mess around. And Zoe had, so to speak—she'd spent six weeks teaching underprivileged high school kids chemistry, and the rest curled up in her childhood bedroom, flipping through papers she found interesting, browsing Harvard principal investigators like a clothing catalog. Sophomore summer, on the other hand, was when your career started. During his, Alex had worked full-time in the lab of the professor under whom he was now planning to pursue his PhD. By that August, he had a first author publication.

Which was why Zoe was nervous, walking to her parents' house with Jack to tell them her summer plans. He had a bouquet of flowers in his left hand that Zoe had bought on her way to pick him up, and he wore, on her request, a plain blue shirt in place of his usual ratty alt-rock band T-shirt. She'd cringed asking, knowing she was making too big a deal of this, that he thought it was childish, how much she cared about what her parents thought. When she'd asked him how his mom felt about the project (she knew it was just his mom at home, had mentioned his parents once in passing and he'd corrected her, Just my mom, and she'd flinched, apologized, and he'd looked at her, amused) he'd snorted, said She's not a scientist, and offered nothing more.

Her mother opened the door before they could reach the top of the steps, wearing an apron.

"Zoe!" Zoe could see her eyes flicking down, hear the words she wanted to say, which were, You look awful, are you eating? You need to do something about those undereye bags. But she would never in front of company.

"Mom, hi." Zoe leaned from her waist into a hug. "This is Jack."

"Nice to meet you," he said. She watched him awkwardly try to shake her mother's hand and pass over the flowers at the same time.

"It is such a pleasure to meet you, Jack! We've heard so much about you." She hadn't, at least not from Zoe.

Jack stepped inside, and Zoe nudged him to take his shoes off, which he did, revealing white cotton ankle socks with gray heels and toes. She could see, walking behind him, that there was a hole in the bottom of one heel. She took a deep breath in through her nose, let it out through her mouth. She had the sudden and profound feeling of trying to be two people at once. Jack's Zoe, and her parents' Zoe.

Her father was in the living room with Alex. They were in the middle of a game of chess.

Zoe had learned but had not been good at chess, always felt this frustrated block in her mind when she tried to see more than one move ahead. She'd sit at the coffee table, exactly where her brother was sitting now, across from her father, who'd watch her coolly. "What do you see?" he'd ask, and she'd stare hopelessly at the board and say, "I don't know," and he'd raise his eyebrows and say, "Look harder."

Alex was a natural.

Jack floated over to the two of them, looked down at the board. It was her father's move, and he didn't break his focus to introduce himself. He looked up at Alex, then back down at the board. Jack clasped his hands behind his back, fingers twitching. Zoe could sense, though she hadn't known he played, that Jack wanted to tell her father what his move should be. The scene went in slow motion. She found she didn't care if he said something or didn't. Her father might be impressed, might be horrified. What did it matter, anyway?

Her father reached forward and moved his knight. Jack nodded once. Alex, practiced, showed no emotion. Her father looked up, stood. "Jack, right?"

"Yes, sir. Jack Leahy. Nice to meet you."

"Professor Kyriakidis. Nice to meet you. Nice to see you, Zoe," he continued, "it's like you're the one at Stanford."

She responded in Greek. "I'm working." His favorite phrase when his small daughter wouldn't leave him alone.

He barked a laugh, shook his head at her. "What're you working on?" he asked in Greek. Her favorite response.

Jack, who had never seen Zoe speak Greek before, watched this exchange curiously. Alex was still staring at the chessboard, planning his next move. Zoe's mother had slipped back into the kitchen and could be heard clinking around. Zoe pictured her clipping the flowers with the small shears she kept in the drawer, putting them in a vase, bringing the vase into the dining room, and replacing the centerpiece with it. Then she would put the finishing touches on dinner, and everything would wait in the oven, keeping warm, until her father was ready—except for the fried chicken, which had to be in the open air so it stayed crispy.

It wasn't how she'd planned it, but she set her jaw and took a breath and met her father's eyes. "The epigenetic basis of aging," she said in English. They always talked science in English.

"You were working on telomeres. No?"

Back to Greek. "Yes. But I had an idea, and was compelled to pursue it." The language made it easier to keep the two Zoes apart.

Alex looked up from the chessboard. "It's a brilliant idea, and they have good preliminary data." In English: he'd never been as comfortable speaking Greek as Zoe.

"This is still with Daniel Fen?" Greek.

"No. Richard Brenna." Zoe ran her tongue along her fixed retainer. She could feel her pulse in her throat.

Her father nodded slowly. "I don't know him personally." He paused. "You have data?"

Zoe pulled it out of her shoulder bag, tried not to let her hands shake. "It's here. I had a whole presentation planned."

"Save the theatrics for your mother." He took the papers, slid the chessboard to the side, laid them on the table, sat back down. "And what does the boy have to do with it?"

"He's my partner. An experimentalist."

Jack could tell he was being spoken about and cocked his head, rubbed the side of his long nose, then shoved his hand in his pocket. Zoe looked back at her father, who was reading the summary. It was quiet enough to hear the tick of the grandfather clock, which had come with the house and would stay with the house, watch over the next professor who lived there. She waited for his eyes to stop moving. When he flipped to study the images and graphs, she said, "He's designing all of the experimentation. I don't have the biology background and he'd be better at it than me if I did."

"You're sure about these results?" He switched to English, addressing the two of them. Jack nodded.

"Okay," he said, taking off his glasses and laying them on top of the papers. "Interesting. But nothing interesting since those. How do you go from yeast to people?" He didn't give Zoe time to answer, clapped his hands together, and stood. His movements were always big, brash, forward. Zoe noticed this even more with Jack beside her, who was always sliding sideways into things. "Let's eat. Meg has prepared something delicious, I am certain."

He walked from the living room into the dining room, and the three children followed him like ducklings. Zoe, then Jack, then Alex.

She gave the presentation over one of her mother's classic southern spreads: fried chicken, corn bread, green beans. Jack chimed in at all his cues. Still, when Zoe paused for what she hoped would be friendly questions and discussion, there was silence. Her father was still eating (he was a one-meal-a-day of twenty-five hundred calories sort of person lately), crunching at a chicken thigh. Her mother was finished (she hardly ate at all, had picked at some green beans and a sliver of corn bread, most of which was still on her plate).

"I want to keep working on this for the summer."

"I think," Alex jumped in, "it's a good idea. I really think they have something big."

Her mother was quiet, looking at her father. Her father chewed, swallowed, nodded. "Sure."

Her mother moved to clear their plates. Then set new, smaller plates decorated with delicate blue cornflowers in front of everyone, disappeared back into the kitchen, and emerged with a blueberry cobbler in an oval CorningWare baking dish, her grandmother's, which matched the dessert plates. She served Jack first—"Ice cream?"—and, while she was scooping, said, "Will you be living at home, Zoe?"

"I'd like to," Zoe said in a small voice.

"Great," her mother said. "I could use the help around the house. Your father plans to host as much as usual."

As they were leaving, her mother walking them to the door, Zoe caught her brother's eye. He had moved to the big leather couch, propped his feet on the ottoman. He shrugged one shoulder, smiled at her. She knew that look: They'll get over it. It was the same one he'd made when he'd shattered their father's windshield with a baseball, when he'd crashed Zoe's car, when he'd brought home his first girlfriend and she was a Southie four years older than him, when he'd shown up past curfew and their father had been waiting on the couch under a lamp, working through equations on a notepad on his lap, when their mother had found his pot stash under his bed in one of his shoes.

But the problem wasn't that they needed to get over it. The problem was that they didn't care. At least about the work. She was taking this enormous professional gamble, this risk that pressed out on her breastbone and up in her throat and made her want to scream with frustration or fear or excitement, depending on the day, and her father had given her sixty seconds of his attention and then shrugged. Sure. Do what you like, it doesn't matter. Just be home to help your mother set the table.

Her mother did care. But only, Zoe was certain, that Jack was a terrible conversationalist, had holes in his socks, and needed a haircut.

Her mother hugged her, and they left. It was a clear night, summery. She took a deep breath. The fresh air tasted good, and Jack's loping walk beside her was deeply familiar. She vibrated between her two selves like they were resonance structures. She mused that as her energy reduced, she'd settle into one. She wondered which. (She knew: Jack's.) They didn't speak as they returned to campus.

12

Zoe'd thought her father would take more convincing, which was why she had told them she'd spend the whole weekend at home, which was why, Saturday morning, she was elbow deep in a pie crust.

"So," her mother said. "Tell me more about your Jack."

"He's not my Jack," Zoe began, then added, "and we aren't dating."

"I have heard that."

Zoe took a breath, cursed Alex. He said he would handle their mother, and now he was gone, on a flight back to the West Coast. Zoe and Margaret hadn't seen eye to eye since—well, since Zoe had shot up three inches taller than her, in about the eighth grade.

"We met in orgo. He's brilliant, and we became friends."

"And why did you let him in on your work?"

"It's more . . . he's the one who helped me get into Fen's lab in the first place. He was there before me." She chewed the inside of her lip. Verbal vomiting wasn't the best strategy, but something about her mother always knocked her off guard.

"I see." Her mother added the sugar to the berries and stirred, cocking her elbow way up. The kitchen was huge and beautiful, built originally for a chef—when her father was given the house, Margaret had already become the favorite cook for department dinners, and the department chair and the dean wrote her a note that said "This one is for you, Meg. We hope you enjoy the kitchen—and we hope to enjoy you enjoying the kitchen!" The note was framed and hung next to the window over the sink. She'd shown it to them with a big, graceful smile at the housewarming party, and everyone had been delighted.

"And how did you end up with—who is this other professor?"

Her mother's memory for names was impeccable. Zoe scrambled to understand why she'd intentionally forget Brenna's.

"Professor Brenna. Jack knew him."

"What do you mean by that?"

"I . . . Jack . . ." Zoe's own discomfort surfaced. She'd forgotten how angry she'd been, that day outside the Biolabs. She swallowed, tried not to let her mother see. "I had this idea, and we approached Brenna about it. He has the space and doesn't have a lot of students right now." Doesn't have any, but her mother didn't need to know he was functionally retired.

"This was Jack's idea, to ask him?"

"To work with Brenna . . . well, yes."

"And how did he know Brenna?"

"I, uh . . . don't know, actually."

"Ah."

They were both quiet. Outside, a breeze was ruffling the early flowers. Daffodils, and those little blue ones that are actually weeds but look so beautiful spreading across the lawn.

"How did he get to know Fen?"

"Well, he worked for him."

"But he's a sophomore, like you, right? How did he start working for him? That seems like a very impressive placement so early in his schooling."

"You're right. I'm not sure." Zoe started to feel ill, the sweet smell of the berries her mother was pouring into the pie crust turning her stomach. The color was a garish purple. Her mother's apron was, as always, unnecessary, remaining starchy white. She handed the wooden spoon to Zoe, who usually liked to lick it clean. Zoe shook her head and placed it back in the bowl.

"Where is he from?"

"Maine." This, Zoe knew.

"Does he go home often?"

"No." Zoe thought of his return to the lab right after Christmas. He hadn't been home since, at least that she knew of. "Not during the semester, anyway."

"Hm. Why not?" Her mother's tone was light, curious. Like they were making small talk.

"I mean, I don't know. Most people don't." She paused. "He clearly doesn't like talking about personal things, so I don't pry. We mostly talk about work."

Her mother set the timer on the oven, slipped off her oven mitts and placed them on the counter, stacked perfectly one on the other. Began wiping down the surfaces. Zoe moved out of the way, and she said, "You have flour on your backside," which Zoe did, a stripe from leaning against the counter, floured from rolling out the dough. Zoe brushed it off.

"Thank you for your help," her mother said, and she knew she was dismissed.

She'd planned to spend the night at home, but now her mother had gotten into her head. That's the problem with mothers, she mused, they're always in your head. They're a part of your head—of every neuron and every other cell, too, flesh of my flesh—but still how is it that a mother's emotions reverberate so precisely, amplified, through a daughter's body from across the house? That a mother's displeasure wraps tendrils around a daughter's throat, and when she reaches a hand to pull them off, she finds them buried under her skin?

Her mother's questions had been her own. Or, her own questions had been her mother's. Who is Jack? Why is he here? Why can he move through this world so easily? What does he want from you?

But weren't those questions just remnants of an entrenched elitism? Her mother's obsession with good breeding and better manners, a troubling relic of the antebellum South?

Except for maybe the last question. What does he want from you. Because maybe all he wanted from her was her father's aura. Maybe that was all she was good for. Maybe her mother was just trying to protect her.

She had a low, annoying headache. She pushed her face into her pillow. It smelled like her parents' home, which, she realized suddenly, no longer smelled like her. She sniffed her own shirt. Yes: detergent and her sweetish sweat and the sterile air of the lab and—was it?— Jack.

Her Jack. He was her Jack, she supposed.

She picked up her bag, slipped out without anyone noticing.

The lights were on when she got to the lab. She stood watching him for a few seconds. He was wearing earbuds, leaning over, typing something on his laptop (a new PC, souped up; Zoe'd always had a MacBook and had no idea how to run a PC). She could see the knobs of his spine through his shirt, his ropey left lat, which was larger than his right. He hooked a stool with his foot and pulled it over, sat, hunched forward, typing furiously.

"Jack," she said.

He turned, startled, and looked at her for a moment before he said, "I thought you were staying with your parents tonight."

"I was." She pulled her own stool over with a screech, sat beside him. She had been hoping for a bit warmer welcome, she realized.

Some reassurance. But he was probably annoyed that she'd made him deal with her parents.

"This is exciting." He didn't ask why she'd left. "I think . . . well, see for yourself when it runs."

They watched the screen, strings of letters scrolling across, both still except for one of Jack's knees, which was bouncing rapidly. A graph popped up. Zoe squinted to read the axis labels, and then her heart jumped.

"I didn't think this was going to be ready until . . ."

"It's preliminary. Super early. I just couldn't stand to wait."

Two human cell lines: one with a knocked-out locus called "I2" (they'd run through the alphabet, and then, as the name suggests, again), the other a control. The factors worked on the second, and didn't work on the first.

Zoe looked at Jack, and his eyes were as bright as hers. She could feel a scream rising in her chest and she clamped her hand over her mouth. "Jack!"

He was laughing, jagged line of his teeth flashing.

Zoe found herself standing, then squatting down, curling herself tight into a ball. He joined her on the floor, took her shoulders in his hands. "You are brilliant."

She wasn't a happy crier, but wished now she was. There was too much feeling to hold inside. She didn't know how to keep her skin from peeling off her body. Then they were both standing, grinning at each other, and her face was in his hands, and he leaned forward and kissed her, hard, and she kissed him back, and the bursting lightness flowed from her to him to her, and when they pulled away they were both still grinning and laughing and then they hugged, and then they went for a walk, because it was too much to be still, Jack's stride bouncy and light, Zoe occasionally, literally, skipping, and they started talking about a name.

Manna, they decided. Sustenance sent by God.

"And it was like coriander seed, white," Zoe read aloud from her phone screen, "and the taste of it was like wafers made with honey."

They both always did have a flair for the dramatic.

Before that night, they'd not spoken about the project as a startup. But Alex was right, Zoe thought: it was the clear next step, the obvious play. These days, one didn't keep something like this inside the hallowed walls of academia. One clutched it tightly to one's chest and ran with it out into the world, protecting oneself with a good IP lawyer, leveraging the functionally limitless funds of people who don't know what else to do with their wealth.

For her, a startup was not about making money. Since she'd grown up in the household of an academic, money had always been secondary to science. Not secondary—irrelevant (at least in the eyes of a small child). They'd lived in shitty small apartments until she was six or seven, but they had fancy functions to go to and she ran around a very rich college's campus in a very rich college town and went to the best public schools in the country, and anyway she liked sharing a room with Alex. Then her dad got tenure, and suddenly they lived in a huge, beautiful house. In some ways she, still young enough to enjoy physical closeness with her family, missed the coziness of the apartments. Anyway, money had never been discussed in front of Zoe, and she'd never wanted for anything.

Jack, however, Zoe was pretty sure, had grown up poor. She'd thought at first that his clothing was a choice: edgy, cool. Because he always seemed so in control. But he never ate out, never bought books, never took public transportation that wasn't covered by Harvard. Shopped at the Garment District and other thrift stores not as a statement, like many of their classmates, but as a practicality.

So as they paced through the north side of Harvard's campus, down Divinity Avenue and through the warren of lab buildings, then back around to the law school, the thing they sketched with their words was both about money and not.

"We can get space in that new building on the corner of Broadway and—what is it? The road sort of loops back on itself. Big glass building."

"Broadway and Galileo, you mean. Turns into Binney."

"That sounds right. And we can hire people. We need to hire people. And get a board. Of advisors. Brenna can chair it, obviously, but who else?"

And so on like that. The sun set, and it was ridiculously perfect, neon pink streaking across the whole sky, light bouncing between the clouds and off windows, turning them to purple and then to dark blue and then to black. They ended up at what used to be the Radcliffe College quad, in a little side garden. Pale flowers seemed to glow in the darkness. They sat and the stone bench was cold through Zoe's jeans and they surveyed the space. In the quiet, Zoe's mind reached back for the data, picked it up and looked at it again, turned it over and over. Her joy bubbled back into her throat. She snorted and put her face in her hands, leaning elbows forward onto knees. Jack looped his arm around her.

"We did it," he said, and then he walked her home.

She could hear her roommates from the hall. Gabby's musical laugh, Hanna's neighing. Sophia would be convulsed but silent. They were, Zoe could tell, drunk (except for Sophia, who didn't drink). She paused before unlocking the door, not wanting to interrupt.

When she did enter, they turned all at once like they were in a sitcom, wearing identical looks of surprise.

"Hey, guys," she said. They were dressed in semiformal wear. "Formal season?"

"Yeah," Gabby said, almost awkward. "Spring Formal."

Of course. Zoe had forgotten it was tonight. She'd deleted at least six emails from the house committee in the past week reminding her to buy her tickets.

"Sounds like you guys had fun!"

Hanna started giggling again. She wore a little, flowy, pale blue dress and had on slightly too much eyeliner, now smudged, which gave her a 1990s rock star sort of look.

"Were you with Jack instead?" Sophia was looking clear-eyed at Zoe.

She didn't want to say yes, but she didn't want to lie, either. She compromised: "In the lab."

Sophia didn't say anything. She looked judgy, and the most uncomfortable in a dress: it was slightly too long, cutting off her legs just above the knee, and she was wearing dark tights with round-toed nude flats. Zoe bristled, thinking, What does she care what I do? and concurrently, meanly, She has no idea how to dress.

Gabby, stunning in something long and tight and purple, grabbed Hanna by the hand and started singing—a recent pop song, probably, but unrecognizable.

"You missed ouuuuut!" Hanna yelled.

"Nah, I had work to do."

Hanna rambled on, "Gabe was there and he's soooo hot and I honestly just want to go back there and, like . . ."

Gabby laughed. "But everyone's drunk."

"Exactly! You think I have, you think I, I"—Hanna was struggling—"courage to talk to him without *at least* three shots?"

Gabby was dancing now, hips swaying, without any music.

Zoe thought of the last time she'd been to a party. The fall, it must've been. She'd gone with the three of them, had put on her tight little black dress and the heels that made her six one, danced until her feet hurt and then kicked off her heels and danced some more. They'd had fun. But now, looking at them, she felt nothing—no regret, no FOMO.

She slipped through them to her door, where she paused, smiling at Hanna. "You should ask Gabe out when you're both sober."

Hanna's eyes were round. "Are you *joking*."

At one time, she wouldn't have been able to hold the good news in: would have blurted it out to them and then basked in their congratulations. Instead, Zoe laughed, and felt very old. "No, I'm not. Sleep tight, guys," she said, and she went into her room and shut the door.

13

Somewhere, and always, and forever, it would be the sweetest parts of that spring. She would be climbing out onto the Adams roof with Jack and his roommates, lying flat with her legs up against a pitch, barefoot, feeling the blood drain from her feet (swollen from standing in the lab for hours), feeling the sun warm her legs, draping her arm over her eyes and closing them (they burned when she closed them), smelling the mild pot that Carter smoked; she would be walking home from the lab alone in the middle of the night, noticing that the trees along Mount Auburn Street had bloomed while she was inside, breathing in their perfume, or else she would be walking home from the lab with Jack in the evening, light lingering later each day, bluish from behind clouds, dorm windows glowing warm yellow, comfortable in tired silence; they would be craning their necks back at the stars, she saying how bright they were and Jack laughing, saying she needed to get out of the city; she would be eating ice cream from Christina's, she and Jack stumbling upon it after a long walk into mid-Cambridge from the Biolabs, waiting for some results, trying burnt sugar (him) and Mexican chocolate (her), each sampling the other's, his eyes wide with how good it tasted, Zoe, used to artisanal sorts of ice cream, still impressed, grinning at the old lady behind the counter (Christina? Perhaps, though unlikely) who said they made a lovely couple, laughing about it as they left, bouncing their way back past the strip malls and apartment buildings that faded into the deliberately shabby, rambling Colonials, pale yellow and blue and white, that fringed Harvard's campus like lace; she would be in the lab looking out the window into the rain, listening to Jack clink around behind her, watching people below, some with umbrellas for the drizzle, others hunching their shoulders up, a silent movie in gray. She would be imagining where they were coming from and where they were going, the things they cared about, the people they were preoccupied with, what they feared. She would be watching the old move carefully, imagining the young blurring into the old in front of her, harried gaits slowing, hair graying, lives turning fragile, translucent, colored with loss, and she would be turning to Jack and to the bright lights of the lab and looking at his face, so young, so smooth, and into his eyes, which would be flicking up to look at her, were always flicking up to look at her, brilliant, and he would be asking her a question, and she would be answering, and she would be pulled back into this time, where they would be dancing.

14

Coincidentally (or perhaps not), when Jack brought up living with Carter for the summer, Carter had just texted Zoe. Wrote a final on Gilgamesh, you should read, à propos de your secret project. She couldn't tell if the thrill that rose in her throat upon reading the text was excitement or guilt.

"There aren't any singles." Jack was talking about the apartment-style housing Harvard leased students for the summer. "And he'd only be there half the summer anyway, but he'd pay for the whole time."

"Why half?"

"He's in DC for six weeks, I don't know." Jack sounded annoyed. She couldn't tell whether he was annoyed that she'd wanted to know, or that she'd expected him to know. Carter and Jack were like opposite poles within the rooming group; both were relatively friendly with Mitchell and Raf and James (though Mitchell and Raf and James were far closer to one another than to either of them), but they seemed to avoid each other.

Zoe did worry sometimes that this was because Jack knew she had told Carter.

"So, sounds perfect?" Zoe said. "Where do you sign?"

"Yeah," Jack said.

Realizing as she spoke what she was trying to do, she said, "We should probably tell him what we're working on, then."

Jack's forehead wrinkled. "Why?"

"Because you'll be living together?"

"We're already living together."

"Yeah, but just you and him? I don't know, wouldn't it be weird to keep it a secret?" Zoe was talking a little too fast. She forced herself to stop, shrug.

Jack's expression was unreadable. "I guess," he said.

They told Carter, and he faked surprise so well that Zoe wondered, for a moment, if she'd dreamed telling him. But of course she hadn't.

He even offered to help. "I mean, if I'd be useful. With any coding stuff."

"Coding stuff?" Zoe said.

"Yeah?"

"Do you . . . code?"

Carter laughed. "Well I am half a CS major. But I'm glad I don't look it."

"Why didn't you tell me Carter is CS? We could've asked him for help with the Python stuff ages ago."

Jack shrugged. "I didn't think of it."

"What do you mean?"

"We could've asked Mitchell for help, too. He's a CS major."

"Okay, great, we could've asked both of them."

"You knew Mitchell did CS. Why didn't you bring that up?"

Zoe closed her eyes, raised her eyebrows, shook her head. Why didn't she? She blushed. "Never mind."

*   *   *

She'd remember four scenes from Gilgamesh, which she read in Lamont, under the too-yellow lights.

One, that each morning of their journey, Gilgamesh's friend
Enkidu would listen to Gilgamesh's dreams and give them meaning.
There was something about that. That your dreams have no meaning
until they are given meaning by another.

Two, that Gilgamesh fails the test, but still is given the prize, the
plant that will make him live forever.

Three, that a snake steals the plant Gilgamesh did not earn.

Four, an image, sparkling behind her eyelids that night as she
faded out of this world. Gilgamesh emerging from the darkness into
the land of the gods, where the trees were hung heavy with fruit.

Zoe texted Carter: Funny story abt Gilgamesh/myth/religion. . . . . . we
actually are calling the project Manna.

Carter texted Zoe: How stereotypically judeo-christian of you.
And then, too quickly to have googled it, and when the children of
Israel saw it, they said one to another, it is manna: for they wist not
what it was.

Zoe smiled down at her phone, texted him back (at once, so that
he'd know she, too, was working from memory): And Moses said unto
them, this is the bread which the lord hath given you to eat.

15

Summer's days were endless. They were trying to confirm l2, the locus, and to investigate how exactly the Yamanaka factors interacted with that locus. It was hard, but not having classes to worry about made Zoe feel significantly better. She felt like her brain was free to spread out, linger over problems. She'd come up with solutions at any time—walking, washing her hair, in the middle of a conversation with Jack about something else entirely—and stop short to write them down. She carried a notebook everywhere. Jack called it the Book of Zoe. When he was struggling with something, he'd say, "Can I consult the Book of Zoe?" It made her smile.

Since they had the lab to themselves, they could play whatever they wanted over Zoe's portable speaker, which had been a birthday gift from her brother. She'd play country-rock and floaty 1960s bands, which Jack found intolerable. "Okay, flower child," he'd say, "when does the free love start?" and she'd laugh. He was into slightly depressing 1990s and 2000s alt-rock: Radiohead, the Smashing Pumpkins, Neutral Milk Hotel, the Goo Goo Dolls. She liked his music, so she usually let him pick.

* * *

It was early July, unbearably hot, when Jack got sick.

They were spending even more time in the lab because it was sort of air-conditioned, unlike Jack and Carter's apartment. That day, the AC was overwhelmed, spluttering and dripping. Jack and Zoe were in the middle of replacing cell culture medium for transfection when Jack said he was feeling odd.

"Go sit down," Zoe said, short-tempered. Her hair was up in a tight ponytail, baby hairs stuck down to her neck and forehead with sweat.

He did, which was unusual, and worried Zoe. So she followed him into the break room when she'd finished the step, and he was sound asleep on the couch.

She stood looking down at him. He didn't look sick, she thought— though perhaps there had been a gradual decline that she'd missed, seeing him every day. But he'd always been pale, skinny. His hair was splayed out in spirals that haloed his face.

He was breathing steadily. Just tired, she thought, and went back to work.

When she checked on him again a couple of hours later, he hadn't moved. She wondered if she should be concerned. Figured probably not, he probably hadn't slept more than four hours a night for the past month. Considered, in fact, lying down beside him. But there wasn't room on the ratty couch and she didn't want to lie on the floor in the office—who knew what sort of weird chemicals they'd tracked in.

At six, she was losing steam. It was hard to work fourteen-hour days without peer pressure. She went to wake Jack up and walk him home.

But he wouldn't wake up. She tried touching him, then shaking his shoulder. Panicked, she crouched, took his wrist in her hands, put two fingers on the inside. Nothing. Nothing? She pushed harder, feeling the bones move under the skin and then, there, a thread pressing up to meet her fingertips. Once, and then again, and again. She steadied herself on the edge of the couch as the adrenaline passed, leaving her limp.

There was that time he'd slept for three days. But he'd woken up when Carter shook him. He'd said he was mildly diabetic. How can someone be mildly diabetic?

"Jack?" and then, louder, "Jack."

She sat back on her heels. If she watched closely, she could see his chest moving.

"Jack," she said again. She touched his face, then grimaced and pinched his arm, hard. He didn't move.

She bit the inside of her cheek, stood. She didn't know who to call—911 felt excessive; she didn't want to call her parents; Brenna would be home, she assumed, or wherever he was 95 percent of the time; his secretary was only in during normal business hours.

Carter? His parents were doctors.

She went into the hall to call him. He picked up on the first ring. "Zoe!"

"Carter, Jack fell asleep in the lab and now I can't wake him up." She swallowed. "He has a pulse."

"Oh." A pause. "That's good," he said, "that he has a pulse. We all need one. Hang on, let me just . . ." She noticed the voices in the background then.

"Oh, god, are you at a dinner or something? I'm so sorry."

"Yes, yes. Well, cocktail hour, very fancy, oldest gentlemen's club in DC . . ." The noises were fading. "Okay. Can you give me some more detail?"

"I'm so sorry, you should go back inside. I didn't know—"

"Zoe, come on. This is slightly more important. Tell me what happened."

"God, I don't know. It was afternoon, I think, but I wasn't paying attention to the time. He said he didn't feel well. I said he should go lie down. When I went to check on him, he was asleep, which I thought was probably good. Looked okay. Every time I checked through the afternoon he was asleep. I was getting ready to go home"—she looked at the clock, embarrassed—"a little early today—"

"Come on, it's six fifteen."

"Right"—she cleared her throat—"and I tried to wake him up and couldn't? I mean, I shook him, I yelled, I pinched him. Hard enough that he started to bruise."

"Okay," Carter said, "that's weird. Do you want me to call my mom?"

"I don't know? Should I call 911? I don't know what to do." She thought distantly that they probably weren't supposed to be in the lab without some sort of supervision.

"Let me call my mom. I'm going to put you on hold, okay? And you can text me if you need anything in the meantime." The line clicked silent. She wondered why she'd gone into the hall to call him. It wasn't like she didn't want to wake Jack. And it was creepy out here. Though maybe creepier in there, with his body. Body? Get a grip, she thought.

She was concluding that she probably did need to call 911 when Carter got back on the phone. "She thinks it's most likely dehydration or overheating, and exhaustion. He might need fluids, so probably getting him medical care is the best thing . . ."

"Jesus." Zoe put a hand over her forehead. The place where her shirt had been pinned in her armpit shifted, soaked and cold.

"I'd try waking him up again. He did wake up that time in the dorm. I'll stay on the phone."

Zoe tried. She yelled as loud as she dared, not wanting to attract the attention of any janitorial staff or other scientists. She shook his shoulder, grabbed his arm and squeezed. Pinched him with her bitten-down fingernails. Nothing.

"Nothing."

"All right. You could call HUHS, but I think they'll just be annoyed and tell you to call 911."

"Ah, fuck. All right. Yes."

"I'll be right here."

On Carter's end of the line, Zoe heard the whoosh of a car going by. Bit her lip. Forced herself to say, "Shouldn't you go back into your event?"

"I'll be here. Call me if you need anything. Even company."

She hung up and called 911. The operator asked if there had been a lab accident: chemical spill, accidental ingestion, glassware cut.

"No. But he . . . he's told me he has mild diabetes? I don't know what that means but maybe it's related."

"Got it," the operator said. He had a Boston accent—"gaht it." Zoe didn't know why she'd expected something different, something generic, stateless, floating in an emergency space untethered to the physical world. "Stay with him. Help is on the way."

Zoe wondered what other calls the operator had taken this morning. How many heart attacks. If anyone had been shot. If anyone had died on the phone; just stopped talking in the middle of a sentence. She swallowed her nausea.

The EMTs arrived, carried Jack out on a stretcher. They seemed calm. But it was their job to seem calm, wasn't it? Zoe trailed behind them, dazed. They asked if she wanted to ride with him to the hospital. She said yes.

When they got to the hospital, they wheeled him away and someone led her to a crowded waiting room. She looked at the other faces, wondered what emergencies had brought them there. Hospitals made Zoe's skin itch. She texted Carter, they took him into a room, in waiting room, and then stared at the wall and tried not to panic. Studied the posters about vaccines and mental health resources, like she'd be tested on them later.

He read the message immediately, and then, a couple of minutes later, her phone rang.

"Carter," she said, "you should go back to your dinner. I feel so bad that I've distracted you so much."

"No, no, no. It's vapid in there. I've had to talk to four different old white men about getting my pilot's license. They're *fascinated*. You know, Black people are like bumblebees? Physiologically, they shouldn't be able to fly."

Zoe snorted, and then started giggling. She covered her mouth, aware that she was in an ER waiting room, but she couldn't stop.

"See?" he said. "If nothing else, I'm great comic relief."

Probably forty-five minutes later, a nurse with a clipboard came out and called Zoe's name.

Zoe stood. "That's me."

The nurse led her back into a room where Jack was lying on a bed, hooked up to an IV drip. When they walked in, he opened his eyes.

"Hey, Zoe."

The relief was so strong her knees buckled. Oh, she thought with a strange distance. I didn't realize.

"Jack." She found herself at the edge of the bed.

The nurse, from the doorway, cleared her throat. "Jack's blood sugar was extremely low, which meant that his brain wasn't getting enough energy. We've given him a glucagon injection and fluids. He'll be fine—but the doctor will be in to speak with him about how he manages his diabetes."

When she left, Zoe sat on the chair beside the bed. The IV was in his left arm, of course, because how would they have known he was left-handed. She felt a rushing downward in her stomach. "Oh, I'm sorry I didn't tell them to put the IV in your other arm . . . that was stupid . . . they shooed me away as soon as we got here." She was tearing up.

"Zoe," he said, "come on. It's not a big deal."

"I feel bad."

"It's really not a problem," he said, and then she was crying, and he was looking at her through half-open eyes. She didn't know what she was crying about, but she couldn't stop.

"Zoe," he said, softer.

She kept crying, bending at the waist to rest her forehead on her knees.

"Zoe." He moved his right hand to her back.

She sat up. "I'm sorry. I'm sorry." She sniffed. "I don't know what's wrong with me."

"I'm fine," he said. "Look at me." He took his hand from her and gestured down his body under the white hospital sheets. "Poster boy for health and fitness." He grinned, and she laughed.

"What the fuck, Jack."

They admitted him to the hospital floor in the middle of the night. Zoe trailed behind the rolling bed, holding her backpack in front of her. He had a private room, so Zoe stayed with him until morning, even though he told her she didn't have to, curled up in the chair. She couldn't tell if she slept, or just slipped into a haze of beeping equipment and shuffling nurses and the blue glow that seemed to come from everywhere. Every time she looked at Jack he was asleep, flat on his back with his IV arm palm up beside him, lips parted. His hospital gown was lower at the neck than the T-shirts he usually wore. He was so thin she could almost see underneath his collarbones.

Around five, she stood and went to the window and watched as the sun came up over the Charles. It hurt her eyes, but she kept looking.

At six, her mother called, at which point Zoe realized she hadn't told her parents she wouldn't be home.

"Zoe? Are you okay?" She sounded like she'd just gotten up.

"Oh no, yes," Zoe stuttered, "I mean, I'm fine, I'm sorry." She often didn't get home until one or two in the morning, so it wasn't like they waited up—but she'd never not come home at all before.

Her mother was silent.

"I'm sorry. Jack is in the hospital, I was up until two when they admitted him and then I just fell asleep here . . . I'm sorry, I should have called."

"Is Jack okay?"

"He's okay now, yes." She didn't want to tell her what had happened, felt vaguely embarrassed by it. Now that it was over, it seemed stupid: kids so full of self-importance they don't eat enough and pass out.

Her mother was clearly waiting for details.

"I'll be home today. I want to talk to the doctor, and then—"

"Shouldn't his parents talk to the doctor?"

"Oh, well . . ." Zoe paused. Didn't correct her mother that it was parent, not parents. Thought about Jack's derisive reaction to the idea of telling his mother about his summer plans. "I'm sure they will," she finished lamely.

"Mm." She could feel her mother's anger seeping from the phone into the side of her head, down her body, into her bones. She shivered.

"I'm sorry, really."

"We'll see you later, then." Her mother hung up.

A bit after nine, Jack and Zoe were watching *Bones*. TV dramas in the morning: a purgatory unique to hospitals and hotel rooms. A new character had been introduced, the father of the wife of the deceased. "He did it," Jack said with certainty.

"How do you know?"

"His face."

A doctor walked in, and Zoe clicked off the TV.

First, he briefed them together. What had happened and why. He asked Jack how he was treating his type 1 diabetes, and Jack said he used insulin but usually didn't check his blood sugar, just calculated how much he should need. The doctor told him he'd used too much and had to be more careful.

"The nurse is going to go over things with you today. You'll stay here for at least one more night. I'm going to refer you to a diabetes management center here in Cambridge, and you should also make an appointment with your primary care provider at HUHS. We'll send them the notes."

Zoe nodded. Jack just looked annoyed.

"Can I speak to you for a moment?" the doctor asked Zoe. They went outside the room and down the hall.

"Are you his girlfriend?"

"I—" She wondered if the doctor could tell her more if she was. "I'm his partner."

"He really needs to start doing a better job managing his diabetes. They told me this has happened before—this is serious. Mistakes like this can be life-threatening." The doctor looked very young, and very tired. Zoe wondered if he was a student. "Do you think you can convince him? He seems like he's just going to go home and keep doing what he was doing before."

"Yeah, I can . . . yes. Can you make sure I get all of the materials and stuff? So that I know what he should be doing?"

The doctor nodded and made a note. "Thank you," he said.

Zoe's eyebrows knit together. "Um. Thank you?" she replied.

16

This was, in hindsight, the turning point of the summer. Zoe started trying to get Jack to treat his diabetes more consistently, and Jack would follow her directions when she was present but then, as soon as she was out of sight, go back to behaving just as he had before—haphazardly counting calories, forgetting his insulin, taking too much to make up for it. She'd walk into his apartment (they'd started coming and going from the lab at different hours) and find him on the couch with a bowl of pasta, and she'd ask if he'd taken insulin, and he'd get this sheepish look on his face that infuriated her. She set up his doctors' appointments, made sure he went, read all of the materials, explained them to him. She felt like her mother. And now he refused to follow instructions without her hovering. She was sure chronic illness was difficult, but it was only made more difficult by mismanagement. And he acted like it only affected him. During his two-night hospital stay, they'd missed their window to check for a particular result and been set back two weeks.

Around this time, Carter came back. Zoe and Jack walked into the apartment together to find him there, sitting on the couch. Jack nodded, and he nodded back, and Zoe stood there awkwardly, like she hadn't been all but living there for a month. He really is hot, she thought, noticing afresh the cheekbones, the dark eyes, the long legs, spread, one bent one straight. Found herself wondering if he was single. Carter's dating life was mysterious: he seemed to always have dates to things but never introduced them as girlfriends. Always just by their name, and usually an impressive accolade. "This is Rita, she qualified for the 2012 Olympics." That sort of thing. Which snapped Zoe out of it, given that she had not qualified for the 2012 Olympics or anything similar, and, even if she had, there was already enough tension with Jack at the moment—she didn't need to make it awkward with his roommate.

So instead, Zoe and Carter became friends.

He immediately, and without seeming to exert any effort, produced precisely the code that they'd needed. And then, without anybody asking, cleaned up the rest of their analysis so that it stopped crashing Jack's laptop. He even took occasional shifts in the lab when Jack had exhausted himself and Zoe was at home helping her mother host dinners, which she had started doing as a wordless apology after the hospital debacle. He nodded sympathetically when Zoe explained her frustration with Jack's lack of diabetes management, though he did not help babysit. (When Zoe caught herself thinking that, she thought, Jesus, why would he? Why am *I* babysitting?) And he listened to Zoe panic, even though she was always panicking about the same things and it must've been horribly boring, the perfect balance of pragmatic and positive. "This is a risk-reward game," he'd say, "and right now, the expected value is still high." Then he'd change the subject, distract her with meandering, nonwork chatter.

When Jack brought up Divya, Zoe was so immediately and incomprehensibly angry that she couldn't even have the discussion.

She didn't know Divya, but she knew of Divya. Premed darling, ran the student EMS services (I'm lucky, Zoe thought bitterly, she didn't show up to give Jack the kiss of life). Also in student government, gunning for student body president. She'd spent some of her childhood in Britain, and clearly worked hard to keep the accent. She was incredibly pretty and possessed a certainty of her own prettiness that made her, to other women, highly irritating and, to men, either magnetic or threatening, depending on their self-esteem.

"What do you think about bringing Divya onto the team?" Jack asked.

"What?" Zoe said, turning from her bench to look at him.

"You know Divya Kaur?"

"I know of her."

"What do you think about bringing her on? She's interested."

"You talked to someone about this without me?"

"I . . . not in detail, no."

"You think"—Zoe gestured around them—"we should bring more people into this mess?"

"Well that's exactly why I thought . . ."

"Bring her on to *what*, Jack? We have *noth*ing, at the moment. Zero large-n data. Preliminary graphs do not a paper make—and certainly not a fucking startup. We can't go around hiring random people."

"She wouldn't get paid. And you brought on Carter."

Zoe flinched. "Carter is your roommate. And he brought himself on."

"But he was your idea." Jack was leaning against the bench, arms crossed. His face was set.

Zoe didn't know what to say. "That's wet," she said, referring to the bench, meaning potentially contaminated. Jack fluttered his eyes shut, shook his head. Didn't move.

They were silent.

"Sure," Zoe said, finally. "But we agreed."

"And you're not agreeing on Divya?"

"I just think we don't need more people."

"We could use another perspective. And she has a lot of startup exposure."

"Oh, *does* she." Zoe was hit with a stab of missing Sophia. Sophia couldn't stand Divya, and neither could Hanna. Sophia because they were both at the top of the premed rat race and Hanna because Divya had had a fling with Gabe. Zoe used to watch them snipe about her with aloof amusement. But now Zoe wished they were here to make her feel better, superior.

"What is wrong with you?" Jack said, and Zoe, embarrassed by her tone and even more by her thoughts, shrunk.

"You're right. I'm stressed. Can we talk about this later?"

"Fine," Jack said, and he stripped off his gloves, dropped them in the trash, and left the lab.

Later, in the apartment, Carter tried to soothe Zoe. "Maybe it's a good idea," he said. "I can't give you fresh eyes on the science side of things. Maybe having someone else would be helpful."

"Jack can't keep his fucking health under control, let alone run a lab. So he thinks he should be making . . . *hiring* decisions? I just don't—" Zoe stopped talking, shook her head rapidly, closed her eyes. "He's completely irresponsible."

"Jack *is* completely irresponsible," Carter said, "which is a good thing, because if he wasn't, you never would have pursued this, and it's going to change the world."

The door swung open and Jack walked in.

"Completely irresponsible? Me?" There was laughter in his voice, and Zoe wanted it to calm her, but instead it put her further on edge. He set his bag on the folding dining table—the plastic picnic kind—and came over to sit beside Zoe on the couch.

"I didn't think this would be that big of a deal," he said.

"I know, and that's what I find so annoying," she said.

"It doesn't have to be a big deal," Carter said. "You're going to hire more people soon anyway."

Zoe threw her hands up. "You're ganging up on me."

"Is two to one really a *gang*?" Jack asked.

"What constitutes a gang? Let's set a definition," Carter volleyed.

"Do we need guns, do you think?"

"No, no, that's not the sense she was using. Although I could see you as a mobster."

"Oh, if only you knew," Jack said, grinning. Zoe's eyes landed on his sharp canines, and she felt a sudden and bizarre throb of desire, remembered that dream. She reached up to rub her temples. When they'd kissed, in the lab. Joy, not desire. Right?

Jack turned to look at her. "Zoe." She faced him. Her brown eyes leveled with his blue. "Are you listening to me?"

"Yes," she said.

"Your theory is correct. We are going to prove it. We have already proven it to ourselves. It is just a matter of time before we have enough data to prove it to everyone else. You *know* how hard experimental design is. I am working as hard as I can. I promise."

She swallowed, still holding his gaze.

"I know this part is on me. You're the brilliant theorist. I'm the clever mechanic."

She resisted a smile, but she knew Jack could see it in her eyes.

"The greasy car-monkey turned heavy-duty machine operator."

"We aren't even using—"

"The hired help, really."

"Stop," she said, but now Carter was laughing, and she was laughing, too.

"And I'm doing a shitty job, and I can't even keep my shitty health together, but I promise I am going to do this."

Zoe was shaking her head and nodding at the same time. "I know you can."

He took her face in both his hands. She stiffened, conscious of Carter behind her on the couch. "Do you trust me?"

She nodded, looked down at the faded blue upholstery, at his faded blue jeans.

"Divya is not a replacement for you."

"I didn't think—" But her guard was down, and so instead of anger she felt insecurity, and it closed her throat.

"She has some of the technical skills, has been working with animal models. Plus her daddy is a VC guy. I thought you knew that."

"Oh." Zoe swallowed.

"So now you understand my logic."

"I . . . guess." They would need venture capital, if they were really going to turn this into a startup. But it wasn't something she'd thought about concretely. "But I still . . ."

"Think about it. And look up her father. Viraj Kaur."

Zoe nodded. Finally, Jack took his hands from her face, but not before tracing a thumb down her cheekbone. Zoe wondered if Carter had seen it, and then wondered why it mattered, and then wondered what the hell it was supposed to mean. She felt weak, like she always did after an argument.

Jack stood up. "Now if you'll excuse me, I am going to check my blood sugar and then stab myself with the magic juice so that I can eat a fucking bagel."

17

Viraj Kaur was high up at Living Ventures, the second largest biotech-specific venture capital firm in the world, with over $5 billion in assets under management. (Zoe would learn later that this does not put Living Ventures in the top five largest biotech *funds*—the assets under management in biotech of NEA and Third Rock are both significantly greater than $5 billion, for example. These sorts of esoteric facts would become her world very shortly.)

Divya brought a degree of enthusiasm to the lab that grated against Zoe so severely she began shifting her working hours to avoid her. Because, in Zoe's opinion, what Divya was most enthusiastic about was how pretending she'd come up with this idea was going to look on her medical school applications. But she had pitched Manna to her father, and he had agreed to a meeting. With all three of them, of course. As though Divya was an equal partner.

Zoe had been fixated on setting the bounds of Divya's ownership of Manna before they brought her on, but Jack had worried that that would turn her off to the whole thing—and anyway, he'd said, "We're going to make so much fucking money what does it matter? You'll have no idea what to do with all of it."

Zoe wasn't worried about money. To her, funding would be a symbol, a trophy. Proof that they were real scientists. Zoe was worried about credit.

"I don't care if she makes a third of the money," Zoe said, "I don't want her to be an equal partner. This is our project."

"You have to give people ownership over things for them to care enough to work hard."

Zoe thought, What do you know about managing employees?

"You weren't worried about this with Carter," Jack continued.

"Carter doesn't see himself as a partner. Carter sees himself as . . ."

"Mm." He tilted his head. "What does he see himself as?"

"I don't know. Not a partner."

A standoff ensued. Jack suggested they table the discussion until they knew whether Viraj would dump a bunch of money on them. Zoe wanted to know why that was a better solution. Jack said, "Because if he does, she's paying for her spot." Zoe detested this idea and said so.

They looked to Carter to break the tie. He said he saw both sides. Super helpful, Zoe said. Thanks a lot. In the end, they held off. Didn't box her in with an employee-style title or even a consultant-style title like Zoe wanted. Missed opportunities: either would have been hilarious to stick on someone who was just of legal drinking age. Of course, they couldn't really offer her anything, title or shares or partnership, because their company did not yet legally exist.

They showed up to Viraj Kaur's Kendall Square office sometime in September.

Zoe wore a black pantsuit with a creamy white shirt all bought new the week prior from the Ann Taylor on Brattle Street. The set cost just under four hundred dollars. She paid for it with birthday money from her grandparents supplemented by her dusty savings account. Zoe figured Jack could lean into the distracted scientist thing, so she told him to wash his jeans and gave him a light blue button-down pinched from her brother's closet. Zoe didn't care what Divya wore, but noted it anyway: dark purple dress cinched in around her tiny waist, matching blazer, black pumps, black laptop bag. Her black hair hung in a smooth sheet to the small of her back.

As for the meeting itself, they had no idea what they were doing or what to expect. And they didn't know how bad their odds should have been; VC firms never really offer preseed funding (that is, funding when all you have is a good idea). Divya told them they should prepare a deck, but Jack didn't think they should show anyone in the industry any data without an NDA, and Divya flat out refused to ask her father to sign one. Later, Zoe would know that they were both right. An NDA before a preliminary meeting is far too presumptuous, at least until you've been covered by major news sources and funded by the biggest names in the space, but handing over your data is asking for a funder to go find someone else they like better to develop your idea. What they needed was a nonconfidential overview pitch deck. But how would they have known that?

So they had a deck conceptualized and organized by Zoe, furnished with data by Jack using code written by Carter, who had otherwise steered clear of the prep for this meeting, and prepared by Divya. It highlighted the theoretical concept, the early data, and Jack's current set of experiments. The work Jack had done right after he'd met her parents was absent—Jack thought the n was too small.

Viraj met them in the lobby, spreading his arms wide open and greeting them all by name. "Jack! Zoe! Divya!" He was slick-looking, South Asian, had a British accent to match his daughter's. He'd been in the United States since graduating from Harvard Business School.

Zoe wondered if he, too, had to work to keep the accent, surrounded by so many Bostonians.

He reached for Jack's hand first, and then Zoe's, and then Divya's, with a wink and a smile and a "call me Viraj!" He led them into his office, "just to chat." It was a corner office with panoramic views of the most innovative square mile on the planet, concrete and glass boxes broken up by the Seussian tilt of the Stata Center, a glint of the Charles just visible in the distance.

"So tell me what you're working on."

Zoe had prepared the elevator pitch. At first, she'd written only about the theory, but Divya said they needed to pitch a therapeutic. Zoe thought this was absurd, since they were nowhere near a therapeutic, but Divya said it didn't matter, the *idea* for the therapeutic was what mattered, and Jack agreed. You can deliver it then, Zoe said, and Jack said, You're way better at stuff like that. Divya broke the tie. Jack spoke.

"Based on a centralized theory of aging developed by Zoe, we are working toward a novel antiaging therapy that, while limited by current technologies, would be functionally unlimited in potential." In other words: we don't think we can make you immortal—yet. "We believe we will produce and introduce to market the first FDA-approved antiaging drug. The market, it goes without saying, is limited in size only by the population of the developed world." Zoe had designed a pause here, but Jack, talking fast, skipped it. "Our work will change the way the world thinks about aging."

Viraj looked at him for a long time. Then he said, "I think your premise is interesting. Can you tell me more about the theory?"

Zoe breathed. She had sweat in her suit in the eighty-degree heat on the walk from the T, and now the climate-controlled interior was making her shiver.

Jack explained in broad brushstrokes. And then Viraj said, "I want to learn a little bit more about the two of *you*."

They hadn't prepared pitches about themselves. Jack didn't speak, seemingly exhausted, so Zoe started in. "We're both juniors at Harvard, where we study chemistry, as I'm sure you know." Viraj was nodding. "We were working together in the Fen Group, on telomeres. But then we started developing the concept we're currently working on, and left the Fen Group to pursue it under Richard Brenna."

Viraj was still nodding. "Brenna, Meselson, and Stahl."

"Yes."

"Where are you from?"

"I'm from here, actually," Zoe said.

"Ah! Where, precisely?"

Zoe told him.

"Are your parents from here, too?"

Clearly he was fishing for it, and she didn't want to tell him, but then again perhaps it was the right answer. Surely he already knew, anyway—surely he'd looked up her last name. "No, my father is Greek by origin and immigrated to New York state as a kid. And my mother is from Texas. He came to Cambridge to take a job at MIT." Indeed, Viraj was nodding like she'd confirmed something.

"His work is very impressive."

"Well, thank you," Zoe said awkwardly.

Viraj turned to Jack. "And where are you from?"

"Central Maine," Jack said.

"Ah, Maine! Where in Maine?"

"Do you have any Maine landmarks?"

"Well, Kennebunkport, I suppose."

"Nowhere near there," Jack said. Zoe thought it was a little too sharp, but Viraj seemed to like it. He leaned forward.

"So where?"

"Hartland," Jack said. "Geographically right in the middle of the state. Small town."

"How many people?"

"In Hartland? A thousand or so."

"Where'd you go to school?"

"Um, Nokomis. Regional high."

"So you went to public school."

"Yes."

"Very interesting. And your parents?"

"What about them?"

"Well, they must be very proud of you."

"Sure."

A pause.

"What are your hobbies?"

"What are my hobbies?"

Viraj nodded.

"Science," Jack said.

Jack and Viraj looked at each other for a long moment. Zoe could feel something shimmering beneath Jack's surface. Anger, maybe? Defiance? Viraj looked pleased. Or hungry. Divya shifted, recrossed her legs.

"Let's talk data," Viraj said, sweeping to his feet. Zoe thought, Why don't you ask Divya where she's from? Are her parents proud of her? Then told herself to focus.

In retrospect, they were lucky. He easily could've taken advantage of them, even helped his daughter take advantage of them. But at root, Viraj was a decent guy, not interested in stealing something from two twenty-year-old kids—or perhaps he thought the idea had the most potential sitting right where it was, they'd never know. He whipped out an NDA, and they walked him through their presentation, and he was nothing but attentive nods and eager uh-huhs and wows.

"There's nothing precedented about this," he said. They must have looked blank because he elaborated. "This kind of therapeutic has never been priced, there are no preclinical models, and the FDA has never approved something similar." Jack and Zoe nodded like bobbleheads. "It's not a bad thing," he added quickly.

Jack said, "We'll have a hundred percent market share as soon as we can get something approved." Zoe looked at Jack. The business-speak sounded silly coming out of his mouth. Like a kid walking around in his dad's dress shoes.

"Certainly," Viraj said, looking amused. Good amused? Or bad amused? "But it will be a long time before you get something approved, and until then there are massive amounts of *risk* here."

Zoe's stomach twisted.

"But I think . . ." Viraj had his legs crossed, hands clasped on his right knee. Over his shoulder, the Charles twinkled. "That we are very much aligned."

Zoe had no idea what that meant.

"I can feel your vision." Can you *feel* a vision? Zoe wondered. Or do you see a vision? "And I want to work with you to make it a reality."

He wanted to buy 30 percent of their company (which meant, Zoe supposed, they'd have to form a company) and a board seat (which meant they'd need a board) for a dollar amount that, at the time, was incomprehensibly high. But Jack blanched at the 30 percent, and when Viraj said, "We'll be partners, you shouldn't be worried about me versus you," Jack bristled even more, held. There goes that, Zoe thought, almost relieved, because this was moving very quickly and she just wanted some time alone in a quiet room to figure out what, exactly, was happening. But Viraj boomed out a laugh, loud and low, stood up, leaned over, clapped Jack on the back, and said, "Twenty it is."

They walked together out of the office, down the street. Zoe hardly registered their movement. She was spinning. What were they supposed to use the money for? Hiring people? *Hiring* people? She had to go to class tomorrow. And how were they supposed to start developing a drug out of this? She didn't know how to develop a drug.

When they were out of sight of the building—they'd for some reason walked away from the Kendall/MIT Red Line stop and landed instead where Main Street met Mass. Ave. in that weird little triangle of roads by the fire station—they paused. Millions of dollars, Zoe thought. In a bank account in Manna's name. This image finally sank in, and she felt a kind of triumph that was so sharp it was almost anger. She couldn't wait to tell her father. She smiled, closed her eyes, shook her head, and turned to say something to Jack— but Jack was facing Divya, who was squealing, throwing her arms around him. Zoe stopped, blinked at the display. Divya released him, and Zoe could see he was smiling crookedly, then she turned to Zoe and hugged her, too. Zoe stiffened, making eye contact with Jack over Divya's shoulder. Something passed between them, and Zoe wanted to ask him right there on the street, over Divya's head, Are you seriously fucking her? But she didn't, she just looked at him, and he looked back at her, and then the moment was broken because Divya had released Zoe and was saying, "Isn't this in*cred*ible? We're really going to do this. This is amazing." Behind her, the "walk" sign had come on and ten or so people all wearing black North Face backpacks branded with biotech logos were speed walking in unison to make the light.

"Thank you, Divya," Zoe said with a tight smile, and she meant it. She really did. Divya squealed again and pulled Jack into a second hug.

"I'm going to go change," Zoe said, "and then head to the lab." Wow, she thought. Why did that hurt so much?

"Me, too," Divya said, gesturing down at her ensemble. "This would be way too much for class, wouldn't it!" She grinned at Zoe like they were girlfriends. Zoe felt Jack watching her. Grinned back.

They didn't part, painfully, until they reached campus. Zoe had nearly ended up in a single this fall, as she'd missed the housing lottery and her roommates had gone without her. "When our number was called there was a better quad than triple, and we figured you wouldn't mind staying with us so we could get it," Sophia told her dryly the weekend after, and Zoe had answered, distracted, "Oh, yeah, of course."

Now she entered the suite and minced through the common space and down the hall, trying not to alert anyone to her presence. She didn't want to talk about what had just happened. She didn't know how to talk about what had just happened.

She stripped off her suit, tossing it over her chair so it wouldn't wrinkle. Pants first, then blazer. The silky white shirt was soaked. She smelled it. Acrid stress sweat. She wrinkled her nose and put it in a separate pile, not wanting the smell to soak into the suit.

She took off her bra, too, as the underarms were damp and clammy, and then her underwear, because why not at this point, and draped herself over her bed, so she wouldn't wrinkle. She lay there for a long time.

She thought of her mother walking into her bedroom one Saturday morning, after she'd been absolutely embarrassed in a debate final the day before (for once she'd been glad that it was only her mother who attended her extracurriculars). She'd been in bed, stewing in self-hatred and mortification, for several hours. By that age she knew better than to hope for a cup of tea and a pat on the head, and indeed her mother had said, "You look awful. Get up, take a shower, put on a nice outfit. Look good, feel good." So she had, and then she'd rehearsed what she'd failed at the day before in front of the mirror until her throat burned.

She grimaced at the memory, and then got up, rinsed off, put on a nice outfit, and went back to work.

18

They both had full class loads, but it seemed like Jack could ignore his and float along fine. Zoe, on the other hand, dragged herself out of bed, ate drooped over a bowl of gummy oatmeal in the dining hall, went to class, took notes, asked questions, went immediately to lab, worked, did her problem sets while experiments were running, went back to her room, and passed out for a sweet, brief five hours, after which she'd wake up feeling like her head had just hit the pillow. Somehow, a whole semester caught in this dizzying loop, blurred by the constant low-grade fear that came from knowing she was in deep enough that it was this or nothing.

Jack was always there when she got to lab, and always there when she left.

They solidified their data on the locus, I2, which should have been thrilling, but instead they were simply on to the next thing. Jack wouldn't even consider publishing what they had. "How do we know it's doing what we think it is if we can't show how it's doing it?" Jack said, and Zoe said, "Could you use fewer pronouns in that sentence," and Jack laughed, but it didn't completely dispel the tension. "I really think we should publish," Zoe maintained, and Jack said, "If we publish before we have the whole mechanism hammered out, someone else might beat us to it."

Divya dipped in and out. She wasn't doing much real work now, citing a "really heavy class load," but she would drop by to ask how specific experiments were coming with a particular edge to her voice that Zoe learned meant "my dad asked." Zoe and Jack had come to the understanding that Divya was his to handle. A kind way to put it: Zoe said, "As long as you're fucking her, you can deal with her stupid questions in the lab." Jack, for his part, did think this was reasonable.

"See," Zoe hissed after one of her visits, "she just wants it on her résumé."

"There is no 'it' without her father's money," Jack retorted calmly. Not that they were using the money yet. It was sitting in a shiny new bank account, waiting.

Then, just long enough after that it wasn't technically a response, he said, "You seem like you need a break. Why don't you text Carter to come hang out with you in the office?"

Carter dipped in and out, too, and yes, he usually encouraged them to take breaks, and yes, Jack usually declined and Zoe usually accepted. But that was Jack's choice. And Carter and Divya weren't the same, Zoe thought, because she and Carter were just friends. She stopped herself, embarrassed. None of this should be about who was sleeping with whom. This should be about who was contributing.

"Carter's actually writing all of our code," Zoe said finally. Jack smirked.

"Thank god for unpaid interns, right?"

Jack would never *actually* argue, never raise his voice, and this pissed Zoe off, too.

December. The ever-darkening days felt like a timer ticking down to some absolute zero, at which point—what? You never hear about the risk-takers whose risks don't pay off, Zoe thought miserably. You only hear about the Richard Brennas. She started to think about who she should beg for a research assistantship in the spring. Wonder if Professor Hall would take her back.

It was a Wednesday. Probably around eight. Zoe had gotten home from the lab an hour before, showered, changed into pajamas, and hunched over her desk to push through a problem set that was due the next day. Her eyes were gritty. Outside it was pitch-black. No snow yet, but cold. She could see the dining hall windows from her desk, the yellow interior giving them a cheerful glow. Her roommates would be there, working on their problem sets together, until late.

Someone knocked softly. Zoe frowned. The resident tutor? Had one of her roommates broken some rule?

She padded over, skirting Gabby's bicycle, which leaned precariously against the couch, and opened the door.

"Jack?"

His face was flushed pink from the cold, making his eyes even bluer than usual, and his hair was tousled high. He was excited—she could almost feel his elevated heart rate, and it pushed her own up. "What is it?"

He handed her three sheets of paper, their usual black-and-white printouts. Color printing was expensive.

"I found something."

Zoe stared. And then she looked up at him. He was grinning. She swallowed, felt tears rising. She blinked. Stared at the papers again. Real, reproduced evidence for her latest theory of how the Yamanaka factors activated the backup.

"Jack, you—holy shit." Thank god, she thought, I did it. We did it.

She wrapped her arms around his neck and pressed herself into him, and he picked her up, swung her around once. When he set her down he nodded, then shook his head, then nodded again, mute. They looked at each other.

After, she wouldn't remember who took the first step toward her bedroom. But they were stumbling there and she was locking the door behind them, and she was taking a deep, surprised breath through her nose because their lips were pressed together, and then sighing it out as her body relaxed, relaxed in a way it hadn't for how long? a year? maybe even a year and a half.

Each moment fit perfectly into the next. There were no hesitations, no points of confusion, no logical leaps to interrogate. She was pressed against the wall and then she was sitting on the windowsill with the window cold against her back and his hands on her thighs and then they were in her bed and she was wrapping her legs around him and he was pausing and pulling away to ask what she wanted and she supposed she should think harder about this, given that it would be her first and weren't you supposed to get really hung up on your first? but there was nothing to think about, this was exactly what she wanted and who she wanted and when she wanted and so she just said, Please, pulled him back to her. She had condoms in her bedside table, the ones the college distributed at the beginning of every semester, there not because she had a concrete idea of needing them but because it seemed like what you did, keeping condoms in your bedside table. He put one easily on himself, which afterward she would take as proof this was not his first time, and then she'd think of course it wasn't, what else would he be doing with Divya, but in the moment and even afterward that was utterly unimportant. He had done this but he had not done *this*. Here, with their bodies tangled together, fights were un-forgotten, but then quickly felt, communicated, resolved.

They were not two creatures but one; they had, for a moment, forever.

Afterward, he lay on his back and she lay on her side against him.

He had a tattoo on his right shoulder that she had never seen before. A snake in heavy black lines. She ran her fingers over it: raised,
slightly. His smell was so familiar she could hardly distinguish it from
her own. They didn't speak. He had his hand tangled in her hair. She
had her hand on his chest.

In the morning, somehow it still wasn't awkward—though Zoe's
anxieties did return. The reproducibility of the data, how to present it
to Viraj, what to do next. What her roommates would say when Jack
paraded forth from her bedroom at 7:00 a.m. If anyone had seen the
data she realized she'd left on her desk.

Jack got dressed, told her he needed to go shower and change and,
he winked, check his blood sugar. They didn't kiss goodbye.

She stood in the bathroom and looked at herself in the mirror and
waited for something dramatic. Some revelation. Because before she
had been one thing, and now she was another.

There weren't any changes she could see. She could hear Gabby
saying, Virginity is a construct, anyway, which almost made her
want to tell her roommates.

Then she remembered why, what Jack had had in his hand when
he came in, and she found herself smiling, and then grinning, leaning
on the edge of the sink.

There is no greater joy than success, she thought. I just want to
feel like this forever.

Her phone buzzed. Thirty minutes to get to class. She shook her
head at herself, bemused by the childish delight in her own eyes, and
started getting dressed.

The first person she called was her father, at the lab because she knew
he wouldn't answer his cell phone.

She'd told her parents when they got the funding from Viraj, which was a way to say, to them and to herself, Look, I didn't just waste my summer. They'd been impressed, and she'd preened, and her father had ruined everything by saying "Be careful, venture capitalists are throwing money at anything that moves these days."

But this was real progress—science progress. She rehearsed her phrasing one last time before she called.

His PA picked up.

"Hi, Beth," Zoe said, "it's Zoe."

"Hey, Zoe," Beth said. "Looking for your father?"

"Yeah, could you get him? Tell him I have some big news."

"Yup, one second," Beth said, and clicked Zoe onto hold. As she waited, Zoe found herself bouncing on her toes.

The phone clicked back on. "I have great news—" Zoe started to say, but Beth's voice cut her off. "Oh, I'm sorry, it's me, he's right in the middle of something. Can he call you back in a half hour or so?"

Zoe deflated. "Oh, right. Yeah. Of course."

They told Viraj, without Divya on the call. Zoe was pleasantly surprised by this, Jack's decision. Viraj just about pissed himself.

They began discussing how to raise more money, as well as how to develop a therapeutic, how to get the therapeutic to market.

They told Carter, and he hugged Zoe before he hugged Jack.

They told Divya, and she squealed, though she must've known already.

Zoe took her finals. Maybe Jack took his, maybe he didn't—what would he care about finals now, anyway?

Jack asked her to go on leave from Harvard with him. They filed the paperwork. They dreamed, giddy, of never needing to return.

The real way losing your virginity is a big deal, Zoe realized, is that suddenly you have a mostly irrational but visceral fear of pregnancy.

The night after she should have started her period and did not, she dreamed she was pregnant. Pregnant enough that she couldn't see her toes when she looked down.

She got out of bed and dressed in a baggy T-shirt and jeans, which she had to leave unbuttoned, and went to the lab. Everything felt ordinary. Except that she ran into a man on the way to the lab who looked sort of like her father and sort of like Professor Brenna but, in combining the two, mostly like neither, and he laughed at her.

She said, "What?" but the man just kept walking.

When she got to the lab, she tried to sit down and work through some data manipulation and couldn't, and when she moved to the whiteboard to focus more on the mechanism, she couldn't do that either. It was like her brain was running through a thick, sticky liquid. No—it was like her brain had forgotten how to walk, let alone run.

Jack came into the office to ask her a question. It was full of jargon that she didn't know. But she should know—it was her project. Confused, she asked him to repeat himself, and he did, but she still couldn't understand. She stood there blinking stupidly at him, and he said, "Zoe?" and she started to cry, and he moved toward her and gently laid a hand on her stomach, and she had the sudden knowledge that she was about to be violently ill, and then she woke up.

When she stood, there was blood in the sheets. She let out a huge breath, light-headed with relief.

Her father had never called her back to ask about the news. And she was already annoyed about the way she knew Christmas vacation would go, her brother and her father retiring to the living room every evening to have drinks and talk shop like old college chums. It wasn't that she wasn't welcome, it was that if she was there, it changed the vibe entirely—wasn't that they didn't invite her to the party, but that it was impossible for her to go. The observer effect.

So, spiteful, she saved up her thunder until two days before Christmas. (She wanted to be dramatic, but not Christmas Eve dramatic.) Her mother carried out a roast. Her father said, "This smells incredible."

Zoe waited until everyone had been served before saying, "Jack and I have made some significant progress in the lab."

"Oh?" Alex looked up at once, excitement in his voice. Her father kept eating. Her mother looked up, too, expression neutral.

"We've sketched out a mechanism by which the Yamanaka factors activate the epigenetic backup, in order to reverse-age cells, and have good data for it." We know how it works! She wanted to stand up, shout it. We know how it works and we're going to figure out how to do it ourselves! But she didn't: she let the facts speak for themselves.

Her father set down his fork. "Really," he said. "That's fantastic."

Zoe waited.

"So, when are you publishing?"

She pushed her chin out. "Soon," she said.

"Good." He nodded at her, just once, before returning to his food.

"And . . ." She realized she'd lost steam. The pleasure of her father's approval—because a warm "good" was her father's approval, even with her brother; he was not an effusive man—had softened her resolve. "And . . . I'm taking a leave of absence from school." She'd planned to say "dropping out" and planned to deliver the statement with much more swagger.

Her father raised his eyebrows. She didn't look at her brother. Her mother set down her fork too heavily, clinking her plate. She pursed her lips at the utensil like it'd been too rough on her china on its own, straightened it carefully. Said, "Do you think that's a good idea?"

"Yes," Zoe said.

"Whose idea was this?"

Zoe knew what her mother wanted her to say. "Mine."

"Mm."

When Zoe didn't offer any additional information, her mother said, "We should talk about this later."

"Sure," Zoe said.

She finally looked at Alex. He was staring at her, wide eyed. He saw her looking and raised his eyebrows, pulled one corner of his mouth back, and nodded almost imperceptibly.

III

MANNA

19

"Hello." Soft smile. She stood in the center of the circular red carpet, elbows bent, hands together. The iconic TED behind her (TEDx, but still). Just like you rehearsed, she thought, just like you rehearsed. "It's nice to meet you all. My name is Zoe Kyriakidis, and I am here to talk to you about aging.

"Let's start with a quick poll: How many of you see aging as an inevitability? Death as a part of life?" Hands went up: first a few, and then most of the room. Zoe nodded. "Good, good. I love a challenge." A smattering of chuckles. "We're going to discuss the biological processes involved in aging, what I believe to be the central cause of aging, and the ways in which we can turn back the clock on our own bodies. I hope that by the time I leave, you will have reframed your understanding. I want you to think of aging not as an inevitability, but as a treatable disease: no different than smallpox, tuberculosis, or cancer. And I want you to leave with hope that we will find a cure." Zoe kept her chin tilted up, arms relaxed, eyes steady and bright, flicking from audience member to audience member. Hold it, she thought, give them the space. Use the silence.

Then she nodded, stepped forward into a pace, and began.

"The story of our understanding of aging has three parts. After we figured out that DNA is the language of life, that our bodies run based on code, just like computers, that is stored in each and every cell, we thought—and this makes sense—that when our bodies stop running, it's because the code has corrupted. We thought that the accumulation of mutations in our genome was the central cause of aging. Ever heard of free radicals?" Pause, let them nod. "That you should consume lots of antioxidants to trap those dangerous buggers, or else they'll fly around, breaking your DNA into pieces?" More nods. "That narrative comes from this theory.

"The idea that DNA mutations cause aging has been disproven. The most concrete evidence is cloning. If the reason the old animal had aged was deterioration of DNA, a clone would have problems. It would be born old, so to speak. But it isn't: when we clone, say, an old mouse, we get a healthy young mouse.

"Too, there's no real link between high levels of free radicals and premature aging. If you're interested, check out John Garcia's work on that. So you can chill on the cranberry juice—although it is delicious." Pause for the chuckle, smile, nod, pace the other direction. "All to say, the free radical theory of aging is dead. Long live the hallmarks theory of aging."

She put her hands in the pockets of her suit pants, cropped to expose her ankles. She wore a silky black shirt underneath. Sharp and monochrome. Designed to be taken seriously. Her hair was down in its natural wave, for balance. She had written the speech for the general public (to be more precise, potential funders via the general public), so she was playing the part of the public scientist. Going for clear, cogent communication, including the audience in the discovery, and focusing on the feel-good story. It was unlike how they'd learned to pitch to VCs, which involved earth-shattering potential, enormous untapped markets, personal brilliance. Being the great man of this historical moment. Jack was much better at that.

"The hallmarks theory of aging—put forward in a 2013 paper by Torres et al. out of Eric Oneto's lab—says that there are nine interconnected causes of aging. The first four are primary damage causers: genome instability, telomere shortening, epigenetic alterations, and loss of proteostasis. Then you have responses to the damage: deregulated nutrient sensing, mitochondrial dysfunction, and cellular senescence. Finally, you have stem cell exhaustion and altered intercellular communication. I would need far more time to do an explanation of those justice. I encourage you to read the paper, and the subsequent work. I, along with Jack, my cofounder, worked on telomeres before Manna.

"It is absolutely true that fighting each hallmark can and will extend life. And there is some extraordinary science going on. For example, Daniel Fen is extending mouse life spans by up to forty percent using TERT delivered by a viral vector. Anthony Dunster is using senolytics to eliminate senescent cells, extending mouse life spans by 36 percent. And that's just to give a few examples. Brilliant scientists are working on every hallmark and making extraordinary strides. And eventually, when these therapies are given together, their cumulative effect, because of the connections between the hallmarks, will be greater than the sum of its parts, both in prolonging life and in prolonging a high quality of life. So not only will we soon be able to give you an extra twenty years, but we'll also be able to give you an extra twenty years of feeling forty." She paused and opened her hands in acknowledgment, and the crowd obliged with applause.

"But wouldn't it be great if, instead of tackling nine discrete problems, each of which is incredibly complex, we could tackle one?" She stopped pacing at this point, back in the center of the rug. Use the stillness, she reminded herself. Move only with your breath. "We can." Pause. Breathe: one, two. "Because the hallmarks theory of aging is also dead. Long live the information theory of aging.

"The information theory of aging says that the single cause of every hallmark is the deterioration of the epigenome. The epigenome is how our cells differentiate. As you know, each of my cells carries the same DNA. The reason my skin cells"—she pointed to her wrist—"are different from my intestinal epithelial cells"—she laid her hand on her stomach—"are different from my heart muscle cells"—she moved it to her heart and left it there—"is because the physical arrangement of DNA in each of those cells tells it what proteins to express. That physical arrangement is analog information, while DNA is digital. If you've ever had a record player, which I haven't"—grin, let the audience relax into a laugh—"you know that analog information inevitably deteriorates over time. While digital information"—she pulled a cell phone out of her suit pocket and held it up—"does not.

"Aging is the deterioration of our body's analog storage system. This deterioration causes all other symptoms of aging. And this deterioration can be reversed." Hold eye contact, keep holding, they aren't uncomfortable, only you are.

"Let me tell you a story."

It was May. Since Jack's breakthrough, five months and $8 million in funding from a seed round that had completely blown up and five part-time employees paid in cash and stock. They'd been in "stealth mode"—that is, no website, no interviews, no press—until Viraj landed the TEDx slot, said it was the perfect launch. And so it was her first real presentation, and so she had been nervous. Really nervous.

But the audience was rapt, eyes locked on her, and she was rapt, eyes locked on them, and they were feeling her emotions—excitement and passion and joy and love—and those emotions were acquiring a life of their own in the room. The audience was one living, breathing creature, enormous and powerful, and it was leaning in, not away. There was no strain of confrontation, of convincing, of pulling a group along; they were moving together, faster and further than she could go alone. When she finished, she held her breath, and there was a moment of fizzling silence, and then they clapped, and then, in waves, they stood. She faced them with her arms limp at her sides, and she had never felt like this before, and it felt good, to be bathed in their applause, to be a supplicant at that altar.

When she got offstage she allowed herself a moment, hand over her mouth, eyes closed, trembling, to think, Yes.

But on the walk back to Carter's aunt's spare rent-controlled apartment on the East River where she'd stayed the night before and would stay tonight, she came back to reality, replaying her own voice in her head like it was on tape, noting that she'd stumbled over this, slurred through that, didn't think the audience had followed there. By the time she reached Turtle Bay, she'd begun to doubt that it had gone well at all. She kicked off her shoes and went straight to the bedroom, answering Carter's "You were brilliant" with a "Thanks" and shutting the door behind her. Then she opened her laptop, found the video, and started watching.

When Carter knocked softly a bit after six, she was on her fourth watch, had three notebook pages full of things to cut, tweak, rewrite, and had already exchanged six emails with Phoebe, her public speaking professor from college who'd helped her rehearse. New comments were flicking up under the video all the time, and she only noticed the awful ones. she sounds like an idiot. this is not a scientist. yay another pretty person who doesn't actually know what she's talking about.

She rubbed her eyes, remembered she was wearing eye makeup, said "shit" under her breath, and then looked up at the door and said "what?" loud enough for Carter to hear.

He cleared his throat. "I, uh. Have dinner reservations for seven."

"Have fun," she said, turning back to her screen.

"For two," he said.

"Who's the hot date?" She'd meant it to come out light, but it didn't. She knew he meant for her to come: it was like Carter to notice she was digging herself a hole and try to coax her out into the sunlight.

"I was hoping you were." He achieved lightness. She smiled without her teeth. Shook her head, stood up, opened the door.

"Ah," he said, "the gods smile upon me."

"How fancy is the place?" Carter was wearing tailored gray slacks and a sweater and was still barefoot, which could mean anything.

"Nice but not cocktail."

Zoe looked down at the T-shirt and shorts she'd changed into. "So probably not this."

"Probably not. Though if you wore that, they'd think you were very rich."

She snorted. "Right."

She slid back into her suit pants and a clean blouse and called it good. "Is my hair okay?" she asked, emerging bent over, putting on her shoes.

"I can't see it," he said.

She sorted her left Oxford out and stood up, turned her face to him.

"Gorgeous."

"Great. Thanks."

He had called a taxi (he didn't believe in Uber), and it was waiting outside. They slid into the air-freshenered backseat, Zoe first, scooting across, and then Carter. Zoe watched the lights blur by, pressing her temple against the cool window to look up, like a tourist. She was a tourist, she supposed. And New York was wonderful: a cliff of glass, rising from the sea.

She had no idea where they were, but when they got out of the car, Carter tipping the driver in cash, the buildings were shorter. The restaurant was on the first floor, behind a black door under a subtle sign. The maître d' was a slight man in a black suit with a trendy cut and loafers without socks. "Hey," he greeted them.

"Hey," Carter said, "two under Carter Gray?"

No Socks tapped at the screen embedded in the top of his podium. "Sure," he said, "come with me."

They were led into the dim restaurant. The ceiling was corrugated metal. It reflected and distorted the lights, which were few, and the fluttering candles, one per table. He sat them in a back corner, at a high top of smooth, dark wood. The floor was unfinished concrete, worn shiny in the paths between tables. "Stacey will be right with you," he said. "Enjoy, guys."

Behind Carter, she could see the rest of the restaurant. It was a decent mix of older adults and young people. The woman at the booth across the way had a blunt silver bob that Zoe admired for a moment, resolving to never dye her hair when she went gray.

"Trendy, right?" Carter said.

"So trendy."

The waitress, Stacey, had a perfect silver manicure. She gave them menus, a single card on a silky leather backing, and set a candle in the middle of the table.

"Have you been here before?" Zoe asked. Carter nodded. "What's good?"

"I can order for us," Carter said, "if you want?"

"Please," Zoe said, resting her toes on the crossbar of her stool and leaning forward onto her elbows, chin in her hands, to people watch. The maître d was leading in a party of four, the first woman wearing a slinky dress and a silk headscarf, loose over her dark widow's peak. She blinked perfect cat-eyes at Zoe. The couple at the next high top were looking moony-eyed at each other, both leaning on the table. Zoe watched the girl reach one leg out, hook the boy's ankle. He smiled at her. Zoe smiled at them, and then quickly hid her expression, looked away.

"Do you like octopus?"

"Too smart," Zoe said. "I feel guilty."

Carter chuckled. "Fair enough."

Zoe zoned out as he ordered. She liked to be surprised.

When the waitress arrived with their cocktails, his clear with a sprig of lavender and a white straw, hers clear with a strawberry and what looked like mint leaves, he raised a toast.

"To Manna," she said.

"To you," he said, candlelight playing in his eyes.

Oh, she thought. Her stomach filled up with something. Excitement? Anxiety? Arousal? All she could think, again, was Oh.

They both took a sip. Hers was sweet and good.

"You never drink, so I ordered something that wouldn't taste like alcohol. It's also not super alcoholic," he rushed to add. "And similar for me, in case you don't like it. So you should try both." He slid his drink across the table. His bottom lip had left a shadow on the opposite rim. "I didn't use the straw."

Was he nervous?

She took a sip of his drink, which was even better. Fizzy lavender, a hint of warmth. "This is really good."

"Good! Keep it. It's a little more off the beaten path, so I thought ordering it for you would be too much of a risk." He smiled. "I was wrong." He reached across the table for her drink.

She pictured the apartment. She pictured Carter unlocking the door, smooth despite the rush, locking the door behind them, and then—

"We can share them both," she said.

She wouldn't recall the main course but would remember one appetizer, a silky, salty, rich mushroom soup that came in a little coffee cup, like a cappuccino, which left a frothy mustache on Carter's upper lip. And of course she'd remember Carter, who glowed brilliant over the food, who ordered them a main to share and saved for her the choicest pieces of everything, who gently led the conversation away from Manna, even though they had plenty of Manna-related things to discuss—he was helping a lot with the admin, thank god, because there was a never-ending pile of admin, what kind of bank account to open and how to run payroll and pay taxes, and they needed like five types of insurance and there wasn't anybody to tell them how to do any of it and Jack was horrible at it, couldn't answer an email to save his life. They talked about other things, it didn't matter what, film and literature and New York and something funny that had happened to Carter on the train. He paid, though she protested, and led her out into the street. It was brisk but not cold, and anyway she could use some cooling down. "A little walk?" he asked.

"That sounds great," she said, and they struck out. "I like this part of Manhattan," she said, looking around at the buildings, mostly brownstones or brick with the occasional funky modern glass front. "You can see the sky." They could: it stretched grayish overhead.

"Mm," he said, "much more manageable than Midtown."

They walked shoulder to shoulder. He led them to a little well-curated park, a block by a block, and they snagged a bench. Zoe loved the magic of being led around an unfamiliar city, each new place coming out of the blue like a surprise gift. "This is lovely," she said.

"Good," he said. He looked at her, smiled, and her whole body vibrated.

It was a bad idea, she knew, to have sex with Carter. It would not be good for Manna. And, of course, in the back of her mind, was the night with Jack. How long ago was that? In her memory, it floated above concrete timelines. Like those vivid snatches of places, conversations, feelings from too long ago to place that rattle around loose, triggered by a smell or sound or piece of clothing.

He and Divya had stopped seeing each other—she didn't know exactly when. But she did know he was sleeping around, enjoying their financial success. There were makeup wipes in his bathroom trash, hair elastics in his truck.

Anyway, as she'd kept telling herself, the sex, which they'd never discussed, hadn't been about them. It had been about Manna.

Zoe and Carter took a cab back to the apartment. The doorman nodded to Carter, and he nodded back. They got in the empty elevator and Zoe took a deep breath. She wasn't really thinking straight. She wanted Carter to touch her: to wrap an arm around her waist, or rest a hand on her lower back, or lean into her and whisper something into her ear.

But he didn't. He maintained a respectful foot or so of distance, and they went inside, and he said good night and dropped her off at the door of the spare bedroom like he was dropping her off at her apartment. They were precisely the same height, a matched set. She looked at him for a long moment. There was a smile in his eyes. He was teasing her, she realized. He was playing a game. She liked games. So she smiled, and said good night back, and went inside, and closed the door.

20

The next week, the TEDx talk blew up. Zoe and Jack sat in silence in an empty conference room in their interim co-working space, side by side in front of a laptop, watching the numbers below the video crawl higher and higher.

Zoe's phone buzzed—Carter, sending a link. Zoe and Carter hadn't discussed the dinner, which had been a date. It would happen, now, and the anticipation was part of the pleasure. MSNBC had run a clip of the TEDx talk on their five o'clock news under the headline "College Students Curing Aging." You look good on TV, Carter's text read. She opened the link and turned her phone to Jack.

"They love it," he said. "They love you."

Then her phone rang. "I have two interview requests, both—oh, sorry, someone else is calling me, hang on—" Carter put her on hold for maybe thirty seconds, Jack looking at her with his eyebrows raised, before Carter clicked back on to say, "Make that three." Carter had the company phone because she and Jack needed a break and their only other options were Raf and James and Mitchell, who were not well suited to phone duty, each for his own reason, and Divya, who thought phone duty beneath her.

"Yes to all," Jack said.

"Great." Carter hung up.

Someone they didn't know walked by the conference room, carrying a tray of vials. Jack's eyes followed. "I can't wait to get a real office," Jack said, and then, "What? You look . . . this is incredible. You were incredible."

Zoe rubbed her jaw, swallowed. "No, I'm happy. I'm happy." Well, she had been, anyway, deliriously so, at least for a few moments—now, the woman on the screen didn't even look like her.

"I'm just . . . I don't know, something about 'college students curing aging.' We don't have enough data for those kinds of statements. It should be, I don't know, 'preliminary work suggests,' 'it is possible that' . . ."

"No, no," Jack said, "I think it's great. Seriously. Communicating with the scientific community is different than communicating with the public. If you couch things like that, they won't get it."

"Do we want them to get it? Do we need them to get it?"

"Well, if we want them to buy our products we do."

"Jack, we are so far from selling anything—we don't even have enough money for our own office yet. And you know how long the FDA is going to take to approve this. There's nothing else like it."

"Exactly. A little public pressure can make this whole process . . . you know, we'll face resistance. From the scientific community, from regulators. If the public is on our side, it'll make it harder for them to slow us down."

"Why are you talking about this like it's some sort of war? Everyone's on the same side here. We're trying to help people live longer, for chrissakes." Jack looked at her, smirking a little, and she realized that was one of his preferred curse words she must've picked up.

"Oh, my Zoe. My darling little professor's brat. Ask your father if everyone is on the same side," he said.

"Fuck you," she said.

A few hours later, Jack found Zoe tucked away in an office, typing frenetically.

"You all right?"

"Can't talk . . . I have two more interviews tonight, like five hours of desk work to do and three experiments running and I need to update the data room and call Laura back, and it's"—she looked at her wrist—"already eight."

"Who's Laura?"

"Our attorney, Jack."

"Ah, right." Jack cleared his throat. "You're, uh, taking the brunt of this, and I'm sorry." A dreary setting for such a pivotal meeting. Two kids in an emptying building, one leaning against the doorframe of a windowless office with a pilling beige carpet and the other curled over her laptop on the floor, the purple bags under their eyes a matched set.

Zoe shook her head. "You haven't slept more than four hours a night in how long?"

"Beauty sleep doesn't do me any good, anyway."

"Hah."

Zoe was trying to sleep. But the closest she'd gotten in a long time was a strange gray state in which her brain thrashed around on work problems. And for the past week she'd been snapping awake around four, trembling, so wired she usually just gave up and went to work.

"I can pick up your experiments tonight," he said, "no problem."

"Yeah, but—" She was going to say, Being in the lab is the only reason to do the rest of it, but her phone lit up. She closed her eyes, slung it across the floor. It came to rest against the opposite wall, buzzing. Then the pressure rose up through her throat and into her sinuses and her mouth pulled down into a frown. She put her hands over her face.

"Hey." Jack was beside her. "What's up?"

"I just—I'm sorry, I don't know why—I should be excited." She took such a deep breath it almost hurt. "This is great. It's really great."

"But it's a lot."

"It's—I can't even keep track of all the things I need to do. I feel like I'm missing stuff. I feel like I'm messing up, and we're going to . . . I'm going to blow everything." It was true. They'd made it, except why did it feel so fragile? Why did it feel like every decision she made had the potential to shatter everything? Her breath hitched in, and she realized she was sobbing, though her eyes were dry. "There's something wrong with me."

"You're doing great."

She shook her head. "I can't do creative work in the lab anymore. It's like my brain doesn't even work. All I can think about is, like . . . taxes. Stupid shit."

"You've already done the creative part, though. It's just grinding in the lab from here on out." Jack paused, looked embarrassed. "And I'm useless with the interviewing stuff, the money stuff . . . Look, I'll pick up the slack in the lab." Jack rested a hand on the middle of her back. His voice was low. "We're gonna be fine," he said. "We're gonna be great."

Two days later, she was on a park bench somewhere in Kendall with Carter when he said, "Darling," half smarmy, ironic, "you're working too hard."

"Yeah, yeah." She was pretty much recovered from the crying-in-the-office thing, which she'd learned, embarrassed, by googling, was probably an anxiety attack.

It was hot out, but still she and Carter sat close enough to touch. It had only been about ten days since Manhattan, but felt like much longer. They still had not slept together. They hadn't even kissed.

"You need to do less."

She looked at him, raised her eyebrows. Thought: from the boy who approaches his leisure—tennis, film, gallery openings, cocktail hours, friends—as seriously as his work? "Mm."

Carter reached up to brush his fingers over the bags under her eyes.

Zoe happened to like them. A mark of how hard she was working. "What, I'm not getting enough beauty sleep to be seen with?"

"As if." His eyes narrowed with a smile, and he took his hand from her face to put his arm around her.

She shook her head, couldn't help smiling back. She was enjoying the tension. "Smooth."

"I happen to think," he said, voice low, into her ear, "that there's no reason for you to be wasting your time filling pipettes eight hours a day like some sort of intern. It's below you."

She paused. Had he and Jack discussed this? It seemed unlikely. They did talk more now. But only about the sterile day-to-day of business management. There was no way Jack would talk to Carter about something so personal.

"It's not below me."

"It is so far below you," Carter said, "that you cannot see it."

A week or so later titles were settled. She chief executive officer, to run the business, Jack chief scientific officer, to run the lab. She couldn't argue with both of them.

And anyway, it was what was right for Manna.

21

Jack and Viraj always acted like best friends until Viraj left the room, at which point Jack's face would, without fail, deepen into a scowl. "What is your problem with him?" Zoe asked, finally, and Jack said, "He's too controlling," and Zoe shrugged, because she couldn't deny it, he was controlling. He was always popping into the lab, making Jack explain things—which took effort, given his background was business, not lab science—and then dispensing orders as though he hadn't just learned what was going on. And Divya was there when he wasn't. She'd never take a risk like dropping out, so she was still part-time, but she was trying to make as much of her association with the rapidly rising startup as possible. She would even post pictures of her bench on Instagram, #MANNA. Zoe's only consolation was watching Jack react to her grasps for his attention, positive or negative, with cool indifference.

Jack said, "I'm worried he wants to replace us." "What do you mean?" Zoe asked, and Jack said, "I mean, you can go grab a CEO and a CSO off Cambridge Street."

Zoe took a deep breath, sighed it out. It was true. Living Ventures had a reputation for dumping enough money on startups to have essentially complete control, and then filling the C-Suite with executives they liked. She thought: I wonder if I'm enough a part of the brand now for it to save me. Then: I can't do this without Jack. Finally: Silly girl. Thinking three or four interviews and a million YouTube hits makes you irreplaceable.

It was Carter, sitting leaned back in one of the wheeled chairs, who said, "I mean, we've been talking about new investor streams. What if you start investigating some? That he's less plugged into. And then you buy him out."

Zoe chewed the inside of her lip. Jack looked at her.

Finally, she said, "Alex did offer." When Carter raised his eyebrows, she added, "To put us in touch with his VC connects at Stanford. Ages ago."

Jack said, "I've heard that West Coast investors are much more founder-friendly. Much more focused on developing *you*, not the idea." Zoe wasn't really listening, was thinking about how much she didn't like the idea of bringing Alex in. How she needed this to be *hers*. But that was selfish.

"Should we call him?" Carter said.

Zoe took a long breath and looked at Jack, and Jack looked back at her. She let it out and called him. Put her phone on speaker. Set it in the middle of the table.

"Hey, Alex. Do you still want to help with our . . . project?"

Alex added his friend to the call. Jack took the lead and was so deliciously vague about the work that by the end the friend was practically frothing with curiosity over the whole thing.

"When can you fly out?" he asked, and Jack and Zoe looked at each other over the phone.

"Uh, when do—" Zoe started to say, but Jack cleared his throat and said, "I have some time-sensitive things going on in the lab right now. How's next weekend?"

"Perfect, perfect," Alex's friend said. "We'd be delighted to have you. I'll have my assistant send over some flight and hotel options, and coordinate a driver."

"Great," Jack said, and everybody hung up.

Alex called back immediately.

"That was fantastic—he loved you."

Jack was bouncing one knee, spinning a pen in his hand. Zoe was up and pacing.

Carter was perfectly still, lounging catlike as he watched them both. "So," he said, "how are you going to handle the pitch?"

Everyone was quiet.

"Jack should go," Zoe said. "I'll stay here. Keep things running."

"It's your theory," Jack said.

"Yeah," Zoe said, "but you're way better at these pitches. Seriously. You go." He was. He was the one who the panel of potential investors always looked to first; he and Viraj spoke a whole language that was foreign to her. This was not Zoe's world of professorships and university funding and dinners with the dean. This was the world of translational research. Of research that matters because it makes money.

"You will have to tell Viraj," Carter said slowly.

"Viraj is the Living Ventures guy?" Alex asked. Zoe had almost forgotten he was on the phone.

"Yes," Carter said, "he's on the board." The board, at that point, was just Zoe, Jack, Viraj, and Brenna. Viraj was very good at holding board seats close.

"Yeah," Alex said. "Okay. No problem—he can come, too. More the merrier."

"Thank you, Alex," Zoe said. "Oh, and have your friend write me—zoe@manna.com. Jack is incapable of answering his email."

Alex laughed, and they ended the call.

"They are obsessed with your TED Talk," Jack said, fresh off a red-eye and high off his new West Coast best friends. "They're like, fuck, she looks so good on camera. What was the word they used—*mediagenic*. Fuck, she's so *mediagenic*."

Zoe rolled her eyes.

"Okay, but how did it go overall?"

"They're super founder-friendly—they kept talking about my *vision*, my *founder mentality*. They really have no idea about the science—it's all these tech investors who want to *diversify*. It's fantastic. They'll actually let us do our jobs." Jack laughed, showing his crooked canines. He was a little punchy, talking fast. "And your brother was great."

"Yeah," Zoe said, "he always is."

"We should talk about bringing him on."

"We probably should." She'd known this would happen.

"No?"

"No, you're right. We should."

The rest of the money they needed came from the family offices, a funding source none of them knew existed. They were approached by a representative of a very wealthy man, a household name, who had seen Zoe's TEDx talk and wanted to speak with her. Zoe said that Jack usually handled investor conversations. The representative said, "But the man would like to speak with you."

They video chatted. The man wanted to fly her out to his Montana ranch. The idea sat wrong with Zoe, and she was considering saying no until Jack said "Absolutely not, that sounds like the start of a horrific cold case. Beautiful young startup founder lured onto wealthy man's estate, never seen again," to which Zoe said, "You wouldn't even think twice if he'd invited you," and so she went.

The ranch was a ridiculous sprawl of dark wood and glass luxury in the middle of nowhere. His wife greeted her at the door, which sent a flush of relief through her legs—irrational, she thought, since wives turn a blind eye to the gross shit their husbands do regularly. She could feel the pepper spray tucked into her right sock.

Except then he was nothing but cordial, delightful. A brilliant conversationalist, a generous host. They had dinner and then retired to his study, bookshelf-lined, where he was all fascinated ears and bright eyes (his body was frail, but his mind was sharp). At the end of their conversation, he said, "I see my investments in the aging space as a kind of philanthropy." She nodded. He said, "I look for founders with vision." She nodded again. He said, "You are a founder with vision." She smiled. He said, "I am going to write you a check. The terms will be very favorable."

She said, "Would you sit on our board?"

He said, "As I said, I believe in founder control." She nodded, and he smiled and said, "Clever girl. I would be delighted."

As soon as the check hit their account, while Zoe was still in a hotel in Montana, Jack bought Viraj out. His daughter went with him.

This meant that Jack and Zoe, together, were majority shareholders again. On the phone, Jack said to Zoe, "Let's not let it drop below fifty," meaning their combined stake.

Zoe smiled. It felt good to have control—real control—over their company again. "Let's not," she said.

Carter picked Zoe up at Logan. When she walked out of the air-conditioned airport into the thick humidity of Boston summer, she could see a bouquet of flowers sitting in his passenger seat. No one had ever bought her flowers before.

He got out of the car to get the door for her, and she said, "Absolutely not," and he laughed, and she laughed, and she said, "I just made ten million dollars," and he said, "I think I'm about to make more. By my valuation," and she laughed, and he laughed, and she took his face in her hands, and kissed him.

22

The office in Kendall Square was Jack's idea, though, as Zoe pleaded, no early-stage startup rents in Kendall, because no early-stage startup can afford it.

Jack didn't care. "We have to be in Kendall. So they take us seriously. And anyway, the board thinks it's a great idea." The board did think it was a great idea. They were all obsessed with the chutzpah of it, sitting next to Moderna or Bayer. Carter agreed, too, saying, "It'll be much easier to hire the best people if you're in the center of the universe."

But still, it didn't sit right. Part of Zoe's discomfort was that this was where she'd grown up. It felt tired, boring. Manna to her was a Harvard thing: born of two-hundred-year-old brick buildings and narrow wooden staircases and rich history. It was about *immortality*. It was something divine. Nothing about Kendall/MIT is mysterious or divine. Kendall/MIT is all clear glass and concrete and fluorescent lights and harried, nerdy-looking people scurrying around with ID cards on retractable belt lanyards. She thought the whole scene was more Jack's aesthetic than hers. Skinny white male socially awkward startup founder with sharp elbows: take one, leave one. She thought she was much more Harvard.

They found a place that Zoe said was way too expensive but everybody else thought was perfect. It was the top floor of an enormous building on the corner of Broadway and Galileo. You could see over MIT to the Charles. There were two different fast-casual salad places on the ground level.

"This can be your office," Jack said when they walked into the huge southeast-facing corner suite. "It suits you."

"Don't be a jerk," she said.

"I'm being serious!"

He was. He claimed a smaller, darker office with easier access to the lab. "Just because it's the story you tell about us doesn't mean it isn't true," he said.

"You're sure?" she asked.

"I'm sure."

Turned out she'd only been on loan to Harvard.

When they left, Zoe looked back at the building. Someone on the second floor had taped paper snowflakes to the inside of the windows. It made her smile.

They signed the lease the next day, then sat cross-legged on the floor of Zoe's empty office, toasted each other with cans of Diet Coke.

"To Manna," Jack said.

"To Manna," Zoe replied.

Zoe's mother showed up with homemade pies as an office-warming present. Zoe's father toured the lab, nodding.

Zoe usually went straight from the office to Carter's summer lease, though she had her own apartment. He rented in Harvard Square, in one of the brick buildings north of Cambridge Common where all the law students lived. It was small but lovely, with a white-painted fireplace and blond hardwood and a cute office into which sun spilled through south-facing windows. Standing beside his desk one afternoon—Carter had an antique desk that was exactly like Zoe's father's, with which his desktop computer and two enormous screens and fancy, modern chair looked alien—Zoe asked, "Why do you do this?"

"Do what?" He didn't stop typing.

"CS."

"What kind of question is that? Why do you do science?"

"Because I love it."

He clicked enter. The computer spat an error at him, and he made a displeased noise.

Zoe looked at the side of his neck. So smooth. Almost golden. She bent down to kiss it.

"Mm," Carter said.

They didn't have *sex* sex, never had, which surprised Zoe, but Carter was the kind of man—boy?—who is almost frenetically dedicated to being skilled at oral sex. In bed he was very pleasant, safe. And incredible to look at. There was no anxiety, anger—also no thrill, desperation. But, of course, she wasn't comparing him to Jack.

Afterward, lying beside her with his arms behind his head, he said "I do it because it's impressive."

"CS?"

"Or because it's hard. No—because it's impressive. Yes. CS."

Zoe said, "Philosophy is hard, and impressive."

"It can be," Carter said, "but the rigor is self-imposed. People already think I just float along. So I needed something with externally imposed rigor, objective rigor, to . . ." He shrugged, gestured. "Be taken seriously. And anyway, what do you do with philosophy?"

"Quote it at the girl you're chasing."

"Exactly." He grinned at her. He had perfect teeth, as did Zoe. Braces from ten to thirteen, both of them.

"You become a professor. You'd obviously be a great professor. But I mean, not yet. We need you."

Carter snorted, then said, "Thanks," which wasn't the snarky response she was expecting, and unnerved her.

Zoe glanced over at him, at the straight nose and smooth face, the long, relaxed muscles of his upper arm, the fine kinked hair in his armpit. He didn't look at her.

"Freshman spring, I got into a competitive philosophy seminar. Based on a written application. I was the only nonsenior undergrad to get in. And someone wrote me this long, anonymous email about how unfair it was that someone like me get affirmative action like that. That I wasn't who affirmative action was meant for."

Zoe didn't say anything. The cadence of Carter's breathing was forcedly regular.

"And then I got another email. And then another. So yeah," he said. "I did want to be a philosophy professor."

"I, uh," she said. "Yeah. I get that, too." It came out lamely. "I mean, woman in STEM, but Daddy is a professor. You know. I wasn't, god, I'm sorry, I wasn't trying to make this about me. I just wanted to . . ."

"I know," he said, and turned, and kissed her on the temple. And then he got up and started making them dinner. He was an excellent cook.

"A fifty-million-dollar valuation, and you're still wearing those boots."

She and Jack were out back of the office, by the freight entrance, leaning against the building. They'd just finished a particularly intense investor pitch, their first without Viraj. They were starting a new raise, Series A. (They'd just finished seed, but as Viraj had always said, the best founders love to raise, the best founders are always raising.) The potential investors had asked lots of difficult questions about concrete timelines, getting better data. Zoe was sweaty, Jack unflappable.

Zoe sighed. "Do you think they have a point? That we need someone at the helm who has more experience?"

"We have Jimmy." Jimmy was who they'd replaced Viraj with on the board. He had sold two of his own tech startups.

Zoe shrugged. The concrete was scratchy against her back.

Jack was smoking a cigarette. He'd started smoking again at some point that spring—he was chain-chewing nicotine gum and then, suddenly, he was dragging on cigarettes. Zoe, on the other hand, had started sipping green juice, running six miles every morning.

"What's the point of Manna, since you're going to live forever anyway?" Jack would say, or, "How's the Silicon Valley pop science? Convinced you to microdose LSD yet?" Or, "I wonder if life span is actually a pleasure clock, so if you're miserable enough, you'll never die?" and Zoe would call him James Dean, say "It's amazing, I thought you were actually smart" or "Wow, you're so continental." If they were outside, he'd suck his cigarette so hard his cheeks hollowed in, moan performatively, and then blow it out in a long, slow stream.

Now, Jack tapped the cigarette against his fingers to loose the ash the same way he tapped his pen, midtwirl. "They're going to give us the money," he said. "They're trying to play with us."

Zoe breathed through her nose. Held in her cough from the smoke.

Jack tilted his head back against the wall, closed his eyes against the sun. "I do need new boots."

"What are you going to get?" She turned her head to look at him, then down at the steel visible through the busted toes.

"I don't know."

"What about cowboy boots?"

"Wannabe rock star?"

"I think they'd look good on you."

"Maybe," he said, "square toe."

"Oh, yes, absolutely square toe."

He stubbed out his cigarette on the wall behind him, leaving a circle of ash. "You're right," he said. "We need a break anyway."

Zoe had been half kidding, didn't believe he'd ever change anything about his appearance. Only she had upgraded and refined her image. In fact, his image was built on the refusal to update. "Okay," she said, "let's go."

They took his truck, an old red and white Ranger with ridged gray cloth seats that he'd always had and that, to Zoe, seemed like something out of a movie. They bounced across the river with the windows rolled down and then she directed him through Beacon Hill to a shop in the basement of a brick building with big windows. There was a cowboy-boot-shaped sign over the door. "Which one is it?" Jack joked.

At that point, they were both recognized sometimes in the Kendall bubble, by MIT students, biotech people. But in the real world they weren't, and Zoe liked feeling the weight of all that money in her pocket—well, the idea of the money—without anybody knowing it was there.

"What are you two lookin' for?" the man behind the desk asked in a Southie accent.

"Jack wants a pair of boots. What do you have that's nice? Square toe?"

The man nodded. "Budget?"

"None," Zoe said before Jack could say anything.

The walls were lined with boots. Zoe took a deep breath of the scent of leather.

"What size do you think you are?"

"Twelve and a half," Jack said. Zoe nodded, looking down. He did have big feet, big hands.

"For dress or for work?"

"Work, but I'm no manual laborer anymore," Jack said, smiling. The guy smiled back. "What did you do?"

"Mechanic."

"What kinds of cars?"

"Old. All kinds."

The guy nodded appreciatively. "Got a 2002 Boxster, bear to find someone to work on it."

"I could do it for you, but I'm not in the business anymore. Just keep my own beater running."

He laughed. "You on her trust fund instead? No budget?"

"Something like that," Jack replied, and Zoe rolled her eyes.

"What's your beater?"

"A '92 Ford Ranger. Four-cylinder. Regular cab."

He nodded appreciatively. "I'm Rick, by the way."

"Jack. Nice to meet you." Jack had slid into a thicker accent than usual. Sort of like a Boston accent, but less heavy on the *w*'s— Bahston, not Bawston. Emphasizing the peculiar thing he did with his -*ous* that was almost Canadian.

"So what kind of work do you do now, Jack?" Rick perused his wall of boots. Zoe had drifted off, was eyeing a pair of sleek booties.

"Lab rat. I'm a scientist."

"Oh yeah? Cross the river?"

"Ayuh," Jack said.

"Have a seat," Rick said, "I'm going to grab a couple pair for you."

Jack sat. Zoe turned to look at him, smiled, amused by how much he was leaning into the country boy thing. Jack smiled back.

Rick came out with three pairs. One traditional cowboy boot, brown, square toe, classic embroidery. One exotic, crocodile leather. And one smooth, plain. "This last one's a roper," Rick said, "took some liberty there."

Jack popped on the ropers. Rick checked the fit. Zoe stood watching.

"Perfect," Rick said. Jack stood up, rocked front to back to front. Took a few strides. They looked good with his faded-out Wranglers.

"Look great with your jeans," Zoe said.

"They're comfortable."

"How much heel slip do you have?"

"Just a little."

"Snug across the top?"

Jack nodded.

"Perfect. That heel slip will reduce over time."

Jack moved over to the mirror at the wall. Rick was nodding, already clearing away the other boots.

"How much?" Jack asked.

"Six fifty," Rick said. "Six even, because I like your truck."

Jack was already shaking his head.

Zoe was prepared for it. "I'll buy them for you," she said. He looked at her like she'd grown a second head. "Don't be sexist."

"I'm not. You're not buying me a six-hundred-dollar pair of boots."

"With what you're doing, they'll last you your whole life. Can resole them as you need."

Jack was sitting down, taking them off.

"Christ, Jack, you're irritating," Zoe hissed.

He shot her a look. "Manna doesn't mean I'm turning into an idiot."

"One pair of shoes does not an idiot make."

He raised his eyebrows.

"He's buying the boots," Zoe told the shopkeeper, "or I'll come back and buy them for him."

Jack looked at Zoe for a long moment. Then he took his wallet out (brown leather, falling apart—Zoe hardly saw it, because he hardly bought anything) and handed his credit card to Rick. "Thank you for the recommendation," he said.

Rick rang up the sale. "Wear them out," he said. "I'll put your old ones in the box."

That night, Zoe and Carter went to her parents' for dinner.

Carter wore slacks in a light wool and a button-down and both of them draped just enough so that he was nowhere near overdressed, especially when he took his shoes off at the door and walked comfortably into the kitchen in his socks and handed her mother a bottle of wine. He'd asked what the meal would be and then chosen the wine to pair with the meal, which was both completely absurd and exactly the right thing to do. He made things so easy for Zoe. She could just trail in behind and let him chat up her mother while she sat on the couch and zoned out, certain her father, marking up papers in his recliner, not only would not expect but would actively be irritated by conversation.

Her mother was laughing. Not her it's-polite-to-laugh laugh, but her I'm-genuinely-delighted laugh. Zoe closed her eyes.

They sat mixed at the table, as was her mother's requirement, Zoe next to her father and across from her mother, Carter next to her mother and across from her father. Which was fine, because Zoe wouldn't have any reason to kick Carter under the table. In fact he was more likely to need to kick her.

"So things are going well, with the company," her father said.

"Yes," Zoe said. An understatement. One must always understate.

"I hear from your brother that the West Coast buy-in continues to be strong."

"Yes. A lot of our investors are from Silicon Valley."

"What luck that Alex was at Stanford, eh?" He smiled.

Zoe thought, I need to scream. She smiled, nodded. So much of her life. Smiling and nodding.

"Oh, it's been great." Carter caught the ball easily, kept running. "Alex, and all of the talent Zoe has been able to pull together in general . . . not me, of course, I'm a drag." Her mother laughed. "But she's just a magnet for talent." He winked across the table at her.

Smile, nod.

"Your roommates—it's so funny, Carter," her mother said, "I could never imagine you living with that group." Understatement. Under the statement: They are so rough around the edges! She twinkled a laugh.

"Well," Carter said, "opposites attract!"

"Hah!" Her mother caught Zoe's eye. Zoe could practically hear her thoughts. He's so *charming*! And so *handsome*. What a lovely young man.

Nod, smile.

They kept talking. But Zoe was walking into Jack's room, that first time, seeing Carter sitting there on the couch, thinking, He is too clean for this place, too shiny. Diamond in the rough. Prince amongst peasants. God. *God*. They must've found Carter so irritating. Jack must find Carter so irritating. Jack with his single mother. How could she have forced him to buy a new pair of boots? Like she was trying to turn him into—

And Carter was the one she'd taken home. Because of course.

They—all of them, Jack, Raf, Mitchell, James—must have found— find—her so irritating, too. Professor's brat, pretty girl. Media darling. On Carter's arm. How obvious. Two kids polished and polished and polished until all you can see in them is yourself.

23

"You know we're going to have to ask," Amy, one half of a famous TV news duo, said, leaning in. "What do you think of all the press around the op-ed? For listeners—I'm sure you've all seen it by now, but in case you haven't—there was an op-ed in the *New York Times* that said"—she pushed up her reading glasses and read down her nose—"'Manna's lack of publications makes it impossible for their work to be discussed and verified by the wider scientific community.' They go on to express concern about your work, and call for publication of your data. Now I know you've responded formally to this, but what say you?"

"Honestly, I think this is what happens when two twentysomethings try to revolutionize a field," Zoe said. "I think there's going to be a lot of concern, a lot of pushback. And that's okay! It's normal! Paradigm-shifting ideas are nearly always rejected for a long time before they, well"—she smiled—"shift the paradigm. Especially when they come from upstart young people who don't even have college degrees." Zoe performed the confidence called for by this carefully crafted response without feeling it. The jab from the scientific community, cosigned by ten leading researchers in the field, had landed square in her gut. She couldn't stop picturing her father reading it, one raised eyebrow, her father's colleagues asking about it. But people were backing Manna up—there was a second op-ed from ten other researchers not saying that Manna was doing valid research, necessarily, but that "just because experiments cannot be replicated by a group of researchers who do not know the methods or procedure does not render those experiments invalid."

"As for why we haven't, and won't, publish," Zoe continued, "while our patents are still pending, it would be very bad business to hand out our ideas." She smiled again, apologetically this time.

"You say upstart young people and, gosh, you are *so* young," Amy said, shaking her head. "How does it feel to be just twenty-one and in the center of all of this? At least you can drink, I guess!"

Zoe laughed, as she should. "I mean, it's challenging because there's experience I very much do not have, and skills that come from that experience that I need. Which is why it's so important to build a great team. That said, though, I do think being young is part of what allowed Manna to happen. I think when you're young, you don't realize what you're trying to do is stupid, and so you do it anyway." She grinned.

Amy said, "We love to see women in STEM, female scientists. Is there anything you'd like to share with the little girls out there who are so excited to see the work you're doing?"

This answer was so rote that her mind, behind it, wandered: Am I a woman in STEM? I do interviews, I read contracts. I hire people. I give pep talks. I talk to rich men. When was the last time I did anything in the lab? When was the last time Jack and I worked on a problem together?

"What kinds of challenges do you face in such a male-dominated space? Women make up less than twenty percent of biotech founders, and are just eight percent of all venture capitalists."

She considered the VC guys (yes, all guys, always, West Coast, East Coast, doesn't matter). That particular look on their faces that said: We're being very polite and respectful of the Woman Scientist, aren't we! They loved Jack's *vision*, his *moon shot vision*, said his *vision* had *gravitational pull*. Said he was a *born founder*. They said that about Zoe, too, but it meant a different thing—meant Zoe was great at this. Midmorning news fluff.

Zoe was, suddenly, looking at the side entrance to the Science Center, watching herself sit on the steps reviewing lecture slides, knees nearly to her chin, arms looped around her legs. A teenage boy comes up to her and interrupts, says "Do you go here?" in a thick voice, and she says yes, pleasantly, politely, and he says "Wow, that's amazing, how did you get in?" and she shrugs and says nothing, and he says "This is my dream," and the way he speaks slowly makes her wonder if he is slightly disabled and she pities him (now, and then), keeps smiling, and says "That's a great dream," and then he keeps chatting at her for a while, and she keeps trying to be nice. She is wearing tight jeans and a baby tee. Maybe it is possible to see a slice of pale stomach when she stretches. Eventually, she stands and checks her phone and says "I have to get going for class," and he says "Oh, okay, maybe I'll see you around," and she says, generously, sure, and he says "Can I have a hug?" and he looks like a child, and she feels like a grown-up, and she's been trained to be kind so she says "Of course," and he moves forward too suddenly and grabs her and wraps his arms around her and runs his hand up the back of her leg, the other down her back, caresses her butt, squeezes. She pulls away, shocked, bile rising in her throat, and turns and hurries up the steps, clutching her binder, wrenching open the door and walking into the air-conditioning, not checking behind her, grateful for a flush of students leaving one of the lecture halls into which she can disappear. What she is most concerned about (then, and now) is whether anybody saw. She hopes desperately no one saw.

Zoe coughed, reached for the glass of water on the table. Thought, Where the hell did that come from. "I just hope that my work inspires other founders, and helps this space become more accessible to women. Because women are brilliant, and have great ideas, and if we get better at helping them bring those ideas into the world, they'll change the world."

They closed on that.

The final decision not to publish had been made way back in January, after a meeting with Viraj and his patent attorneys. Zoe had been overwhelmed; the conversation was mind-numbing and confusing and terribly stressful all at once. They wouldn't file a patent yet, because you don't patent a theory, you patent a drug. But everyone was talking like there was already a drug, and even derivative drugs.

Zoe and Jack were sitting alone in the conference room, waiting for Viraj, who'd needed to take a call and was pacing up and down the hall with his phone to his ear and one hand in his pocket.

"How do all of these NDAs work with the paper?" Zoe asked.

"What paper?" Jack asked.

"The paper . . . with the mechanism?"

Jack looked incredulous. "No way we publish this now."

Zoe looked incredulous back. "Why wouldn't we?"

"Because as soon as we do, twenty labs are going to start gunning for the same drug we are. And we might not get to it first." He paused. "Like what happened to Russo," he finished, though he didn't have to. The story had been everywhere for the past year or more. Marie Russo put in years of work on a novel vaccine type, and then another scientist took the final application step first and filed a patent. Russo subsequently filed for patent interference, but rumor was that she was going to lose. And then, on top of that, she'd been pushed out of her own startup by male cofounders, left to slink back to academia with her tail between her legs.

Zoe and Jack had seen her speak at Memorial Hall their sophomore spring. Zoe hadn't been into dumbed-down science presentations— funny, now—and had daydreamed through the talk, but Jack was rapt. After, he made a beeline for the stage. Zoe stood in the middle of their empty row, watching Jack talk earnestly at Russo, looking deeply vulnerable and somehow pathetic. Zoe worried Russo would say something dismissive just to get him to stop talking—oddly half wanted her to do just that, so the sheen would crack for him—but instead she nodded seriously. They made a strange picture—Jack in his worn thin jeans and T-shirt, through which you could see every hard line of his frame; Russo also hard, lean, but in an impeccably cut suit—and, looking at them, Zoe realized she was jealous. Why? She wasn't jealous of someone like Fen. Or maybe she was? But this was different—this was more visceral. She found herself nitpicking Russo's appearance, the way she spoke. Thinking of reasons she shouldn't be where she was.

The group of students behind Jack were getting annoyed. Russo noticed and gestured at them, cutting Jack off, but then pulled a business card out of her back pocket and handed it to him. When he returned to Zoe, he was glowing.

"She thinks we're asking the right questions," he said.

"I know we are," Zoe replied.

Uncomfortable, that memory. Why had she been so cruel, if only in her mind? She answered herself: because there's only room for so many. And you wanted it to be you.

And now it would be. Zoe vowed to succeed where Russo had failed. "You're right," she said to Jack. "No paper."

Zoe and Carter went out to dinner in Manhattan with a big group of his friends and friends' friends the evening after the big interview with Amy. He always drank to a buzz before social events, "to take the edge off," and so he was slippery beside her, easy, laughing, while she felt coiled tight and buzzing. He introduced her as "my Harvard dropout," and she could feel people staring, could feel people's jealousy, which she usually enjoyed. She liked how they looked together. But tonight it made her feel hot, gross.

She was developing a headache when someone, a young woman, said, "But you have to tell us more about this Jack—he's so mysterious! I have a friend who slept with him once"—she tittered—"and she said he lives in this shithole in the middle of, like, what's the town beside Cambridge?"

"Boston?" Carter joked. The girl hit him on the arm.

"No, come on."

"Somerville," Zoe supplied, though Jack's apartment was actually two towns over, in Medford.

"What's up with that?" the girl said. "And she said he has, like, roommates? I mean, not to be rude, but how much are you guys worth?"

"Jack's past saving," Carter said, and laughed.

"Is he hard to work with? I've heard he's hard to work with."

"Well, you know," Carter said with a nonchalant smile, a one-shouldered shrug. Zoe was stiff beside him.

"God, I mean, imagine having an idea like that and living in some dump in Somerville!" Zoe had no urge to correct her. The less she knew of Jack, the better.

"It wasn't his idea," Carter said, "it was Zoe's. Jack just runs the lab."

Zoe's headache was worsening, crawling forward from the base of her skull to just over her left eye. "It was our idea," she said. Why was she upset? She *wanted* credit—she hated when people assumed all of the science was his. "I'm going to head out, I think—I have some work to do before bed."

"Oh!" Carter said, turning to her, eyes searching. "I'll come with you."

"No, no. You stay, have fun." But he followed her out anyway, asked her what was wrong, and she said, "Nothing, nothing, I just don't feel well," and she didn't, especially now on the damp Chelsea street, which smelled like trash and pee and something sort of metallic, and he kissed her on the temple and said, "You didn't eat anything, let me cook for you when we get home," and then draped his arm heavily over her shoulder and walked in lockstep with her back to his aunt's apartment, Zoe the whole way resisting a twitching urge in her legs to run—Where? Away. Away.

When her dad called the next day, she said "Fuck" softly before sliding her finger over the screen to answer.

"Hi."

"Zoe," he said.

She took a deep breath, closed her eyes, held it, let it out.

"When are you going to publish?"

"We want to wait until we're closer to a working therapeutic."

"Hmm."

Her mother was thrilled by Manna, by Zoe as a frontwoman, by her two children working together. She told all of her friends about Zoe's TV appearances, enjoyed dropping the names of people Zoe had been interviewed by, met. Her father wasn't so easily impressed by pomp and circumstance, or by money.

"I don't . . ." she said, and then, "I know. But the investors are telling us not to."

"What you have to understand," he said, "is that these investors don't care about you. They care about their money making more money."

She sucked her cheek between her molars, slowly started biting down.

"The whole startup thing, it's not rigorous. You're not building a reputation in the community." She bit down harder. "You and Alex could publish together." She forced herself to stop biting before she started to bleed.

She wanted to say, You mean you're not building *the right kind* of reputation in *my* community. She also wanted to say, You didn't *really* care what I was doing until your *boy* was implicated. Except she didn't, because she didn't have that kind of disrespect in her and also because she wasn't sure if all of this anger really had anything to do with him and also because she was scared he was right.

Monday was staff meeting. They started with all-staff—that included Carter, Rafael, who'd been on a clinical trial team, James, who could do finance, Mitchell, who was a software engineer and into data analytics, plus Phoebe, for PR, who they'd hired full-time once they could afford her, and Alex, plus twelve additional hires, mostly lab rats—and then pared down to Alex, Carter, Phoebe, Zoe, and Jack ("exec"), Alex calling in from the West Coast. She and Jack didn't need a formal meeting: their lives were an ongoing conversation about Manna.

As they were wrapping up exec, Zoe said, "What do we think about publishing something?"

"Why?" Jack said.

"To nip the criticism in the bud." She shrugged. "We publish, show them what we have, and they all shut up. And at this point, are we really worried about someone outrunning us?"

The room was quiet.

Jack said, "I see no reason to kowtow to stupid people. And I still think it's too big a risk."

Zoe looked at Carter. "Carter?"

"I'm not a scientist—I don't know." He was looking down.

She rolled her eyes. "Alex?" She wanted to tell him what their father had said, but not in front of everyone else.

Alex, grainy on her laptop screen, chewed the inside of his lip, a habit she recognized as one of her own.

"What would the West Coasters think?" Jack asked, and Zoe turned and said "Shut up, Jack, let him decide."

Alex tilted his head one way, then the other.

"Yeah honestly—it's just so cutting edge, Zoe," he said. "And it's not like the funders are complaining that we need to be publishing." He cleared his throat. "It kind of feels like a high-risk-no-reward thing."

"You think there's no reward because you don't take shit on TV about it," Zoe said.

Alex shrugged, nodded. "Yeah. That's true."

Zoe said, "Fine," stood up, and left.

24

They finished the raise and all four of them, Zoe, Jack, Carter, and Alex, went to California to meet with the West Coasters, for no particular reason other than that they could: they could buy business-class seats and drink champagne on the flight and stay in suites in a fancy hotel. The firms wined and dined them, for no particular reason other than that everybody was making tons of money. Zoe forgot the publishing quibble, found herself thinking: This is exactly what I want. This is exactly what I want forever. She'd look back on the trip, later, and shake her head, and smile. Young and hot and surrounded by three men who adored her, her three best friends, and taking over the world. No wonder.

The day before they were scheduled to go back, Zoe was hanging out in Alex's hotel room. He'd just told her he was going to put his PhD on hold to work full-time at Manna—she was both thrilled and not, even though it had been her idea; mixing family and business is complicated—and now they were talking about nothing. Some high school classmate who'd just had a baby.

"My god, can you believe it? Do you remember when he made fart noises at you in front of Mom?"

Zoe laughed out loud, remembering her mother's scandalized face. "Oh, man." She rubbed her forehead. "And now he's raising a child."

"Well, you're raising a company," Alex said.

Zoe laughed again. "Yeah. Me and Jack. Great parents."

Alex's phone buzzed. He picked it up. "Group of Stanford and Berkeley people are having a get-together tonight." It buzzed again in his hand, and he laughed. "They're inviting me, but only because they think that means you'll come."

Zoe rolled her eyes. "Not true."

Alex turned his phone to her. Indeed, the text read, think Zoe might make an appearance?

Zoe wanted to be cool, but the smile crept across her face anyway.

"Carter will want to go," she said.

In the end, Carter and Alex went together and she stayed at the hotel with Jack. One, because it felt even better to turn down the invitation than it would have to accept it, two, because she was jet-lagged, and three, because she and Jack hadn't had a night to hang out and relax for a long time. Plus, Carter and Alex got along great, and were both actually fun at parties. They'd enjoy running the Silicon Valley scene together for a night.

Meanwhile, Zoe and Jack sprawled across his bed and watched *Mulholland Drive*. Zoe gave it three stars. "Too opaque."

"Three stars," Jack agreed. "Not opaque enough."

25

Around the end of August, Merck started sniffing around, and so
they started debating the merits of a potential acquisition. Jack
thought it was way too early, as did Jimmy. The West Coast VC
guys thought it was slightly too early. They were desperate to get M,
the therapeutic, "into the hands of a commercialization partner who
can get it to the patient population," but only after the next inflection
point, the next valuation jump. Brenna couldn't understand why they
would ever sell. The ultrawealthy would have just followed Zoe, but
Zoe wasn't sure, and so they weren't either.

As Zoe slowly climbed the five flights to Carter's apartment, passing the bikes and scooters of the resident grad students leaning on
the wrought iron railing at each landing, she was thinking that she
agreed with Jack, that it was too early, but not for financial reasons.
More because she didn't feel like they were *done* yet. M was still in
such an early stage. People still doubted her—doubted them. How
could Merck have enough to go on?

She unlocked Carter's door, went in, dropped her bag, sighed.
Strode over to his soft leather sofa and sat, curling her legs up under-

neath herself. Carter came out of the kitchen with two mugs, handed her one. Her favorite tea. She smiled at him as he sat beside her.

His face was serious, but his face was often serious. He might be telling her something inane: the grocery store had stopped carrying her preferred nondairy milk, the apartment had said he couldn't get a dog after all, he'd noticed she was developing a verbal tick in her interviews and needed to pay attention to it. She smiled at him. He was so beautiful. He always looked like he was glowing slightly. She reached up to pluck a piece of lint from his shirt, pushed a twist encircled by a gold ring behind his shoulder on the way down.

"Zoe, I have something to tell you." His voice sounded strange. She met his eyes as she drew her hand back, too fast, wrapped it around the mug.

"I'm leaving Manna."

In the silence, Zoe's ears started ringing. "You're what?" She set the mug down on the glass coffee table.

"I'm leaving Manna." His face was set and he'd steadied his voice, but after he said it he swallowed hard enough that she could see his Adam's apple jump.

She leaned back. Her feet were numb. "I don't understand."

"Zoe, you guys are doing great. You don't need me anymore."

"What do you mean we don't need you?" Her voice arced up, and she took a deep breath to try to bring it back down to the smooth cadence she cultivated. But instead, it just came out quiet. "I need you."

He opened his arms, and she leaned forward into his chest.

"It's okay," he said, rubbing a hand over her shoulder, "you're okay."

Her head was spinning. She wanted to ask him why, but this was clearly a conversation in the context of their relationship, not their work, and since they'd started dating they'd followed a no-work-talk-at-home policy. Did Why are you leaving my company count as work talk?

The panic was rising from her feet up her legs and into her lower abdomen. Was he breaking up with her? She wanted—needed—him to say, I'm breaking up with Manna, not with you. But if he did, she knew she'd say I am Manna, eyes shiny with fury and tears, and so what good would it do?

"I—" He started to speak. He took a deep breath, and she moved with it. He paused for a long time. She couldn't bring herself to sit back and look at his face. "Just think it's for the best."

He was breaking up with her. Over his shoulder, she could see into his kitchen. The lights were on their lowest setting. She could feel his heartbeat. She thought, I have been pulling away, haven't I. Since when? Since that party we left early? Or before that—since I brought him home to my parents? Why? He couldn't be more perfect. Alex loves him. My mother loves him. I love him. *I* love him. Don't I?

An elegant, flared crystal vase was sitting on the island, one white lily in it. She'd bought him the vase for his birthday. He was a Leo, just. July 24. It was expensive, Baccarat. He'd loved it.

Afterward, she was curiously numb.

The interaction felt like it had been staged. Like they had spoken and moved and breathed as scripted by someone else.

She kept expecting to feel sad. Instead, she felt panic. How-can-I-function-without-him panic, and how-can-Manna-function-without-him panic.

But panic is different from grief. Panic is a practical emotion possible to problem solve through. So by the time Jack stalked into her office, she had made a list of what they needed to do (first on the list: two new hires to do Carter's work), and there wasn't anything else left.

He slammed the door. The door, hydraulic, resisted slamming. Slowed and then sucked itself shut on its own schedule.

Zoe looked up. "What?"

Jack didn't say anything, so Zoe looked back down at her desk, glanced at her notes. "I just interviewed that candidate for your lab opening—Mira? MIT, biochem, experience in drug design. She seemed great. Do you want to speak to her, or can I bring her on? Actually, I might catch her before she gets out of the building . . ."

"You knew about Carter?" Jack said.

Zoe breathed in, pulled her shoulders back, looked up at him. "He told me a few days ago." She coughed. "We'll be fine. We don't need him."

"You didn't tell me?"

"He wanted to tell you."

"Well he just fucking told me."

"I was upset, too."

"Yeah, can't have your little boyfriend running errands for you anymore. Getting you a matcha latte or whatever the fuck you're drinking." It was a matcha latte on her desk. Guilty on one count.

"I had an intern get this, actually."

Jack sat down hard in one of the chairs in front of her desk, clear plastic scooped things that looked very futuristic. They'd seemed necessary when furnishing the biotech office that was going to cure aging. He turned his shoulders to the side, and it felt like his anger went with them, pointed outward from the two of them instead of at her, and she relaxed.

"Do you know where he's going?"

"He told me he was looking for a job."

"Regenera."

"Oh," Zoe said. Regenera was a much larger, much older biotech firm specializing in drug development as well as genome sequencing. Jack was right. That didn't look great.

"He's taking our fucking shit to Regenera."

Zoe swallowed. "He didn't tell me."

"Well he told me. Couldn't resist—had to tell me what he was getting paid."

In Carter's defense, Zoe thought, if she knew Jack, he'd have started it, said something like How dare you leave the greatest biotech company the world has ever seen, you're nothing without us. She tapped her pen on her desk. Swallowed again. Her mouth was quite dry, she realized. And she was nauseated. The smell of the matcha was making it worse. She pushed it away.

"I'll talk to him."

"Talk to him about what?"

"About what he's taking to Regenera."

"He's not fucking taking anything to Regenera. I already confiscated his company phone and laptops, and he'll be hearing from our lawyers."

"He hasn't breached contract yet, Jack."

"And he won't, because he'll have heard from our lawyers."

She kept tapping her pen. She was mad. And wounded. And scared, now, that they'd have Regenera breathing down their necks. Regenera taking her ideas. The thought came with another wave of nausea. She closed her eyes, took a deep breath, concentrated on relaxing her face. She didn't have a right to wear her emotions like Jack was. This was her fault, her mess. She needed to clean it up.

"I'll talk to him," she said again.

Jack looked at her for a moment before standing up and leaving her office.

She had to go find Carter physically, because, of course, Jack had his company phone and it didn't feel right to text his personal. He was cleaning out his desk.

"Could I speak to you in my office?"

It might've been the most direct order she'd ever given him.

He followed her.

He sat in the chair in front of her desk. Up straight, feet shoulder width apart and planted, hands clasped in the same seat where Jack had just sprawled sideways, one knee bent and one straight, arms splayed over the edges.

"I'm sorry about Jack," he said, "I hope he didn't take it out on you."

Zoe hadn't realized exactly how angry she was until he was sitting in front of her like he hadn't lied to her face. And that comment made it worse. What business of his was the way she and Jack interacted? "Of course he didn't."

Carter nodded slowly. "What did you want to speak about?"

"Did Regenera hire you to bring them our IP?"

He met her eyes. But he always met her eyes. Unlike Jack, who was shifty in conversation. Carter was as well trained as she was.

"No, they didn't. They recruited me like any other senior, offered me an enormous hiring bonus, and I felt I couldn't say no."

"We could have matched them, and you know it."

"I would never ask for a raise from my girlfriend."

"Jack would have matched them."

"I definitely wouldn't ask him."

"You're making a shitload of money. Have you tallied up your shares lately?"

"I don't want shares. I want cash."

Zoe shook her head. "The shares are worth infinitely more. The shares are going to be worth double—triple—what they're worth now in two years."

Carter was silent.

"You think they won't be?" When did he start to feel this way? She supposed she wouldn't know: the no-work-at-home rule meant she didn't get his unfiltered opinion on their prospects anymore. But how could it be the case that he'd been so optimistic when they'd had absolutely nothing and now, when they had so much, he'd lost faith?

He didn't answer her.

Zoe's heartbeat was thudding in her teeth. "Why are you worried about your stock package." She spat it out.

His words were measured, tone even. "I would just feel more secure with cash in the bank."

She stared at him. He stared back. Behind him, through the glass wall of her office, she could see some lab rat in a white coat carrying a tray of test tubes carefully down the hall. Her eyes followed him, and then flicked back to Carter.

"Fine," she said.

He left the office. She followed him about a half hour later. He drove, and she'd usually ride with him, but she couldn't stand the thought of sitting in his Mercedes. Also, she didn't want to be seen leaving together. It'd be bad for morale, she thought. She could take the T.

She waited on the corner of Main Street, Vassar, and Galileo. The walk sign came on, and with it the voice, singsongy and familiar:

"Walk sign is on to cross *Vass*ar Street." A woman scurried across carrying a Styrofoam cube.

Zoe found herself walking past the Kendall/MIT stop, hands jammed in her pockets. She slipped onto campus and looped west. She needed some air.

It was strange to walk through MIT itself. Kendall had become another world to her, distinct from the familiar paths of her childhood.

She came to the library, Killian Court. Where most summer afternoons as a kid she'd go with her mother to bring her father lunch. Just the two of them, because Alex was always busy, at camps or playing summer sports.

Professor Kyriakidis's office was at 182 Memorial Drive, which hardly means anything because 182 Memorial Drive includes a cluster of buildings expanding raggedly backward, only one of which actually touches Memorial Drive. It is more useful to say that Professor Kyriakidis's office was in Building 6, also called Eastman Labs, because it borders Eastman Court.

But they didn't go to Eastman Court to meet her father for lunch, they went to Killian Court, because, her mother said, it is much more beautiful. And who would argue with her—Killian Court is headed by the Great Dome, the neoclassical library facing the Charles with "Massachusetts Institute of Technology" on the front (except all the *u*'s are *v*'s) that you'll find on the cover of any MIT brochure. Zoe's dad called it "the library," and for years after, if someone mentioned a library to Zoe, she'd picture an enormous limestone domed-and-columned building. She would learn later that most libraries are much more modest. She would also learn later that MIT students call the Great Dome "the center of the universe."

Her father would stride out of Building 4, taking the steps down two at a time. He would grin at Zoe and crouch down and ask her how her morning was, and Zoe would answer him. And he would ask for details, like "What did you learn from coloring that picture?" or "What was the most interesting thing you saw while you rode your bike?" and she would ponder these questions like her conclusions were singularly important and he would watch her and nod seriously like he felt the same way. That was one thing about her father: when he was paying attention to you, he was really paying attention to you. It was just that he was often paying attention to something else, and more and more often as she got older.

And then he and she and her mother would sit somewhere sunny, on the steps of one of the buildings or on one of the sculptures in the court, and open the intricate picnic lunch her mother had packed, first containers of cut vegetables and separate containers of dressing, and then a coleslaw or potatoes or some other side with the main course, which varied by day and season, followed by a dessert. Zoe's favorites were tomato sandwiches and peach cobbler, though eating the cobbler on a picnic wasn't quite as nice because they couldn't top it with ice cream.

After they'd eaten, her father would grin and say "Delicious!" and her mother would smile at him and he would say "Zoe, what did you think?" and Zoe would always say "I thought it was very good," because it was, even if it wasn't tomato sandwiches, and her father would say "Four-year-olds don't lie," and kiss her on the forehead. And then he would kiss her mother on the lips, say "Thank you, my love," and she would lean into him and say "You're welcome," and then they'd get in the car to go home, where her mother would start cooking supper.

Eventually, Zoe made her way back to the Red Line. The train's swaying further upset her stomach, which was already roiling. She gasped when she was aboveground again in Harvard Square, clearing the baked air from her lungs.

By the time she knocked at Carter's door she was soaked with sweat under her jacket.

He let her in, didn't say anything. He'd already gotten her a glass of water, left it on the coffee table. Two pairs of her shoes were lined up by his door.

She sat. He sat.

Her heart was fluttering.

"What's going on?"

Carter shut his eyes. "I just think it's time that we parted ways."

"Why?"

"Look, you and Jack—it's your thing. It's not my thing. It's your thing."

"What about Alex?"

"What *about* Alex? He's your brother."

Zoe shook her head. "I meant—what the fuck was it supposed to mean, about your shares?"

"I don't . . . I just . . . I think that Jack's projections are unrealistic." He said it quickly.

Zoe's anger leaped into her mouth. "You think our projections are unrealistic? Us and every other biotech startup? Why do you think Merck is hinting at an acquisition, then?"

"You think everything Jack does is right because you love him."

Zoe blinked like she'd been hit, and then thought, You were asking for him to say that, weren't you? So why are you surprised? Why did it hurt?

"So this is all a possessiveness thing. I thought we were better than that."

"It's not a—"

"You're jealous of our relationship. Jack and I have never been

anything more than colleagues." A lie, of sorts. But one she believed.
"And so you're shitting on my work. But also, you're bringing it to
Regenera? How does that even make sense!"

He said, "You're not listening to me."

"I'm hearing you loud and clear."

They had both stood, at some point.

He held his hands up, showing his pale palms. Soft hands. She
wanted to grab them, put them on either side of her face, lean her
forehead into his. But she didn't.

"You know what, Zoe. Whatever. Like I've ever been able to tell
you anything."

She wanted to say, Get the fuck out of my apartment, but it
wasn't her apartment. She wanted to throw something in his face.
You think everybody in biotech, no, the whole fucking country, is
wrong and you're right? But she didn't.

He took a deep breath, fluttered his eyes shut, breathed out
through his nose.

She said, "All you ever wanted from me was to be cooler than you
are. You acted like the housewife"—she flung a hand out, gesturing
toward his kitchen—"but I was the trophy. So I don't know why you
think you can accuse me of—" She didn't know what she wanted to
say. He'd been a trophy, too. A shiny toy to bring home to her mother.
The perfect person to be dating. Smart and beautiful and wealthy
and accomplished. Was that all they were to each other? An ego trip?
His face was twisted up. He struck her, suddenly, as pathetic. She
thought, He's a wannabe. But she didn't say it. She stood up, and
she left.

He called her the next day, and she let it go to voicemail. He left a
message that he'd clearly rehearsed. "Zoe, I'm sorry. That conversa-

tion was too loaded. I should have kept things separate, and I didn't. We should speak again. About Manna, and then about us." A long pause, and then, "Call me back."

She didn't. She moved her stuff out while he was in class.

26

At the beginning of September, Jack had to go home for a funeral.
His uncle, or his mom's uncle, or something—he was vague.

When he told Zoe, in his office, she was retrieving some updated
data for a slide deck she was putting together. She said, "I'm so sorry,"
and he said, "I didn't know him that well."

And then, as she was leaving his office, data in a thumb drive
in her hand (they didn't use any cloud-based sharing for security
reasons—Jack was obsessed with data privacy, had hired an IT guy
to keep things totally locked down, which meant IT was one of the
only things Zoe didn't have to manage, and she was grateful for it),
she said without thinking, "Want company?"

He looked up from his computer.

"Yeah," he said. And he smiled, just a little.

Which is why Friday after work she tossed a duffel into his truck and
they headed out of the city on Route 1, then got on I-95 going north,
Jack running the aux, just like he used to when they were alone in
Brenna's lab.

"I really don't mind staying with your mom," Zoe repeated from the passenger seat, but he maintained that it would be better not to. Zoe kind of wanted to meet his mom, or, really, wanted him to want her to meet his mom, but she certainly wasn't going to ask directly. So she booked a hotel. Well, a motel—there weren't any hotels where they were going, not even a Red Roof Inn or Super 8.

Their lodging, a shabby place called Prays Motel (no apostrophe), actually made the whole thing more interesting, in a Coen brothers sort of way. They got there in the dark, so all Zoe saw of central Maine after getting off the highway in a place called Waterville was long roads hemmed in by tall, dark trees and then the interior of this motel, which was all one floor, terribly campy, with yellowish lighting, green carpet, and those tiny frilly curtains at the tops of the windows. The walls had wood paneling on the lower half and the two full beds had floral sheets and the toilet had a wooden seat. It was clean, though, and smelled okay.

When Zoe emerged from the bathroom, wet hair twisted up in a towel, Jack was sitting at the head of his bed on his laptop. The blue-white light cast a black shadow off his nose, making it look even craggier than usual.

"Blue light is terrible for your sleep," she said, taking the laptop from him. He let it go limply, watched her. She turned on night shift, and the screen warmed, and then clicked down the brightness. "There. Marginally better."

"Thank you," he said.

She crawled into bed, slid her silk sleep mask on, and pulled the blankets over herself. The only sound was the whisper of Jack's fingers over the trackpad. Probably reviewing materials coming from or going to Merck.

She tried to quiet her mind and realized that the room was painfully silent. Like there was something in her ears. She rubbed them. Like the room was filled with a huge, pillowy cube, pushing against every surface, pressing her against the bed. Like the cube was expanding into cracks and crevasses: the space between the trim and the ceiling, the nightstand, between her fingers, inside her ears. The inverse of an insane asylum.

She jerked awake. Something was chirping—a bug? a frog?— which for a moment dented the silence. The creature was answered by another, farther away or just quieter, with a slightly different tone and rhythm. The silence rebounded to fill the hollows the noises had left. Perhaps it was made of memory foam (the silence). It looked like memory foam, in her mind, in one of those commercials, a handprint pressed in slowly erased. A glass of wine sitting on the top, not falling.

She ruminated like that, half awake, for a long time until, around midnight, she faded into real sleep.

Zoe didn't go to the funeral itself. She'd offered, but Jack turned her down. "You don't need to sit through that," he said, and then repeated, "I didn't even know him that well."

So she hung out at the motel. There was an in-ground pool with dead leaves in the corners. On the side of the road, a sign advertised the "Harmony Free Fair." She'd ask Jack about it when he got back. It was a strange temperature out, both hot and cold at once. She walked a lap around the nearly empty parking lot, wondered what types of people usually stayed here. Probably a motel couldn't subsist on college kids coming home for funerals. Though, she thought, I guess we aren't even college kids. Are we.

She leaned against their door, warm, dark green, and stretched her arms over her head.

She was still standing like that, eyes closed, arms up, basking, when she heard the rattle of Jack's Ford. Then the scrape of him turning sharply to park, the engine stop, his door open, shut, his steps across the parking lot, louder until she could feel him a few feet from her.

"Someone could sneak up and abduct you."

"I heard you from down the street." She kept her eyes closed, a small smile on her lips.

"You heard *me*. I wasn't trying to be quiet."

"I don't know quite who would want to abduct me."

"I don't know," Jack said, "I hear banjos."

"What?" Zoe said, opening her eyes.

Jack just laughed.

"Do you want to go for a drive?"

The first truck they met—which was after the sign that said "Bingham 7 Jackman 57 N Anson 8 Canada 70," the gas station with the old-style pumps that Zoe'd never seen except in movies, Agency Liquor Store, Guns & Bait, and Solon Elementary School—was ancient. The paint job was matte, like it'd been done with gray primer, except for the driver's-side door, which was rust colored. The driver was wearing a trucker cap, and Zoe could see something swinging from the rearview. She squinted at it. The driver had the window down, elbow out. As the car approached she could see the hanging thing was furry.

"What's that on his rearview mirror?" she asked. In her side mirror, she watched the truck recede, bouncing. There was something in the back covered by a blue tarp that flapped up at the edges.

"Some sort of critter," said Jack.

Another sign: "Bingham, ME, Halfway Between North Pole and Equator."

"Huh," Zoe said.

They drove for a while. She was half certain Jack was trying to tell her something with the drive, that the drive was a narrative of images and at the end she'd understand.

A dead skunk on the side of the road, raven swooping down to land on it, hopping around to a choicer side.

Her phone screen, no notifications except one: failed to send, 1x in the top right corner.

A pond maybe a hundred yards to their right, ripples on the surface.

Sign after flag after sign for the far-right candidate who'd lost the last presidential election. She'd never seen one used unironically before.

A deer floating through the ditch. Like gravity wasn't real.

A falling-down gray barn, the middle of the roof caved in.

The painted September sky.

A field full of old cars, grass growing through the windows.

A ruddy-faced kid standing in front of his house—trailer, actually, Zoe realized after they were past, two trailers pushed together—pants unzipped, penis in pudgy hand, peeing toward the road.

The dark pines silhouetted against the dusty red sunset, everything turning pinkish orange, including Jack's left hand on the wheel, Jack's left arm, Jack's right hand on the stick shift, Jack's face. Head tilted back against the headrest. T-shirt drapey on his shoulders. Seeming looser than she'd seen him in a long time.

Zoe had expected to bring up Carter. Banish the last knot of tension. But, she realized, it was already gone.

Outside, the sun a burning red ball too much to look at. Look instead somewhere beside it to watch it sink, line by line, until there's only a glow in the sky to tell you it was there. And then she must have dozed, because now there was darkness, and they were still driving, but Jack seemed to have planned this, because they came to open fields of what looked like grass in the headlights, drove through them, crested a hill. Zoe had the sense that if it was light there would be a view. Jack flicked on his blinker for no one and pulled into a driveway, just two dirt ruts.

"Are we going to your house?" Zoe asked. She was still out of it, lulled by the constancy of road and motion.

He was slowing down, putting the truck in neutral, pulling the parking brake, switching off the lights. The darkness was deafening.

"No."

The giggle that rose in her chest was confused. "Did you bring me here to kill me?" Was she dreaming? Of course Jack wouldn't hurt her.

He opened his door with a creak, swung to the ground, tilted his head to look up. Leaned back into the truck. It was cold—Zoe could feel the night rushing in around him.

"You coming?"

"Coming where?"

He pointed up.

She got out of the car and fumbled her way around to his side, and then finally got around to looking where he was pointing, which was at the sky, which was spangled—finally, a sky so ridiculous as to be worth the word—with stars. Stars, not just hazy pricks of uniform light—all different sizes, some closer, some farther away, different shapes, different colors, pulsing with varying rhythms. No. Dancing.

"Oh," she said.

She could see in the stars the curve of the sky over her, and so she could feel the curve of the earth under her. She had a vague notion that this was supposed to make her feel small, but it didn't, really. Just made her chest ache.

Jack had retrieved something out of the back and was wading into the grass. The earth was so dark when she tore her eyes from the sky. He was trampling the grass into a square, laying a blanket down. She could barely see him, a smudge of moving dark against still dark. The smudge sat, then lay down, without motion invisible. She went toward him, tripping on nothing.

"I can't see." She laughed, and the laughter was real this time.

"You're almost there. Your night vision is terrible."

She bent down, brushed at the grass with her fingertips, not wanting to step on him. A blind mouse. A city mouse. A blind city mouse. A few more wobbly steps and her hands met rough wool, and she folded forward gratefully, sat too hard.

"There's the Big Dipper," Jack said, and from this angle she could see part of his arm by how it blocked out the stars. She followed where he pointed, and the shape was there, drawn on the sky. She could use the Big Dipper to find the Little Dipper, she pulled from some distant elementary school memory. But the Little Dipper must've been beneath the tree line. She shivered, chilly. There was the smoky smell of fall underneath the summer smells of life and rot.

She flopped back onto the blanket, cushioned unevenly by the clumps of grass below, and stared up into the dizzying lights. That was the Milky Way, wasn't it, arcing over them. Jack lay down beside her.

"This is what you meant about being able to see the stars here."

She heard him breathe out, quickly, through his nose.

"There's Hercules," he said, by way of answer.

27

They were headed home, moving toward Kendall, a sweet flush of relief in Zoe's mouth.

The aux cord came unplugged and the radio fuzzed on. A familiar guitar riff. Jack moved to plug the aux back in, but Zoe exclaimed, "No! I love this song."

He sighed and rolled his eyes.

"Lighten up while you still can—come *on*, Jack, everyone likes this song."

He was smiling, with his teeth, leaning his head back against the headrest. He drove with the seat way back, so his arms were stretched out, wrists resting on the top of the wheel. The highway was a blur of sun-faded gray. Zoe leaned toward him and poked him in the stomach. She knew he had no tolerance for her country rock.

But now, to her delight, he chimed in with an exaggerated twang. "Come on baby, don't say maybe," he sang, looking over at Zoe with a furrowed brow and wide, sarcastic doe eyes. She laughed aloud.

She joined him on "we may lose and we may win," closing her eyes and swaying her head back and forth with the beat. Jack watched her and shook his head, smiling. It was midsummer in the car, though outside fall was looming: the smell of sun on asphalt, flowers bursting into leaf, sweat on sunburned skin, hot berries ripening on the vine.

The joke, of course, was all well and good—except both of them realized afterward that they had jolted dangerously off their parallel tracks. This was much more real, much more consequential, than that first night with the data. Maybe this needed that night, maybe that night cradled them like a catalyst, moved them into position for the reaction. Maybe not. It didn't matter, and the mixed metaphors only confused things. There'd been a moment in the car, probably, when they both were leaning precariously, that they could've pulled the brakes, righted themselves. But Zoe had poked him, and he had sung.

28

There were an awkward few days right after they got back from Maine when neither of them knew exactly what was going on. And then she went to his new apartment—he'd finally broken the lease on the shitty place in Medford and found somewhere in Kendall. One moment they were sitting on opposite ends of the couch, and the next they were horizontal, breathing each other's air, faces together, offset so their noses were side to side. Zoe ran her hand up the back of his neck and buried a hand in his hair, and they both started laughing. At what? Nothing. Everything. She realized she was shaking.

They slept there, on the couch, that night—neither willing to move. The next morning, Zoe woke up and all she could smell or feel or see was Jack and it was perfect, it was absolutely correct, and the feeling that swept over her was so much that tears rose in her eyes. Jack murmured into the top of her head, "I'm not going to work today," and she said, "Me neither," and he said, "I'm going to call my boss, let her know I'm sick," and she laughed, and he cleared his throat and said, "Hello? Boss? I've come down with something." And she said, "Wow, that's weird, me too," and he said, "Perfect, I'll see you tomorrow, then," and she thought I love you, I love you, I've loved you this whole time.

They spent the time they weren't at the lab tangled up.

To be pressed against him didn't feel good, necessarily—it felt like relief. Like the rest of the time her body was craving it, had been forever, and she just hadn't known. "Probably," she said quietly one evening, "this is what drug addicts feel like."

She didn't need to ask if he knew what she was talking about. She knew he knew. Half the time, they didn't need to talk to communicate. In fact, sometimes words just got in the way.

"It's absolutely what drug addicts feel like." He shifted his left arm, which was under her, away from her rib cage to press into her more pliable waist. "Isn't that what neurobiologists say? Something about addiction pathways. You're the neuroscientist."

"Not anymore," she said. And then, "Speaking of addictions. When exactly did you switch back to nicotine gum?"

She felt him chuckle. "August."

He shifted onto his back, rolled her on top of him. Her nose in his neck. She wished there were a way to press so close that they'd merge, atoms making way for atoms, become one. Wasn't there some sort of myth about how couples were originally one person who'd been split apart, doomed to spend their lives searching for their other halves?

What took us so long? she thought.

"What took us so long?" she said.

Jack laughed. "You were dating the pretty rich boy."

Zoe propped herself up. He was grinning. "*I* was? You were with the pretty rich *girl way* before—" But before she could finish Jack reached up to kiss her, which shut her up.

She revised her opinion on the sex they'd had back in January. It hadn't been about Manna. It had been about them.

She didn't tell her parents. She wasn't totally sure why.

It wasn't the breakup with Carter that she didn't want to share. In fact, telling her mother she dumped Carter might have felt good. Screw the match you thought was *right* (it was amazing how her mother had adjusted her prejudices to her East Coast environment—a biracial man could be the right match, but someone without the right academic and financial pedigree could not).

She and Jack were out for a walk on a rare shared gap between meetings when they ran into her mother. She was headed toward MIT, probably to bring Zoe's father something. Dinner, perhaps, if he was staying late in the lab.

Zoe tried to dodge her, but it was too late. There was only one other person in the courtyard, and the sandy bricks against the sandy stones of the buildings left no place to hide.

"Zoe!" her mother called.

Zoe waved a limp hand.

"And Jack," her mother said, nodding, "nice to see you."

"Where are you headed?" Zoe asked.

"Oh, just to bring your father something to eat. He's got caught up, department meeting and then a postdoc needs something."

Zoe nodded. "Cool."

"How's Carter?" her mother asked.

"Um," Zoe said.

Jack was quiet beside her. She didn't want to look at him.

Her mother was looking at her. Her tongue was slow and fat in her mouth.

"He's fine," she said.

"Oh," her mother said, and she could tell her mother knew. Knew what, exactly, she couldn't say. But knew. "Well, I hope we see him soon. I'll get this to your father now"—she tapped a finger on the lunch box she was carrying—"before it gets cold."

Zoe nodded and watched her mother walk away, half-wishing Margaret would walk more slowly so that she could stay suspended in this preargument moment for longer.

But her mother turned the corner out of sight, and Jack said, "Shall we?"

Her stomach stayed knotted for the rest of the silent walk. When they got to his apartment, she turned to him. "I didn't tell them about Carter."

"I gathered."

"I didn't want to add to the drama."

"Makes sense."

They looked at each other.

"Are you not . . . mad?"

"I know your mother doesn't like me."

Zoe blinked. "So you are or you are not mad?"

He shrugged, raised his eyebrows. One of his curls had dropped onto his forehead. Her whole body felt cold. It was like half of herself being mad at the other half of herself. Except if that were it, at least she'd know that neither half could leave.

She thought about saying to Jack, You clearly are embarrassed enough of me that you won't let me meet your mother. But she didn't really think that was true.

She woke up in the middle of that night to find him awake, too. Without speaking she pulled him onto her and kissed him and he kissed her back and her relief mixed with her desire and she wrapped her hands around the back of his neck and her legs around him and sucked his lower lip into her mouth and held it between her teeth and dug her fingers into his back until he groaned. When she let go, triumphant, he propped himself up away from her on one arm and ran his fingers up and down her body with his other hand until she was shivering, pulling him to come back, to close the gap between them, at which point he leaned down, teeth against her ear, and whispered, a laugh in his voice, "What would you like?"

That her mother didn't know came up again only once. They were out for ice cream, walked all the way to Christina's. Zoe pretended she didn't eat ice cream now, so Jack would order a medium with one scoop of her favorite flavor, burnt sugar.

Zoe was taking her first mouthful of the ice cream when she noticed Jack holding back a smile.

"What?"

He nodded up at the ceiling, and then spoke the words along with the song that Zoe hadn't realized was playing.

"Said your mother told you all that I could give you was a reputation." Paused. Cocked his head. "But did she ever say a prayer for me?"

29

Just how and why the *Vogue* feature happened was a bit of a mystery to Zoe; it seemed that someone at *Vogue* had become fascinated by her and then convinced some famous photographer who had convinced everyone else.

They'd been shooting all morning, with three different outfits, and it was past lunchtime, and the novelty had worn off, and Zoe was bored and annoyed. Which was why when the photographer said "You look gorgeous, stunning" for what must've been the tenth time, she opened her mouth to say, "Is gorgeous really the point here?" and they got the shot. Looking straight into the camera, thumb and two fingers framing her face, hair curving up over her brow and back, lips parted to speak, steeliness in her eyes.

"Perfect," the photographer said, looking down at his screen. "*Perfect*. Finally caught your edge."

The headline was FOREVER YOUNG: ZOE KYRIAKIDIS ON ENDING AGING. The day it ran, the office was flooded with calls. NPR, Fox Business, CNBC, CNN. *USA Today*. The *Times*. TED, without the x. Zoe had thought that the *Today* show was a big deal, and before that, she'd thought TEDx was a big deal . . . it's all relative, she supposed.

She and Phoebe were midargument over the women's magazines—"My photo will not be on the cover of a magazine next to 'How to Lose Ten Pounds' and 'What to Wear So Your Ex Will Want to Fuck You.'" "They've moved away from stuff like that—it's really no different from *Vogue*." "Are you joking? It's nothing like *Vogue*—Serena Williams has been in *Vogue*. And Hillary Clinton"—when Alex called.

"They love this out here," he said. "Great job, kiddo. Bad*ass*."

"Thanks, Alex," Zoe said.

"And Mom's gonna piss herself."

Zoe made a face.

"Don't get it framed for her, I'm doing it for her birthday."

"Fuck's sake," Zoe said. "Later."

"Love you."

"Love you."

She hung up. Phoebe, she noticed with displeasure, was still in her office. "It'd show your range."

"My range? I run a billion-dollar company. That's range enough."

"And you're gorgeous, and feminine. You want to show young women that they can be both."

"Do I?"

She thought of the letters, addressed to their office, from young girls. *I want to be just like you, you inspired me to do science. I love biology in school. I want to start a business, too. Science isn't just for boys!* They made her cringe, for some reason. She made sure they all got replies, though she didn't write the replies, only signed them.

She thought of her face in *Vogue*, hanging in her mother's immaculate living room.

*   *   *

When she came into Jack's apartment at the end of the day (really, their apartment—at that point she had pretty much moved in), there were three copies of the magazine sitting on his kitchen table. It was quiet—he wasn't home yet. She smiled at the gesture, flipped open to the feature, looked at it for a while. She didn't see herself, but it wasn't not her, either.

Jack came in. Must've seen her leave the office and followed.

"Hey."

"Hey." He came up behind her, rested his chin on her shoulder.

"What do you think?"

"What do I *think*?" His voice was buzzy so close to her ear. She laughed, leaned back into him. He caught her, wrapped his arms around her.

"I can't decide if I hate them."

"If you do, you're wrong. Which would be unusual." He spun her around and looked her in the face. "I do have a very serious question."

She flinched. "What?"

"What kind of celebratory takeout should we order?"

Everything just kept getting bigger. More money, more investors, more legit press. Harvard Medical School asked her to join their Board of Fellows. They could probably sell and retire and be rich for the rest of their lives, but why would they? What could be better than this?

There are four idols, said the happiness professor guest on the podcast Zoe listened to sometimes on long runs. Four false gods: Fame, Power, Money, and Pleasure. She supposed the professor would say hers was fame. But it had more to do with respect. Or being taken seriously. Maybe power, too. Jack's was probably money. Perhaps power, in a way. Certainly not fame—even when journalists begged him for interviews, which they did, everybody fascinated by his mystery, he turned them down. Too much to do in the lab, he'd say. Before they were together—that is, physically a couple—she wouldn't have thought pleasure for either of them, but now, certainly. Together, then, they covered all four. It made sense with that Greek myth. A whole person, before being separated into halves, is plagued by all four devils.

But all gods are false. And Zoe wasn't trying to be happy. What a simplistic emotion to chase. She wanted more than that. She wanted this. She wanted exactly what she had. And if the therapeutic was approved—it was coming, slow but sure, they had preclinical data almost finished—they could actually, literally, have this, forever. Be young and rich and brilliant and beautiful and together, infinitely. Maybe that's why they didn't start using like the other founders, no bumps of coke or microdoses of psychedelics. They didn't need anything to get them through the sixteen-hour days. There was no more potent drug than the one they had.

They weren't looking for a house. But they were out for a walk one afternoon, taking a break from the office, and it was sunny and warm—a March thaw, hint at another spring to come. It smelled good, like melt, like soon things would be alive again. In fact, there were blades of grass poking up through the dirt, tiny flowers budding.

"It's kinda sad, that they're just going to die in a couple days when the temperature drops again," Zoe said.

"Nah," Jack said. "Don't be sad. It's happy. They're happy. Making hay while the sun shines."

They were in Cambridgeport, wandering tree-lined streets with big old Colonials and brick apartment buildings and the occasional modern-looking new build. They didn't hold hands. Carter had always wanted to be touching, but she and Jack didn't really do PDA. Didn't have anything to prove. Still, they proved it, by the way they moved, not in sync but to the same inaudible rhythm.

There was a For Sale sign in front of a small house, brick, with double-height windows. Zoe pointed it out. "That's cute."

"Do you want it?" Jack asked. She looked at him, smirked. Two could play at that game. She pulled out her phone and dialed the number on the sign.

"Yes," she said when the real estate agent picked up, using her CEO voice, "we want to look at it right away. How about this afternoon?"

"I can be there in a half hour," the real estate agent said.

Zoe grinned. "Sounds great. See you then." She hung up. Jack looked at her.

"She'll be here in thirty. Want to get coffee while we wait?"

The real estate agent was a bubbly woman in her thirties who, when she saw how young they were, was clearly annoyed to have come. Zoe didn't like to be underestimated and, she'd realized as she and Jack sat in the coffee shop, she sipping her matcha, Jack sipping his coffee, her feet up in his lap, she wanted the house. She wanted the house and she wanted to decide to want the house with him and she wanted to force him to give his opinion on what color couch to get, even though she knew he did not care, and she wanted their names side by side on the deed and she wanted to stand in a kitchen together in the morning that was theirs and look at him and think, Yes.

So, partly to entertain Jack and partly to torture the real estate agent and partly because she actually wanted the answers, she walked slowly through the downstairs, the big airy living room, big airy kitchen, asking very specific questions. "What cabinetmaker did they hire?" and "But is the kitchen floor heated?" and "Would the permitting allow for an additional bathroom to be put in? Could you show me where the plumbing is?"

They took the stairs up to the master suite. There was a deck off the bedroom, looking into a small bricked-in yard that caught the sun and held it. The real estate agent had stayed downstairs, and they could hear her on the phone. They stood on the deck, side by side.

Zoe's hands were shaking. She leaned into Jack and, before she could worry too much about what he'd say, whispered in his ear, "I love it."

Jack turned and kissed her. "I love it."

"Let's make an offer," she said, eyes wide, without moving her lips from his lips. "Real estate is a great investment."

"How much?" Was he just playing? Or was he serious?

"Asking?"

"Come on," he said, "ten under."

"Ten over. I want it."

"I thought it was an investment?"

"Mm," she said, and looked up at him.

"Twenty over," he said, wrapping his arms around her waist. She smiled, first with her lips and then with her teeth. And then she let out a little whoop, because the feeling was too much to hold in.

They offered ten over, cash. They laughed out loud at the look on the real estate agent's face. They put the money down that evening.

30

By the day they would have graduated college, they employed 150 people. They joked about throwing a "graduation" party for so long that they decided to actually have one. Labor Day weekend they rented out some hip new barbecue place that was three minutes from their office, hired a DJ, told folks to bring plus-ones. Looking out over the crowd, Zoe felt a kind of triumph. She was running this. She was putting food on the table for all these people. She was standing in front of them making a toast to their great work. She was surrounded by a gaggle of nervous, starstruck interns (many of them just a year younger than she was), the new guard, and she was listening politely to their ideas and looking them in the eyes and nodding seriously. Yes and–ing them, telling them that not only did they need to think outside the box, but that they had left the box entirely, that here they would be allowed to truly *create*. Her phone buzzed. She glanced down. The head of the foundation of a man worth two billion dollars. But the man wouldn't meet with Zoe himself. Kept insisting she meet with this lackey. She rolled her eyes. Give me the respect I deserve, she thought, or give someone else your money. She sent it to voicemail. She was wearing a custom suit and a gorgeous new pair of dark gray-blue Santoni loafers and she'd just been featured in the *Times*. She was living with her—soul mate sounded ridiculous, new-age-y, but it was true—soul mate. After the party they would go home to sleep in the new house, freshly remodeled, for the first time. She was watching Jack speak to a couple of the lab higher-ups from across the room, and she caught his eye and grinned at him, chest filling with warmth, and he grinned back.

So when Mira approached her and waited quietly for her to be free, Zoe was not at all in the right frame to take what she said seriously.

"Mira, right?" Zoe said after she'd extracted herself from the interns, proud that she remembered. She'd interviewed Mira the previous fall on recommendation from Gabby (Zoe wasn't in touch with her other two former roommates, but she occasionally did brunch with Gabby, who would start at Harvard Medical School the following year). Mira slouched and didn't dress well, but it'd taken just one interview question for Zoe to realize that she was utterly self-assured, spoke firmly and clearly about her work and thoughts, quietly so that you had to lean in and listen. Zoe was impressed by her.

"That's right," Mira said. "It's nice to see you."

"It's nice to see you, too." Zoe raised her glass. "How are you doing? I hope you're enjoying the food!"

"It's delicious," Mira said. "I hope you find some time to eat. I'm sure you're incredibly busy at things like this."

"Oh, it's no problem. I love talking to everyone."

Mira just nodded, looking at Zoe. She's comfortable with silence, Zoe thought. Maybe that's what makes her seem so confident.

"Can I talk to you?"

"Absolutely." Zoe smiled expectantly.

"Perhaps outside?"

She would've said no, but she wanted to make Mira feel appreciated. She wanted all the staff to feel appreciated. So she followed her out to the street, which was quiet. There was a group in the door, perhaps getting some air. People were already a bit drunk. Zoe smiled, satisfied. She wanted everyone to have a good time.

Mira walked her nearly to the corner.

"Is everything all right?"

"I'm sorry to do this here, tonight," Mira began, "I just . . . wanted to speak privately, without everyone seeing."

"You're always free to schedule time with me." Zoe was confused.

Mira cleared her throat. "Jack asked me not to."

"Jack asked you not to?"

"I brought the concern to him first, and he told me not to raise it to you."

"What do you mean?" Indistinct alarm bells rang.

"Zoe, M doesn't work. It doesn't work at all."

Zoe held in her laugh. "Well, it doesn't work perfectly yet, that's for sure! Or else we'd already be getting it in people's hands."

"No, listen—Jack's data . . . I haven't been able to reproduce it. I started running into some issues, some glitches. I'm working on bioavailability, so I'm totally separate from the therapeutic effect people. Which seems a bit silly, because those two things are tied, as I don't have to tell you. Anyway. I was struggling a bit on my end, so I went to talk with the efficacy people. That team is almost entirely new. As in, hired in the last few months. And they're all fresh out of college. Not a single graduate degree."

"Oh? Well, I don't have time to do all the hiring. Only the most talented recruits." Zoe smiled generously.

The flattery didn't derail Mira. "None of them has a full picture of what they're working on. Jack has each person doing only one small part of the experiments. No one person does a whole experiment. Are you hearing me?"

Zoe's expression must have been blank. She smiled politely. This girl was crazy. She'd made a mistake hiring her. She wondered if she'd talked to Carter somehow, if Carter was spreading rumors about Jack to get back at him. "Jack is a brilliant scientist. He knows what he's doing. We have a lot of concerns about . . . employees leaving, and taking intellectual property with them. We've had some issues with that in the past. And of course you understand that the proprietary knowledge we have is extraordinarily valuable. That's why he doesn't have any one person working through the whole process."

Mira paused, waited for Zoe, who was looking over her shoulder at the party, to make eye contact with her again. "When I tried to piece things together, employee by employee, and replicate the whole process, I could not get any of his results. I think you're brilliant. I know you're brilliant, I've seen your work. I know you haven't been in the lab a lot, because of how much you're doing running the company. I'm just asking that you spend some time in the lab, see what's going on. I think there are some problems that need to be addressed." Zoe nodded vaguely.

"I'll see what I can do. But in the future, you can just schedule a meeting with me, okay?"

"When I brought my concerns to Jack, he said that I could either be a team player or he'd fire me."

This got through. Zoe frowned. Jack could be unreasonable in his passion, at times, but Mira didn't deserve to be on the end of that. Mira's face was open, pleading.

"Okay," Zoe said. "I understand. I think there's probably some miscommunication happening. We're all under a lot of stress, of course. But I hear you." She nodded forcefully, wanting to show how seriously she was taking this. "And I will investigate. Personally. Okay?"

Mira nodded slowly.

"I'm going to go back inside," Zoe said, gesturing at the door with the glass of water that was still in her hand (she wasn't drinking—

she and Jack would joke that it was "because of the baby," meaning Manna). "I'll see you in the office. And don't worry, I can handle Jack."

Zoe swept off down the sidewalk and back into the lights and music. Mira stood on the corner and watched her go.

31

Zoe was "taking Sundays off," which was how she described working from home on Sundays. She had been looking forward to her first one in the new house, replying to emails leisurely from her new home office, taking breaks to prepare herself lunch, do some yoga. Except now all she could think about was what Mira had said. It was annoying. She was annoying. Zoe had better things to do than worry about something so stupid as this.

After lunch and ten minutes of attempted meditation in a pool of sun on the living room carpet, Zoe gave up. She was nearly certain Jack, who was in the lab, wouldn't have eaten yet—it was only one. So she went back to the kitchen. Took the sourdough from the bread box, cut two slices, toasted them with olive oil in the cast iron. Took a mozzarella ball from its bath in the fridge, sliced it. Then a fat, fresh tomato (it would be one of the last of the summer, she noted), taking pleasure in her exquisitely sharpened chef's knife. She'd taken a liking to cooking, or at least preparing raw vegetables, which is mostly what she ate. Had produce delivered from the farmers market every week. Plucked a few basil leaves from the herb garden in the kitchen window (that was Jack's little pet—Zoe had no green thumb). All on the bread. Drizzle of olive oil to finish, press the two slices together.

It smelled so good she wanted to eat it herself. But she'd already had her five-hundred-calorie lunch and wasn't scheduled to eat again until six, so she just leaned down to inhale the scent, letting it linger in the back of her throat before exhaling.

It didn't escape her, as she walked toward the office, that she was being very like her mother. In another life, she'd have refused to do this, thought of it as an overly gendered assault on equality within the relationship. But not with Jack—she and Jack were precisely equal. Two sides of the same unweighted coin. And anyway, she needed to talk to him about Mira. She'd resisted the urge Friday, wanting to enjoy their first night in the new house, and then talked herself out of bringing it up yesterday, because she didn't really believe it, did she?

She picked up her pace, so the sandwich wouldn't get soggy.

The office was empty and quiet. She and Jack didn't want folks working seven days a week—they both saw that as a ridiculous startup culture fad that had gotten out of hand and didn't actually add productivity—and so they shut off everyone's key cards at noon on Saturday and left them off until six Monday morning. That is, everyone but the two of them. They both had too much to do. Especially this weekend—Jack was finalizing a bunch of things for a deadline next week. The big preclinical data package, which had already been pushed back by months. A really exciting step; next would be working with the FDA to set up clinical trials. She breathed in the clean, filtered-air smell, took the seven flights of stairs up to their floor (as always). She skirted the wet lab, and went into Jack's office.

The lights were on, but he wasn't there.

There was an Excel sheet up on his desktop monitors, and printouts scattered over his desk. He was always nagging Zoe not to leave things lying around, for security reasons. She floated over to his desk, glanced down at the printouts, and then up at the sheet.

She chewed the inside of her lip.

How long had it been since she'd actually dug into their data?

She sat down in his fancy office chair, leaned forward. Looked like the printouts were graphs of the most recent performance data of mice fed M. She felt a little buzz of excitement. Like what she imagined a parent would feel, looking at their kid's report cards. She ran her fingers over the graphs. Hard numbers, to prove that they were on their way to really doing this. To making people live much, much longer.

Except then she really looked at them. There were six, labeled 23 through 28. She squinted. They were messy, noisy. He'd drawn a best fit line through the middle of each, but that was wishful thinking. There was no linear association—except for 24, which looked sort of okay. A handful of the mice in that trial had had increased performance. But, she sucked on her teeth, not to the degree they should, given how well it was going with M. He must be missing something, failed to control for something, need a better model.

She looked up at the sheet. Jabbed at the keyboard. It took her a few tries to produce a graph with the right variables (god, it'd been a long time since she'd done any of this stuff), and the Excel version of the graph was way jankier than the version he'd coded, but it matched 24. She nodded to herself, skimmed through the numbers. Played with it for a while. A weak linear association. No mistake she could find that'd make it stronger.

She looked back down at the graphs, eyebrows knit together. The others were far worse. Concerningly worse. These must be the worst sets. Maybe lab techs had made mistakes? And he was seeing if he could figure out what'd happened?

As she stared at 24, she noticed the shadow of something written on the back side. She flipped it over.

At the top, in Jack's handwriting. "KEEP." It was circled.

She felt the realization before she saw it, creeping up behind her.

She opened his computer's trash, which was full.

M_PD_082515_23. M_PD_082515_25. M_PD_082515_26. M_PD_082515_27. M_PD_082515_28.

And there were more. 20–22, 29–52, 56–70.

Thirty-nine. He'd thrown out thirty-nine sets of results to keep one.

Her hands went numb.

She minimized the sheet. Behind it was a deck for a presentation to the board. There was the graph of 24. Y axis stretched to make the results look dramatic. Beneath it, bullet points that he hadn't yet fleshed out. "Promising preclinical data. Representative sample."

She let out a shuddering breath. Her heart was beating so hard now she could see it, vision pulsing.

Fuck, she thought. You idiot.

She knew she was going to throw up. She pulled the trash can from under his desk, put it between her knees. Each movement felt like it was taking years.

She looked down at her hands. They were shaking. On her left wrist, the sleek Cartier watch he'd just given her. "Happy anniversary," he'd said, and she'd known exactly what he meant. Closed her eyes and was back in the car, singing along to the Eagles.

Was she going to throw up? Or cry?

How long had he been doing this? She had worked on the first sets, the theory stuff. So she knew that was right, didn't she? This had to be recent, this had to be about the drug. But what if it wasn't? She was walking into the lab, he was showing her what he'd found. That evening after her mother had ripped him to shreds. Zoe had been a fire needing putting out. He was picking her up and kissing her. He was coming into her dorm room with printouts. The printouts that proved her a genius. She was in his arms. They were in her bed. That couldn't have been—but how would she know? And even if it was just the data related to the drug. Was there no drug? What had they been selling people? What had she been selling people?

She saw herself on TV, looking serious, talking with her hands.

Liar.

How long?

She opened her eyes. Realized she was standing—when had she stood? Turned around. Looked straight at Jack.

IV

THE FALL

So he drove out the man; and he placed at the east of the garden of Eden Cherubims, and a flaming sword which turned every way, to keep the way of the tree of life.

—GENESIS 3:24

"O Gilgamesh, there never has been a way across,
Nor since olden days can anyone cross the ocean."

—EPIC OF GILGAMESH, TRANSLATED BY
ANDREW GEORGE

32

Evening. Their house milky with streetlights, the windows uncov-
ered. She was in their bedroom (what would be worse? Their bedroom
or one of the offices? She had wanted to sleep at her parents'—well,
she hadn't wanted to go back to theirs in the first place, but where
else could they talk? And then, when they were as finished as they
could be, she had wanted to go home, she called it home, not her
parents' house, which hurt, but he could see in her face she wouldn't
be able to hold it together in front of her parents and the whole thing
would come spilling out of her and so she stayed). He had promised
to sleep on the couch. He had been able to hear her crying for a long
time, tiny, hitching, too-fast sobs. He wondered if she might hyper-
ventilate, then reminded himself that if she did she was already in
bed and passing out would be a fine mode of self-protection. So he
stayed where he was and listened to her and studied the backs of
his hands, the palms of which he pressed flat to the top of the fancy,
modern-looking table that Zoe had picked out from some interior design catalog and ordered custom to the dimensions of their dining
room.

The biggest scar was on his right middle finger, diagonal from the tip to his first knuckle through his fingernail, which was dented and wavy and would never grow right again. He had been, what, twelve? and using the electric metal shears, didn't know the correct hand position for holding the piece (didn't know he shouldn't really be holding it at all, better to clamp it). He'd watched himself press the blade right into his own flesh, the blood slower to come than he thought it'd be, the laceration wide open and pale inside, felt the panic of believing, for a moment, that he'd cut off his own finger, which he had not. It's not the kind of panic you can forget. In fact, he felt it flare now, in his rib cage. Or had it been there for a while, and he was only now noticing?

Other, smaller scars were too common to remember.

She'd asked him why, and he hadn't been able to tell her. Looked straight into her face, and there were no words for it. The only ones he could think of were *I love you*, which he had never said to her before and could not let himself say now.

He might have used the tragic backstory. That Night, they'd call it after. He had been something like six. Tiny, skinny. The height would come later. The bulk would come never. Tangled curly hair. Kids at school would say, when they were old enough for this sort of thing, "jew fro," though he was not Jewish. He would wonder if his father had been Jewish, before discovering on a bulky white desktop computer in the library searching for some tie to something that Judaism is matrilineal anyway.

It is close to four in the morning when the cops show up. They show up because he called them. He asked the 911 operator if they could say someone else called. Like a neighbor. The operator hadn't seemed confused by this request. He will suppose, later, that 911 operators have heard just about everything. That they must be hard to confuse.

Blue lights flash through the window into the dark room. The kitchen light is on, but no one has bothered to turn the living room light on. He crawls out from behind the saggy couch when he sees the blue lights because he is nearly certain he is the only one conscious in the house and because he is afraid they'll come and go and leave him there with It. There is a long burn on his left arm that he is thinking hurts a lot. And something is wrong inside his right shoulder. But he won't remember, later, the actual pain. Just the idea of it.

The cops come in the door, which they don't have to break down or anything, it's unlocked, and he is looking straight at them over It, and one of them comes to him, stepping around It, and kneels down and asks if he is all right, and he must say something about his arm and his shoulder because the next memory is the back of the police car and then an emergency room, and he must say something about his great-grandparents, too, because his great-grandmother is there.

The hospital lights are so bright and the sheets are so white and the nice doctor with soft hands says You partially dislocated your shoulder but you are so small and it is so slight that I can just fix it in just a—and then, in the middle of his sentence, he does something that hurts blindingly (this pain he will remember), but his shoulder feels fine after and he doesn't even cry, crying being, he well knows, for girls and pussies. And the doctor speaks quietly to his great-grandmother, who has been sitting in the chair beside the bed the whole time. And then a nurse with huge pillowy breasts puts a cream on his arm that is cool and feels nice and then wraps it up. And then they also find a big lump on his head where he hit it and also a cut on the back of his knee. And then, all inventoried, he gets in the back-seat of his great-grandmother's car and she keeps turning to look at him, her face a weird gray color. It is morning when they get to her house, clear, cold morning. Spring. She asks if he wants to go to bed and he shakes his head no, so she sets him up on the couch under a blanket with a couple of granola bars and a glass of milk and says she'll make him any food he wants. It is a school day but there is no mention of school.

And then there is that strange time after when he has to go back to his mother's house, which is empty and has a weird smell, like the smell after you clean up vomit, which is just vomit mixed with cleaning supplies. The carpet that soaked up most of the blood is gone. There is a stain on the floor, which Jack's eyes go to as soon as he walks in, a dark stain, but if you didn't know you wouldn't know what it was. You could think it was beer, for example, Jack thinks. His mother looks at him with big eyes and speaks to him like a stranger, like she is afraid of him. Eventually she gets a phone call that makes her cry, and grabs him in her arms and squeezes, and it hurts his burn, even though it's almost healed, shrinking and crusty. And that afternoon she tells him to pack up his favorite things, which include his T-shirt with the dinosaurs on it and his rock collection. It does not include the teddy bear, ratty and torn, that sits beside his pillow. Because he is too old for that. But when he is sure he is alone, he squeezes its paw goodbye.

When she drops him off, she gets on her knees and hugs him and her tears and snot get all over his shirt. His shirt feels cold and wet and when he gets inside his great-grandmother asks if he wants to change it. He will not remember if he says yes. He will remember feeling strange when his mother is on her knees hugging him, his great-grandmother standing in her doorway with her arms crossed. He doesn't have a name for the feeling. He wants the whole thing to be over, but after she's driven away, he wants her to come back.

That night, he holds on to a pillow and wishes he'd brought the bear.

The next night, his bed is freshly made, and the bear is sitting on the pillow.

Except that wasn't why he did it. That would be a cop-out, woe-is-me sob story excuse, and he couldn't bring himself to lie to her and use it. Couldn't bring himself to lie to her. Hah. He felt the corners of his mouth pull back in a grimace.

He thought, You couldn't have waited to ruin everything until you'd at least enjoyed the house for a few months?

He sat at the table until morning.

33

When the boy first moves in, the great-grandmother asks him what
he'd like for dinner and he shrugs, how school was and he shrugs, if
he wants to go outside and play and he shrugs. He can see her getting
frustrated but he isn't really sure why, since a shrug is a perfectly
good answer to all of those questions, meaning as it does some combination of "fine" and "whatever."

His great-grandfather doesn't ask him any questions, and Jack
appreciates that very much.

At his parent-teacher conference (parent-teacher, hah), his teacher
says quietly to his great-grandparents—his great-grandmother sitting
up primly with her hands in her lap, his great-grandfather wearing a
clean shirt that she'd forced him into—as though he can't hear, "We
think Jack is very bright, but he can be difficult to engage. In fact, he
never speaks. We're really going to have to think about holding him
back, or putting him in a separate classroom." And so on. After that,
his great-grandmother starts trying to encourage him to do schoolwork
at the kitchen table, plus doubles down on her efforts to talk to him.

He always does what adults tell him to do. So he sits in front of the schoolwork, looks down at it, holds the pencil. Motionless like that, for hours, until his great-grandmother looks at him and sighs and says he can go off and do whatever he likes, and he goes and sits in his room, curls up on his bed or on the floor in the corner, and what?

Jack supposed, remembering, he must've been thinking about something. Daydreaming. But he couldn't imagine what he would've dreamed about.

His great-grandfather is a mechanic, and Jack knows from the conversations that flow over his head that for extra money he takes clients outside of the shop, which the shop doesn't like but can't really do anything about. (It was never that Jack wasn't listening, just that he didn't think he needed to say anything and, in fact, was finding that the less he spoke the looser adults were with their gossip around him, for example his great-grandmother the other day told a friend at the kitchen table that Nicky was thinking about going to rehab, and the friend said Oh isn't that great, and his great-grandmother winced and shrugged and sighed and glanced over at Jack, who made sure his eyes were trained on the television screen and glazed over for good measure, and said Maybe but I just don't want them to think she's competent again, to have Jack. Jack didn't know what *competent* meant, but he could figure out the gist.) Jack's great-grandfather works on these extra cars one at a time in their dooryard or under this structure he built that he calls a garage but is really just two walls and a roof to keep off some of the snow in the winter.

After some long stretch of time, Jack starts creeping out quietly to sit on an old tire or block of wood or whatever is kicking around beside his great-grandfather while he works.

The slow constancy of the work is soothing. The repeated, predictable images. His great-grandfather fishing around, shoulder deep in the engine, pulling his arm out triumphantly, holding something small and shiny, hand blackened with grease. Lying on the square of wood with wheels so he can slide around under the car on his back. Holding four bolts in his mouth while he cranks a fifth down. And the best part: he never talks to Jack. He mutters a string of swear words occasionally, when he drops something or can't find something or what have you. The same string every time, like one word. An incantation. A mantra. A poem, even. "Mother-fucking-cock-sucking-sunnuva-bitch-shit-fuck." But that is it for utterances.

Jack likes the way his great-grandfather always knows what to do next.

He will hear his great-grandmother tell the story later, when he is in high school and she is bragging about how much of a genius he is, how he is going off to Harvard. She'll say, Little Jack, so tiny then, you'd never know it now with how he's sprouted up, he'd sneak out and sit beside Jim. And Jim, well you know Jim, wicked quiet, wouldn't say nothin' to the boy at first and that was fine 'cause Jack didn't want to say nothin' either. And they became friends without talkin' at all.

His great-grandfather, after some additional long stretch of time, starts narrating. Just small things, sounding like he's talking to himself. "Aight, tomorrow I'll get that hose back on" or "tire rotation's the last thing" or "start with the leak test after dinner." Then more, speaks a bit as he works, like "this bugger doesn't want to come off" or "battery's corroded," stuff like that, and Jack starts to move closer to the engine so he can peer inside and see what his great-grandfather is talking about.

It is winter, and his great-grandmother snags him in the afternoons when his great-grandfather gets home from work to bundle him up in a coat and hat and mittens before he slinks outside. And his great-grandfather's hands are lit in sharp white with dark shadows by the combination of the big light he has attached to the top of the garage and the light he wears on his head in the wintertime when it gets dark early. Jack creeps up to see better, and when his great-grandfather pulls his hands away and pauses, Jack points and says "What's that?" which are his first words since That Night.

34

Jack alternated between watching his own blue-gloved hands and glancing back at the gaggle of new hires behind him. All very young: straight out of college. They were to work on synthesis of M, the drug. He switched to a larger pipette, picked up a tip, started moving a pinkish liquid into a clear liquid. Their faces were round and rapt. His hands made the pipette look small. Their faces were nodding. He finished, discarded the tip, laid down the pipette, took off his right glove, then shucked his left with the right inside directly into the trash, brushed his hands together. "Questions?"

First, a decent one about refrigeration of materials. Then, a good one about whether they'd thought about substituting one reagent for another. Jack was careful to reward both, but the first more than the second. Good rule followers, he'd found, didn't make trouble. Good creative thinkers could sometimes get too creative for—not necessarily for their own good. For Manna's own good.

None of them asked about the step after synthesis, which would be testing. Probably because they assumed that efficacy data would be fed back to them so they'd know if they were making mistakes. When they didn't see that data is when they would ask, and then he would act like they were asking an incredibly stupid question, tell them that startups didn't work that way, that for security reasons each team was a closed circle. That what they were doing was top secret, and what the teams who worked with the mice across the hall were doing was top secret, too. And he'd imply that perhaps they hadn't fully read the employee manual (150 pages), despite having signed it, and narrow his eyes like he was suspicious they had broken their NDA already. "Have you been sharing your data with other teams?" he'd say slowly. They'd scurry from his office, terrified, and they would not ask again.

Which was good, because if they saw the raw efficacy data, they would know that everything Manna was saying to the media about the treatment they had in development, everything they'd seen on national news or read in *Vogue* or the *NYT* or *Forbes* about the drug that wasn't going to *cure* aging, of course, we can't do that but, wink wink, but might as well, a course of which would knock fifteen, twenty years off your biological age pretty much immediately, was at this moment something between extreme exaggeration and outright lie.

Jack smiled at them, no teeth, and said, "Then why don't we move on to the next step?" As he was saying it, he caught movement through the glass wall behind them. He knew before his eyes had focused that it was Zoe. Purposeful stride and perfect posture, unchanged since he had watched her walk to Professor Norton's office hours that very first day. Her hair was twisted back into a knot, exposing her long neck. He pulsed with something. Longing. She must've seen him out of the corner of her eye but did not look. He glanced back at the new hires. They'd clearly noticed her, too— some were still staring. He and Zoe should've greeted each other. The reputation was that they were inseparable. They should keep up appearances, or people would know something had happened.

He watched her turn the corner into her office. With so many

panes of glass between them, she was just a shadow sitting down at
her desk.

Perhaps it didn't matter. Let the employees distract themselves
with gossip about a lovers' quarrel.

He turned and carried on with the demonstration.

At the end of the day, he went home. Zoe had taken out a lease on
a one-bedroom in Kendall weeks ago. The night she went, he had
things delivered to her he knew she might need. Toilet paper, paper
towels. A white noise machine, which she couldn't sleep without. A
few groceries, including the matcha and oatmeal and fancy nondairy
milk she needed for breakfast. A bouquet of flowers, which he thought
she'd probably launch out the window but he felt compelled to send
anyway (out of what? cruelty? tenderness? what's the difference?).
Left the note blank. She relented on the building address but wouldn't
tell him her apartment number, so he just used her name, and it all
found its way.

He pulled off his boots and then lay down on the couch. It was
enormous, one side more than long enough for him. Zoe had picked
it out. He had an alarm set on his phone already, and his ringer off
except for Zoe, whose calls were set to come through no matter what.
Not that she would call him. He fell asleep at once, sucked downward
into blackness that slurred into the piercing beep-beep-beep of nine
o'clock. He stood, trudged to the kitchen, leaned into the fridge, pulled
out a prepackaged dinner. Removed the plastic, put the tray in the
microwave, punched three. Into the fridge again, pulled out his insulin,
flicked off the cap, pulled up his shirt, pinched the skin on his stomach,
injected. Flipped open the sharps container Zoe had gotten cleverly dis-
guised as a drawer in the kitchen and tossed the used syringe. Closed
his eyes and dozed against the counter while he waited for the microwave. Pulled the tray out with bare hands, fingers too many times

burned to feel the heat. Grabbed a fork. Sat on the couch. Rested the tray on his knees. Looked up at the television, thought about turning it on. Stared at the empty screen. Did not turn it on. Forked up a bite of whatever this was. Rice, chicken, something greenish. Blew on it. Too hot to taste. Just as well. Shoveled the whole thing down. Stood up. Got a glass of water from their fancy refrigerator, which had a built-in filtered water dispenser. When he was a kid, he'd thought those kinds of refrigerators were for rich people. Which now, he guessed, he was. But the fridge hadn't been that much more expensive than any other fridge. Anyway.

He pulled his boots back on, shrugged on a light jacket. The nights were cold. Checked his watch. 9:35 p.m. Left the house, locked the front door, got in his truck. He had a new car, a BMW. But since Zoe left, he'd been driving his Ranger again. Sank into his body print, etched forever into the seat. The drive was easy, streets empty. Ten-ish on a Wednesday night is the perfect time to drive into Kendall. Parked at the lab. Went up. Unlocked. His key card was the only one that worked after seven now. Went inside, flicked on the lights. Took a big breath, pulling his shoulders up, and sighed it out. Retrieved his stuff from the locked storage closet. Sat down at the bench and picked up where he'd left off last night.

35

He'd worked crazy hours before. Maybe he was just tired because he was getting old.

He'd been working crazy hours the fall he met Zoe.

He would go to Fen's in the morning. Wake up, grab a bagel, eat it on the shuttle. Spend six or so hours working. He was the only undergraduate, and only there because a postdoc in Fen's lab had worked for his PI at JAX for a summer and owed the PI a favor, which meant he felt he had to keep up with the PhD students and postdocs. So he'd said, when Fen had mentioned time commitment, that he had all the time in the world. That he wanted to be working there forty, fifty hours a week. Fen had been pleased, nodded with this small smile. Fen didn't think there was much value in undergraduate classes. But that had all been at the end of his freshman year—before Jack knew Brenna and what Brenna would offer him. So when Brenna did offer it—it being a place in his nearly empty lab, one-on-one mentorship, a shortcut to the top of the ladder—he had to keep up what he'd been doing for Fen before, because he certainly couldn't tell Fen that he was also going to work on antiaging with another PI.

Back to Adams House, grab a meal, sometimes. Or else just stuff some food in his bag for later. Attend his evening class, a grad seminar that met six to eight. At least for a few weeks, until he realized he couldn't do as much as he needed to be doing in both labs and also go to class. At which point he stopped attending. Hike north of the Science Center to Brenna's. Flick on the lights. It'd be empty—the only postdoc worked normal hours and anyway was nearly finished with the paper he was publishing so mostly worked from home. Put in another six hours or so. Eat whatever he'd put in his backpack—usually some kind of makeshift sandwich. Back to his room. Work on Fen stuff on his computer for a few more hours, or else research, read papers. Sleep when he had to. Four hours was a decent night.

The evening he ran into Zoe his schedule was all fucked up, which is why he almost gave himself away.

He'd done his usual day at Fen's, then headed straight to Brenna's. But his postdoc at Fen's, Jerry, emailed around eight saying that he needed him to come back, they had to rerun something, what he'd done wasn't clean, etc. He was only even checking his email because Jerry had said he'd send over questions and changes on the PowerPoint that Jack needed to finish before tomorrow's group meeting (at which Jerry would be presenting Jack's work, to be clear, but that's how it goes). Pissy email. Jack thought what he'd done was solid. But fine. He looked at the experiment he was running, blew air through his nose. If he left it, he'd have to start over. Two hours of work down the drain. But what could he say? I'm in class? As soon as there was a problem with the presentation, he'd be presenting it. He emailed back that he was in his dorm, that he would get on the next shuttle. Another popped up in his inbox when it refreshed automatically: the orgo TF, emailing his midterm grade. Right. He supposed he hadn't been back to class since to pick it up. An 81, which would be a B plus, probably, on the curve. Cool, he thought. Then he cleaned up, threw shit in the trash or down the drain—useless now, anyway—slung his worn backpack over his shoulder, turned off the lights, locked up.

He was hustling across the Yard when he saw Zoe. He knew it was her immediately: tall, for a woman, and with this ramrod posture. Plus the hair: that wavy black mane. I mean, sure, of course he thought she was beautiful, in an untouchable way. Like some sort of Greek sculpture. But mostly he found her interesting. So much worse, to find someone interesting.

This was not the night he wanted to run into her. They hadn't had a real conversation yet—had pretended to ignore each other as they wrestled for the intellectual upper hand—and he wanted to have something to say when they did. He wasn't sure what, exactly. Something.

But she cut across the Yard toward him, clearly altering her path to meet him. He swore internally.

He made some inane comment about his work with Fen, because of course he never told anyone about Brenna, she with one eyebrow arched. He was certain she was bored. Her voice, when directed right at him and not at him through their orgo professor, was melodic. She must've asked where he was coming from. He would've rather she kept talking, so he could keep listening. He said he was coming from lab, pointing behind himself to emphasize, and she smirked slightly like he was an idiot and said, "Fen is across the river, no?" nodding backward, and he felt himself blush, a hot blush that he knew would turn his face splotchy like he'd gotten into something. He wouldn't even remember how he responded, probably laughed awkwardly and said "Yeah," or something equally unhelpful. And then he scurried off like some sort of nervous wildlife, spooked in the night. A deer. Or, better for Cambridge, a rat.

36

When Zoe'd asked how long he'd been lying, he'd said "It doesn't matter," and she'd said "What the *fuck* do you mean, of course it matters." And they were both right.

"The investors aren't investing in the theory, they're investing in the application. The application is not fully working, and we're telling them it is, and that's what matters," Jack said.

"But if the theory is a lie, too, *all* we've done is defraud them. We've made up a pretty story and put a bow on it and handed it to them and they bought it. What am I saying—*I've* made up a pretty story and—" She'd choked on her sentence.

He'd wanted to grab her shoulders and pull her into him, but knew she'd wrench away, swear, Don't you dare fucking touch me, and so he hadn't.

"Your theory is right," he'd said. "My application is failing."

"I don't believe you," she'd said, and whirled around, but still he saw her face collapse on itself, anger to agony.

He thought when she found out she'd go straight to the board. But she didn't. Instead, she waited a week or so and then they met about what to do, just like they'd met about everything else. About the original idea, Viraj, dropping out, hires, the lab space, the board, and on and on and on.

"I can't give an opinion when I don't know the full story," she said. "You have to tell me. Or else how can I contribute to"—she gestured broadly—"this."

"Life is a game of incomplete information." He'd already told her he wouldn't share the details of what he'd done and when. So that she could be more convincing onstage, he said. But really he wanted her to have plausible deniability. He thought she probably wanted that for herself, too.

They looked at each other. What was that supposed to mean? He didn't know. She didn't either. Her eyes were flat, dull.

"I just need more time," he said. "I've only ever needed more time."

She shook her head. The corners of her mouth were tight. Why wasn't she saving herself? Why was she sitting here with him, in what used to be—would have been—their kitchen? (A memory, painful: she playing "Our House" over the kitchen's built-in speakers as they unpacked, he rolling his eyes—he'd always made fun of her music taste, since the very beginning when they were fighting over the aux in the lab, he calling her a hippie, she laughing.)

She took a deep breath. He took one, too, waited.

"Startups spin off all the time," she said. "Take Saytrex—they started in antiaging, and now they're in cancer therapeutics."

He let out the breath.

She was here because she would go with him.

His throat closed and he cleared it, looking away from her.

They settled on the obvious. They were the biggest, most well-funded startup in the antiaging space. They could take any antiaging technology in development and run with it, get it to clinical trials before the others just by nature of their firepower.

"So we do that," Zoe said. "Pick the lowest-hanging fruit."

Jack nodded.

"How long do you need?"

He closed his eyes. "Maybe a year and a half?" He knew what he was asking her for. He did not believe she would say yes.

She said yes.

The strange thing about Zoe finding out was it made it easier to keep up the lie in some ways, i.e., logistically, but harder in others, i.e., emotionally. Because before she knew, it was just a part of the process. Just giving himself time to make things work. Which they would. Work. Things would work, and soon, and he just needed more time.

But once she knew, and she was the one buying the time, and it was to be spent on somebody else's ideas, not on M, he realized, suddenly and without warning and without the possibility of unrealizing, that he had been deluding himself. That in fact he was never going to make M work, that in fact he was never as good as he said he was, that in fact he was never good enough for her.

37

No one on their board was really paying attention to the science.

They only had West Coast VCs, and mostly from outside of biotech. As Jack learned early with Viraj, East Coast biotech VCs ask too many questions. They don't understand the science, but that lack of understanding makes them try harder to catch you in a mistake so they can prove they're smarter than you. He and Zoe used to laugh about the gibberish they'd come up with, but it was irritating. Made it impossible to get things done. Too many cooks in the kitchen, and half of them having never touched a chef's knife. Plus, they're always ready to replace you. So Jack and Zoe had replaced them, instead, with "founder friendly" West Coast VCs—"founder friendly" meaning they want to cultivate *you*, aren't interested in pushing you out and finding someone else to develop your idea. So—much less engaged in the science.

Zoe's ultrawealthy group had been a pleasant surprise. The scuzzy old men were completely enchanted by her, just wanted to give her money. Perfect: put as many of them on the board as possible.

Brenna was the only scientist, and he'd been checked out since the beginning. He'd show up to about a quarter of board meetings and gripe, "All of this money talk is an incredible waste of time, really too bad it's the only way you can get things done these days." But his name was as much scientific justification as anyone needed.

In any case, it was no surprise that their first board meeting since That Day, the day she'd found out, went fine.

They'd decided they wouldn't mention that Jack was starting work on a new drug. Too suspicious. They'd wait for proof of concept and then pitch it as a happy accident. Say it's so promising, we should invest in it. And then what? If it went well, hope everyone would just forget about M, the real thing? They didn't discuss that. It took all the faith they had just to imagine the first step.

So now they showed the board the one data set that made M look sort of promising. Jack made a vague statement about clinical trials. And the patent applications? someone asked. Yes, sir, we have them all in. These things just take time.

Before, he'd worried Zoe would accidentally ask a hard question. Now he worried she would break character. But she was a much better actress than he'd realized. They asked her something fluffy about marketing, and she said, "I'm always thinking about how to help people understand the revolutionary nature of our work without fearing the mad scientist trope. I want people to see us as physicians, if possible. Healing, not experimenting. Especially as we transition into the clinical trial stage, and get closer to getting this drug in people's hands." Jack nodded along. Her public speaking was so cultivated, smooth, consistent. Which made it even more of a delight when, before, in his apartment, in his bedroom, her laugh jangled rough from her throat; when she relaxed, leaned into him, and her voice spiked up and down with her emotions, like a song.

Those long days after they'd left Fen's lab and were working together, alone. When the next breakthrough was just past the tips of their fingers. They'd fill sheets of paper with notes and diagrams and then shuffle the papers around and then tear them up and stuff everything in the trash and start over.

Zoe, when she was really focused, lost that perfect posture. She'd slump forward, shoulder blades pushing back through her shirt like wings, elbows on the desk, face in her hands, spine curved long. Her hair would frizz, as if reacting to the electricity from her brain. She'd peek through her long, splayed fingers at the papers in front of her.

When they were talking together, his words blurring into hers, they went more than twice as fast. Felt like being a kid and running downhill, arms pinwheeling, legs barely able to keep up with the forward momentum, strides lengthening into leaps.

Sometimes they'd stay up, bounding over the flat at the bottom of the hill. Other times they'd stumble, roll forward, fall onto a shoulder, back, side. Limp away laughing with grass stains on their shirts.

Walk it off. Pace through Cambridge. Up Plympton to Mount Auburn, then left past the darkened storefronts, past the homeless guy who slept in the doorway of JP Licks, to the T stop, then right and up Mass. Ave. Or down Mount Auburn to the furniture store with the huge painted chair on the side, then north into narrow residential streets. They kept weird hours, so the city was quiet, which made it theirs. When it was going poorly, Zoe would walk like she had somewhere to go. When it was going well, she'd sing whatever he'd had playing in his room before they left. In his memory, that Vampire Weekend song. The one about dreaming of Boston all your life.

One night, set on edge by coming out of his room to see Carter rubbing her shoulders, he showed her the Adams tunnels. Watched her watch the walls. That wry smile she got when she was intellectually amused. They talked about dying. About living forever. Was it possible? Jack thought so. He was sure of it, in fact. The problem was just that evolution hadn't had cause to select for it—but what did evolution matter now? Or, one might say, medical science is evolution, just of a different type. A species preserving itself. Especially because the longer a person lived, the more things they could accomplish. That was part of the problem, Jack mused, with science now—you have to specialize so deeply, walk so far to reach the cutting edge, that by the time you get there you're dead.

"I think we'd forget how to be human, though. If we lived forever." She said it without looking at him.

"Why do you say that?"

She sighed through her nose. She looked sad. Then she smiled, turned to him, and said, "Don't you always work better on a deadline?"

He laughed.

I love you, he thought.

When he walked back into his dorm after that visit to the tunnels, having left Zoe, slightly high, outside of Lowell, Carter was on the couch.

"Hey."

"Hey."

"God, she's stunning," Carter said. Jack nodded, shrugged.

"You don't think so?"

"She's my partner," Jack said. He leaned against his doorframe, thinking of the papers on his desk. Big, messy handwriting for such a put-together woman. It conjured her voice in his head. When he was working now, it was often her voice in his head that answered his questions. Her handwriting scrawling across the inside of his eyelids when he closed his eyes.

"I mean, sure, but you can't ignore how gorgeous she is. That hair? Those eyes? Those legs?"

"Ask her out, then," Jack said, and he turned into his room and shut the door.

38

How could he have been so careless? Leaving raw files up on his laptop when he knew she could wander in anytime? After he'd hidden everything from everyone so perfectly for so long?

The obvious answer was that some part of him wanted her to know. That he just couldn't keep it from her any longer.

39

The dinner with her parents was a disaster.

And why wouldn't it be? He was an outsider, an intruder. He was walking into their house and trying to remove their daughter from the path they'd wound her up and set her on—the path that led straight to tenure at Harvard, MIT. He came into their enormous, beautiful, clean home like a pest carrying a raft of diseases: that chip on his shoulder too big to miss, the stink of poverty, the hunger for risk. He might as well have been trying to steal their silver—so much worse, to try to steal their only daughter.

They'd like Carter much better, he thought when Zoe's mother looked him up and down, when Zoe and her father switched into rapid Greek to speak over and around him, when he fumbled with which fork to use.

He almost thought Zoe would stay there, leave him on the front steps, go back inside to her perfect, brilliant family. But instead her mother dismissed them both with a prim little hostess smile.

He stole anxious glances at Zoe in the grainy half-dark between streetlights. She was so deep in thought she didn't notice him looking.

He dropped her off at her dorm and went straight to the lab.

Couldn't settle; kept flickering from anger to embarrassment to fear to anger again.

Should've told her father what move to play in the chess game. He'd known immediately what it took the old man several long minutes to understand. Should've shown him what he could do.

He slammed around for a bit. Taking things out and putting them away. If they had more good results, maybe her parents wouldn't have been so disbelieving. And that was his fault. That he couldn't make this stupid shit work now. And he was sure it could—sure it *should*. Mother-fucking-cock-sucking-sunnuva-bitch-shit-fuck. His great-grandfather's voice gave him a smile, and then a near-immediate shaft of pain. Still hurt when he laughed.

He sat down at his computer, ran his hands through his hair, which was already standing on end. Opened his latest Excel sheet. Flicked over to a graph.

If only it were a little cleaner. If only they had a little more.

He stood up and started gathering things to rerun their most recent experiment. He just needed to tweak that one step in the middle, and then maybe it would work.

He spent the night there and then most of the next day. The sun was high, noonish, when he was done with the first part. He had a headache but wasn't tired. It was Saturday, and Zoe had planned to go back to her parents' to sell them on this by herself. Was going to spend the night there tonight.

She should've done the whole thing without him, clearly. She and her brother, with his goddamn ease. The way he moved like he owned

every room he was in. Talked like everyone always cared about what
he had to say. And he was so pretty, too. They could be twins. The
two of them like an advertisement for Gap or something equally
preppy.

So he'd be alone. Which meant he could set up the second experiment and then sleep on the couch while it ran, for four hours or so,
and then work the data in the evening.

He knew it was no better before he'd even looked at the numbers.
But he tortured himself by running analyses anyway, pulling up a
graph, calling forth a P value. He felt the fear and anger and embarrassment he'd been able to push away as he worked come slouching
back. Not even taking turns with him anymore: all sitting together
in his belly, having drinks and making jokes at his expense, getting
louder and more raucous as the night wore on.

He looked, sandy-eyed, at the spreadsheet. He could see what
it would have looked like, if the experiment had worked the way he
wanted it to. This number would look like that, this like that.

Zoe was going to leave him. It settled into his mind and then
sank through the rest of his body. Zoe was going to leave him and the
project and he would have nothing.

He shut his eyes.

He just needed more time. Just a few more months. He saw himself, begging her for it. Saw her shaking her head, saying, My parents are furious, there's no way, I have to get a real summer job. I'll
help out when I have the time. Which would mean: We're done, I'm
through, good luck.

His headache was blinding.

He squinted at the screen and started typing into the spreadsheet.

He was finished when he heard her come in, but it still froze him.
He hadn't decided if he was going to go through with it. Had put
the new sheet in his computer's trash bin and then pulled it back out

twice already. But she was behind him. She was going to break the news. He swallowed the clump of sticky liquid that kept collecting in the back of his throat. His heart was thrumming in his hands. He knew they were shaking, but that could pass for excitement. He turned to her.

"Come here," he said, "I have something to show you."

40

There were things he didn't tell Zoe to protect her, and things he didn't tell Zoe because he was too embarrassed. And things he didn't tell Zoe because he didn't want her to leave. He had plenty of time alone, now, to contemplate which was which.

He didn't tell Zoe about Divya because he wanted to protect her.

Divya and Jack had known each other since freshman year. They, and Sophia, Zoe's roommate, had been in LS50 together, this overly intense freshman science sequence that promised independent research opportunities. Jack found those opportunities to be not at all independent, and the other students to be insufferable—playing, all of them, some perverted version of king of the hill where the goals were all wrong and part of the game was pretending you weren't playing. They seemed to want the professor to *like* them the best, and to get the *highest* A. Jack thought this was idiotic. What was the point of being the best at being a Harvard student? What, exactly, did that get you? A pat on the back? Jack knew even then that he wanted to suck up all the knowledge and resources he could, make a breakthrough, get out, and start making real money.

Divya was no different from anyone else, except that the professor was extremely nice to her. At first Jack thought it might be because she was beautiful, and the professor was a man in his fifties. He operated under that hypothesis until Divya sent him a friend request on Facebook (how? why? Jack didn't think too hard about it—he'd found since he checked out of the whole dating game that being aloof made him more appealing. She was not the first girl to have searched him out and struck up a conversation on social media, from this class or his others), at which point he saw her last name, which he recognized, did a quick Google search to confirm. Threw out his old hypothesis, replaced it with a new one: the professor either had a startup or was on the board of a startup, and he either was funded by or wanted to be funded by Divya's father, Viraj Kaur, who was what Jack's great-grandfather would've called a high muckety-muck at Living Ventures, a huge biotech VC firm.

The new hypothesis changed Jack's calculations. He accepted Divya's friend request.

The next class, she sat one seat over from him, in the back row. As though the one-seat buffer made it seem less like she was coming to sit with him when she was really a sixth-row sort of student—not in the front, because she wasn't *trying*, but not in the back, because she wasn't *checked out* or anything.

She leaned over halfway through the class to whisper a question. Jack answered.

He didn't accept the invitation, later, back to her room, because he was playing the long game. If he slept with her now, the mystery would be broken and she'd either want to date or to wash her hands of him and neither would give him what he needed. So he stayed half in touch, had dinner with her occasionally, even texted her first once or twice. Kept her on ice until he and Zoe had a real concept. Mid-summer after their sophomore year.

She texted him. you in cambridge?

He was. She knew he was, probably had asked someone else about his plans. He had given out enough information for people to be in-trigued by what he and Zoe were working on, but not enough that anyone actually knew what it was.

Yeah he texted back. u?

having a party tn at my apt, 25 grant st., swing by if u want.

Jack swung by.

She met him at the door, squealed over the bass. "Jack *Leahy,* since *when* can anyone get you out!" He smirked.

She and her roommates (two other girls, both of whom cooed over him, *Jack,* it's been so *long,* where have you *been?* I feel like I haven't seen you since *LS50!*) had a whole house, a warren of narrow hall-ways and bedrooms and bathrooms with just enough room to stand and piss, full otherwise of the myriad trappings of twenty-year-old women, a pink shaggy bath mat and four hairbrushes full of different-colored hair and at least fifteen soaps. The house was nestled between Mass. Ave. and the Charles, easily walkable from any Harvard sum-mer housing, which was certainly the point.

The complicated part was Zoe's face when she realized. He hadn't expected to feel so much—so much what? Relief, satisfac-tion, and then also hurt, because her hurt was his hurt. But they needed Divya's father's money, and he was getting it. Just like they needed Brenna's support, and sure, he'd gone behind Zoe's back, but he'd gotten it. And like they needed that first data set, and yes, it'd been unauthorized use of materials in Fen's lab, but Brenna wasn't set up for yeast, and Jack needed yeast. And, sure, Fen had been pissed beyond words and had functionally fired Jack (this, he supposed, Zoe still didn't know). But he'd gotten the data and they'd gotten their start.

Can't make an omelet without breaking some eggs.

He didn't tell Zoe that Carter had introduced him to Dick Brenna because he was embarrassed.

Jack met Carter early. Freshman fall. It was just cold enough to start wearing a jacket. Jack had gone to see this talk about starting a business, and the speaker was using a bunch of words he didn't know, and Jack realized that, if he was going to start a company—which, as far as he could gather, was the quickest way to money that he could access, given that he obviously did not fit into the group that was planning on going into finance—he would need to speak this language, or else he'd get fleeced.

Harvard did not have a business major, but all of those finance types planned on studying economics. This was before Jack was working in a lab, which meant he had plenty of free time. So he started going to Ec 10a—in Sanders, the honeyed-wood chandelier-lit amphitheater, which seemed like a ridiculous place to hold an intro-level course—and sitting in the back. Just to listen.

A few weeks into this project, a cool-looking, khaki-clad Black guy slid into the seat next to him.

"I'm Carter," he said.

"Jack," Jack said. He tapped his pen nervously. He didn't know if this was technically allowed, this sitting in on a class that was not his. It did feel, a little bit, like stealing, and he was afraid now that Carter was going to call him out on it.

"Do you not take notes?" Carter asked.

"Oh, I'm . . ." Jack paused. Should he lie? He looked down at Carter's scuffed-up dress shoes.

"You must have an incredible memory." Carter filled in the silence, smiled. Jack smiled back.

And then what? Carter kept coming to sit next to him, and, eventually, Jack said, "I'm not actually taking this class," and Carter laughed out loud and said, "You're sitting through this and not even getting the credit?" and Jack shrugged and said, "I just wanted to understand business a bit better," and Carter said, "Why?" and Jack shrugged again and said, "I don't know, I just feel like it's a good skill to have," and Carter looked thoughtful, and nodded, and said, "Yeah, I mean, I'm not going to study Ec, either. So I guess we're doing the same thing." And then he paused and added, "But I want the class on my transcript, for my ego," and Jack didn't know if he was supposed to laugh at this until Carter grinned, said, "Resist, brother." Jack smiled back.

That spring, they sat together all through Ec 10b. This time neither of them for credit. "You're right," Carter said of this, "we seek knowledge for the sake of knowledge." And then he'd asked Jack, sort of sheepishly, if he'd like to be in his blocking group, which were groups of freshmen who formalized their social cliques so as to be sorted into the same residential houses for their sophomore through senior years. And Jack, who didn't really have any other friends, and figured Carter was the type of person with an abundance, had been so *happy*.

Their sophomore fall, Carter offered to introduce him to Brenna. "My dad worked under him during his undergrad," Carter said somewhat sheepishly. Jack put on a nice shirt, not wanting to look grubby next to Carter, who was always impeccably dressed. Carter, across from Brenna, was so deferential—"This is Jack, the smartest person in our class"—and Jack—pathetic!—was barely able to keep the smile off his face. Brenna was interested, so they continued the conversation in a second meeting, without Carter, and Brenna offered him the job, and the rest was history.

But then, about a month later, Jack heard Carter's voice in the dining hall. "Well, it wouldn't be very *transformative* of me to just room with all of you guys, would it?" This was like Carter, to react to the fact that he should not be saying something by saying it louder, and in public.

Jack stopped, listened. The group Carter was with, all polished to the same high shine, chuckled as one. They were pretty, in the way eighteen years of braces and acne treatments and tailored clothes and perfect grooming makes you pretty no matter what you started with. If Carter recounted the story, he would have mentioned being the only Black man in the group, but Jack couldn't have told you what color anybody was. To Jack, rich was rich.

The boy across from Carter looked skeptical. "I mean, I guess," he said, "it's not like you don't see them in class."

Carter shrugged. "They're all brilliant," he said. "You guys are placing silly little hundred-dollar bets on the next Zuck in the dining hall—I'm voting with my feet, as it were."

Jack could feel his heart beating in his teeth.

"In-ter-est-ing," said the girl beside the boy across from Carter, leaning forward. "So who's it gonna be?" The girl was looking at Carter's lips, not at his eyes, Jack noticed, and by the way he leaned back in his chair, widening out his shoulders, it was clear Carter had noticed, too.

"I don't know," Carter said. "I don't have to."

"Oh, come on."

"Unicorn?"

"No, don't be silly."

"Carter's a smart man."

"So who'll it be, Peter Thiel?" The boy across from him.

Carter shrugged. "Mitchell," he said. "But it's close."

"Should we put money on it?"

"That's just because he's the only one in CS, right? I mean that's an obvious bump."

"You asked me for a probability, I gave you a probability, which takes into account the fact that Mitchell is in the field where the most startups are happening. What do you want from me?"

Jack had heard enough. He didn't even consider walking through Carter's line of sight—just turned and left. He didn't know what was worst: that Carter had gathered him up in a group of potential startup founders; that Carter had introduced him to Brenna for his own gain—no, that wasn't quite it—that Carter hadn't told Jack his intentions, like Jack was some sort of puppet; or that Carter did not think, despite this introduction, Jack was the most likely to make it.

Also, Jack had thought he and Carter were friends.

Much later, when Jack understood better exactly what Harvard was, he could look back and see that the thing Carter's roommates all had in common was edge. Rafael's from being Afro-Latino and from San Jose, so close to San Francisco but so far from that group of polished San Fran kids with their particular nasal accents. Mitchell's from being fat and being from the Midwest, worse than being from rural Maine because of coastal privilege. James's less obvious, from being insecure about his own privilege, constantly trying to prove that he deserved to be at Harvard, that being milky white and male and blond and freckled and an economics major and from some suburb in the Northeast didn't mean he'd been let into these hallowed halls because he looked like the only people they'd been open to for hundreds of years.

Zoe and Carter were so inevitable it was funny. In fact, Raf and James and Mitchell had an unspoken joke, communicated in smirks and raised eyebrows, about how Carter, who never hung out in their room, always happened to be there when Zoe was. When Jack caught the edge of the joke they'd cringe, shrug. Sorry, dude. We feel your pain. What're you gonna do.

So Jack knew long before they were officially together, long before they'd gone to New York for the TEDx talk, Carter casually offering up his aunt's place (who has an aunt with a place in Manhattan just sitting there, empty?), where of course she'd stay, hotels were expensive, and why wouldn't he go with her, in fact it would be weird if he didn't, because somebody had to get the key and know the doorman and show her where the garbage chute was.

Jack knew way back that first summer, when he accepted Carter's offer to live together because he'd waited too long and didn't really have another option. And he'd tried to picture Carter and Zoe in bed together, as a sort of punishment for lying to her. Except the image was slippery, and each time it began he slid behind Carter's eyes, and it was he with her, not Carter, those were his hands on her stomach, that was his name in her mouth.

When they hired Carter, he took pleasure in it. Thought, If he's going to hang around, he might as well be my goddamn employee.

41

It went something like this.

Preseed, that was Viraj, back in the fall of their junior year. They were developing a theory, so they stayed in Harvard's labs. Using Harvard's money until there might be a patent, and then getting out of Dodge. They'd been honest with Viraj, actually, about what they had and what they did not have. Completely honest. Jack told Zoe that the data set he'd shown her after the dinner with her parents was too small-n to bring, or something. He'd sworn, then, that he'd never do it again. That it was a onetime thing, to buy himself the summer.

Of course, it's never just once.

Between every raise, you need what industry people call an inflection point. Which is what it sounds like. A big step forward on which you base your next valuation. For each raise, you must up your valuation so that you don't completely dilute yourself and your investors.

Here was the thing: by December, they really hadn't progressed beyond what he'd said he'd done way back in May, and so he was losing Zoe again. Viraj, too, was getting antsy. He couldn't take back the money, but he could pull support. And if he pulled support, it was over—he was a big enough name in biotech that nobody would jump on once he'd jumped off.

Then, a miracle: an experiment illustrating the mechanism came through just well enough. Sure, it wasn't as perfect as Jack led Zoe to believe. But it was close. Definitely enough for industry, even if it wouldn't stand up to peer review.

They dropped out. Started to raise seed. And to get real hype.

They had a plan for a drug based on the mechanism, but no proof of concept. Unusual, but it was so new, so exciting, the promise of immortality, that people were throwing money at them anyway.

Jack figured out quickly what they wanted him to be. They'd already written the script, and now they were casting the roles. The Mad Scientist was driven by a tragic backstory, like a classic American superhero. That is: fucked up. Bootstrapped from nothing, which would give him that *run-through-walls mentality* (a favorite phrase). Obsessive, disheveled. Aloof, apart from the masses—thinking his own brilliant thoughts while mere mortals bothered with mundanity. Always sliding away from the camera but hesitating just enough for it to catch a glimpse. That is, naive to his commercial potential—a *founder who doesn't realize that he could be a great founder.*

He was reckless. They wanted him to be reckless. You have to *think long-term.* You have to *want it.* It has to be a *moon shot.* One of them, he couldn't remember which one now, said, "Well there's the CEO, and there's the scientist standing behind the CEO, saying 'You can't say that!'" And they'd both laughed, because, of course, he was the scientist and the CEO was Zoe (her role, too, already written) but they were the opposite, he was the one one-upping the guys in the conference rooms, assuring them that they *could* say that, they *could* do that. He just needed time. He just needed money. Or, the tasteful way to put it: *runway*.

Zoe was so by-the-book, so academic, that the way industry worked—the hype, the positive spin, always selling, selling, selling—was incomprehensible to her. Their experiments weren't going as well as he'd suggested, and she was overwhelmed, panicky, and he just needed time to get everything straightened out, and he'd have so much more time to do science if he wasn't also arguing with her about what they were saying to investors. So when her TEDx talk blew up (of course it did, Jack had known it would), he took the opportunity to say: You run the company, I'll do the dirty work.

But it pained him, to push her away from the thing she loved. The thing she was so good at. Especially when everybody else was pushing her away from it, too. He always called it Zoe's theory, Zoe's work, Zoe's idea, because it was, but nobody cared. The part of the scientist was written male.

It pained him enough that, when she resisted, he couldn't push again. But Carter could. Carter—for his own reasons, probably the same reasons he introduced Jack to Brenna—also thought Zoe should be focusing on the PR. And at that point they were dating. And so she agreed.

Meanwhile, Jack was trying, trying, trying in the lab, no progress.

They rushed into Series A because everybody told them they should ride the wave.

They had an incredible amount of cash. But you can have all the cash in the world and no working drug.

Their projections involved steps toward a minimum viable product that summer and then real proof of concept the following fall. What would have been their senior year.

You can't show up at the end of your timeline empty-handed. Money has to keep coming in, you have to keep raising. You come empty-handed, what do you raise on?

He couldn't do that to Zoe. Not after she'd followed him this far. He couldn't let it all fall down. Not this thing that they had built together.

And so then. Again.

Not as badly as the first time, after the dinner with her parents. This was just cherry-picking. He never typed fake numbers into spreadsheets. It was just selling. Spinning. He could even sometimes convince himself it was what the board wanted him to be doing. They wanted another big raise, too, because that's how they made money. Everybody was on the same team.

Plus, how else were you supposed to do it? They wanted *moon shot*, but also that you hit every prestated target. They wanted *vision*, but that you do things the same way everybody else does. The real thing takes time. Takes trust. Takes belief.

He thought it'd be just once, again. To give himself more runway.

He never stopped believing. The breakthrough was always right around the corner. Always.

But once you start. Once you start.

By the end of that summer, Carter suspected.

Maybe Jack should've told Carter what he'd overheard, way back in their sophomore year. Let Carter defend himself, instead of keeping quiet and opting to use Carter back—for his rent money, that first summer, and then his coding skills, his business savvy. Because maybe then they'd have worked it out, become friends again, or at least genuine collaborators, and if they were, then maybe Carter's intervention might've worked. Maybe Carter could've caught Jack in the nosedive, helped him level out the plane.

The closest Jack had come to initiating the conversation was accusing Carter once of not being all in on Manna—which wasn't actually what he meant, what he meant was that Carter was using Manna for his own goals. Carter said "I don't quite have the luxury of dropping out" and Jack said "Excuse me?" and Carter said "I need a degree, I don't get to be a Harvard dropout," and Jack said "I'm not sure I understand what you're saying" and Carter said "Exactly" and walked out. Carter liked to make his points like that. With a lot of subtext. Like if you couldn't decipher his clues you weren't worthy of knowing what he was trying to say.

But realistically, as soon as Carter saw Zoe, and Jack saw Carter see Zoe, and Carter saw Zoe see Jack, there was no chance of them working it out, anyway.

It was early August when Carter came into Jack's office with a stack of papers. Jack hated meetings, so he didn't have a second chair. Carter stood.

Jack spun around, looked up.

"Have a second?" Carter asked.

"Sure," Jack said. They never spoke one-on-one. "Should we grab a conference room?"

"No," Carter said, "let's stay in here. I'll get a chair."

He left the papers on Jack's desk, disappeared. Jack stared at them without seeing.

Carter returned carrying a chair. Set it down. Sat.

He looked at Jack steadily. "What are we going to do about Series B?"

"What do you mean?"

Carter spread the papers across Jack's desk, which was already covered with a layer about an inch thick. Raw data. It was unavoidable, that Carter had some access: he was running their analytics team. Carter left his hands splayed flat, covering the numbers, for a moment. As though he didn't want to look at them. His fingernails were perfectly uniform, just the right size crescent of white at each tip, and had a soft glow to them.

Jack cleared his throat.

"You know what I mean," Carter said finally.

"I don't."

Carter said, "You can keep it from Zoe all you want, she's too busy to think straight, but I actually have time to look at the numbers."

"And? We have some good data. We'll have more soon." Which he believed. Always.

"We have some sort-of-okay data. We do not have . . ." He worked his mouth. He wasn't looking at Jack. "What we promised seed and A investors."

"Who is this 'we'?" Jack said.

"You, then," Carter said. "This isn't a power trip for me, Jack. I'm worried."

"Don't be."

Carter looked at him.

"It's not your job."

"I . . ." Carter licked his lips, shook his head. "Look, I'm not trying to run your company. But it does affect . . ."

He seemed to have expected Jack to interrupt him, but Jack was leaning back in his seat, hands clasped in his lap. Just watching.

"Yes?" he said.

"I mean, this affects everybody."

"Well," Jack said, "if you can't handle risk, you probably shouldn't be in this field." He turned back to his computers. "You're more cut out for middle management at a Fortune 500 company, methinks. Or management consulting. And, I mean, there's always law school."

A pause. Then Carter said, "God. Fuck you, man."

Jack let himself smirk.

But then Carter said, "Look. Whatever. I'm out. But if I'm right . . . it's not fair, what you're doing to Zoe. She doesn't deserve to be dragged down with you. If you . . ." He paused. "If you let her take this fall, I'll . . ."

Jack tensed, refused to turn and look at Carter, clenched his jaw hard enough that it clicked.

Later, he would think, Is the love of my love my hated? Or is the love of my love my loved?

He heard Carter open the door. The air quieted—that distinct unnoise of being suddenly alone in a small space.

The door shut.

He would've been really worried if Carter had access to all the raw files. But he didn't. Jack threw out the actually bad stuff long before it hit the analytics team.

Still. Jack wouldn't sleep until Carter had told Zoe.

When Divya had left, after they'd bought out her dad, she'd screamed in his face that she knew it was all to get rid of her because she was smarter than Zoe and more attractive and would be way better on TV and he knew it and Zoe was brainwashing him into protecting her by pushing her out. It was a little bit pathetic, because at that point she really didn't have anything to do with anything. She'd slapped him hard enough that it hurt, and he let his eyes close and his head turn and left it there, at a ninety-degree angle to her.

When Carter announced his departure and Jack stormed into Zoe's office, hiding his fear under anger, to see that Zoe, under her usual layer of professionalism, was furious at Carter, he felt such relief that when he left her office, his legs threatened to give out and he had to steady himself against the wall, left fingerprints on the glass.

42

They asked her to speak at Harvard, in Sanders Theatre.

He was with her when they called. Her eyes fluttered shut and she looked like she might vomit, but her voice came out clear and strong and she said I would be so honored. Because of course she could not say no.

The afternoon of, he sat in the benches on the floor so that he had to tilt his head back and look up at the stage.

He thought about seeing Marie Russo there, years earlier.

He turned to scan the audience while he waited. There, in the balcony, were her parents and Alex.

He looked away immediately, not wanting them to notice him. But they were preoccupied: her mother chatting to an older gentleman in a suit on her left, her father in deep conversation with Alex on his right. Her mother was gesturing toward the stage, beaming.

When the chair of the chemistry department adjusted the microphone and began reeling off Zoe's achievements, Jack risked one more glance back at her family. Alex was leaning forward, elbows on his knees. Her mother had a little smile on her face. And her father—even her father—was nodding along. When the department chair finished, her father was the first to applaud.

Jack forced himself to look away again. Could not bear to see their faces when she took the stage. The sadness was so deep and so blunt that he thought he might throw up, all over the 150-year-old wooden benches.

But then she walked up the steps, all eyes on her, and she said, "My name is Zoe Kyriakidis, and I'm here to tell you a story." And she paced across the stage under the yellowish lights, and her voice, her hands, her eyes—she was captivating. He tilted up his chin and looked into the face of the divine, and, for a moment, he forgot.

43

The boy's mother moves apartments a lot but always stays in town, near the old tannery. The boy's great-grandparents live far enough out of town that you can't really walk in, especially because it's a main road, speed limit fifty-five, which they hope will keep him out of trouble and does.

Starting in about the seventh grade, he works at the mechanic's (the big peeling sign that leans precariously over the road reads "Buddy's Auto"—quotation marks included) where his great-grandfather works.

He likes it: the smell of engine oil, the sound of power tools, the constant rotation of cars. Nice ones, sometimes, Jeeps and new pickup trucks with ridiculous lift kits and the local doctor's Mercedes. At first, he runs errands, answers the phone, fetches things for his great-grandfather. After a while, his great-grandfather lets him do small tasks on his own, and then larger ones. Turns out all that time watching, he was paying attention. He is good, and this is satisfying. And then they ride home with the rattly air conditioner on high, and his great-grandmother feeds them supper, and they eat quietly and she doesn't try to get Jack to talk now because his teacher says he is doing just fine, though she isn't too impressed by the crowd he runs with.

Jack is annoyed by that last comment, thinks it shows just how little the teacher knows about how to survive. It is this or no crowd—white trash has limited options. He might have been in with the athletes, but he doesn't play sports. He might have been artsy, but he isn't gay. She implies he could befriend the smart kids, because he is smart, but she seems to forget that the only boys in that group are rich: the doctor's son and the son of the guy who runs the local construction company. That leaves him to the kids on the edge of things. Only a group by virtue of not being part of another group. The angry kids, the hungry kids, the potheads.

"I don't care what company you keep," his great-grandfather says, "so long as you keep your goddamn nose clean and grades up."

He does.

Or anyway he does until he moves back in with Nicky the summer before his freshman year. Her home has been deemed safe enough, the caseworker says. That particular drug dealer–boyfriend is in prison now, it's true. He looks at her from behind blank eyes.

When she's gone, Jack sits with his hands pressed flat on the table. The idea of leaving, having to go to Nicky's apartment without the promise of returning here, puts a knot in his stomach.

That night, he hears his great-grandparents talking about it quietly in the living room after he's shut himself in his bedroom and turned off the light and lain fully clothed on his bed, hands folded on his stomach, eyes shut.

His great-grandfather's voice is an irritated rumble, his great-grandmother's high and upset. He could make out the words if he tried, but he doesn't.

After a while, he hears his great-grandmother crying.

Tale as old as time. From the boy, everything is taken. Then the boy builds something new, and is happy, but everything (oh it must be!)

is taken away again. Cruel! think the ladies in the audience, dabbing their eyes. His great-grandparents try to fight it, and that makes it worse. His mother crying, yelling. How dare you steal my child from me. In the end he won't even be able to visit them. It would've been better to just let it be.

So he moves back, a ball of resentment. They won't let him work at Buddy's that summer. His mom's boyfriend senses both the anger and the intelligence in him and so he picks. Starts small. Saying nasty things, ordering him around the house. When Jack retreats to his room, the boyfriend pounds on his door, rattles the handle ("What are you doing locked in there alone all the time, huh?"). One day Jack comes home and he's taken out the doorknob, leaving an empty hole peering into Jack's space, the door swinging easily.

Jack doesn't have much reason to hold back. And he's grown. Over six feet now. Sure, lanky, and underfed in his mother's house, where there is never anything in the cupboards but peanut butter and cigarettes and the occasional dusty can of something. But he knows how levers work. The boyfriend is in his forties and short-limbed and carries around one of those hard, oblong beer guts.

One night the boyfriend grabs his cheek and squeezes, called him some name. A girl, or a pussy, or a bitch, or a fag. What does it matter. Jack stands up and says "Get the fuck out of my face," and the boyfriend says "Sit your ass down," and Jack can smell the tang of beer on him, and doesn't say anything, and the guy hits him, and Jack hits him back, and pretty soon they are tangling, chest to chest. The guy is stronger than Jack had bargained for, harder, with wiry old man muscles. Jack is young and long but too supple, and he doesn't yet know how to inflict pain. Still, a pretty even match. Nicky is screeching, yelling at them to stop, crying, carrying on. Jack half wants (shameful, this) to hit her, too, to tear down the whole house and his mother with it, leave everything in a pile of rubble behind him.

She calls the police and both men are dragged in, like the fifteen-year-old should share the blame. Jack will remember sucking the blood out of his split lip in the back of the cruiser.

First of many. Fights, that is: fisticuffs with her boyfriend, screaming matches with her (he will never hit her, not ever, not even when she hits him, not even when she throws a beer bottle at him, not even when she burns him with a cigarette). When school starts, fistfights in the parking lot. Because why not. Half the time with guys he'd been friends with before and will be again. They're all just young and full of red, red anger.

He is suspended for fighting, which is too bad, because he likes school. Especially math and science, which he finds easy and satisfying. He spends the week roaming town with the gaggle of boys who've already dropped out.

He comes back to school. He smokes weed hanging out the window of the men's bathroom, goes to class high. He gets suspended again. Back to roaming. The worst part about being suspended is that he doesn't get free lunch, and since he's moved back in with Nicky he's tried to eat enough lunch at school that it suffices for dinner.

Somewhere in here he gets a stupid tattoo, lying on a folding table in somebody's garage. Later, when he's rich, he'll make an appointment to get it removed, but Zoe will beg him to keep it. "It's part of you." He'll roll his eyes but cancel the appointment.

He goes back to school. The next time they catch him with pot they give him an in-school suspension, which is when they want to suspend you but they know that you'll get up to worse shit outside school than in. This is fine with Jack. He sits in the vice principal's office and reads and does the worksheets he missed while he was out, and it's pretty pleasant, actually. It's satisfying to figure things out, have the information snap into place in his mind like puzzle pieces.

The year is a shitshow, but somehow his grades are fine. Not good, but not terrible. He doesn't work at home, but when teachers hand out assignments he sits there while the rest of the kids chat and whips something out and hands it back to them. He never studies, but if he shows up for tests he does well.

Ms. Brady intervenes when the year is coming to a close and the junior parking lot is a mess of ruts and murky puddles that the boys drive through at full speed to try to splash the girls, who squeal and jump away.

She asks him to wait after the bell, and he wants to ignore her but he likes her, thinks her class is interesting. They dissect things, frogs first but then things brought in from outside or from nearby farms, a baby deer, a calf that died in birth. He was genuinely upset when one of his suspensions meant he missed the second day of the calf dissection. He is fascinated by the way Ms. Brady connects the things they learn in chemistry to the things they learn in biology, the way he can follow how molecules interact all the way to how the bodies on the table worked.

She says, "Jack, you're very talented. You could make something of yourself."

Sure, school is pretty easy for him, if that's what she means by talented. But in his experience that's not what separates the smart kids, the kids who are going to "make something of themselves," from everybody else. So he shrugs. Looks at the door. He could go for a smoke.

"Have you thought about being a doctor?"

He starts to laugh, but then he sees she isn't kidding, and she says, "But you've got to focus, you can't get distracted with all of this bullshit." She waves her hand at the door where he'd been looking a moment ago, and he wonders if she read his mind about wanting a smoke, and also thinks there is something really cool about a teacher who swears. She has this big coiffed 1980s hair that she must've had since, well, the 1980s.

"I know you can do better than this," she says, pointing to the exam she'd handed back at the end of class that Jack now holds, crumpled, in his left hand. He loosens his grip, not wanting her to know he'd been about to throw it in the trash. He missed a couple of questions, ended up with an eighty-five or something. That was fine with him—she has a reputation for hard tests. But she's shaking her head like she's disappointed, so he nods.

"You're very smart and you're good with your hands. You just need to apply yourself. You like my classes, don't you? You like science."

Jack leans against the table, then straightens up self-consciously. He does like her classes. He pictures the only doctor he knows, who he went to when he broke his arm in the fifth grade. Whose son has the perfect blond hair and plays basketball and gets good grades and can do no wrong, parks in the senior parking lot as a junior, cuts class, comes back with Dunkin' Donuts but brings the secretary a coffee and she giggles, writes him an excused absence and a hall pass. They are already talking about him going to *Harv*ard.

"I don't think my grades are good enough for that," he says.

"They aren't right now," she says. He feels like one of the dried butterflies she has pinned to a corkboard behind her desk.

He surprises himself then. "What would I have to do?"

"Sit down," she says, "let's talk."

Step one is a summer internship at the Jackson Laboratory (JAX).

First, the problem of transportation. He took his driver's test as soon as he turned sixteen (that spring—they held him back a year in elementary school at some point when he still wasn't talking much), but he doesn't have a car, and the commute to JAX is two and a half hours each way. Ms. Brady's husband has an old Ford Ranger that isn't running, and Jack tells her about his work at Buddy's and she says if he can fix it up he can drive it to JAX and back for work. Then looks at him hard like, Don't even think about driving it anywhere else. But they are already talking about his college applications, how to get him into a good school with a good scholarship as far away from Hartland as possible, the last part Jack's requirement, and he is completely convinced, isn't planning on driving anywhere else anyway.

He doesn't have the tools he needs to fix the truck, so he sneaks back to Buddy's, hitching a ride with a girl he's half-dating (sure, he dated all through that year, which is maybe surprising but shouldn't be—he was the least dangerous of the dangerous crowd, and the girls could smell it, liked to have the edge without actually getting beat on or screamed at), asks Buddy himself (well, Buddy the second—it was his father's shop, first) if he can borrow some things, and Buddy takes pity on him and says sure. He doesn't see his great-grandfather while he's there.

He gets the truck running. It's a five-speed, so he has to teach himself to drive a stick. This he does alone and by feel, crunching and lurching through Hartland with his teeth clenched.

JAX's stipend is not quite enough to cover his gas. But Ms. Brady asks him to do some odd jobs—trimming bushes, cutting the lawn, cleaning gutters. Her weekly envelopes of cash, "Jack" scrawled across the front in black pen, just happen to perfectly make ends meet.

Jack, with Ms. Brady's guidance, enters the statewide science fair. There is a five-thousand-dollar scholarship for the winner, which becomes ten thousand if used at the University of New England. Jack doesn't want to go to the University of New England, because it is in

Maine and therefore not far enough away, but ten thousand dollars sounds like a lot of money.

Jack's experiments are not perfect—he ran many trials, and got conflicting results—but Ms. Brady assures him that this is fine. Good, even. That this is how science works, and that it is even more interesting to discover something is more complicated than you thought than it is to find a simple "right" answer.

He cannot make his experiments perfect, but he can make his poster perfect. So he stays up all night, tearing it apart and putting it back together. Makes sure that no paper is crumpled, every edge is straight, no ink is smudged, every word is correct.

"This is fantastic," Ms. Brady says before they get in the van to go to the science fair. "You should be very proud." Jack just feels anxious. There's one other kid in the van, a girl he doesn't know well. She is typing on a Mac, her own personal laptop. He thinks, I need this and you do not, and he is angry—no, bitter.

At the fair, he sets up his board and then goes to the bathroom. He tries to calm his hair by wetting it, which only makes it curlier. He is so nervous he can taste sour bile.

He stands up very straight when the judges come to him with their clipboards. Calls them ma'am and sir. Hands them a stapled packet each: his work in the form of a scientific paper. This was not a requirement, but he wanted to do it. Wanted to make it real, like the work at JAX. Thought they would be impressed.

"What is this?" the woman says, and he explains, and she says, "It isn't part of the judged materials," and sets it down on the table like it's contaminated.

Jack doesn't say anything.

They study his poster.

"So, what's your conclusion here?" the man says.

"Well," Jack says, "I conclude that my results are, at the moment, inconclusive. And that more experiments are needed." He goes on, lists the variables he tested, the ones he struggled to isolate, the limitations both of his own equipment and of measurement generally, describes the changes he made to his original hypothesis over the course of the work, offers his current revised hypothesis. When he stops speaking, and they Mmhmm, frowning, make marks on their clipboards, thank him politely, and walk on, Jack knows that he lost.

He stands there, stiff beside his poster, as people—other students' friends and family, he supposes—walk around looking at the work. Sometimes they glance at what he has done, but the cramped type, the complicated graphs, and the lack of color or drawings or exclamation points seem to deter them.

Then two elderly people approach him. They are purposeful. And familiar.

"I didn't know you were coming!"

His great-grandmother hugs him, and he leans down to hug her back.

"How did you even know where to come? Or what time? It's such a long drive."

"Oh, we have our ways," his great-grandmother says. "Look at this!" His great-grandfather is already studying the board, leaning in to read the text.

She continues, "How did it go? We saw the judges come over, they looked very, what would you say, stern."

"They were," Jack says. "I don't think they liked it very much."

"What? Why not?"

He shrugs. He doesn't want to talk about it. But they're making him feel better already.

His great-grandfather is still reading. Jack and his great-grandmother watch as he studies everything on the board, and then picks up the stapled packet and reads that, too.

Then he holds the packet so Jack can see it, and points to the first piece of jargon he doesn't know.

"Okay, Jack. What's this?"

Jack doesn't even place. His results sheet shows he lost a quarter of the possible points for "lack of a clear, definitive conclusion."

Ms. Brady tells him they're scientifically wrong. That no conclusion is a conclusion. Files a complaint.

Jack throws the board in the trash before she can rescue it.

Things go better at JAX. He starts in mouse production—JAX is famous as a supplier of lab mice—but quickly gains a reputation among the lab techs as helpful and gets recruited to work on all sorts of projects. His favorite has to do with kidney failure. That is, renal oxidative stress. He is transfixed. It's like tearing apart an engine, but the engine is alive.

He comes up with a potential solution to a problem they are running into with drug delivery, scribbling iteration after iteration in his notebook. He talks it through with Ms. Brady until the whole thing is polished and perfect, and then, hands sweating, he brings it to the PI. The PI is impressed. The idea, of course, wasn't as polished as Jack thought, but it does contribute to the real solution and also to the PI realizing that Jack exists. When the summer ends, the PI asks Jack to come back weekends and vacations during the school year. Jack says yes.

He does anything they'll let him. Clinical and research services— antibody evaluation, safety and efficacy studies, oncology drug discovery candidate validation. Cutting-edge 3D genome mapping. He understands machines better than the other researchers, and soon becomes the person to call when something isn't working quite right. Ms. Brady gets him permission from the school to spend half his time there (they create a program for him modeled after the kids who are learning a trade at the local tech school). The principal's logic is that the only thing worse than an angry troublemaker is an angry, *smart* troublemaker, and that this seems to keep him out of trouble. He isn't overly grateful to the school for this, but he should be.

His success pisses off Nicky's boyfriend, who picks on him for going to the lab, for driving Ms. Brady's husband's truck. "You fucking her?" he says. "She keeping you around to fuck her?" He refers to Mr. Brady as "the cuck." He beats on Jack indiscriminately. But now Jack knows he can't get arrested or he'll lose his job, fall off the bridge Ms. Brady has strung over the abyss in front of him, and so he doesn't fight back. The lack of retaliation inspires even more anger. So Jack goes to school and work with bruises on his face, back, arms. Doesn't explain them to anybody.

Nicky hardly speaks to him. When she does, he calls her Nicky with an edge in his voice. He makes sure she knows he thinks of Ms. Brady as a mother. Nicky is using more than ever, passing out on the bathroom floor so often he doesn't even bother to call 911.

44

A bit more than a year after Zoe found out, Jack became certain she was using.

Large pupils, runny nose. Disappearing in the middle of a meeting to go to the bathroom. A new habit of bouncing her knee under the table. She'd been skinny, always. Of late, very skinny—Zoe fancied herself a bit of a Silicon Valley mogul, like Steve Jobs or Elon Musk, and so bought into their weird health obsessions. Perfect body, perfect soul.

But this was sunken skinny, forgot-to-eat skinny, puking skinny. Drug skinny.

He wanted to be surprised, but he wasn't. What else had he expected? She was standing in front of everybody, lying to their faces, while he was tucked away in his safe little lab. How else did he think she would keep going?

He thought maybe he should tell Alex. Alex had stayed in California, their boots on the ground with the West Coasters, so he could be excused for not realizing. And anyway, how would he know what an addict was like? But telling him felt like a betrayal.

* * *

She'd scream, cry, scream again. The same things every time. *Groundhog Day*. Most recently, she'd gotten in her new Porsche (she'd bought a 911 Carrera 4S to go with her new apartment—begrudgingly, Jack loved the car) and squealed after him to his apartment. He'd sold the house.

"You've ruined my career! You've ruined my *life!*"

Jack just nodded.

"I still don't know what to fucking believe, but if I'm not crazy and if what we had to begin with was real, and I had published it, at least I'd have something! At least I could get the fuck out of here and go— and go try to get back into academia as a stupid—as a naive theorist who got—"

Jack was sitting at the table, Zoe standing over him.

"How much of it? How much of it did you—I don't even have a college degree because of you—"

He didn't answer her.

She moved away.

"You're a fucking monster. And you've destroyed my life." She picked up a glass from the coffee table, still half full of water, and then turned and flung it at him in one motion. The water arced across the room. The glass hit his arm with a dead thunk, bounced off the edge of the table, shattered on the floor.

"I hate you," she whispered.

She melted into his couch and put her face in her hands and cried. He stayed where he was. Resisted the urge to go put his arm around her, rub her shoulder. He could almost feel the delicate bones underneath her skin. Like a bird.

Then she got up, went into the guest bathroom, rustled around for a while. Came out with dry, red eyes, sniffling.

"What if we go back to Merck right now?" she asked. "I could call Mr. Framer." Everyone else used first names all around, even for people like the CEO of Merck, but Zoe could never bring her-self to.

"What?" This was a new addition. A step further than she'd been willing to go before.

She wiped her nose with the edge of a tissue. "You know as well as I do everybody here is just gambling. VCs and pharma. You think they thought we were a sure thing a year ago?" She paused. "Was it a year ago? When was that?"

Jack hummed. "Maybe two. I don't remember. I think it was one."

"Whatever. They knew there was a good chance M wouldn't pan out. They acquire ten, one works, they make money off it. How is it any different now? The only person who knows, who didn't then, is me. We sell this to them tomorrow, and it's not our problem. I don't even think it would be, necessarily, much different than what other people do. Depending."

Depending on what exactly Jack had done and when. He heard her loud and clear. He rubbed the delicate skin underneath his right eye. "I think we can do it."

"Do what."

Like most of their conversations now, this one went unfinished. Jack swept up the broken glass. They left together for another fund-raising dinner.

45

A few weeks later, Phoebe walked into the lab with a folder in her hand and a look on her face that sucked Jack's stomach into his feet.

"I have Zoe in the conference room," she said, and he got up and followed her.

Zoe had stopped sitting on his side of the table during meetings. So he picked a chair across from her, and Phoebe shut the door, and the room quieted.

Phoebe put a printout in front of Jack. He spun it halfway so Zoe could read it, too, but she said, "I've read it," so he spun it back to himself.

The *Wall Street Journal*. FORMER EMPLOYEE SAYS HOT STARTUP MANNA LAB CULTURE FLAWED.

Jack read.

The "former employee" was really a former intern. Jack remembered him. A whiny rich boy, with a baby face and a Vineyard Vines polo, legacy at Harvard. He'd snooped around, asked a lot of questions. Not even the right ones—he seemed to think Manna was hiding some kind of horrible side effect issue. Jack had been dismissive. And so, evidently, the kid had gone to the *WSJ*.

Well. That'd kill the Merck idea.

Halfway through the piece, Jack put his palm on it and swiveled it back to Phoebe. "This is bullshit."

"You didn't even finish it," Zoe said.

"I don't need to. It's ridiculous. He's pissy that I didn't treat him like some sort of a god just because everybody else has his whole life."

"It doesn't really matter why he's done it, it matters that people now think Manna's culture is 'secretive,' 'siloed,' and that 'employees are not allowed to speak to their coworkers about the science,'" Phoebe said, indicating direct quotes by gesturing with two fingers.

"So we're a billion-dollar startup—of course we're secretive."

Phoebe opened her folder, removed another paper, slid it toward him.

Also the *Wall Street Journal*, an op-ed, cosigned by ten of the biggest names in the life sciences.

"They've done this before," Jack said, referring to the negative op-ed that had come out the summer before what would've been their senior year. "It blew over."

He was looking at Phoebe, not at Zoe. He couldn't look at Zoe.

"I've been fending off this reporter"—Phoebe tapped the first piece—"for weeks, but now we're going to have to do some sort of damage control."

"So we do damage control."

"I can't believe you're being so fucking chill about this," Zoe said. He looked at her. Her lips were pressed together so tightly the blood had gone from them, leaving no color in her face at all. "If you had any concept of how hard it is to stand in the shitstorm that I'm about to stand in, you wouldn't be acting so goddamn arrogant. Get your fucking act together." She stood abruptly and left the room.

Jack swallowed.

"Well," Phoebe said. "Since you're not inclined to read it, you should know that the op-ed says no other scientists have been able to reproduce Manna's claims, that some of said claims should be scientifically impossible, and that an investigation should be initiated into the scientific practices of the company." She cleared her throat. "So. Get your lab ready for that investigation." Then she left, too.

They got on a conference call with Alex about it. Alex said the West Coast investors would understand, would be flexible. Jack could see Zoe losing her cool and then, abruptly, she sobbed aloud, and Alex went silent, and Jack flinched. When they got off the phone, she said, "I know, I know. He doesn't—he won't guess."

Zoe asked Jack to come backstage with her before the first big damage control interview. So, he thought, he still had something to offer her, even if it was just being the only other person who knew, and that thought gave him such pleasure, and the pleasure such disgust.

She was wound so tight she shimmered.

The prep team was trying to coax out a sob story. "So how did you get interested in the antiaging space?"

"Actually, Jack was working in antiaging first. He brought me on. I was interested in neuro, consciousness." She didn't look at him, but he could read between the lines: I might've been a brilliant scientist if not for you.

"But you must have something in the family . . . age-related illness, even the death of a loved one? This issue touches all of us."

"Am I myself impacted by the day-to-day problems of mortality? How dare you suggest as much." She smiled tightly, and they laughed in a chorus. "No, but I'm very privileged. All four of my grandparents are still alive. Of course, they are aging."

"But no deaths . . ." A tinge of disappointment. Jack cracked his knuckles.

"No deaths, no."

"What about you?" One of the lackeys, another TV journalist wannabe with a smooth, pretty face, turned to Jack, and suddenly everyone remembered he was there.

"Hmm?"

"If it was you who was interested in aging first, you must have had a reason."

"Yes," he said.

They all looked at him expectantly. He couldn't read Zoe's face.

"What is it?"

"Does it matter? Zoe's doing the interview."

"Some of your story might add some color."

"I am pretty fucking colorful," Jack said, and Zoe shifted. He could feel her annoyance.

She prodded. "Well, Jack?"

Well.

The summer after his junior year in high school. His great-grandfather was in his mid-seventies. His great-grandmother a bit younger. He was eighteen.

He worked two jobs that summer. One at JAX. Had wanted the other to be at Buddy's, where he knew he could make good money and see his great-grandfather more, but his mother's boyfriend said if he went to work there, he wouldn't let him work at JAX.

"How's that," Jack replied from his seat at the dining room table.

"I'll call the school and I'll tell 'em I found drugs in your room, co-cayne, that we're disc'plin" (-*ing* lost somewhere in the ether, repeated sounds too much for his brain) "you for the summer."

Jack didn't say anything, just looked up through heavy eyelids.

"Or better yet. I'll tell 'em we found a gun in your room, that you've been threat'nin us." Us vs. You. As though Jack and his mother weren't of the same flesh.

The cruelty in retrospect seemed so random, so absurd. In the moment, though, it had all made perfect sense. The adult male, threatened, chases the adolescent from the pack before the adolescent is large enough to kill the adult. And Jack never missed the chance to stage small rebellions. Use words he couldn't understand, speak over him at the dinner table, call him by his first name, remain silent when spoken to. So, in a way, it was Jack's fault.

Anyway, he got a job at the Dollar Tree across the street for minimum wage. He'd get home from JAX and work the late shift there and then go to bed for a few hours, up at five thirty and directly into his truck to drive to JAX, there nine to five, rinse and repeat. A couple of times he was so tired at the end of his day at the lab that he called in sick to the Dollar Tree and slept in his truck in the JAX parking lot, windows cracked and summer breezing in, in the passenger seat because the driver's seat sometimes wouldn't move and he was afraid it'd get stuck all the way reclined and then he wouldn't be able to drive.

The reason he worked two jobs was so that he could make payments to buy the truck off the Bradys.

Which meant that he could use the truck for things other than driving to JAX, which meant he sometimes used it to visit his greatgrandparents.

It was awkward, at first. Especially with his great-grandfather. He thought it was because it had been a while since they'd spent any real time together, and neither of them were very good at talking. And because Jack was too big and awkward, took up too much space. And because his great-grandfather had aged, and the mismatch between the man who worked six days a week and the man who sat on the couch, fading into it, was confusing to Jack.

But really it was because his great-grandfather was dying, and they didn't tell him.

Jack showed up at their house one Sunday afternoon and both his great-grandfather's truck and his great-grandmother's little Toyota were in the yard, but they weren't inside.

He'd been in the empty house before, of course, but it felt strange that day. The couch had a pillow and blanket on it, and they were sort of tossed around, the blanket trailing on the floor. Someone had tracked in mud (it had rained all night) and hadn't cleaned it up.

His great-grandmother was impeccably clean.

He knew before he knew. He guessed that one of them had been taken away by ambulance and the other had gone with. And he could have guessed that the one who needed the ambulance was his great-grandfather, who had done manual labor his whole life and also was older. But he didn't let himself get that far. He just cursed the fact that neither of them had a cell phone, got back in his truck, and drove to the closest hospital.

He was lucky to have arrived when he did, because his great-grandfather was soon to be transferred to another, larger hospital. And lucky that he shared a last name with them, that two generations of unmarried teen moms had passed on their own names without knowing quite what else to do, and so the secretary was willing to go get his great-grandmother for him. With her arms crossed over her stomach, she looked so small, so fragile. Jack hugged her, and then he forced himself to ask her what had happened and what he could do.

Which was when she told him that this wasn't sudden at all, that his great-grandfather had been struggling for a while, had been diagnosed, in fact, at the beginning of the summer, which was when the anger rose. Right there in the waiting room, bright red against the brown carpet, brown curtains, brown chairs, and three other people, in his memory all dressed in brown, only one even pretending to read a magazine.

"Why didn't you tell me?"

"We didn't want you to worry." She smiled at him, gently. "It wouldn't have helped."

"I could have helped you with care. I could have—I understand more about treatments, now. From working at JAX."

"The doctors are taking very good care of us."

Us. An Us that did not include Jack. He thought, You didn't tell me because I'm not a part of your family. And he began to cry.

That evening, his great-grandmother authorized him to speak to the doctors. He asked what the treatment plan was.

"We're more just making him comfortable," they said (surely it had been one doctor, but there were so many and they all said the same things and so in his memory there was a chorus).

"What do you mean."

"He has not chosen to pursue an aggressive course of treatment."

"Why not."

"Your grandfather is suffering from multiple age-related conditions, and his quality of life is diminishing. He understood that it would only diminish further if we moved forward with treatment. So he chose to focus on palliative care."

Hospice hung unsaid between them.

"How long—"

"I don't know yet. We'll need some time to address the acute symptoms he's been experiencing the past few days, and then we can have that discussion."

Jack stood at his great-grandfather's bedside like a guard dog, loomed over the nurses and asked sharp questions. The nurses, used to angry, bereft family, ignored him. His great-grandmother stood in the doorway and watched.

They brought a hospital bed home. They put it in Jack's room.

In the master bedroom, gathering his great-grandfather's things to bring to him, Jack found a copy of his science fair paper. Kept clean between two blank white sheets. The printout was soft from being flipped through, the top corner where it was stapled creased almost to tearing.

His great-grandfather's pain increased, and so did his pain medication. This meant his lucidity decreased, precipitously.

When his great-grandfather was mostly unconscious, his great-grandmother said, "Jack, you should go back to work. That work you're doing is so important."

He looked at her with all of the anger he felt, and she flinched and fled to the kitchen.

His great-grandfather died two weeks later.

He knew he should've stuck around to support his great-grandmother. But he blamed her for losing the summer he could have spent with his great-grandfather, if he had known, instead of working eighty hours a week.

He didn't say that to her. If he had, she would've said that Jack's future was more important than an old man's death. And he would have thought she was stupid. Might have said so. An eighteen-year-old boy cannot comprehend the perspective of a seventy-year-old woman.

The rest fell into place. Only greater focus, nothing here for him anymore. Everything echoed: get me out get me out get me out. His obsession with JAX grew, because it became his way to fix what he saw as having caused his great-grandfather's death: the failure of medical science to treat aging, the flawed mindset that age was a reason to give up.

He applied to MIT early. He was certain he'd get in. He'd done everything, he'd fixed his grades, he only got straight A's now, got a near-perfect SAT score (missed one question on reading), had a full schedule, plus was nearly full-time at JAX even during the school year. His name was on his PI's most recent paper, which had just come out. Ms. Brady and his PI had written his letters of recommendation.

When he didn't get in, he broke down in tears inside his truck.

He poured his hurt into the lab. Was made of energy drinks and anger. Was going to be first author on the next paper. Was going to show them what they'd missed.

Applied to twenty-three other schools regular decision. Anywhere that would give him money and get him out of central Maine, out of Maine entirely if possible.

He was waiting for an experiment to run when he got the call. It was 3:00 p.m., a Wednesday. "This is Kitty, and I'm calling from the Harvard admissions office. Is this Jack?"

"This is Jack." Frozen in place, pen in hand. Had he made a mistake on his application?

"I was the reader of your application, and I just wanted to be the first to tell you that we think you're incredible, and we would love to have you at Harvard."

Whole body vibrating.

"You'll receive what we call a likely letter in the mail in a few days, but for now I just wanted to call to congratulate you personally. You have had such an amazing upward trajectory—your teachers and mentors have nothing but incredible things to say about you. I really hope you'll come join us at Harvard."

Jack realized he was silent. "Uh, I—I don't—thank you."

"You're very, very welcome. And while you won't receive your financial aid letter right away, you should know that our office meets all demonstrated financial need—you won't need to worry about costs."

"I—okay. Yes, thank you, that's . . ." He couldn't find anything to say. "I'm sorry, I don't know what to say," he finally managed.

The woman laughed. A twinkly laugh. A twinkly laugh from a

fairy in a faraway fantasy land. "That's okay! I'm sure this is over-whelming news. I just wanted you to know that it was my pleasure to read your application and to advocate for you in front of the committee."

"Thank you so much. Is there anything I—is there anything I need to do?"

"Not at all. The hard work is over. I hope you do something fun to celebrate."

When she hung up, he set his phone down. His hands were shaking.

He put his face in them. He curled over himself and started sobbing. He cried for a long time, in time with the refrain that thrummed steady in the back of his mind, that would never stop. Don't blow it don't blow it don't blow it don't—

"It's a great story." Someone from the team was speaking. "Jack, why don't you join her today? You lead with that—everyone will love it."

He'd forgotten they weren't alone. "Oh," he said. "I don't really . . ."

"Jack doesn't do public speaking," Zoe said. She looked exhausted.

"Well what if we just . . . Zoe could tell it. We could just make a few tweaks, so it fits her background."

Jack laughed out loud.

"Tweak away," he said, shaking his head. "Knock yourselves out."

46

Alex took leave from his post, went back to Stanford to resume his PhD.

Sure, it didn't help anything. But Jack couldn't blame Zoe for wanting to protect him or him for wanting to protect himself.

He and Zoe didn't speak about it.

47

Finally, the investors started to yell.

The West Coast VC guys, usually so chill, Jack's best friends, were "concerned." Externally, of course, everybody was positive. Defuse defuse defuse. But there was chatter, only making its way back to Zoe through her loyal ultrawealthy group, about replacing her and Jack with someone who might "run a tighter ship," "make sure the house is in order." The one with the Montana ranch would reply to these email chains with blunt rejections. "Frankly, it offends me that you would suggest . . ."

When Zoe showed Jack the emails, he promised her they were almost there. He was close to proof of concept on the new drug, Beta. So, so close. He just needed more time.

She closed her eyes, raised her hands to rub her face, took a deep breath, and held it in as she nodded.

They put a board meeting on the calendar for the next Friday.

On Wednesday, she rang his doorbell. He answered the door. It was midnight. He'd just gotten home from the lab. She hadn't been in the office since Monday. She was a mess. Her eyes were wide and wild, her hair was knotted. She was wearing a T-shirt, though it was

December, thirty-some degrees. He could smell her from several feet away. It wasn't her sweat, which to him was sweet and earthy, but an acrid, chemical smell. A fear smell. It reminded him of lab mice when they were dying.

"I can't sleep," she said, and her voice cracked.

"Come inside," he said. "Are you okay?"

She stumbled in. He didn't know if he should touch her, but she leaned precariously, bumping him in her stagger, so he caught her around the shoulders and moved with her inside. He'd barely furnished the place, but there was a couch, which he sat her on. "Nice couch," she mumbled.

He disappeared into his bedroom, where his only blanket was on his bed, returned with it and handed it to her. She put it on herself without bothering to untwist it, which left one leg and one shoulder out. Jack gently tugged at it until it covered her whole body, then sat down beside her, a foot or so away.

"Can't sleep," she muttered again.

"Yeah? Why not?"

"They stopped working."

"What stopped working?"

"My red pills."

"Mm? What red pills are those."

"Downers. So I can sleep."

He nodded. It wasn't like he didn't know.

"What else have you had today?"

"What do you mean?"

"What other pills have you taken today?"

"God, Jack, I don't know." She shut her eyes. "I can't . . . remember." Zoe of the perfect memory. Zoe who could recall every element on the periodic table (and who knew it was a fairly useless skill). Zoe who didn't make mistakes. It hurt him.

"Do you have something that will make me sleep?"

Jack looked at her steadily. Took a deep breath in.

"No, I don't. I have weed."

"'s not strong enough."

"I know."

She started crying. Her breaths came fast. She put her hands to her throat. Gasped, mouth open, like a fish.

"I can't—"

"Shh," Jack said, "shh. You can." He moved closer to her, to catch her in case she passed out, make sure she didn't pitch forward onto the coffee table. She was shuffling her feet around like she was trying to stand up.

"I can't br—"

"You're having a panic attack, Zoe. You're all right." He wasn't sure of that, didn't know if perhaps she wasn't overdosing in front of him. It flashed into his mind, unbidden: that was the last thing they needed on the front page of the *Times*. "Manna founder in hospital after drug overdose." A picture of Zoe snapped from the bushes, like this. Then he scolded himself. This is your *partner*, he thought.

"Let's put your head between your knees, okay? Can you breathe with me?" He started dictating breaths. "In—" Breathed in himself, a long breath. "Out—" Breathed out himself, equally long. She'd try, hitch up on the in, then cough, choke. She was shaking violently.

He stood up to get the phone. Realized his own hands were shaking.

And then it was over as quickly as it had started. Her breaths got longer, whistling on the way in. She turned her head to the side and vomited, a clear stream that hit the floor and splashed. She coughed, then said, "Oh, god, I'm sorry," voice raspy.

"It's all right." He kept his voice quiet and calm. "It's all right, I'll get it. You're okay." He moved back to sit beside her, then paused, went into his bathroom to grab his towel, threw it over the bile on the floor. "You're okay." She was nodding too fast, taking big breaths now, like she couldn't get enough air.

"I couldn't breathe."

"I know. But you can now."

"I can now."

Her eyes were big and empty. He tried not to think of his mother, curled up on the bathroom floor.

He sat with her until her breathing had regulated, until there was something behind her eyes again.

"Do you want to take a shower?"

"I don't think I should by myself."

He didn't want to offer to help. It was implied.

"Let me clean up," he said, nodding down at the floor. She winced.

"I'll get it."

"Don't be ridiculous."

He went into the kitchen, grabbed cleaning supplies from under the sink, paper towels from the counter. Returned. The liquid had mostly been sopped up by his towel. And it was only liquid. He wondered when she'd last eaten. He sprayed the floor, rubbed it, sprayed again. Took the whole bundle to the trash. He could buy a new towel. Wrapped up the bag and tied it, put it by his door. Returned to Zoe. Her eyes were closed.

"Will you help me?"

"Of course."

He led her to the bathroom, sat on the closed toilet while she undressed. Averted his eyes like he'd never seen her body before. She turned the shower on, stepped past him and in. He caught a glimpse of one hip bone, skin sunken in to meet it, curved like a flower petal. He held out his hand in case she needed it.

"You don't have to close your eyes, Jack. Like you've never seen me naked." A bit of her old sharpness back. It helped him feel better. He looked up. The water was running off her matted hair, which did not want to wet. He tried not to flinch, looking at her. He could count the ribs on her chest. He wondered if he was going to throw up, too.

She soaped her body, rinsed. Then her face. Spat again and again into the drain. Worked her fingers into her hair. Dropped her hands after a while. It was cleaner, not clean. He gave her a towel, a clean T-shirt, a toothbrush. She slept that night on his couch.

The next morning, while Zoe was in the bathroom, he checked his email.

Deus ex machina. One of their patents—the one for M, the drug that had never worked—had been approved.

Well. The USPTO doesn't usually question whether something works, only whether it is patentable. And, indeed, the drug they might have created was useful, novel, and not obvious.

When Zoe came out he said, "Look," and she came over to him, and he could feel the heat from the shower still radiating off her body as she leaned over his shoulder, and she almost laughed in his ear, though it came out more like a huff, and said, "Well there. That'll shut them up for a few months."

She slept on his couch again Thursday night. Friday before the board meeting she did her makeup in his bathroom, hiding the dark under her eyes, the paleness of her face. Took a handful of pills. Jack did not comment.

She was going to go in alone and play good cop. Jack was going to remain outside, bad cop.

He could not hear what she said. But when everyone emerged, heads were nodding. The board dispersed. He went in, and she was sitting at the head of the table. She looked exhausted.

"I'll remain CEO," she said. "And you CSO. I convinced them that I can do it."

He didn't know what kind of magic she'd worked, but he could see what it had taken out of her. He nodded. Sat down beside her, their backs to the glass wall. He was reminded of sitting beside her in another glass conference room, after she'd convinced Fen to hire her. Lifetimes ago.

She cleared her throat. "I told them that it's a leadership problem, a management problem. That you're a genius, the genius, that there's no company without you, but that you can't run a lab, and you'll leave if they hire someone over you. That I've been too absent, too focused on spreading the message. But that I'll be here, and I'll fix things." She paused for a bit, and then added, "Wouldn't have worked without the patent news, though."

"Patent news wouldn't have worked without you."

She nodded.

She had bought him time. He would buy her her life back.

They sat together for a while, looking out the window over Cambridge.

48

That night, Jack didn't go into the lab. Stayed home, allowing him-self to hope that she'd come back to his apartment.

That first winter they lived together, she had traveled a lot. The apartment had felt so empty without her. And dark. Literally—she liked to have all the lights on, while Jack, if he was alone, wouldn't bother. He'd get home late and walk through the darkness to the bedroom, where he'd just turn on the bedside lamp and wait half-asleep for her to call him after whatever event where she'd been wined and dined by people with money or people who have control over money, and she'd say, "You'll never guess what happened," and he'd say, "Bernard told Edward that he had the *personal* cell phone num-ber of so-and-so, who is a Lebanese *prince*," and she'd say, "Well, it might be his cousin's personal cell," and he'd say, "Isn't that what I said? And, also, Edward was *just speaking to* Elon," and she'd say, "Musky, baby—how did you know?" and he'd laugh and say, "How was it?" and she'd say, "Same shit, how was the lab?" and he'd say, "Same shit," and he'd listen to her brush her teeth, wash her face, and he'd say, "Did you eat?" and she'd say, "There was food at the event," and he'd say, "So no," and she'd say, "So no," and he'd get online and order her room service and she'd act surprised when it arrived, even though he did this every time. And then they'd fall asleep without hanging up the phone.

At first, when she'd just moved out, and now, again, he tried to trick himself into believing she was on a really long business trip. And for some reason just couldn't call.

She didn't come Saturday, either.

He gave up around midnight and lay back on the couch and let his eyes slip shut and then he was in the lab, in Brenna's lab, and there were things that might be memories or might just be dreams, Zoe's hand shaking his shoulder, being loaded bumpily into an ambulance, Zoe's voice insisting she ride with him, an EMT with a thick accent— Indian, maybe? and then he was opening his eyes in a hospital room, three summers ago. There was an IV in his arm. There was a nurse. He asked her if there had been an Indian EMT and she said What? His head was killing him, throbbing so hard with his heartbeat his vision pulsed purple. He coughed, and the nurse offered him a paper cup of water.

"Your girlfriend is in the waiting room," she said. "Would you like me to get her?"

"Yes. Please."

On Sunday Jack thought, I really need to go back to the lab.

He had to keep making progress on Beta. But was he making progress? He found it hard to trust his own work.

He closed his eyes, saw Zoe.

What does it mean to betray yourself?

Stepped back and looked at his own loneliness. An ugly thing, to be so alone. He thought of his great-grandmother. Her forgiveness. "You were young, and anger is part of grief," she'd said. Her own descent was into madness. Still alive, but not. Worse, if anything could be worse. The house had been sold. She lived in a home. He knew he should visit.

Someone knocked. Jack startled. "Zoe?"

He got up, went to the door, opened it, squinted out into the carpeted hall. Nothing. One of his neighbors, perhaps, or a TV. Or he'd fallen asleep, and she had knocked in his dream.

He sat back on the couch, stared across the dark room. Laughed, a little, at himself.

"Is there—*is* there balm in Gilead?—tell me—tell me, I implore!"

His voice sounded strange in the silence.

He must have slept, because when he stood to get himself something to eat it was eleven. He pulled a microwave dinner from the freezer. Was standing in front of the microwave in a hum-induced trance when, he was certain of it, someone knocked. That is, he was certain that he heard a knock. So either someone had knocked or he was having an auditory hallucination.

He froze. He did not want to open the door, because if he had imagined the knock—

The microwave beeped.

Jack flinched.

The person knocked again.

Jack shook his head.

Jack moved, opened the door.

She had a duffel bag over her shoulder, and her head cocked to one side.

(Prophet! said I, thing of evil!—prophet still, if bird or devil!)

"Zoe?"

"Yes?"

"Are you—"

"I don't—" "you didn't—" "—have to—"

They both fell silent.

"Do you want to come in?" He was mortified, suddenly, by the food waiting for him in the microwave. Too-hot mashed potatoes, sad strips of chicken, rubbery broccoli. The apartment already smelled like the broccoli, and he wondered if it was grossing her out.

She stepped over the threshold.

He closed his eyes and breathed in and he was opening them that weird morning (was it morning? afternoon?) when he'd slept for hours and hours, half in half out of dreaming, monstrous things floating around his head and dancing through his dorm room, devils, angels, equations, to see her, another apparition surely, except she spoke and kept speaking, though he couldn't remember now what she'd said. Just that he was trying to keep his eyes open and also do math, because she was talking about dates and days and times and how long he'd been asleep and he had been, before this sleep, in Brenna's lab for over twenty-four hours and the one thing he could remember in this weird morass of anti-thinking was that she did not know he was also working with Brenna and he did not want her to know, not yet. He watched her watch him with those big dark eyes and fucked up his math on days, nights, how long he'd been sleeping but that was plausible because he was hardly conscious, sleep kept pulling him back underwater where it was cool and calm and quiet and then she'd drag him back up again, back into the harsh bright sharp air. He blinked and saw Carter there, too, Carter looking at Zoe looking at him, and he thought Fuck, and then someone was handing him a juice and he was sitting up and drinking and then he was awake, actually, and the edges of the room were no longer made of strange, living, pulsing darkness, and his head was killing him.

She took him to dinner.

He wasn't ready yet. He'd wanted to have a finished idea to present to her. But sitting there across from her in the dining hall he could see how easily she might leave him, how much of a mess he looked, and he knew he had to do something to pull her in. So he said, "Don't you want to know what I was working on that kept me up all night?"

He didn't know they'd figure it out just like that. He didn't know he had only glimpsed the edges of her creativity, which was something purer, truer than his own. His a bumbling trial and error, brute force, take things apart and put them together. Blue-collar, more perseverance than anything. So plain in the face of this flickering energy behind Zoe's eyes that leaped up at his challenge and danced.

He expected the worshipfulness he felt to make him want to have sex with her, but that night his only thought was that he must not do anything to break the delicate silvery threads that had sprung from nowhere and wound themselves from her to him and back. He sensed they needed time to set up: a cool, dark place. No heat of passion. No sudden movements.

Maybe if he had been stronger, he wouldn't have let her move back in with him. Would've been sure it was in her best interest to stay as far away as possible.

But he couldn't help giving himself too much credit. Thinking maybe it was the other way around.

As she was settling into his bedroom, he snagged yesterday's *WSJ* from the table. SECOND MANNA EMPLOYEE BLOWS WHISTLE.

He carried it over to the trash, opened the lid, and then held it for a long moment, staring.

It wasn't that he thought she didn't know. He just wanted—

"Jack?" Zoe called from the bedroom. "Do you have another extra toothbrush I can use? I forgot to bring one."

"Yes," he said. Of course. And a second pillow, and an extra towel, and a heated blanket for when he was in the lab at night.

His eyes were drawn to the killer line: "One employee was instructed to throw out a data set that appeared to shed negative light on the therapeutic." The stupid thing was it wasn't even true. He always did the throwing out himself. But how do you come back from that?

How do you come—

He began to realize something. A realization that might rise to the status of revelation, epiphany. He stood there looking at the paper while it swirled, a thick gray mass threatening to take shape.

"Jack?"

"Mm?"

"Um, toothbrush?"

"Right," he said, and he let go of the paper and it fell into the trash can, but it was faceup, so he reached in, flipped it over, shoved it under an empty takeout container, let the lid shut, turned on the faucet, washed his hands. "I'm coming."

49

When they received notice that Harvard was filing suit for breach of contract they laughed until they cried.

Harvard's claim was that they had done work on the drug while enrolled, and thus Harvard's IP policy—which says that any patent on an invention conceived "with direct or indirect support from Harvard" is Harvard's property—was active, and thus Harvard had the right to the patent, and thus, by not signing the patent over, they had breached contract. But they hadn't worked on the drug at Harvard, just the theory. They owed that to Viraj, actually. It was his lawyers who had hustled them out of Harvard labs as soon as they started thinking about drug development.

At the time, Harvard's IP policy hadn't felt fair. But now, thinking about how much money they must've burned in Brenna's lab just fucking around, thinking about how much time they'd spent begging for that same money since they left—well, maybe they'd screwed Harvard, actually. Or would have screwed Harvard. Maybe Harvard was itself a sort of venture capitalist.

Fen was filing suit, too. That his name should be on the patent.

"None of the experiments were even done in Fen's lab, were they?" Zoe asked.

"Well, the original yeast," Jack said.

"Right," Zoe said. He shrank, but she was laughing. "Of course. Brenna wasn't set up to do yeast then. How did I never realize. What did you do, sneak in during the dead of night?"

He laughed, too, grateful. Oh, the forgivenesses he did not deserve. It helped, probably, that his first real results from Beta had come back beautifully. And she'd watched him do it, seen no sleight of hand. He was far beyond being hurt by her lack of trust. "I mean . . ." He shook his head. "Yeah, I did."

She laughed louder. "Are you serious?"

"Yes."

"You snuck into—how'd you even get in?"

"I had a key."

"They gave you a key?"

"I was in a lot at weird hours."

"Oh my god, Jack."

"I'm charming," he said, "what can I say."

She leaned her head onto his arm.

"To a fault," she said.

And then, "I thought this was a tragedy," she said. "But maybe it's a comedy."

"The difference," he replied, "is entirely in the framing."

The irony (comedies and tragedies, both rife with it) was that the patent dispute actually brought more investors knocking. Which further soothed the board. They only needed people to keep putting money in. That was the beauty of it. So long as the pyramid keeps growing, it doesn't matter what's inside. There was again talk of selling. There were formal discussions opened with Merck.

The first time she kissed him again, he cried. She just shook her head.

"We can do this," she said.

"We're doing it," he answered.

They had never said the *L*-word. But if they did, he would have. He hoped she might have, too.

50

Four years nearly to the day after he'd started this whole mess, he sat at his computer and finalized the data package that would present Beta as a promising new drug.

This was the first time the Yamanaka factors had been used successfully as a total-body treatment in mouse models without inducing severe tumors, and, if things kept going well, would be the first Yamanaka-based therapeutic to move forward into the clinic. Approval—like all gene therapy approval—would be a nightmare. But his projections were showing—really showing—meaningful potential human life span increases of one to two years. No more than that, because higher concentrations became toxic. And it was only for use in old age, before which the benefits would not outweigh the risks.

And, of course, it wasn't M. It wasn't based on Zoe's theory.

Jack chewed on the inside of his cheek, which was ragged.

He knew, sitting alone in the lab, alone in reality, without the belief of others to get drunk on, that it didn't matter. This was the realization (revelation, epiphany) that had been waiting for him with that newspaper in his kitchen trash: by itself, Beta was not enough. Not with the employees who had gone to the press, and how much money they had and how long they'd lied to get it, and the vitriol from other scientists. As soon as they came out with a pivot, the world would say Aha! It would be as good as an admission of guilt. And then the world would demand judgment, punishment. Atonement.

But Beta, plus him. That was enough to give Zoe a way out and forward. The relief he felt, clicking save and then backing everything up on an external hard drive, made him dizzy.

One to two years sounds modest until you get there, at which point it probably sounds like an eternity.

He sat for a long moment. Looked at the clock in the top right of his screen. 11:11 p.m. He shut his eyes for a second. Made a wish.

Then he dragged the files into an email, subject [INTERNAL] BETA.

Breathed in.

Sent it to zoe@manna.com.

Breathed out.

He couldn't remember if he'd asked her to come with him to Maine, or if she'd asked him to go. He did remember she and Carter had just, finally, broken up, and that Carter had left Manna.

It didn't matter who'd asked who anyway. One's thoughts from the other's mouth.

He didn't really think about how a meeting between her and Nicky would go. He couldn't imagine them in the same room. When he tried, he flushed with embarrassment. For who? For himself? Secondhand for his mother? What if she had bruises on her neck? What if she showed up with some prick who would inevitably—god—take a pass at Zoe?

When he said he'd get a hotel she'd said "I really don't mind staying with your mom." But he insisted that they get a room. Made up some stupid excuse about there not being enough space. He worried she'd think this meant he didn't want to introduce them. Which of course was true. But he worried about all the reasons she could think up of why that might be.

When she asked to go to the funeral, he said he hardly knew the guy and was just going to support his family, anyway. Which was true insofar as no one knew him that well, except maybe his ex-wife, who was long dead herself, because he was a drunk, shunned social contact, and lived in the middle of the woods. But Jack didn't go into detail.

When he got back from the service, which had been held at the ugly little white Baptist church his uncle had occasionally attended, Zoe was standing against the hotel room door in the sun with her eyes closed. Like she was posing for something. Her hair had gotten long and she'd let it fall into her face. She had her hands palms out. The lines were sort of elegant. She looked, against the green, with her shirt caught up on her shoulders to expose a strip of belly and the tops of her hip bones over her low-rise jeans, like some sort of hippie rock star trying to make it in the 1970s. Or maybe that was just because Fleetwood Mac had been on the radio.

She kept her eyes closed as he came up to her, left her arms up.

"Trying to get abducted?" he said.

She was trying not to smile. "By who?"

"I don't know," he said. "I can hear banjos."

It was the first time he'd seen Nicky since that boyfriend had given him a black eye. Merry Christmas. Explaining it to his postdoc had been such a great gift. She had a new boyfriend now. Didn't look too much different. He had a cold, sweaty handshake.

Nicky looked pathetic, wrung out. She clung to his shoulder and said, "Jacky, it's so good to see you." He wondered if she'd been drinking, didn't think she had. Which only made it worse.

She must've seen Manna on TV. But then again it was all Zoe's face, and sure his name was there sometimes, but his mother had never paid attention to detail.

"How is school, darling?"

He didn't bother telling her he'd dropped out. He didn't bother telling her he was worth half a billion dollars. He had been sending her more money, a lot more, but she didn't ask how he was getting it. He could be selling coke to the rich boys at Harvard, for all she cared. Hell, that would probably make more sense to her than Manna.

Maybe she never asked because it didn't matter how much he sent, she would always call asking for more, voice thick like she'd been crying. He'd step out so whoever he was with wouldn't hear. His team at the lab, Zoe, whatever girl he was sleeping with. He'd wonder if a boyfriend beat her until she called. The fury was so far from him now, or so deep that he couldn't feel it. He wondered why she ended up with violent man after violent man. Was it something about her? Just that she had been a pretty thing, and the only thing men can do with a pretty thing is break it? Was it something deeper? Something inside her that asked to be broken? That whispered to her to go back home to the one that hit her, and when he left, to find another; to drink the liquor; to breathe in the powder, or, better, faster, to warm it carefully and slide it into her own vein? Was it in Jack, too?

"Fine, fine."

He saw her eyes on his boots, the only thing he'd changed about his appearance. He'd thought about taking them off. He still had the old ones, the secondhand ones with frayed holes to the steel toes, buried in his closet in Kendall. He was, though he didn't like to admit it, sentimental.

But putting those back on felt too dishonest.

"Nice boots," she said, "they look good on you. Such a handsome boy."

And that was it.

It left him itchy. He wanted to drive. He wanted to drive all the way back to Kendall and pretend the whole thing had never happened, but he didn't know what Zoe would think of that, especially since they had the motel for another night. So instead he drove her around, watching her wide eyes. He avoided the cluster of Hartland, with its abandoned tannery and its druggies on the street. Better the tragic beauty of being poor in the middle of the woods. He wondered what exactly he wanted her to see. Didn't realize until the sun was going down. He wanted her to see the stars.

And then she wanted to see the fair.

It was Labor Day weekend, the weekend of the Harmony Free Fair. And so there were signs in Athens. And so Zoe had asked, "What's the Harmony Free Fair?" and Jack had explained, and her eyes had widened and she'd said, "Can we go?"

"Well, it is free," Jack said.

They went in the afternoon, the day after the funeral. The nights had been cold, Jack waking up in the motel in the morning facing Zoe's bed opposite him to see her curled up tightly, gripping the comforter around herself, tip of her exposed nose pink. He'd walk softly to the window to watch the sun burn off the fog while she slept. The cold made him melancholy; the change from summer to fall gave him an anxious buzzing feeling in his fingertips. Not one thing or another.

Today it was summer again, hot, over eighty, and it seemed the bugs had taken this as a last hurrah, so when they drove into the center of Harmony (Jack could hear Zoe thinking, *This* is a town?, though she didn't say it) and parked on the lawn outside the elementary school and hopped out of the truck they were engulfed immediately by a cloud of blackflies. Jack grimaced. "You sure you care enough about this to brave the bugs?" he said, wiping away one that had gotten itself trapped in the corner of his eye.

"Absolutely," Zoe said, though she didn't seem to know quite how to swat them and instead was moving her head side to side like she might avoid them, shuddering slightly when they landed on her exposed legs (she was wearing shorts, unusual for her, little yellow midthigh shorts and white socks that came just over her ankles, which made her look young and gangly, nothing like one of the *Time*100, Founder of the Year, woman featured in *Vogue*. She was paler than most of the rednecks, even though she was half-Greek— she'd asked Jack, once, if he saw her as white, and he'd said Yes without even thinking, what kind of question is that, and she'd laughed and said Carter said she was *leukōlenos*, white-armed, and he'd rolled his eyes). She put Jack in mind of a filly shivering its skin to keep the horseflies off.

They walked down over the embankment and up onto the fairground, which was really just someone's field that was too wet to bother growing anything on. It was full of white tents and framed by a handful of wooden structures, white with green trim, that housed some livestock, a food vendor, exhibitions, the bathrooms, and the band. The last had "Harmony Free Fair" painted on it in green. There was a pile of round bales right as they came in with probably twenty kids crawling over it like ants, playing some relatively nonviolent version of king of the hill.

"Here we are," Jack said. He wasn't embarrassed because this wasn't his place. He'd come maybe twice as a kid, once with the dead uncle, once, he thought, with his mother, though she didn't often venture far out of Hartland.

The sky was a hard, empty blue.

It would have been worse to take her to the Bangor fair. Where he'd spent the dregs of every summer after he had enough of his own money to pay the entrance fee, starting maybe in the sixth grade, with the grungy group of boys he ran with before Ms. Brady. The lean ones, shadowy, twelve and already with the kind of edge that made teachers nervous. Two of them were named Brandon. He couldn't remember the name of the third.

They'd go to the fair because it was an unsupervised gathering of kids just old enough to start having sex but too young to otherwise have access to each other's bodies. Someone's mom would drive them, wanting to go with her boyfriend who was already half in the bag to bet on some horse racing, or something.

Kyle. That was the third one's name.

Bangor wasn't like Harmony—it was a real fair, with flashing neon lights and those clanking metal rides that are the same everywhere you go. The Zipper. The Ferris Wheel. The swings that raise up high. Zero Gravity.

He and the Brandons and Kyle would walk past the rides (music blaring, pop from three seasons ago, Rihanna "S&M," Pink "Raise Your Glass," Jason Derulo "In My Head" nostalgic forever for him now), seek out the gaggle of kids under the grandstand. Puff themselves up trying to look older than they were for the skinny girls with their low-rise jeans and belly button piercings and heavy eye makeup. Some of them with a badly done tramp stamp already, tantalizingly half-visible. Jack recalled the lust he'd feel staring at those four inches of flat belly between jeans and little T-shirt.

Several summers of puking on the Gravitron and washing his mouth out with Gatorade *just in case* before he actually got any. By then he was going into eighth grade (or was it ninth?), and had finally started growing, and he towered over the girls, which meant he was, to his shock and delight, suddenly noticeable, in fact blow-job-able. (It was, he would learn, partly because they sensed he was now tall enough to buy them beers. He didn't actually look twenty-one, but the twenty-five-year-olds sloshing alcohol into plastic cups didn't care so long as they weren't obviously serving a minor.) He walked that particular girl (Sami, her name he would remember, she wrote the *i* with a heart for the dot when she doodled it in pen on his arm like a brand) around for the rest of that night and then the next day, his arm around her waist, marveling at how the taut skin of her belly felt under his hand after years of looking. Brandon and Brandon glared. Kyle didn't care. Kyle had been having sexual success since the sixth grade. Something about the wavy blond hair and the lean build and the thinly veiled anger in all his movements and the roll of cash in his wallet already and the way he talked to girls like they were dirt. Kyle only smirked at him like they were in on something together now, handed him a condom in a tattered package, winked. Which whirled Jack back into an even older memory, how one of his mother's boyfriends had slurred too close to his face, he couldn't have been older than ten, Don't get a girl knocked up, they tell you they're on birth control, they lie to ya, and then they get knocked up just like they wanted and then you're trapped, and how he'd wondered about his mother, who'd been fifteen when she got pregnant, wondered what man she'd been trying to trap, and how he'd gotten away.

Anyway, Bangor was straight trailer trash: dirty concrete, sneakers with the tongues pulled up, white poor people either really skinny or really fat, self-medicating with drugs or food respectively. At least Harmony had the kitsch novelty of the hyper-rural, backwoods types.

Oh, Zoe, he thought.

They walked through the tents. She had her hands in the pockets of her little dark blue windbreaker, probably to keep the bugs off. Occasionally, she'd raise one to the back of her neck and scratch. Jack imagined the flies crawling up under all that hair.

She stood eye to eye with an alpaca for a good five minutes. "I think he hates me," she said finally, and Jack said, "They hate everyone," and the alpaca snorted as if in response and moved away with its strange bouncy, wobbly stride. Behind them, a teenage boy wearing an orange shirt with "Volunteer" across the back was picking up a piglet by its hind feet and the piglet screamed, which made Zoe flinch.

"It's okay," the boy addressed Zoe as he tried to adjust his grip on the pig's ankles, losing purchase, "it don't hurt him none." Zoe nodded thoughtfully.

They meandered back through the tents. Vote no on two, various salsas, crappy made-in-China clothes with printed slogans. A wood carver with some primitive-looking bears, a sign that said: "All burglars must carry ID so that we can notify next of kin." A tent selling far-right political paraphernalia, which Zoe didn't blink at. Jack supposed she'd seen enough already, knew people had to buy it somewhere.

They stood for a while and watched a blacksmith craft a five-pointed-star brand.

"I can make the two of you a heart, afterward, if you stick around," he said with a wink. Zoe laughed, Jack shook his head. Two barefoot kids went sprinting by. They meandered on.

The band had paused, and the lead singer was speaking. "It's my forty-fifth birthday,"—applause, whoops—"and I did the best thing I could have done. I went to the First Congregational United Church of Christ and I got baptized this morning." Louder applause, more whoops, at least two big AY-MENs. Jack tried not to laugh. He didn't know what was so funny. Zoe, you ain't in Cambridge anymore, he thought.

"Is that the same church the funeral was at?" Zoe whispered to him, an edge of excited recognition in her voice.

"No, no," Jack said, "that was the United Athens Christ Church."

"Oh," Zoe said, "my bad."

"There's plenty," Jack said, really almost laughing now at some joke he couldn't put into words, "to choose from."

They bought an enormous fried dough to share. Zoe ordered, but then looked at Jack helplessly when the attendant, a crunchy-looking woman in her sixties, asked what toppings they wanted.

"Butter and powdered sugar," Jack filled in.

"He knows what he's doin'," the woman said to Zoe, who smiled and handed her a twenty.

They stood at one of the tables, old spools tipped up on their sides and painted with flowers and clouds and bees, alternating tearing off pieces of the hot dough, dabbing up butter and sugar, and stuffing them in their mouths, then licking lips and fingers. "This is really good," Zoe said seriously.

"Gourmet," Jack said, and then, "I'm going to go to the bathroom, I'll be right back."

At the urinal, he let his mind go blank. The bathroom was a pleasant reprieve from the blackflies. He could still hear the band, muffled.

When he emerged, Zoe was standing alone, waiting for him (of course she was—what was notable about that?). The band changed songs. A familiar guitar riff. *Well I'm a-runnin' down the road* . . . The sun was behind the trees, and she was half silhouetted, all leg and tousled, wavy hair. She stood balanced on one haunch, the other knee slightly bent. She tore off a piece of dough as he watched. *Take it easy*. Grinned at him. *Take it*, raised it to her mouth, *easy*.

When he reached her, he realized he was smiling, full-on, with all of his crooked teeth. She was swaying with the music. *Come on baby.* He was full of something, something warm and complete, and he found he didn't particularly want to leave. Didn't want to leave, ever. *I gotta know if your sweet love—*

"You ready, kid?"

There was a fleck of powdered sugar on her lower lip. "Sure," she replied with a sweet, sweet smile.

51

The reality of it came suddenly. Truth is simple and easy and all at once.

The logistics of it were slower. She would need the notes, at least two of them, and he would need the third, and it would take him at least some minutes to write them, at most the rest of his life.

He was already dead, so what did it matter. We all are.

He had known for a while, hadn't he? The highway was in front of him, long and straight. He had passed its last exit. It was just that he hadn't pictured where it led.

But the reality of it—the act—the physicality of it—the brutal detail. Cells dying after cells dying after cells dying until. That was only decided in doing. It wasn't done and then it was.

He did it in the lab because that's where he was.

He did it efficiently because he knew how.

He is driving down a back road somewhere in central Maine. It is summer. Must be late summer, because the leaves have that hint of brown under their green gloss that says fall is coming, and after that winter.

Down a long, slow hill. The road is heavily crowned, paved a long time ago, and the lines are faded away. He meets a car, in it a woman. He feels a pull toward her, thinks perhaps he recognizes her, but they are both going too fast for him to see. She doesn't wave.

The road is familiar. He knows where he is going, though his destination isn't front of mind. He also knows the music that is on the radio, flowing out to fill the truck, but not well enough to sing along.

He is approaching a massive tree overhanging the road. Its thick green crown has been worn by passing tractor trailers, shaped such that the negative space forms the top of a rectangle. He remembers asking his mother once if trees are cut like that on purpose to let trucks through. She told him she didn't know. Later, he asked his great-grandfather, who told him no, the tractor trailers just wear the tree down over time. Then his great-grandfather took him out to an alfalfa field and told him to look at the tree line and asked what he noticed about the bottoms of the trees and Jack said, They're all the same level, they're really flat, and his great-grandfather said, Do you think trees all naturally grow the same level like that? About five, six feet from the ground? And Jack said, Probably not, and his great-grandfather said, Nosah, that's just how high the deer can reach.

Still, it looks like a paper tree that someone cut from. A square hole for a square peg. A children's toy, a puzzle piece. He marvels at how crisp the lines are. He wonders if the tree minds. If it hurt, the trucks wearing the branches away like that. If any had broken. If it had been violent, or if the tree had just grown that way, aware of the pressure of the passing vehicles and reaching its tendrils only into safe space.

On his right, he can see some body of water. On his left, only trees. No houses. A raven is pecking at a dead skunk in the other lane. It raises its head to look at him. Doesn't so much as flinch when he passes.

The shape of the tree is like the top third of a picture frame. And the fact of the frame means something is framed, which gives the road through the tree a strange flat quality. Or is it that this side is flat, and beyond has depth? Looking through the tree makes his eyes do strange things.

It becomes clear to Jack that he is sitting still and the road framed by the tree is approaching him. It starts to rain, and a few drops perch, trembling, on his windshield. He is so focused on the image framed by the tree that everything around and before that is blurred. It looks just like it always has, the road after the tree, but somehow he knows it is not precisely the same road as the one he is on now.

And then he reaches the tree, or the tree reaches him, and as soon as he touches the plane he finds he was imagining, the glass in the frame, in the beat where he should've moved seamlessly through and shaken his head and thought, Hey, that was weird, the whole thing clicks off. That is to say, there is nothing.

V

JUDGMENT

"Icarus, Icarus, where are you? Where should I be looking, to see you?"

—OVID'S *THE METAMORPHOSES*, TRANSLATED BY A. S. KLINE

Zoe,

I want first to thank you for being an incredible partner and scientist, and second to apologize.

While you have been busy running the business we built, I have been maintaining the appearance of progress when progress was not always present. It is difficult to say where reality ends and fiction begins. I do not have time now to try. There was never anything wrong with your novel theory of aging. I still believe it is correct, and I still believe in Manna's mission to leverage that theory to help people live longer, healthier lives.

For the past months, I have been working on a different line of experiments. This line is less ambitious, and it is not what we promised our investors. And it is not what I promised you, because it is not a treatment based on your theory. However, I have been successful. I hope that you put the team on this project. I believe my results are reproducible.

I am sorry. I am sorry to the investors, and the public, and to myself. But mostly I am sorry for lying to you. Please see attached an addendum which gives what might have been my testimony. That is, that you are guilty of nothing but trusting me.

I hope you share it with whoever you need to.

And please go back to work. You are too brilliant to waste.

I will miss you.
Jack

Zoe,
I love you
Jack

The New York Times

May 10, 2017 Updated 7:23 a.m. ET

LIVE: Manna Cofounder and CSO Jack Leahy Found Dead in Kendall Square Lab. He was 24.

The New York Times

May 23, 2017 Updated 2:35 p.m. ET

Zoe Kyriakidis, Cofounder and CEO of Manna, Enters Rehabilitation Center in Utah

The Wall Street Journal

Updated May 29, 2017 6:34 am ET

WSJ NEWS EXCLUSIVE: Manna CSO Suicide Note Contains Evidence of Data Manipulation

The New York Times

May 29, 2017 Updated 7:03 a.m. ET

LIVE: Manna Under Fire for Possible Data Manipulation, Kyriakidis Resigns

Biotech Today 06/01/17

Was Antiaging "Revolution" All a Lie?

The Wall Street Journal

Updated Jun. 01, 2017 12:23 pm ET

Manna CSO Leahy Left Shares to Kyriakidis

The New York Times

Jun. 03, 2017 Updated 7:03 a.m. ET

Who Was Jack Leahy?

New York Post

June 05, 2017 10:42 AM

"SHE STOLE MY SHARES" MANNA CSO'S MOTHER SPEAKS OUT

The New York Times

Opinion Guest Essay

Jun. 21, 2017, 5:00 a.m. ET

Kyriakidis: New Musk to New Madoff

The Wall Street Journal

Updated Jun. 23, 2017 1:15 pm ET

Embattled Startup Manna Makes Bid to Regain Confidence

The New York Times

Jun. 26, 2017 Updated 10:00 a.m. ET

Startup Manna Under SEC Investigation

The Wall Street Journal

Updated Dec. 13, 2017 2:52 pm ET

WSJ NEWS EXCLUSIVE: Zoe Kyriakidis Indicted on Criminal Fraud Charges

Billboard, Route 1, North of Boston

If you invested in biotech startup Manna, you may be eligible for compensation. Call 1.800.429.2299.

The Wall Street Journal

Updated Dec. 3, 2018 4:14 pm ET

Why We Believed Her: The Wish for Women in Biotech

SUBSTACK

The AB Show

Kyriakidis Precis

February 23, 2019

102 Likes 42 Comments 9 Shares

We anticipate a verdict in the Kyriakidis trial any day now. In case you've been living under a rock, here's your five-minute rundown of the trial that has taken four months.

First of all, Kyriakidis pleaded not guilty.

Her defense has hinged on Jack Leahy's suicide note and self-titled "addendum," which state that Kyriakidis is "guilty of nothing but trusting [Leahy]." Other important witnesses included Carter Gray, former CBO, and Alexandros Kyriakidis, Zoe Kyriakidis's brother and former Manna employee. Both left the company before the fraud allegations. Both provided strong statements that, to the best of their knowledge, Zoe Kyriakidis was unaware of any alleged fraud.

The prosecution pushed on Gray's romantic relationship with Kyriakidis, which took place from the spring to the fall of 2014, and on Alexandros Kyriakidis's departure from Manna, which occurred approximately six months before Leahy's death. When asked if he was warned about any issues at the company, Alexandros Kyriakidis said he "knew of the negative press."

Key witnesses for the prosecution included a laundry list of ex-employees who substantiated the questionable lab practices of the company, as well as a veritable who's who of academic scientists in the field who discussed the infeasibility of Manna's claims. The defense answered with their own scientists, primarily from industry. (This has sparked much discussion about scientific integrity in biotech more broadly. **Who decides what a reasonable interpretation of data is without peer review?   How do we balance expectations of scientific rigor with investor expectations of positivity and belief in the vision?**)

Ex-employee Mira Joshi's **diaries** have proven pivotal for both sides—they make it clear that Kyriakidis was warned about the fraud, but also indicate that Kyriakidis did not take that warning seriously.

The last to testify was Kyriakidis herself. She offered a vulnerable description of her path to fame, including details of her own obsessive tendencies, eating disorder, drug use, and insecurity. "Ultimately," she said, "I didn't know what was going on in the lab. I was really no different than an investor. And I still don't know what was going on in the lab. It was a mistake: I should have never made claims that I couldn't back up with research I had seen and touched myself. But I did."

On cross, however, Kyriakidis stumbled. When the prosecution asked, "Is it possible that Leahy lied in his note to protect you?" she appeared to become emotional, struggled to speak, and shook her head. When asked for a verbal yes or no, she began to cry, and the judge called for a break.

Absent entirely from the trial has been Manna's board of directors. This, too, has **sparked debate** around what duty early investors have to verify the claims they are promoting, the ways in which early investors are **incentivized only to build hype**, the **lack of scientific background** among venture capitalists, and, more generally, the **shocking amounts of money** poured into biotech every year.

You can find more about the trial in this **coverage timeline**, and live updates on the deliberation **here**.

COMMENTS:

@BrianBrian: This trial has been better than reality TV, seriously.

@WSSK: Kyriakidis is such a whore. Can u even imagine screwing your CBO and then your CSO. and clearly some of her investors too

@phyllis_bb: loool when do we find out Carter Gray and Leahy also dated

@ObieK: over under on whether Carter Gray, Kyriakidis, and Leahy were a threesome?

@StantheMan: This didn't age well. **VIRAL VIDEO Zoe Kyriakidis on New Antiaging Startup**

@GlenSS02: You know it's bs when the CEO is tlking about the science but has no experience except dissecting a frog in hs

@DrRachelM: who thought it was a good idea to give two 20yos 9 bil

@JennyGoHome223: Glad to see this bitch exposed finally.

@blosh: I hope she dies

@GiannisVal: This whole thing is kind of sad.

[see more]

CNN

Published 4:13 PM EST, Tuesday February 26, 2019

Breaking: Manna Cofounder Found Not Guilty

After seven days of deliberations, the jury found Zoe Kyriakidis, cofounder and CEO of Manna, not guilty on all counts.

When she heard the verdict, Kyriakidis remained stoic. She nodded to the jury before leaving the courtroom.

VI

THE RAVEN

Subject: Student Researcher Interested in Theory of Aging

Dear Ms. Kyriakidis,

My name is Lily Harmon, and I am a second-year PhD student at MIT.

I am working in the lab of Dr. Kapir on the epigenetic basis of aging. I am aware of the scandal that happened around your startup, Manna, but I am still very interested in what you were working on and your ideas about reverse aging and the physical location of epigenetic data.

I was wondering if you might be willing to speak over coffee about your work.

Sincerely,
Lily

Afterward, everything was so quiet.

The whole duration of the trial she'd wished for it to be over, for them to stop reopening the wound so she could stop limping home to bleed all over the carpet, stop crawling into bed exhausted and in tears, stop getting up and putting on the face again.

But when the end did come—when she'd been found not guilty and the IP suit had been dismissed and she'd signed off on selling said IP to Merck (how funny, twofold, one that Merck still wanted the IP and two that it was she signing off even though they'd ousted her—she wasn't CEO anymore but she still owned 51 percent of the company, which of course was the deciding vote in the boardroom) and the money had gone straight to the investors and everything in the offices had been sealed up and carted away (Zoe never went back, even though she thought about it all the time, thought maybe seeing the place where it happened would be a relief) and the company had been dissolved, a whole legal person gone just like that, into the ether like it had never been real in the first place, and the media coverage had slowed from firehose to stream to trickle to the drip, drip, drip of a leaky faucet, the only noise in a house in the middle of the night—she realized she'd been wrong to wish for it.

Some thoughts she had in the darkness:

Am I real if they aren't writing about me?

Was I ever the person they were writing about?

Am I the ghost of that person? Am I the ghost of some other person?

Am I real more generally? As in, am I alive? As in, is this hell?

Zoe was jogging. Nowhere in particular. She wore a baseball hat and sunglasses. Her mother was tracking her phone and waiting for her at home. It was a busy time of day, the beginning of the evening commute. The sun was starting to ooze golden.

She came slowly into a square, somewhere in Somerville. Five roads meeting. She squinted at the building diagonally across. The space was deeply familiar but not quite, like emerging into a dream. Like an ice cream place that you half-remember going to as a child except this is not where you grew up.

There was, she realized jarringly, an actual ice cream place in the building, the neon sign in the window turned off. She must have been here before. The air smelled smoky, like falling leaves. Her hands tingled.

She was certain she'd never been here before.

She had been rereading the *Epic of Gilgamesh*. Why? For the same reason you listen to breakup songs after a breakup, she supposed. If you rub salt in the wound, at least you control the pain. And she preferred sharp pain to dull pain. Sharp pain made her feel like a person. Dull pain made her feel like dying.

Had she been to that ice cream place with Jack?

A raven landed on the sidewalk.

Differences between Uta-napishtim in *Gilgamesh* and Noah in Genesis. Noah sent out a dove, and the dove came back with an olive leaf, and so Noah knew the flood was over. Uta-napishtim sent first a dove, but the dove came back, and so he knew the flood continued. Then a sparrow, but the sparrow came back, and so he knew the flood continued. Finally a raven, and when the raven did not come back, he knew the flood was over.

She was at the point in the jog where she couldn't really feel her legs, so it was like she was floating. If she slowed to a walk, the magic might be broken, so she didn't.

She was sure they hadn't been to that ice cream place.

Samenesses. More than the differences. When the flood was over, each man burned offerings. *And the LORD smelled a sweet savor; and the LORD said in his heart, I will not again curse the ground any more for man's sake; for the imagination of man's heart is evil from his youth.*

But the Gilgamesh version was better. *The gods did smell the savor / the gods did smell the savor sweet / the gods gathered like flies around the man making sacrifice.* And some were angry, and some were regretful, and some were sad, and one blessed Uta-napishtim and his wife with immortality.

The raven jumped up, flapped its wings, rose away.

She kept jogging.

The raven did not come back.

She swallowed.

Like flies around the man making sacrifice.

A sob rose in her throat. If there was a god, she'd be like Alanis Morrisette. If there were gods the air was thick with them and they were hungry for pain. She saw Jack in front of her, clear as day. The raven did not come back. The sob ripped from her throat and she folded over for a moment before forcing herself to stand, to move. A homeless man sat on a bench and watched her pass.

The whole scene receded and she had the sense that if she turned around, she wouldn't find the square again.

One late morning, after spending 6:00 to 11:00 a.m. in her pajamas, she caught a glimpse of herself in the mirror, bending over to pull on jeans. Tilted, it distorted her proportions, giving her a huge hunchback, a shrunken pale folded belly. She stood up and her reflection snapped back to normal.

She'd taken to raiding her brother's closet and dressing in his old clothes, rolling them and cuffing them and belting them to stay on her body. She pulled on a pair of his khakis, worn to thin softness, and one of his rugbies.

He had somehow escaped the fallout. He was doing fine.

She could hear her mother moving around downstairs. Starting lunch, probably.

She wondered, again—no, not again, as there was no line between the last time she had wondered it and this time, it was a continuous wondering—what she was supposed to be doing.

The first time her mother visited her in rehab the news hadn't broken yet, but still Zoe couldn't look her in the face. She sat down beside the bed, and Zoe started to cry. She hated crying in front of her mother, but she'd learned that the tears were irresistible, like the weather.

"We don't have to talk," her mother said.

Zoe closed her eyes, nodded.

Her mother came back the next day with her father, who stood awkwardly in the door. Zoe hadn't slept at all the night before and was out of it, couldn't keep her eyes in focus, so he was two people, and then one, and then two. She fell asleep, and when she woke up her father was gone but her mother was still there, reading a magazine.

The next day, her mother brought a puzzle. Zoe sat up in bed, and they did it together.

The next day, Jimmy, from the board, called to tell her the news had broken. When she hung up, she just kept shaking her head. Shaking and shaking and shaking.

She did not expect it, but her mother came anyway. She sat down beside Zoe and took her right hand and held it.

Ever since, Zoe had felt like she was seeing herself through other people's eyes. Her nurses', to whom she was just another fucked-up superstar, until she wasn't, until she was a fucked-up superstar fraudster. Awful, to be sober for that. She wanted nothing more than downers, downers to make her sleep and sleep and sleep.

Her father's, to whom she was weak and then, after the news broke, weaker still. He looked at her with disappointment, with revulsion, but mostly tried not to look at her. Even worse to be sober for that, but they'd deleted her dealer's number from her phone. She thought of texting one of the younger VC bros to get it back except then she'd remember that none of them would reply, that she was an exile now. Cast down. Gates barred behind.

Her mother's. To whom she was nothing more or less than a daughter. Wounded and in need of care, but the same girl she'd always been. Was that better? Or worse?

Through the whole thing she read the news and it hurt her and she'd swear she was going to stop reading it except the next day she'd pick up her phone and read it again. It did not feel like a choice. If she did not look through other people's eyes, she could not see herself. Because except through other people's eyes, she did not exist.

It'd been strange to see Carter on the stand. She hadn't seen him in years.

He looked okay. The relief at this was stronger than she'd anticipated.

He had known. Of course he had known. Or known enough.

He said, "I have no reason to believe that Zoe was aware of any fraud committed by Jack while I was employed by Manna," and she stared at her hands.

She imagined what she'd looked like to him, that day she stormed out of his apartment. She had believed so completely that he was the irrational one. That he was jealous. That she was untouchable. That they were gods.

At least then she had been beautiful in flames. Now she was just burned. A ruin.

She saw, with a sort of detached surprise, that her hands shook.

She wished she could say thank you. She knew she could not. She should at least meet his eyes, but she couldn't even offer him that. If she met his eyes she might see herself and she could not bear it.

She wished she could say Why didn't you save me. But she knew he had tried.

Mira's journals were even worse—Mira who she didn't even really know—read aloud in court and then published word for word in the *Times* and quoted in blogs and videos and op-eds and tweets and, and, and. Zoe had studied them enough (couldn't resist, like rubbernecking at an accident, like pressing on a bruise) that she could recite whole paragraphs. *She was surprised/dismissive. Figures. She's never in the lab. Funny how everyone sees her as a scientist. I think the idea of another person (woman) telling her something she doesn't know about J was maybe offensive to her, or maybe just funny. Not exactly the type to feel threatened by someone like me. Have to say I am curious how long they've been sleeping together. Is it, like, a since-the-beginning thing? Can't imagine starting a company with a sophomore year in college boyfriend. I almost feel bad for her.*

It had been so disgustingly easy to tell her story to the jury. Not really any different from telling the story of Manna to the public. Except before it had been an epic, and now it was a tragedy. And before she had been the hero, and now—

Funny how everyone sees her as a scientist.

She didn't even have to lie on the stand. Not really. Jack had made sure of it.
Jack had—
Jack—

I almost feel bad for her.

Too often, she sat in front of her laptop and googled her name.

The most recent piece was from weeks ago. She'd already seen it. Does This Outfit Make Me Look Guilty?

She clicked anyway. There she was. In profile, eyes on the ground, headed into the courtroom. It was true, she had changed her costume. Gray slacks and a pale blue shirt that washed her out. Her hair, dull, tied back. No makeup. She hardly recognized herself.

In the past months Zoe Kyriakidis, Mardi G, and Hillary Hall have all shown us how to use clothes as communication in court . . .

She looked so old. So pathetic. Dead woman walking.

There is a clear connection between light neutrals and simple, modest clothing and the version of the self the defendant wishes to portray. She is respectful of the court, innocent, youthful, and hardworking. Ms. Raston said that she advises clients to dress for court "like you're dressing for church."

West to the Yard down Mass. Ave. from where she'd parked, over past the Harvard Art Museums.

Through the gates. Enter to Grow in Wisdom. Thought, campus is so green this time of year. Cut right between Lamont and Widener. September, so the Yard was full of new first-years. Widener was taller than she remembered. Stared up only for a moment before realizing she looked like a tourist.

She couldn't stop looking for Jack's height, his hair flopping to the side, his loping gait. (She had buzzed her own hair short like a boy's. Amazing how no one recognized her now. Like a woman is entirely her hair.) She expected him in every student who came into her view.

She wandered into Sever (even with whatever masochism this was, couldn't go anywhere near Divinity Avenue). Why had she come? She was so old. She was certain that the security guard would stop her. Ma'am, what are you doing here? But he didn't, just nodded.

In every face, she looked for Jack. She was nauseated.

Why had she come, to see their faces, which were her face? Round, anxious, sad, wild. All trying to hide something under something else.

When she meandered back the other way, some kind kid asked if she needed help finding a classroom. How was it possible she looked enough like one of them to need help finding a classroom? Her mind spun. She does. She does need help. She is eighteen, she is looking for a gen ed. She is nineteen, she is looking for Phoebe's public speaking class. She is twenty, she is looking for Jack, she has something to tell him. She is nervous, the smell of fall in the air, the vibration of so many bright children packed so close together. They are so young. We are so young. The kid asked, "Are you okay?" And she said, "Oh, I'm sorry, I don't need help, but thank you." She heard her own voice, smooth and polished. The kid gave her a strange look. Her voice must have betrayed her age. Twenty-six. So many years past. Expired. Or perhaps he just sensed she was lying.

It was a lie, wasn't it.

Procedure:

Reagents: Intelligence, youth, desire, undeveloped prefrontal cortexes. Add arrogance (you're the best in the world, handpicked to be here). Evaporate off true confidence (suddenly, you're just one of many). Distill. Repeat x1600. Combine first in small batches (rooming groups). Then larger (freshman dorms, large lecture classes). Allow to rest. Synthesis products: competition, anxiety, insecurity. Secondary products: love, lust, or both, depending on initial conditions (variations to include: culture, wealth, poverty, physical beauty, trauma, prior education, charisma, mental illness, relationships with parents, physical illness, etcetera). Place under pressure. Add: expectations, belief, promises. You can be ___. You could make ___. Look what ___ is doing. One of us will ___, someday (imply: why not you?). You will change the world. We will change the world. You will change the world.

Add: Money. Add: Power. Add: Fame.

Combine all and shake.

Caution: Gases may be explosive.

Possible products: World-changing innovation, anger, fabulous wealth, abject failure, nervous breakdowns, brilliant art, bitterness, money, depression, burnout, fame, flight, world-saving political leadership, cheating, lying, stealing.

Fire, broken glass.

Death.

Caution: Reaction at all steps is highly volatile, flammable, explosive. Avoid excess friction, pressure, sound, light. Reaction at all steps produces a highly toxic, colorless, scentless vapor. Perform under fume hood. Wear personal protective equipment at all times.

Alex came to see her once in rehab when she was so whacked-out on the replacement drugs they put you on—that's how they do it, they drug you to undrug you—that she couldn't even speak to him, just drooled on the pillow and mumbled something that could have been "Missed you," and he said something and smoothed her hair back from her forehead—that was the other thing, when she'd really stopped eating a lot of her hair had fallen out and then when they put her on IVs it started growing back which meant she had all of these weird short hairs—and then he'd left, and she had not looked into his face and so, blissfully, she had not seen his pity.

Then, during the trial, she hadn't been allowed to see him because he had been called as a witness.

But now that the trial was over, he could come home. Zoe, upstairs in her bedroom, heard him arrive, heard her mother greet him, heard his low voice answer. Zoe was in bed (she was usually in bed), though she had changed out of his clothes. She was scrolling through Facebook looking at photos of Hanna and Gabe's wedding. There were Gabby and Sophia, smiling for the camera, on either side of the bride. In her profile picture, Sophia wore a Harvard/MIT MD-PhD Patagonia.

All three had refused to be interviewed for the big profile on Zoe that had come out the day of the verdict. A kindness she had not earned.

You have to get up, she thought, but her limbs refused to move. And then she heard his feet on the stairs and managed to sit up, swing her legs around so that she was perched on the edge of the bed. Not much but better than being prone, horizontal. The body of his sister rather than the real thing.

He knocked. "Come in," she said.

"Hey, Zoe," he said.

She met his gaze and saw herself. And she was flooded with his pity. And it was unbearable.

"Hey, Alex."

He sat beside her. She was shaking.

"How are you?" she said, and then "Congratulations, Doctor." He had successfully defended his dissertation at Stanford, taken a job as an assistant professor just down the road at Berkeley.

"Thank you," he said. "I won't ask how you are."

"Best not to."

How was it possible that they hadn't really spoken since? To speak to him now was to resurrect the self that had existed before. It was almost a hopeful feeling.

"I, uh," he started. She knew he'd rehearsed something, and also that what he'd say would not be what he'd rehearsed. "Oh, fuck it," he said. She nodded. There was satisfaction in knowing someone that well. In being known that well, too.

She saw out of the corner of her eye a dark wave of missing Jack. She held her breath. It passed over her.

"I just want you to know that I . . . understand. Or, as much as I can, I understand. And I don't . . . I'm sorry."

She looked at him.

"How could he?" she whispered.

Alex took a deep breath, and she looked over and saw that he was crying. She had not seen him cry since they were kids. It sat oddly on his face.

"Isn't it obvious?"

"I would have rather gone to jail," she said, "I would have rather been locked up for the rest of my goddamn life with him alive than—" She was yelling, she realized, screaming, and her face was distorted, monstrous, she could see it through Alex's eyes, red and wet and horrible.

"I hate him," she said.

"You don't," he said. "I don't. But I wish he . . . he couldn't see another way. That was his flaw. But he gave you another life. So, look, that's what I wanted to say. Well, I had something better planned, a whole speech, much more indirect, but that was what I wanted to say to you. Was that he gave you this, so. You should use it."

"I don't want it."

"Too bad," Alex said. "You can't take it back."

"I absolutely—" She stopped herself. She could not, would not. Alex was right. That would be the ultimate betrayal.

She thought about Jack's note. She had it memorized, of course. *Please go back to work. You are too brilliant to waste.*

"I can't," she said. "I can't go back to work. I'm empty."

Funny how everyone sees her as a scientist.

"You're empty because you can't go back to work. Not the other way around."

"No one would hire me."

Funny how everyone sees her as a scientist.

"Let me help you."

"You need to help yourself."

"I'm fine. Just—I wouldn't do anything without asking you first. So that's what I'm doing. Asking. Can I help you?"

Zoe closed her eyes. She was back in the conference room in that stupid rented office space with Jack, and she was saying "My brother Alex did offer," and he was looking at her, and she was picking up the phone.

"Okay," Zoe said. She swallowed. "Okay. But not at the expense of—"

"Trust me."

"Okay." She couldn't look at him. All the forgivenesses she did not deserve. "Thank you."

Zoe opened her email.

Six unread from the same girl. The stupid kid. Lily.

Hello, the most recent one read, Just following up on the above. I am fascinated by your work and would love to have the chance to speak to you about it. Thank you so much . . .

Persistent. Although how many emails had she sent Stephanie, Daniel Fen's PA, with no replies? At least six, she thought, maybe more.

She stared at the screen until it faded to black and she was just staring at herself. Past the shaved head to the big nose, dark eyebrows, dark eyes.

Well. Same girl. Somehow.

Too brilliant to waste.

Happy to get coffee, she typed, Tatte? Anywhere but Darwin's. What is your schedule like? She hit send too fast for her thoughts to catch her, hold her back.

The girl replied within five minutes. My schedule is completely flexible, I'm sure you're really busy. Zoe almost laughed.

How about this afternoon? 4 p.m.?

That sounds perfect. Thank you so much. See you then!

She needed to shower. She closed her laptop, fully intending to stand up, go to the bathroom, turn the shower on, step in. In fact, she envisioned herself doing all those things in such detail that she was genuinely surprised when, half an hour later, she was still in bed, in her pajamas.

She licked her lips, chewed off a flake of skin. Opened her laptop to cancel.

And then she saw the six emails, and she saw herself.

And she got out of bed.

They sat down at a two-person table, Lily sliding onto the bench and Zoe taking the chair. Lily hadn't recognized Zoe until she heard her voice, for which she'd apologized profusely.

"So," Zoe said. "What can I do for you?"

"Well, I'm a second-year PhD student in the Kapir Group," she said, "and he has a project on the epigenetic basis of aging that I've had the chance to work on." She was nervous—kept clasping and unclasping her hands, folding and refolding the scarf she'd unwound from her neck. She must've been around twenty-three, but as she launched into an explanation of the project she lit up, seemed no older than fifteen.

When she finished, Zoe said, "Do you have figures we can look at?"

Lily's eyes widened. "Yes!" She pulled a folder from her bag, spread some sheets across the table. Zoe studied them.

She had thoughts, immediately. And questions. And an idea was floating around somewhere—she could feel it hovering just behind her right ear. If she turned, she knew it'd disappear. She had to be patient, work into being worthy of it, let it slip into her mind on its own time.

She hadn't felt an idea like that in—she stopped herself from thinking it.

"Does Dr. Kapir know you're here?"

"He, uh . . ." Lily paused, and Zoe could see the answer was no.

"Look." Zoe frowned. "I think you're doing great work. You shouldn't jeopardize it."

"No, but—" Lily looked so desperate. And the idea was buzzing around, now, moving from side to side. "I'm just—it would be so stupid to waste your expertise!" She blushed. "I mean—"

Too brilliant to waste. Zoe swallowed the nausea. Wondered if she was going to cry, now, here, in front of this kid.

She stood. Lily's face fell. And then she slid around to the other side of the table, so that they'd be facing the same way, pulled one of the figures closer.

"Do you have a pencil?" she asked. Lily rooted in her bag, handed one over, and then pulled out a second for herself. She was left-handed. "Okay," Zoe said, beginning a numbered list. "Let's start with your fundamental questions."

Driving on a highway north of Boston, somewhere it'd shrunk to two lanes and the trees rose on either side like banks of a river, like the gray asphalt was calm water. Not Maine, because this was early—long before he'd taken her to the funeral. She couldn't remember where they'd been going. Maybe nowhere.

Blinding, early summer sunshine, deep blue sky turning, slowly, to dark. The rain clouds were creeping up beside them, and so they did not notice the wall of near-black climbing into the sky, but it was there. With the first sprinkle (she was driving, he was in the passenger seat), he craned his head back and said, "Look at that."

She peered out. "Wow." She cracked her window, inhaled the clean smell of summer rain. "Ugh," she said, letting it out, "that smells so good."

The rain turned from friendly to sharp, rat-tatting on the roof. A rumble started, low and soft, building into a rip. The highway curved into the cloud bank, and there were brake lights in front of them, fading into the wall of water. Zoe hit the brakes, too, and the water broke over them. Like the ocean. Not wrathful, just indifferent.

"Christ," Zoe said, braking harder, the windshield a wash. The car in front of her swerved to the left, narrowly avoiding a car in front of it that was pulling over. "Fuck. What should I do?"

She looked at Jack, who was looking out the side window, eyes wide, a stupid grin on his face. "Look," he said, "it's hail."

"Should I pull over?" Her irritation flared. There had almost been an accident right in front of them, and the rain was only falling harder now, building up several inches deep on the road, the car squirrely through it. "I can't see."

"Sure," he said, and so she did, spinning the wheel furiously and parking, crooked, in the breakdown lane behind three or four other cars who had opted to wait it out. She prodded her hazards on. Tiny balls of hail bounced off the hood. An eighteen-wheeler screamed by, rocking the car on its axle, and she flinched.

A flash, a crack. Her chest full of more adrenaline. She thought of the lightning show at the Boston Museum of Science. The guy in the cage touching the insides of the bars while electricity crackled yellow down the outside.

A clearer strike, a tear in the sky, exposing the light behind.

She looked over at Jack, and he looked at her, and they were both grinning, and then they were both laughing, and Jack rolled down his window, soaking the inside of his door and his leg, and leaned his head out, still laughing, mouth open to catch some of the sky. The trees were dark, perfect green, the grass flattened by the rain, the sky heavy, the road reflecting it, so that the whole world was gray-black and green. And blinking red hazards. Zoe was laughing so hard she couldn't tell him to Get your head in the window, stupid, you're going to get struck by lightning. And the rain was falling so hard it was splashing all the way over to her side, leaving tingly little cool spots on her right arm, and she reached a palm over him to catch some of it. He pulled his head back in the window and his dark curly hair was pasted flat to his forehead, his eyelashes stuck together, framing those pale blue eyes, and it was like he was the storm and the clear sky at once, grinning, and he shook his head like a dog and splattered her with water and she tipped her head back against the headrest and smiled.

"I fucking love lightning," she said, turning to him.

"Me, too," he said, and he leaned his wet forehead onto hers, and she could taste the rain dripping from his hair, and their eyes held identical wonder.

In her imagination (she knew it didn't happen, but why not) when the rain let up and she pulled back onto the wet road, that Tom Petty song came on the radio. The one she'd been listening to since he—she couldn't even think the words. And she thought, I hope you're somewhere you feel free.

Picture it.

He is walking her home. They are only just getting started.

He stops. She keeps walking for a step, and then realizes he isn't beside her, stops, turns. He is framed by brick. She looks up at him. She is tall but he is taller.

"Do you want to live forever?"

It might not have happened this way. She might only have imagined it.

She remembers being taken aback. Thinking about it. Not knowing for sure.

He remembers her meeting his eyes. (If a false memory, a shared one.) "Yes."

Dear Jack,
I love you
Zoe

Acknowledgments

To Katie Greenstreet and Melissa Pimentel and the Paper Literary team, Deb Futter and the Celadon team, Lily Cooper and the Penguin Michael Joseph team, AH, DH, Ski Krieger, Maryam Hiradfar, Noel Austin, and Jonathan Taylor: thank you, thank you, thank you.

To Carole Gopsill: wish you were here.

And to everyone else who supported / listened to / distracted / fed / housed / otherwise helped me through this process: thank you. You are numerous, and I am grateful.

As noted, this is a work of fiction and *everything* in it—all of the characters, scientific developments, organizations, etc.—is either a product of my imagination or is used fictitiously. But I would like to give credit to some of the scientists whose actual discoveries will be recognizable to some readers:

The Yamanaka factors come from a real paper used fictitiously: Kazutoshi Takahashi and Shinya Yamanaka, "Induction of Pluripotent Stem Cells from Mouse Embryonic and Adult Fibroblast Cultures by Defined Factors," *Cell* 126, no. 4 (2006): 663–76, doi: 10.1016/j.cell.2006.07.024. Shinya Yamanaka and John B. Gurdon won the 2012 Nobel Prize in Physiology or Medicine "for the discovery that mature cells can be reprogrammed to become pluripotent."

"Brenna" is a fictional scientist—Meselson and Stahl did *not* have a third partner. Meselson and Stahl's real paper, used fictitiously, is: Matthew Meselson and Franklin W. Stahl, "The Replication of DNA in Escherichia Coli," *PNAS* 44, no. 7 (1958): 671–82, doi: 10.1073 /pnas.44.7.671.

The "Byrne" paper ("Byrne" being a fictional scientist) that "Zoe" and "Jack" refer to on page 65 is a real paper used fictitiously: Alejandro Ocampo et al., "In Vivo Amelioration of Age-Associated Hallmarks by Partial Reprogramming," *Cell* 167, no. 7 (2016): 1719– 33.e12. doi: 10.1016/j.cell.2016.11.052.

"Mark Fraser" is a fictional scientist, but the information theory of aging (pages 67, 94) is a real theory used fictitiously. See: Jae-Hyun Yang et al., "Loss of Epigenetic Information as a Cause of Mammalian Aging," *Cell* 186, no. 2 (2023): 305–26.e27. doi: 10.1016/j .cell.2022.12.027.

The papers "Zoe" refers to in her (fictional) TED Talk on pages 155–58 are the following real papers, used fictitiously:

Ryan Doonan et al., "Against the Oxidative Damage Theory of Aging: Superoxide Dismutases Protect Against Oxidative Stress but Have Little or No Effect on Life Span in Caenorhabditis Elegans," *Genes & Development* 22, no. 23 (2008): 3236–41, doi: 10.1101 /gad.504808. ("John Garcia," to whom she attributes this work, is a fictional scientist.)

Carlos López-Otín et al., "The Hallmarks of Aging," *Cell* 153, no. 6 (2013): 1194–217, doi: 10.1016/j.cell.2013.05.039. ("Torres" and "Eric Oneto," to whom she attributes this work, are fictional scientists.)

Dabbu Kumar Jaijyan et al., "New Intranasal and Injectable Gene Therapy for Healthy Life Extension, *PNAS* 119, no. 20:

e2121499119, doi: 10.1073/pnas.2121499119. ("Daniel Fen," to whom she attributes this work, is a fictional scientist.)

Ming Xu et al., "Senolytics Improve Physical Function and Increase Lifespan in Old Age," *Nature Medicine* 24, no. 8 (2018): 1246–56, doi: 10.1038/s41591-018-0092-9. ("Anthony Dunster," to whom she attributes this work, is a fictional scientist.)

The description of poetry "Zoe" remembers on page 65 is indeed Emily Dickinson, in a letter to Thomas Wentworth Higginson on August 16, 1870. "If I feel physically as if the top of my head were taken off, I know that is poetry."

The student artwork in the Adams tunnels that depicts "the Abyss" mentioned on page 81 is really there—or at least it was when I last went down.

On page 156, "Zoe" offers cloning as evidence against the free radical theory of aging. There are two sides to this argument. The National Human Genome Research Institute does cite the early death of Dolly, the first cloned sheep, as potential evidence of age-related DNA deterioration, specifically shortened telomeres, in young clones (see "Cloning Fact Sheet," National Human Genome Research Institute, NIH). However, Wakayama et al. find no evidence of shortened telomeres over six generations of cloned mice (see Teruhiko Wakayama et al., "Cloning of Mice to Six Generations," *Nature* 407, no. 6802 (2000): 318–19, doi: 10.1038/35030301).

On page 226, "Zoe" listens to Professor Arthur C. Brooks being interviewed on *The Tim Ferriss Show*.

On page 323, "Jack" quotes from Edgar Allan Poe's "The Raven."

"Zoe" and "Jack" sing snippets from "Take It Easy" by Jackson Browne and Glenn Frey on pages 217 and 339–40. "Jack" sings a snippet from "Only the Good Die Young" by Billy Joel on page 223. On page 264, "Jack" reminisces about the song "Ladies of Cambridge" by Ezra Koenig, Chris Baio, Chris Tomson, and Rostam Batmanglij.

On page 16, "Zoe" walks into Harvard Yard through a gate that reads "Enter to Grow in Wisdom." There is such a gate, Dexter Gate, but it is on the south side of the Yard. "Zoe," here, is coming from the north. The gate she'd be walking through is Meyer Gate, which has a much longer, less punchy quote.

Sanders Theatre is real, but I believe that dressing room to be a convenient fiction.

About the Author

Austin Taylor graduated from Harvard University in 2021 with a joint degree in chemistry and English. *Notes on Infinity* is inspired in part by her undergraduate studies, peers, and lab work in Harvard's chemistry department. She has also worked as a public speaking coach and in science policy. Austin is a private pilot, a Registered Maine Guide, and a bassist. She grew up in central Maine, where she now lives and writes.

CELADON
BOOKS

Founded in 2017, Celadon Books, a division of
Macmillan Publishers, publishes a highly curated list
of twenty to twenty-five new titles a year. The list of
both fiction and nonfiction is eclectic and focuses
on publishing commercial and literary books and
discovering and nurturing talent.